To So Few

Victory

Books by Cap Parlier:

Anod series

The Phoenix Seduction (1995)
Anod's Seduction (2004) [reprint of The Phoenix Seduction]
Anod's Redemption (2004)

Apocalypse Endeavor (2019)
Indulgence (2021)

To So Few series

To So Few – In the Beginning (2014)
To So Few – The Prelude (2014)
To So Few – Explosion (2015)
To So Few – The Trial (2016)
To So Few – The Verdict (2017)
To So Few – Frustration (2018)
To So Few – Deflection (2019)
To So Few – Hunter (2020)
To So Few – Struggle (2021)
To So Few – Overlord (2022)
To So Few – Victory (2023)

Non-fiction

Sacrifice (2000)
The Clarity of Hindsight (2016)
and with Kevin E. Ready:
TWA 800 - Accident or Incident? (1998)

Coming soon from Cap Parlier: Anod's Glory, 3rd book of the Anod series.

These and other great books available from Saint Gaudens Press
Post Office Box 405
Solvang, CA 93463-0405
URL: http://www.saintgaudenspress.com
Visit Cap Parlier's Web Site at: http://www.parlier.com

To So Few

Victory

by
Cap Parlier

SAINT GAUDENS PRESS
Phoenix, Arizona & Santa Barbara, California

Saint Gaudens Press
Post Office Box 405
Solvang, CA 93464-0405

http://www.SaintGaudensPress.com

Saint Gaudens, Saint Gaudens Press and the Winged Liberty colophon are trademarks of Saint Gaudens Press

Print edition ISBN: 978-0-943039-67-1
Ebook edition ISBN: 978-0-943039-68-8
Library of Congress Catalog Number - 2023935879

Printed in the United States of America

The TO SO FEW series books are works of fiction. Any reference to real people, objects, events, organizations, or locales is intended only to give the fiction a sense of reality and authenticity. Other names, characters and incidents are the products of the author's imagination and bear no relationship to past events, or persons living or deceased.

Dedication

—

This volume of the To So Few series is dedicated
to all the patriots who won the fight against
the fascist Axis nations in the most horrific war
in human history.
May God bless their immortal souls.

—

Acknowledgements

———

As has been the case across this series, John Richard freely offered his curiosity, sense of history, critical eye, and inquisitive mind to challenge me to do better and to tell a more compelling story. He has consistently pushed me to dig deeper into the extraordinary details I have tried to capture in this series of historical novels. I owe John a debt of profound gratitude that can never be repaid for his critical and constructive review of the manuscript. Thank you so very much, John.

Jeanne remains my steadfast and irreplaceable partner in life. Her support and care sustain my writing. I cannot imagine life without her.

I am blessed to work with the editors and staff at Saint Gaudens Press who continue to impress me, offering invaluable support and assistance along with incomparable skill and attention to detail to produce a better book.

Thank you all.

———

List of Terms

As a consequence of complex, evolving, military operations, a consolidated list of operational code names and abbreviations is provided for the reader's benefit. These are terms used throughout this story, and this is not a comprehensive list for the era.

1MC	1 Main Circuit – general ship-wide broadcast address system
AEF	Allied Expeditionary Force
AFRL	U.S. Army Air Forces Research Laboratory at Dayton, Ohio
AGO	*Apparatebau GmbH Oschersleben Flugzeugwerke* (Machine-making Aircraft Works Company in Oschersleben)
ALBERTA	code name for leadership unit, also known as the Tinian Joint Chiefs, to support and enable the atomic bomb deliveries
ANGEL	TS-SCI compartment for all classified material associated with listening to German POWs (fictitious code name)
ARGONAUT	Allied Summit Conference in Yalta, Crimea, Ukraine (4/11.February.1945)
ATA	Air Transport Auxiliary – British aircraft ferry service
ATS	Auxiliary Territorial Service –women's branch of the British Army
AUTUMN MIST	Operation AUTUMN MIST (*Unternehmen Herbstnebel*) – code name for the German winter counter-offensive in the Ardennes Forest region of Belgium and Luxembourg (16.Deember.1944); became known as the Battle of the Bulge; originally known as *Unternehmen Wacht am Rhein* (Operation Watch on the Rhine); name changed in early December, two weeks before execution
BAGRATION	Soviet spring offensive of 1944, named for Russian General of Infantry Prince Pyotr Ivanovich Bagration
BAS	Bainbridge Air Services, Inc. – Drummond's airline company (fictional)
BBC	British Broadcasting Corporation – national broadcaster of the United Kingdom

BC	Bomber Command, Royal Air Force
BDST	British Double Summer Time, time shift two hours ahead of astronomical time from 25.February.1940 to 7.October.1945
BIS	Bank of International Settlements, Basel, Switzerland
Boniface	code word used predominantly by the British to refer to ULTRA Enigma decrypted messages
BSC	British Security Coordination – organization base in Manhattan, New York City, with broad charter of intelligence, logistics coordination, and lobbying reporting to the prime minister
CAVU	aviator acronym for Clear And Visibility Unlimited, pronounced "cav vu"
CEC	Civil Engineering Corps – one of numerous U.S. Army specialty branches of service
CHOKER II	planned Allied Expeditionary Forces (AEF) airborne and glider landings near Worms, Germany (not executed)
CIC	U.S. Army CounterIntelligence Corps
CIGS	British Chief of the Imperial General Staff (Army); equivalent to the U.S. Army Chief of Staff
CinC or CINC	Commander in Chief, pronounced 'sink'
CINCPAC	Commander-in-Chief Pacific, pronounced 'sink pack'
CINCPOA	Commander-in-Chief Pacific Ocean Areas
CINCSWPA	Commander-in-Chief Southwest Pacific Area
CO	Commanding Officer
COI	Coordinator of Information -- strategic intelligence service, predecessor of the Office of Strategic Services (OSS)
CORONET	Allied operation plan for the invasion of the Honshu, Imperial Japan, part of Operation DOWNFALL (tentatively scheduled for March 1946, the second part of DOWNFALL)
CNO	Chief of Naval Operations
DETACHMENT	Allied operation, invasion of Iwo Jima (19.February / 26.March.1945)
DFC	Distinguished Flying Cross
DIAMOND	code name for Trevor Thomas Andersen (fictitious)
DNI	Director, Naval Intelligence

DOWNFALL	Allied operation plan for the invasion of the Home Islands of Imperial Japan (tentatively scheduled for November 1945)
DRAGOON	Allied Forces amphibious landing at St. Tropez, France [15.August.1944]
DSC	Distinguished Service Cross
EBW	Exploding-BridgeWire detonator used in implosion-type atomic explosive
ETO	European Theater of Operations
FAAA	First Allied Airborne Army
FAILINGS	TS-SCI compartment for all classified material associated with Operation UNTHINKABLE (fictitious code name)
Fat Man	second deployed atomic bomb [Nagasaki, Japan; 9.August.1945], an implosion design with plutonium core
FBI	Federal Bureau of Investigation - United States domestic intelligence and security service
FHO	Foreign Armies East [*Fremde Heere Ost*] – German military intelligence organization covering Russia and Eastern Europe
Gadget	Manhattan Project engineering test unit detonated at Trinity Site to prove the implosion design [16.July.1945]
GC&CS	Government Code and Cypher School (AKA Bletchley Park, Station X) [predecessor of British Government Communications Headquarters (GCHQ)]
GRU	*Glavnoye Razvedyvatel'noye Upravleniye* ([Soviet] Main Intelligence Directorate) military intelligence and special operations agency
GUMPS	**G**as-**U**ndercarriage-**M**ixture-**P**rop-**S**peed – pilot's quick landing readiness acronym
H-Hour	designated initiation hour for a military operation
Hg	mercury –inches of mercury used to measure pressure
HMG	His Majesty's Government
HMS	His Majesty's Ship
HUNTER	TS-SCI compartment for OSS air support information and Bainbridge Air Services operations
ICEBERG	Allied operation to seize Okinawa

IJA	Imperial Japanese Army
IRON CROSS	code name for an OSS special operations mission into Obersalzberg, Germany, to disrupt the Nazi Redoubt potential, and to capture or kill Adolf Hitler
Jedburgh	code-name for joint special operations units within MI6, SOE and OSS
JIC	Joint Intelligence Committee – representatives from various departmental organizations within the U.S. Government
JCS	Joint Chiefs of Staff – military service chiefs
L-Day	Landing Day
LFA	*Luftfahrtforschungsanstalt* (Aeronautical Research Institute, AKA Hermann Göring Aeronautical Research Center
Little Boy	first deployed atomic bomb [Hiroshima, Japan; 6.August.1945], a gun-type design with enriched uranium core
MAGIC	TS-SCI compartment for decrypted messages from the Japanese Purple encryption device
Manhattan Project	Allied nuclear weapons development program
MARKET GARDEN	Allied operation to cross the Rhine River at Nijmegen and Arnhem
MC	Medical Corps – U.S. military medical services branch
MD	Medical Doctor
MI5	Security Service – British internal security service, roughly equivalent to the American FBI
MI6	Intelligence Service – British Secret Intelligence Service, responsible to collection, analysis, and distribution of foreign intelligence information
MI19	British interrogation service of German POWs
MP	Military Police
MPH	Miles Per Hour
MTS	British Mechanised Transport Corps
NAPLES II	planned Allied Expeditionary Forces (AEF) airborne and glider landings near Cologne, Germany (not executed)
NKGB	*Narodny Komissariat Gosudarstvennoi Bezopasnosti* ([Soviet] People's Commissariat for State Security) responsible for foreign intelligence operations

NKVD	*Narodny Komissariat Vnutrennikh Del* ([Soviet] People's Commissariat for Internal Affairs) responsible for internal security
OCTAGON	Allied Summit Conference in Quebec City, Canada (12/16.September.1944)
ODESSA	*Organisation Der Ehemaligen SS-Angehörigen* (Organization of Former SS Members) – secret Nazi SS support group
OLYMPIC	Allied operation plan for the invasion of the Kyushu, Imperial Japan (tentatively scheduled for November 1945), the first part of Operation DOWNFALL
OP	Observation Post or OutPost
OSS	Office of Strategic Service [predecessor of the Central Intelligence Agency (CIA)]
OTU	British Operational Training Unit – second stage pilot training
OVERCAST	American operation for exploitation of German specialists in science and technology in the United States; later became Operation PAPERCLIP (3.September.1946)
OVERLORD	Allied Expeditionary Forces (AEF) amphibious, airborne and glider landings in Normandy, France (6.June.1944)
PAC or Pac	-- Pilotless Aircraft -- Pacific
PACCOM or PacCom	Pacific Command
PACKARD	one of numerous Jedburgh joint OSS/SOE teams sent behind enemy lines to aid resistance units
PAPERCLIP	U.S. post-war operation to recruit German experts in a wide variety of engineering, scientific, and counter-intelligence fields to assist U.S. development and operational programs
PARAMOUNT	TS-SCI compartment for all classified material associated with the Manhattan Project (fictitious code name)
PhD	Doctor of Philosophy – a high level education degree
POINTBLANK	Allied strategic air forces operations to diminish Nazi German fighter operations
POW	Prisoner of War
PTO	Pacific Theater of Operations

PURPLE	TS-SCI compartment for decrypted messages from the Japanese naval code from the JN-25 device
RADAR or radar	RAdio Detection And Ranging
RAE	Royal Aeronautical Establishment at Farnborough, Hampshire, England – British aviation research organization, roughly equivalent to the aviation segment of NASA
RAF	Royal Air Force
RaLa	contraction of radioactive lanthanum (^{140}La) and a broad, general descriptor for implosion technique experiments within the Manhattan Project
RN	Royal Navy
RODEO	fighter sweeps over enemy territory
SAS	Special Air Service – British special operations service
SCDW	*Saikō Sensō Shidō Kaigi* (Supreme Council for the Direction of the War) – the Japanese equivalent of the British War Cabinet or Defence Committee
SCR	Set, Complete, Radio – a general U.S. designation for a variety of radio frequency units
SHAEF	Supreme Headquarters Allied Expeditionary Force
SILVERPLATE	509th Composite Group – atomic bomb delivery unit
SIS	Secret Intelligence Service (AKA MI6 and the Intelligence Service)
SOE	Special Operations Executive – secret espionage agency of the Economic Warfare Ministry
SS	*SchutzStaffeln* (protection squads, AKA Black Shirts) – Nazi Party paramilitary organization under Himmler's command
TERMINAL	code name for the Potsdam summit conference with Churchill (Attlee), Stalin, and Truman (17.July to 2.August.1945)
THUNDERCLAP	-- Exercise THUNDERCLAP was a SHAEF staff tabletop simulation exercise to assess the readiness of the Operation OVERLORD amphibious assault plan -- Operation THUNDERCLAP was an Allied operations plan for the strategic bombing of German cities
TNT	TriNitroToluene – an explosive substance

Trinity	code name for the full-scale test of atomic explosive (Gadget) at Alamogordo, New Mexico
TS-SCI	Top Secret – Sensitive Compartmented Information
TUBE ALLOYS	British nuclear weapons development program collateral to the Manhattan Project
TWA	Transcontinental & Western Airlines (predecessor to Trans World Airlines)
ULTRA	TS-SCI compartment for decrypted messages from the German Enigma device
UNTHINKABLE	British planning project for military operations against the Soviet Union to push the Soviets back to the pre-war border
U.S.A.	United States of America
USA	United States Army
USAAF	United States Army Air Forces (predecessor of the U.S. Air Force)
USAFFE	United States Army Forces Far East
USAR	United States Army Reserve
USFET	United States Forces European Theater
USMA	United States Military Academy, West Point, New York
USMC	United States Marine Corps
USN	United States Navy
USNA	United States Naval Academy, Annapolis, Maryland
USO	United Service Organizations Inc. – American nonprofit-charitable corporation provides live entertainment to members of the U.S. Armed Forces and their families
USS	United States Ship
USSR	*Soyuz Sovetskikh Sotsialisticheskikh Respublik* (Union of Soviet Socialist Republics)
VARSITY	Allied Expeditionary Forces (AEF) airborne and glider landings near Wesel, Germany (24.March.1945)
VENONA	highly classified signals intelligence program to penetrate Soviet encrypted communications
VHF	Very High Frequency radio band
VHF-AM	Very High Frequency – Amplitude Modulation – a type of radio commonly used by aviation units
VHF-FM	Very High Frequency – Frequency Modulation – a type of radio commonly used by ground units

VIP	Very Important Person
VMI	Virginia Military Institute
WAC	U.S. Army Women's Auxiliary Corps
WATCH ON THE RHINE	Operation WATCH ON THE RHINE (*Unternehmen Wacht am Rhein*) – planning code name for the German winter counter-offensive in the Ardennes Forest region of Belgium and Luxembourg (16.Deember.1944); became known as the Battle of the Bulge; name changed to AUTUMN MIST in early December, two weeks before execution
WILD	TS-SCI compartment for OSS Director travel itinerary and progress reports (fictitious)
X-2	OSS Counterintelligence Branch

British honors:

bar	second and subsequent award
Bart	Baronet - member of a British hereditary order of honor, not peerage
BEM	British Empire Medal
CH	Order of the Companions of Honour
DFC	Distinguished Flying Cross
DL	Deputy Lieutenant
DSO	Distinguished Service Order
FRS	Fellowship of the Royal Society
GC	George Cross

<u>Most Honourable Order of the Bath</u>

GCB	**K**night Grand Cross, Most Honourable Order of the Bath
KCB	**K**night Commander, Most Honourable Order of the Bath
CB	Companion, Most Honourable Order of the Bath

<u>Most Excellent Order of the British Empire</u>

GBE	**K**night Grand Cross, Most Excellent Order of the British Empire
KBE	**K**night Commander, Most Excellent Order of the British Empire
CBE	Commander, Most Excellent Order of the British Empire

OBE	Officer, Most Excellent Order of the British Empire
MBE	Member, Most Excellent Order of the British Empire

<u>Most Venerable Order of the Hospital of Saint John of Jerusalem</u>

OStJ	Officer, Most Venerable Order of the Hospital of Saint John of Jerusalem

<u>Most Distinguished Order of Saint Michael and Saint George</u>

KCMG	**K**night Commander, Most Distinguished Order of Saint Michael and Saint George
CMG	Companion, Most Distinguished Order of Saint Michael and Saint George

<u>Royal Victorian Order</u>

CVO	Commander, Royal Victorian Order
MVO	Member, Royal Victorian Order
Kt	**K**night Bachelor - basic rank granted to a man who has been knighted by the monarch but not inducted as a member of one of the organised orders of chivalry
LM	Legion of Merit
MC	Military Cross
MP	Member of Parliament (an elected member of the House of Commons)
OM	Order of Merit
PC	Privy Council – selected advisors to the King/Queen
TD	Territorial Decoration
VC	Victoria Cross

—

Prologue

Major Brian Arthur Drummond, USAAF, had been flying frontline Allied fighter aircraft since the autumn of 1939, after he left his childhood home in Wichita, Kansas, to cross the Canadian border and join the Royal Air Force as an American volunteer pilot. A fellow fledgling aviator, Jonathan Kensington, completed Operational Training Unit Seven (OTU7) together and joined No.609 Squadron, flying Supermarine Spitfires through the Phoney War and the greatest aerial battle in history—the Battle of Britain. Brian and Jonathan became friends and lifelong members of The Few—memorialized by Prime Minister Churchill in his 20.August.1940 speech to the House of Commons.

> "Never in the field of human conflict was
> so much owed by so many to so few."

During one of his several episodes of being shot down during the great air battle, he was rendered unconscious when his Spitfire disintegrated, and he miraculously landed still unconscious and seriously injured under his parachute in a farm pond. A widowed woman and owner of the pond jumped in and nearly lost her life saving his. For her courage and selflessness, King George VI awarded the George Cross to Charlotte Grace Palmer, née Tamerlin; Brian had been awarded his first Distinguished Flying Cross at the same ceremony. Charlotte resisted, but their relationship grew under Brian's relentless insistence. They married in December 1940, and their first-born came the following June—Son Ian Malcolm Drummond.

Early on New Year's Day 1941, after celebrating, Brian's parents had been killed in a freak traffic accident. Beyond the shock of losing both his parents at the same time, he was shocked to learn that they had accumulated a substantial estate that he inherited. The new resources had enabled Charlotte and Brian to expand Standing Oak Farm and take on a huge U.S. Army contract to produce vegetables for the war effort in Europe. Those inherited resources also enabled Brian to form Bainbridge Air Services, Inc. (BAS), a quasi-airline in direct support of the national intelligence agency, the Office of Strategic Service (OSS).

Relationships blossomed during the war. Brian's best friend, Wing Commander Jonathan Andrew Xavier 'Harness' Kensington, CVO, DFC, who now served as the commanding officer of RAF North Weald, was expecting his first child with his wife Linda Kensington, née Mason. Like his brother-in-arms, Jonathan was also a decorated ace fighter pilot who held a further distinction of being chosen as a service exploitation pilot. He had flown all of the captured German aircraft held by the Royal Aeronautical Establishment.

Brian's British mentor was Air Vice Marshal Sir John Henry Randolph Spencer, KCMG, DFC, Air Officer Commanding-in-Chief of No.37 Group, flying Supermarine Spitfire fighters in support of the 15th Army Group fighting Germans in Italy. Sir John collaborated with his best friend and brother-in-arms from the Great War, and Brian's American mentor and flight instructor Malcolm Bainbridge, who died in a freak winter aircraft accident in March 1940. Sir John was also the nephew of Winston Churchill, whom he introduced to Brian before the war. Sir John was married to Mary Elizabeth Ann Spencer, née Armstrong, and they had a young son, Malcolm Ian, and a younger daughter, Charlotte Mary.

Brian and Jonathan's flight instructor at OTU7 was by now Group Captain Lord Jeremy Robert Kenneth 'Mud' Morrison, Esq., younger brother of the 8th Duke of Cottingstone, and Commanding Officer of RAF Hamble, a major repair and delivery center and home of the Air Transport Auxiliary (ATA) – the British aircraft ferry service. Independent of their duty, Jeremy met and eventually married ATA Third Officer Marilyn Powell, an American volunteer ferry pilot on an exchange tour who decided to remain in England when she met Jeremy.

Intelligence field agent extraordinaire, Trevor Thomas Andersen, had begun his professional career after graduating from Cambridge University. He had been given the code name DIAMOND when he joined Naval Intelligence, and he retained that code name when he was transferred to the Special Operations Executive (SOE). Trevor spoke several languages fluently in addition to English—German, French, and Polish. He ran or participated in numerous important operations including the capture of a functional German Enigma cipher device before the war, the attempted capture or assassination of General Rommel with a Special Air Service (SAS) unit in North Africa, the potential recruitment of the White Rose dissent student group in Münich, and the sabotage of a German armor reconnaissance unit with the local French Maquis group in support of Operation DRAGOON. Trevor used numerous aliases in the field including Robert Henry Stone Johnston, François Deschamps, and Tobias Weber.

The Western Allies had landed successfully on the Normandy beaches of France in the spring of 1944, while the Red Army had fought hard against the dwindling German war machine to the Vistula River in Poland. Two weeks after OVERLORD began, the Red Army began their long-awaited Operation BAGRATION – the final push in coordination with the Western Offensive. East and West were in a race to Berlin and the unconditional defeat of the last Axis power in Europe. The joint British and American Manhattan Project had retained its focus on development of an atomic explosive and shifted their application from Germany to Japan. The Germans carried out a surprisingly secret and aggressive last gasp winter offensive that became known as the Battle of the Bulge. Lieutenant General George Smith Patton, Jr., USA [USMA 1909], commanding general of the U.S. 3rd Army, shifted one armor and two infantry divisions for a thrust north to relieve the surrounded 101st Airborne Division at Bastogne, Belgium. The German advance had been thwarted, and the enemy was being pushed back. The Western Allies were ready to initiate their final spring offensive to finish off the Germans. The end was near, and the Japanese were not far behind.

General of the Army Dwight David 'Ike' Eisenhower, USA [USMA 1915] had been the supreme commander of the Allied Expeditionary Force (AEF) since January 1944. Ike knew there was still hard fighting ahead, and the war was not over, yet, but he had begun devoting more attention to the occupation and denazification of Germany, and the transfer of the bulk of ETO forces to the Pacific for Operation DOWNFALL—the invasion and defeat of Japan. The war in Europe was not yet won, but the focus of the leaders had already begun to shift to the Pacific Theater of Operations (PTO).

President Franklin Delano Roosevelt had been in declining health for months. Everyone knew it. Even the president recognized the reality, although he refused to acknowledge his weakening state. He had just been elected to an unprecedented fourth term as president. Roosevelt had also agreed with his friend, compatriot and fellow traveler, Winston Churchill, to make the long arduous journey to Crimea for the ARGONAUT (Yalta) Conference. He was not looking forward to the trip, but he knew he had to do it. Stalin refused to fly or take a ship, so the Western leaders had to go to him.

Prime Minister Winston Leonard Spencer Churchill, CH, TD, FRS, MP for Epping, had held his position as the King's first minister and the leader of the coalition War Cabinet since the German invasion of the Low Countries and France in the spring of 1940. He had inspired the nation he led and the Commonwealth in those dark days of 1940/41 with his words alone. Churchill had reached out to the leader of the United States during the peak of the isolationist years before Pearl Harbor to unilaterally send vital secret military technology to America. He also gained the president's support and consent for an exchange of British western hemisphere basing rights for 50 surplus Great War destroyers needed for the life-threatening Battle of the Atlantic. Churchill's prescient insight continued to play a major role in international affairs.

Director of the Office of Strategic Service Major General William Joseph 'Bill' Donovan, USA, was a successful lawyer and Medal of Honor recipient from the Great War. He was often referred to as Wild Bill for his aggressive style, or Big Bill in contrast to his relationship with Churchill's principal intelligence liaison in the United States, William Samuel 'Bill' 'Intrepid' Stephenson, MC, DFC, who was comparably known as Little Bill for his stature beside Donovan. President Roosevelt was a law school classmate and turned to Donovan to create a strategic intelligence agency to provide him a top-level international intelligence perspective. Under the president's direction, Donovan formed the Coordinator of Information (COI) in 1941 and began constructing a strategic intelligence apparatus. A year later, after Pearl Harbor, again at the president's direction, Donovan transitioned COI to the new Office of Strategic Services (OSS)

And so, here begins our story.

—

Chapter 1

I like the dreams of the future
better than the history of the past.
-- Thomas Jefferson

Monday, 1.January.1945
USAAF Station F-356 (formerly RAF Debden)
Saffron Walden, Essex, England
United Kingdom
07:20 hours

"Well, gentlemen," Arnie began, "this is a different one, and we don't have much time. First, Happy New Year to all of you reprobates." A few muttered comments did not stop him. Lieutenant Colonel James Averell 'Arnie' Clark, Jr., USAAF, had been the commanding officer of the 334th Fighter Squadron for a year and led the pilots through the difficult operations of last year. "Intel has reliable indications that the Germans are likely to execute a major aerial attack on Allied forward airfields and support facilities today. According to G-2, they may well throw everything left at the Western Front to counter our successes of the last couple of weeks. We are likely to see 109s, 190s, 163s, and 262s," he said, referring to Bf109 and Fw190 front line fighters, and the Me262 jet and Me163 rocket fighter variants. "Our primary mission priority will be to keep the fighters off our troops. Our secondary task will be to destroy as many attackers as possible. Group had indicated that we should be prepared for elements to be released to tail the enemy to their bases. Most of Fighter Command will be airborne today to oppose the expected German air offensive."

The 4th Fighter Group would operate initially as a group under the command of Commanding Officer Colonel Donald James Matthew 'Horseback' Blakeslee, USAAF. The group would use a familiar tactic of rotating stacked squadrons with the highest squadron providing top cover, the middle squadron spotting for the low squadron that, in this instance, would take on the attacking Germans when they were spotted.

Arnie covered the expected weather and deployments of U.S. forces in the squadron's assigned sector, which was over the U.S. 3rd Army, having redeployed from Nancy to Luxembourg City, Luxembourg, and the southern flank of the German salient that was slowly being whittled away. They would ingress into their operating area as a group and then separate. The 334FS would be the initial low squadron. Then, if the Germans did not show, Horseback would release them for ground attack missions at the frontlines on the northern side of their sector. The intelligence and the plan had the makings of a good hunting day.

The 4FG took to the air by section in the dark of pre-dawn to place them in their sector air space at or near dawn. A group of 50 P-51D fighters was a formidable instrument of war, and they were one of ten fighter groups in the first wave over the Western Front, with other groups timed to arrive and maintain a constant cover over the Allied lines. If the Germans did show, they would be coming from the morning sun and more difficult to detect, but the Americans were ready.

At their ingress altitude of 15,000 feet, the western horizon began to lighten before they could see the ground. Occasional flashes appeared ahead of and below them. Artillery. Horseback adjusted their heading slightly to the south. We're early.

"Cobweb, Cobweb Six. We're entering a broadside five-mile racetrack." A holding pattern at the western boundary of their assigned sector. They would remain stacked by squadrons with step down 1,000 feet apart. It's awkward but workable. "We'll get the sun shortly. Throttle back for fuel. We'll wait for the sun to reach the ground or bandits arrive. Eyes out."

Blakeslee took them into the holding pattern. As the first low squadron, the 334FS was at the bottom of the stack, and Brian's 'B' Division was the lowest of the 334FS aircraft. The sun rose on the eastern horizon and illuminated the array of fighter aircraft assembled above the battle zone. Brian switched to his shaded goggles to improve his ability to see approaching Germans coming out of the sun. Yet, he saw none, and that made him more than a little antsy. It would take another 20 minutes or so for the sunlight to reach the ground below them.

As the pine trees became discernible below them, Horseback broadcast, "Cobweb, Cobweb Six, descend to your initial positions."

Arnie took the 334FS down to their low perch at 2,000 feet. The 335FS would be immediately above them at 5,000 feet, and the 336FS and group CO would be at 10,000 feet. Arnie signaled each of the division leaders to assume their spread positions. Each division entered a 25-mile-long west-east racetrack with each section opposite the other. Brian's wingman, Second Lieutenant Karl Eugene 'Corn' Eiger, USAAF, of Hershey, Pennsylvania, held a perfect combat spread position, one mile off Brian's left wing. Each division assumed a similar pattern five miles apart. Per the mission briefing, they kept their speed in the mid-range.

When they could see troops on the ground, they were generally moving north and nearly universally cheered. They appreciated hearing and seeing the graceful Mustangs roaming over their heads—very reassuring.

Brian constantly scanned the sky above them and the ground ahead of them. *Looks like there's more business north of us. Nothing here so far. Corn's still good.* Brian turned back to the west. Corn crossed over to hold his spread position. About halfway back, they saw the Red Flight Second Section going east. First Lieutenant Gerald Adam 'Hole' Horten, USAAF, of Omaha, Nebraska, served as section leader, and Second Lieutenant Jackson 'Horn' Lee, USAAF, of Richmond, Virginia, was Hole's wingman.

"Cobweb, Cobweb Six, rotate."

Brian immediately located Arnie as he pulled up into a climb. Both divisions began to rejoin. Brian's 'B' Division reformed before they took up a position a half mile behind and a few hundred feet below Arnie's 'A' Division. Arnie leveled off at 10,000 feet. Horseback was 1,000 feet above Arnie.

Something is definitely happening to our north. Black smoke trails in the sky and explosions on the ground seemed to validate Brian's observations. *Damn, he could have given me a heads up.*

The group cycled through the three levels four times. eventually called the group's bingo as the 78th Fighter Group checked in on station. They returned to Debden without any difficulty. Blakeslee ordered a quick turnaround—mostly fuel, but a few needed a top-off of ammunition. Most of 334FS were able to debrief since there was not much to offer. The group repeated the mission two more times, departing the sector at sunset. The return to base was simple enough and without incident.

Arnie insisted upon gathering the pilots in the Operations building after they completed their debriefings for the day. They had already missed the evening meal sitting in the Officer's Mess. "I'll make this short. It's late, and we've already missed dinner. Colonel Blakeslee has been relieved of command and transferred to 8th Air Force Headquarters. As a result of that transfer, I have been relieved of command of the 334th to assume command of the 4th Fighter Group. As a consequence of my transfer, Major Drummond has been chosen to become the commanding officer of the 334th Fighter Squadron." Cheers erupted. Shouted congratulations shook the windows.

Brian received numerous punches in the shoulders or thighs. Damn, he could've given me a little head's up. Arnie held up both hands. The room quieted. "Since we've missed dinner, the truck will take us to The Cocks. I'm buying dinner and drinks, although we can't stay long. We've got a repeat of today's mission early tomorrow. Let's be safe." The Fighting Cocks Public House remained the pilots' favorite pub in the Debden area. Shepherd's Pub in London still held the status as the fighter pilots' number one bar and grill, in American parlance, but The Fighting Cocks served their purpose closer to home base.

—

Monday, 1.January.1945
Springwood Estate
4097 Albany Post Road
Hyde Park, Dutchess County, New York
United States of America
16:35 hours

Roosevelt had been working solo in his office since lunch. His friend and political confidant Harry Lloyd Hopkins and his military chief of staff, Admiral William Daniel 'Bill' Leahy, USN [USNA 1897], had been in and out sporadically throughout the afternoon. Things were going well in Europe. The German winter counteroffensive had been stopped and was being pushed back. Even in the Pacific, the Nimitz island-hopping plan was progressing well.

The president put one report in his Outbox and picked up the next report from his Inbox. The knock on the door brought a sense of relief. "Enter."

Leahy stepped inside, closed the door behind him, and extended his left hand with a folder to the president. "We just received a personal for you from the prime minister."

"Thanks, Bill," Franklin answered and took the folder.

TOP SECRET

```
DS
EMBLON NR 003
TS 010903Z JAN 45
FM US EMB LONDON FOR PM UK
TO POTUS
T O P   S E C R E T   P E R S O N A L
ROUTINE
BT
PM TO POTUS PERSONAL EYES ONLY NUMBER 871
HAPPY NEW YEAR TO YOU ELEANOR AND FAMILY STOP
THIS COMING YEAR IS THE YEAR OF OUR LONG
AWAITED VICTORY STOP WE SHALL BE DELIGHTED IF
YOU WILL COME TO MALTA PRIOR TO ARGONAUT STOP
I SHALL BE WAITING ON THE QUAY STOP YOU WILL
ALSO SEE THE INSCRIPTION OF YOUR NOBLE MESSAGE
TO MALTA OF A YEAR AGO STOP EVERYTHING CAN BE
ARRANGED TO YOUR CONVENIENCE STOP NO MORE LET
US FALTER STOP FROM MALTA TO YALTA LET NOBODY
```

```
ALTER BREAK
YOUR TRUE FRIEND BREAK
WINSTON END
BT
NNNN
```

TOP SECRET

"Have you read it?"

"No sir."

Roosevelt handed the message to Leahy, who read the missive before giving it back to the president. "I truly appreciate his enthusiasm, but sometimes I wish he would leave me alone," the president offered.

Leahy chuckled visibly, not audibly. "Would you like me to draft a rejecting reply to the invitation in a respectful manner?"

Franklin laughed more boldly. "Nice thought, Bill." The president lapsed into contemplation. "I genuinely appreciate your initiative and generosity, but no, thank you. I am tired. Part of me just wants to stay here, or the White House, or Warm Springs. But, the other part of me knows I have no choice. If we are to win the peace, I must convince Joe Stalin to honor our Tehran agreements. Winston has not given up on him, but he holds a rather cynical view of Uncle Joe's motives in Eastern Europe."

"If I may ask, Mister President, has your opinion changed?"

Roosevelt chuckled. "I would like to say no, but the truth is, Winston's incessant mantra is wearing on me. I give the man the benefit of the doubt until I have reason not to do so. I want to see the good in the man."

"Winston definitely sees the bad, but he also recognizes that we must work with the fellow. We cannot end one war only to enter another."

"Truer words cannot be said. However, I must confess my admittedly perhaps naïve hope that I can find a way to connect with him and move him to a more democratic approach."

"I guess there is always hope . . . until there isn't," Leahy said in a rather matter-of-fact manner. They both laughed.

"I suppose that should be the watchword for all of us," the president declared.

The two men remained quiet for a few minutes. Then, Leahy looked at the house and stood. "I'm getting the signal that dinner is ready for us."

"Then, let us be off. We don't want to keep the ladies waiting."

Sunday, 7. January. 1945
Forward Headquarters, 12ᵗʰ Army Group
Zonhoven, Limburg
Liberated Belgium
10:15 hours

General Officer Commanding-in-Chief, 12ᵗʰ Army Group, Field Marshal Sir Bernard Law 'Monty' Montgomery, KCB, DSO, decided he needed to hold a press conference to comment on the ongoing Allied counterattack in answer to the German counteroffensive that had become known as the Battle of the Bulge. Accordingly, Montgomery consulted with Chief of the Imperial General Staff (CIGS) Field Marshal Sir Alan Francis 'Brookie' Brooke, GCB, DSO, and gained permission for his intended news conference.

Several scores of British, American, and other Allied journalists gathered at the 12AG forward headquarters for a press conference called by Field Marshal Montgomery. The headquarters support staff had set up a large field tent just for the press conference. The muffled conversations between friends and colleagues ceased immediately when Montgomery entered the tent 15 minutes late. He did not wait for the commotion to settle.

"Good morning, gentlemen," Monty said in a commanding voice. "Thank you for attending. Let me start by saying that the battle for the salient is not yet over, but General von Rundstedt's forces are being written off. When General von Rundstedt attacked, he obtained a tactical surprise.

"As soon as I saw what was happening, I took certain steps myself to ensure that if the Germans got to the Meuse, they would certainly not get over the river. The situation had begun to deteriorate, but the whole Allied team rallied to meet the danger and national considerations were thrown overboard.

"General Eisenhower placed me in command of the whole northern front. I employed the whole available power of the British group armies, which were brought into play very gradually. They were brought in in such a way as not to interfere with the American lines of communication. The force has finally put into battle with a bang. The British divisions today are fighting hard on the right flank of the American 1ˢᵗ Army."

A rumbling among some attendees caused Montgomery to pause, but he clearly was not done or interested in questions or even recognizing the disturbance.

"The first thing to do was to see the battle on the northern flank as one whole, to ensure the vital areas were held securely, and to create reserves for counterattack. I embarked on these measures: I put British troops under command of the Ninth Army to fight alongside American soldiers, and made that Army take over some of the First Army Front. I positioned British troops as reserves behind the First and Ninth Armies until such time as American reserves could be created. Slowly but surely the situation was held, and then finally restored. Similar action was taken on the southern flank of the bulge by Bradley, with the Third Army.

"General von Rundstedt must have scraped together everyone possible reserve for his job, and he has not achieved a great deal. General von Rundstedt was really beaten by good fighting qualities of the American soldier and Allied teamwork.

"I first saw the American soldier in battle in Sicily and formed then a very high opinion of him. I saw him again in Italy. And I have seen a very great deal of him in this campaign. I want to take this opportunity to pay a public tribute to him. He is a brave fighting man, which stamps the first-class soldier. All these qualities have been shown in a marked degree during the present battle.

"The battle has been most interesting and possibly one of the trickiest I have handled, with great issues at stake. The first thing to be done was to head off the enemy at vital places. The next thing was to see him—rope him in and make quite certain he did not get the places he wanted, also that he was slowly removed from those places. He was, therefore, headed off, then seen off, and in now being written off.

"General von Rundstedt has now turned to the defensive and is faced by forces properly balanced to utilize the advantage he has lost. Another reason for the failure of General von Rundstedt's air force was that although he is still capable of pulling a fast one, he cannot protect his army. Our tactical air forces were the greatest terror to the German army.

"A great deal remains to be done. The battle has some similarity to that of August 31st, 1942. when Rommel made his last bid to capture Egypt and was seen off by the 8th Army. What is General von Rundstedt trying to achieve; nobody can tell for certain. The only guide we have is the order he issued to his soldiers before the battle began. He told them that it was the last great effort to try to win the war and that everything depended on it;-they must go all out. The gains on the map there did not win the war; they are likely to slowly and surely lose it all.

"Let me tell you that the captain of our team is General Eisenhower. I am absolutely devoted to Ike. We are the greatest of friends. It grieves me when I see uncomplimentary articles about him in the British Press. He bears a great burden and needs our fullest support. He has a right to expect it, and it is up to all of us to see that he gets it. Let us rally around the captain of the team and so help to win the match. Teamwork wins battles and battle victories win wars. On our team, the captain is General Ike."

Again, unintelligible, muffled exchanges of words disrupted Montgomery's speech. Finally, he paused for a moment to allow the chatter to dissipate. One journalist tried to ask a question, but the general waved it off dismissively. He was still not willing to entertain questions.

"One last point, nobody objects to healthy, constructive criticism, but we must put an end to destructive criticism, which was impairing Allied solidarity, and for the breaking up of the team that was helping the enemy. Let us have done with the destructive criticism that aims a blow at Allied solidarity.

"I have said what I needed to say. I've got a war to fight, and I must leave, so no time for questions. Thank you for coming." Field Marshal Montgomery marched smartly out of the tent. The assembly erupted into a cacophony of unintelligible shouted questions and protests. Monty did not hesitate or respond.

In the aftermath, Field Marshal Montgomery claimed he was well-intentioned, but the press conference did not sit well with American military leaders and singularly soured Anglo-American military relations for the remainder of the war and beyond.

The Germans exploited Montgomery's words of self-promotion by developing a fake BBC broadcast amplifying the implication that Montgomery had singularly thwarted the German counteroffensive. The broadcast, although false, gained traction among American leaders predisposed to believe the reporting on the British general, many thought was overly cautious and prone to self-promotion. By the time the Allies figured out what had happened, the damage had been done.

—

Sunday, 7. January. 1945
Site Y (Los Alamos National Laboratory)
Los Alamos, Los Alamos County, New Mexico
United States of America
09:30 hours

Commanding General of the Manhattan Project Major General Leslie Richard 'Dick' Groves, Jr., USA CEC [USMA 1918] arrived earlier in the morning, knowing what was scheduled for the morning. The technical team under the scientific director and head of the Site Y laboratory Julius Robert 'Oppie' Oppenheimer, PhD (Physics), had supervised a series of tests since September of last year to develop and refine the implosion technology needed for the plutonium bomb to function. Since September 1944, the team at the Site Y Laboratory had been working on the mechanics for the implosion technique.

Three designs made it through the gauntlet of physics, engineering, and manufacturing scrutiny to achieve the development team's focus. Each design had one objective—remain stable and safe until the instant came to achieve critical mass at the desired moment. Critical mass was a state of nuclear physics when fissile material attained a sustained chain reaction with an associated enormous energy release. Robert 'Bob' Serber, PhD (Physics), gave the three surviving designs their code names: Little Boy for a gun-type uranium device, Thin Man for a gun-type plutonium weapon, and Fat Man for an implosion plutonium bomb.

The Thin Man design had been abandoned in July of last year when the instability of plutonium 239 (^{239}Pu) proved insurmountable. The Little Boy design met all the design criteria, but uranium 235 (^{235}U) was difficult and slow to produce. Serber proposed an implosion technique to compress a plutonium sphere to its critical mass density. The first of a series of experiments had shown promising but not acceptable results last fall. The series of experimental detonations were called the RaLa experiments because they used radioactive lanthanum (RaLa, ^{140}La) to validate the implosion technique scientifically based on the measured neutron flux upon compression by the conventional explosives. While the initial event had been promising, subsequent attempts convinced the team that using a multipoint detonating cord system would not achieve the necessary compression precision.

To gain the needed exactitude, the team developed what became known as an exploding-bridgewire detonator (EBW), also known as an exploding wire detonator. The electrical current required to activate an EBW traveled at the speed of light. To achieve the precise symmetrical compression of the plutonium sphere, the EBWs inserted into 32 accurately shaped explosive lenses had to detonate as close to the same instant as possible, causing the shockwaves to hit the target at the same instant with the same force. The symmetric shockwave would compress the softball-sized core to the size of a tennis ball sufficient to achieve critical mass.

This morning's RaLa test was the first full-up implosion shot on the radiolanthanum target using the EBW detonated implosion. General Groves and Doctor Oppenheimer arrived 30 minutes before the planned event. Groves was familiar with Technical Area 10 (TA-10) in Bayo Canyon.

"Good morning, General. Director," Serber said, as the two men entered the test block house.

"Good morning, Bob," Dick and Oppie said in unison.

"We're ready."

"Proceed," ordered Oppenheimer.

The team stepped through their checklist to ensure one more time that the firing circuits were ready. The instrumentation array was ready. And all of the safety precautions were satisfied and complete. Finally, the test technician radioed the network to take their safety positions for the shot. Serber looked at Oppenheimer, who nodded his head. Bob responded with his left thumb up, and then he patted the technician on the shoulder and said, "Go."

The technician broadcast, "Fire in the hole. Ten. Nine. Eight. Seven. Six. Five. Four. Three. Two. One."

A large white flash of light replaced the small metallic ball a mile away at the bottom of the canyon. The shockwave hit the block house, shook the building, and knocked dust off everything inside the facility. Groves and Oppenheimer continued to look out the heavy window until the dust began to settle, and then they turned to face Serber.

The two senior leaders waited patiently. Oppie's inclination, as a scientist, was to look over the shoulder of the instrumentation team to see the strip charts himself, but he resisted for one reason only. He did not want to distract the test team from their task. Of course, he would eventually see the strip charts himself, but if General Groves got too close, he would want to understand what he was looking at. And that would be a distraction.

Neither the general nor the director spoke as the half dozen men of the test team huddled over the strip charts. Muffled conversation accompanied their undivided attention on the data.

Twelve long minutes later, Serber straightened up and turned to face the leaders. The stern expression made it look serious. No one spoke. The hint of a smile on Bob's face grew and bloomed into a broad, ear-to-ear, all-teeth grin. "The gamma-ray burst was greater than calculated and tighter than we've yet seen."

"My, my, my, that is very good news, Bob," Oppie said. The director looked over his left shoulder at the general. "That is the metric we wanted to see. We'll have to retrieve the core once it cools, carefully measure the dimension, and examine the data minutely before we know. The gamma-ray burst tells us we most likely achieved satisfactory compression."

"The next series of tests," Serber interjected, "will establish consistency— the repeatability of the results is essential."

"The data will tell us whether we have an acceptable design," added Oppenheimer. "It will take several days before we can examine and measure the core. Are you going to stick around for the results?"

"Nope. I've got to get to Site X with an intermediate stop at Site W before ending up at the Pentagon by Friday."

Only a handful of people knew that Site W was the Hanford Engineer Works on the Columbia River in Washington State and the site of Reactor B, the world's first plutonium production facility. Site X was the Oak Ridge National Laboratory in Oak Ridge, Tennessee, and the location of the centrifuge array enriching uranium 238 to isolate its fissile isotope, uranium 235. The facilities and code names were rarely associated, and even then, only by a few Manhattan Project leaders.

"I'll send along the results once we have them, but the preliminary results are quite encouraging."

"Thanks, Oppie. That should do nicely. We might have a functional design."

"We appear to be substantially closer than we were yesterday, but we still have some hurdles to cross. As we have discussed previously and given the sensitivity of the physics, it is looking like Bob Serber is correct. We're going to need a test of the full-up design."

"We can support that, I do believe. I'll confirm the production rates at Site W tomorrow. We need enough for your experimentation here as well as two or three devices by late spring. But, none of that matters without a viable design."

"Agreed. If we can duplicate these results with the next two shots, I think functionality may well be within reach. But, at the bottom line, only a full-up test will prove the science."

"We'll shoot for that. I'll prepare the secretary for that potential, and we need to blend that test shot into our timeline."

Oppenheimer nodded his head. "Now, mindful of the clock, we must get you to the airport."

The two leaders thanked the test team and departed. They dealt with some remaining business, and then Oppenheimer accompanied Groves to his waiting plane.

—

Monday, 8.January.1945
Chequers Court
Ellesborough, Buckinghamshire, England
United Kingdom
10:30 hours

Prime Minister Churchill decided to make a slow day of it. He needed to take the extra time to finish studying the ARGONAUT plans prepared by the Foreign Office, including the agreed agenda, negotiating positions pluses and minuses, and the avoid areas. Only one item was on today's agenda . . . well, two, if you count the evening meal. The War Cabinet was scheduled to meet at 16:00, and the dinner/social event was planned with Lord and Lady Selborne, and General Gubbins, at No.10.

Major General Colin McVean Gubbins CMG, DSO, MC, had a renown and decorated reputation as a special operations leader long before he became Director of Operations and Training at the newly formed Special Operations Executive (SOE) in July 1940. His reputation only grew from there.

Roundell Cecil Palmer, 3rd Earl of Selborne, had served in several governmental posts before he became Minister of Economic Warfare in February 1942. Within his ministerial domain was SOE, in which Lord Selborne immersed himself. While Gubbins would attend the prime minister's dinner unaccompanied, having divorced from his wife of 25 years after the death of their oldest son at Anzio on an SOE support mission in 1944, Lord Selborne would be accompanied by his wife of 35 years, Grace Palmer, née Ridley, Countess of Selborne.

Churchill remained sitting up in bed. The morning breakfast tray had been removed an hour earlier. He had completed his morning Inbox and rang the handbell.

"Yes sir," said duty Private Secretary John Rupert 'Jock' Colville.

"I finished the morning pouch. There are a number of follow-up actions in there," Winston announced as he handed the leather case to Colville.

"What do you want to do now, Sir?"

"Frankly, I think I will doze a little before my bath and dressing. We'll leave for the city in time to make the War Cabinet meeting, which means I shall forego my afternoon nap and opt for another snooze during the drive."

Colville responded, "I shall see to it." He was gone only five minutes, just enough time to fluff his pillows, scoot down, and nearly achieve the dream world of sleep when the door knock brought Churchill back to abrupt consciousness. "Excuse me, Sir, a special courier has arrived."

"Show him in," Winston said as he sat up and adjusted his robe. He instinctively checked for the key around his neck, and then he retrieved and donned his glasses.

The prime minister stepped through the case opening process and removed a single pink paper.

MOST SECRET - ULTRA

```
MOST SECRET ULTRA
DATE 0323 08 JAN 1945
TO PM UK FM FO
```

```
FROM STATION X
SUBJECT MOST URGENT ULTRA
SENSITIVE
DATE 1007 07 JAN 1945
TO ARMY GROUP B
FROM THE LEADER
COPY RSHA OBW OB WEST
BREAK
YOU ARE HEREBY AUTHORIZED TO CONDUCT A
FIGHTING WITHDRAWAL FROM AUTUMN MIST TO
DEFENSIVE LINES AT RHINE BREAK 6 TANK ARMY
DIRECTED TO DISENGAGE AS SOON AS POSSIBLE AND
MOVE AS SWIFTLY AS POSSIBLE FOR DEFENSE OF
HUNGARY BREAK SPECIFIC ORDERS TO BE ISSUED
FROM ARMED FORCES HIGH COMMAND BREAK HAIL
VICTORY HAIL HITLER END
SENSITIVE
DECYPHERED 1901 07 JAN 1945
MOST SECRET ULTRA
```

MOST SECRET - ULTRA

Churchill returned the message to the case and locked it. The courier confirmed the case was locked. The prime minister asked, "Has this message entered the normal distribution process?"

"I'm afraid I don't know, sir. I can check as soon as I return to Broadway."

"Not necessary, young man. Simply ensure that it does. I need this message for the War Cabinet meeting at four this afternoon."

"Yes sir. Is there anything I can do, sir"

"No. Thank you. Safe journey."

When the courier opened the door, Colville stepped just inside the door. "I'll stand guard."

"No. The moment seems to have passed. Fetch Sawyers. I'll have my bath now."

Frank Sawyers had served as Winston's valet since 1936. He was a short, balding bachelor of a man who remained devoted to his charge.

"I'll fetch him straight away."

"Thank you, Jock. After I'm dressed, we'll have lunch, and then we'll head into the city."

As Churchill waited for Sawyers, his thoughts turned to the fallout from the Montgomery press conference yesterday. He knew he had to address it straight away with the War Cabinet. The Boniface message might soften the impact a little, but the feedback he had heard so far was unanimously not good. The outrage among the Americans undoubtedly meant he would have to address the issue in Commons, and his inclination told him he should raise it with Franklin next month before he did. Monty had embarrassed Great Britain.

Sawyers entered and asked, "You are ready for your bath?"

"Yes, I'm heading back to the city early."

———

Monday, 15.January.1945
Supreme Headquarters, Allied Expeditionary Force
Trianon Palace Hôtel
1 Boulevard de la Reine
Versailles, Yvelines, Île-de-France
Liberated France
11:45 hours

Field Marshal Brooke requested the private meeting with now five-star General Eisenhower. No agenda had accompanied the request, but Ike presumed he knew the principal topic. Brookie had to have heard the rage of American generals regarding Field Marshal Montgomery's press conference a week ago that had become widely known. The Allied counter-counteroffensive continued to make good progress.

Ike's chief of staff, Lieutenant General Walter Bedell 'Beetle' Smith, USA, knocked once, entered, and closed the door behind him. "Brookie has arrived. He'll be up here in a few minutes. Still no idea what this is about?"

"Only a guess, Beetle. I've never known Brookie to ask for a personal meeting without an agenda or at least a topic. I suspect that press conference a week ago."

"You will soon know. I'd better get outta here before he knocks on the door."

"Thanks, Beetle. We'll talk when this is done."

Smith departed. Eisenhower put his working papers aside. His aide-de-camp, Major Julius 'Juli' Calhoun, USA, from Macon, Georgia, who had been with the general since arrival in England, knocked and opened the door to announce Field Marshal Brooke.

"Great to see you again, Brookie," Eisenhower said with a positive tone and extended his right hand. They shook hands, and Ike gestured to the facing couches.

"I would like to say it is great to see you, Ike, but I am afraid I come with hat in hand." Eisenhower nodded. The two men sat opposite each other. "I shall step into it straight away.

"I come to offer the apologies of the King, the prime minister, and His Majesty's Government for the inappropriate and uncalled-for words of Field Marshal Montgomery a week ago." Eisenhower started to respond but stopped when Brooke raised his hand. "He had called me to gain permission for the press conference. He said he wanted to dampen divisiveness in the press and coax them to contribute to Allied unity."

"He did not accomplish the stated objective."

"No, he did not. I am here to mend fences."

"There are fences to be mended. There are near-universal calls for me to relieve him of command for cause and send him home."

"I know. I hear the same calls. Monty has always been a bit headstrong and competitive, but he achieves results. He and Georgie are two peas in a pod."

"Personality-wise, yes. They are both highly competitive and successful field generals. They are both prone to self-promotion. And they apparently both run their mouths when they should just keep their opinions to themselves. I appreciate his efforts to defend me and Allied unity, but it was not necessary. I suppose American generals are more accustomed to the aggressiveness of the press."

"Perhaps so."

"Apologies accepted. I will also say that my rational side is not inclined to relieve Monty."

"Prime Minister Churchill asked me to make this journey and instructed me to inform you that he will address the matter in Commons tomorrow. He is on your side. I am on your side as well, Ike. We will do what needs to be done to repair any damage done by Monty's words."

"Thank you, Brookie. It is water under the bridge. We've got major river crossings ahead of us and the spring offensive to defeat our enemy."

"Which brings me to my next topic. I want to offer one last plea on behalf of His Majesty's Government to abandon the pivot to Vienna and Austria. In this, I think the prime minister's position is correct—Berlin is the objective, not Vienna."

"I've heard all the arguments, Brookie. Even Patton agrees with you, although I suspect his motivation is quite like Messina. He wants to beat Monty and the Soviets to Berlin." The two generals chuckled with memories of the induced competition between Montgomery and Patton to reach Messina, Sicily first. "My assignment from the leaders of our countries is to command the Allied Expeditionary Force to victory as soon as humanly possible. There is no debate that Berlin is important. However, given the intelligence and the situation, my concern is that taking Berlin will not win the war."

"Humph," Brooke reacted and paused. "M-I-6 is not convinced the rumors of the Alpine redoubt are practically realizable."

"And they may very well be correct. My problem is that the independent facts offer stronger indications than we had a month ago, and we are just now returning to the lines of a month ago. Hitler withdrew the 6th Panzer Army to Hungary. They are mostly *Waffen-S-S*. They are not enough to stop the Red Army, and their natural line of withdrawal is Obersalzberg. All the signs are pointing to that Nazi redoubt in the Obersalzberg region. The rumors may not be true. We doubted the indications of WATCH ON THE RHINE and AUTUMN MIST, and we got burned because we doubted or discounted the intelligence. We must not make that mistake again. We are not going to ignore Berlin, but we must interdict those S-S units and especially the 6th Panzer Army from reaching the Obersalzberg."

"So, your mind is made up?"

"Brookie, I appreciate your candor and argument. I also recognize, understand, and appreciate why the prime minister is so focused on Berlin and the Red Army. I do not doubt or dispute the prime minister's position, but my orders are to end the war as quickly as we can with the forces we have. My orders are not to end part of the war but the whole war in Europe. The potential of a pocket of Nazi fanatics with powerful weapons continuing to operate is not ending the war in total."

"Very well, Ike. We all respect your position and decision. To summarize, the 21st Army Group will press on across Northern Germany to Berlin, and the 12th Army Group will penetrate Southern Germany to Austria and potentially Hungary."

"I will only add that as long as the situation and intelligence generally remain the same, it is my intention to head the 1st Army to Berlin once they are across the Rhine to hold Montgomery's right flank, and the 3rd and 7th Armies will pivot to Austria and potentially Hungary."

Brooke nodded his acknowledgment. "We will do our best to help you achieve victory as soon as possible."

"Thank you."

"What is your top-level view of the situation at the front?"

"We are making progress on the bulge. We estimate that in another few weeks, we will have collapsed the pocket. Monty has a toehold on the east bank of the Rhine in Holland. As soon as the front stabilizes, we'll rest and replenish units for the spring offensive. We've reviewed the crossing plans in each sector. We'll be ready when the weather breaks."

"Excellent. Now, I'm afraid I need to be on my way. I must get up to Brussels and give Monty the dressing down he deserves. I appreciate your candor and forthrightness . . . and shall we say tolerance. I shall do my part to rein in Monty's mouth."

"And you will probably have as much luck as I have had with George Patton." They both laughed at the comparison.

The two generals parted with respect. Eisenhower jumped into his paperwork. He knew Beetle would be in shortly to get his assessment of the conversation.

—

Friday, 19.January.1945
Standing Oak Farm
Winchester, Hampshire, England
United Kingdom
15:25 hours

The distinct sound of a horse's hooves on the gravel stones of the forecourt meant the earlier than expected arrival of Mabel Jane Bloodworth, who was the supervisor of the Brownfield greenhouse complex. Charlotte waited inside by the fireplace.

June Sorvon Cranston, the farm's accountant and bookkeeper, had already departed for the day. *She has been a godsend. They all have. I'm so grateful.*

Mabel entered the house a minute or so later, presumably turning over her horse's care to Jacob. She joined Charlotte at the fireplace. "I presume Todd is upstairs with Edith."

"Yes."

Mabel nodded her acknowledgment. "We've prepared another crop delivery of tomatoes, cucumbers, carrots, onions, lettuce, and cabbage. The Army agreed to pick it up tomorrow."

"Excellent. Good work, Mabel. Please pass along my gratitude to the crew."

"I will. The Americans keep pressing me for more vegetables, but we are producing as fast as possible. We implemented a staggered planting scheme to spread our deliveries rather than one big shipment. Local distributors are crying for more as well. We can increase our planting in the spring, but we are at full capacity of the greenhouses during the winter months."

"We need more greenhouses, but until then, we'll do the best we can with what we have."

"We have the water and the soil. The wood gas generators work perfectly, but we'd need more of those units, too. I took the liberty to call around to material suppliers. Unfortunately, there is no way to gather up the necessary materials with wartime restrictions."

"What about the American Army?" Charlotte asked. "They built the buildings we have."

"I've not raised the matter with the Americans. Perhaps I should."

"Tomorrow's pick-up may be an opportunity. Do you want me to open the discussions with the Americans when they arrive?"

Mabel thought for a moment. "I suppose the answer depends upon whether you trust me to make and close the deal with the Army."

"Oh, Mabel, I am so sorry you would even think I doubted your ability. You've done an exemplary job with the greenhouses. You know best what is needed. You have my complete backing. I only offered my help if you want it or need it."

"Thank you, Charlotte. I do appreciate your confidence."

"You have it . . . without qualification, Mabel."

"Thank you again. Now, I'd better go hug my son, or he might think I've abandoned him." Mabel stood and ascended the stairs.

Charlotte did not react when her thoughts went to a very dark place. *I'd like to hug my son, too . . . but I can't.* Charlotte felt the tears welling in her eyes, but she felt no urge to stop them from descending her cheeks. She stared at the flickering flames and glowing coals. The tears continued despite her best efforts to divert her thoughts from the terrible loss of their three-year-old son, Ian Malcolm Drummond, four months ago tomorrow. When the footfalls descending the stairs came to Charlotte's awareness, she quickly dabbed her eyes and cheeks, and then, she sat up straight, forcing a smile as broadly as she could manage.

Todd was the first to reach the landing, followed by his mother and Edith. The preschooler ran to Charlotte and wrapped himself around her neck. They exchanged words of affection, for which Charlotte was immensely grateful. Todd's innocence had done so much to help her recover, in addition to Brian's love and encouragement as well as the ladies who had diligently watched over and tended to her in the three months after the tragedy.

When Edith hit the landing, she nearly ran to the kitchen. "I am behind," she declared.

"My fault," Mabel added.

"Momma was helping me on my project," Todd added to defend his mother and Edith.

"Not to worry," Charlotte said.

"The dairy crew will be here shortly, and they will be hungry," Edith observed. Mabel jumped in to help. They chopped up vegetables from the farm's greenhouses and grated the farm's cheese.

In a surprisingly short amount of time, the two women had a large bowl of nutritious salad with fresh sliced bread on the table when the front door opened.

Lionel Bridges, Horace Morgan, and Jacob Holden entered. They reported on the afternoon's production. The laughter and light-hearted exchanges at the extended table brought a deep family feeling to the dinner. The process alone renewed and refreshed Charlotte. While she had her dark moments, every day seemed to be improving.

—

Monday, 22. January. 1945
Bureau of Engraving and Printing
14th and C Streets, Southwest
Washington, District of Columbia
United States of America
22:05 hours

Ferdinand Magellan, the president's custom-built, well-appointed and armored, special Pullman railcar, sat on the private underground siding. Porters were loading the baggage. The president's private car was just one of six cars that would eventually be coupled to a soon-to-arrive locomotive and tender.

President Roosevelt transferred from his transport wheelchair to a unique custom-built plush leather oversized chair in the salon. He really liked the chair, and every time he had the opportunity to sit in the chair, he thought about obtaining copies for Hyde Park, the White House, and Warm Springs. It was an exquisite piece of furniture.

The Cabinet attendees, diplomatic and military staff, were traveling by separate means—mostly flying. Others would meet the president and be aboard the USS *Quincy* when he arrived at Hampton Roads, Virginia, at 06:25 tomorrow morning. They would soon be en route to the ARGONAUT conference in Yalta, Crimea, Liberated Ukraine, scheduled to begin in two weeks. The summit conference of the Big Three would set the guidelines for post-war peace.

Roosevelt did not want to make the arduous journey, but his sense of duty drove him to find the least complicated or risky means, thus the heavy cruiser *Quincy* and the small task force to protect her.

An unusually small entourage would accompany him on the overnight train, stay with the president throughout the long journey, and included:
-- Admiral Bill Leahy, Chief of Staff to the President of the United States,
-- Vice Admiral Wilson Brown, Jr., USN [USNA 1897], Naval Aide to the President of the United States,
-- Major General Edwin Martin 'Pa' Watson, USA [USMA 1908], Senior Military Aide to the President of the United States,

-- Vice Admiral Doctor Ross T. McIntire, USN MC, MD, White House Physician,

-- Lieutenant Commander Doctor Howard Gerald Bruenn, USN MC, MD, dedicated cardiologist to the president.

Yet, to the ailing Franklin Roosevelt, the most important member of his onboard train traveling companions was Mrs. John Boettiger—his daughter Anna—who had become far more than his daughter. She had grown into his confidante, hostess, social advisor, and all-around Girl Friday. In large measure, Anna had virtually replaced Harry Hopkins as his Mrs. Fix-It.

The president began to nod off in the posh comfort of his chair when Anna finally joined him.

"Looks like we need to get you to bed, Papa," Anna said before she sat across from her father.

"We should be pulling out soon."

"Bill's on the platform waiting on the locomotive. All the baggage is loaded, so as soon as we get an engine to pull us, we'll be on our way."

"I'm tired, Anna. I'm should head to my compartment. I trust Admiral Leahy will tend to our transit."

Anna stood and secured the wheelchair as the president transferred himself to the mobile chair. She pushed her father to his plush, completely contained, larger than normal berthing compartment. "Would you like my assistance, Papa?"

"No, thanks, my darling. I can handle it."

Anna kissed her father's cheek and closed the compartment door behind her. Before she could take her seat, Anna felt the car lurch, which meant the locomotive and tender had just coupled with the assembled rail cars.

Admiral Leahy entered the car and joined Anna. The car lurched forward this time. "We are on our way," Bill announced.

—

Thursday, 25.January.1945
Hôtel-Dieu de Marseille
Marseille, Côte d'Azur
Liberated France
14:00 hours

General Marshall's aide-de-camp stood when General Eisenhower and Major Calhoun entered the lobby. He saluted the general and then gestured above them. They took the elevator to the third floor but did not talk since they were not alone. They walked to the end of the L-shaped corridor to Suite 301.

Again, Marshall's aide did not speak, unlocked the door, and only gestured for Eisenhower to enter. Marshall was standing to greet Eisenhower.

Marshall extended his right hand and said, "Great to see you again, Ike."

The two generals shook hands. "Likewise, Chief."

Marshall gestured to facing upholstered chairs. "Thank you for making the journey down here."

"You've come a long way and have a long journey ahead."

Both men sat. "What's the latest on our situation?"

Eisenhower gave the chief of staff an executive briefing summary of the Western Front situation. The Germans had been pushed back across the border and behind the Siegfried Line. They would keep the pressure on the Germans to prevent them from an orderly retreat. Ike also summarized the AEF plan for the spring offensive.

"Thank you for the summary, Ike. I think we can all understand Churchill's and the British focus on the Soviets. The Germans are done, but the corporal's ego will not let it end. Bill Donovan has given the president the details of the Nazi Redoubt and ODESSA business. The president, the secretary, and I agree with your decision to cut off the S-S."

"Thanks. Patton is not happy."

"He wants the glory of Berlin."

"Not much left of Berlin after the 8th Air Force and Bomber Command have done their work so well. There's not much left."

"The O-S-S believes the corporal has descended into his bunker below what's left of the Parliament building and remains there. Yet, they also find enough indications that the government, including the leader, will move to Berchtesgaden and his mountain retreat, the Berghof, to justify preparing for a special operation called IRON CROSS. Donovan has withdrawn one of his most successful field operators for a disruption mission near Berchtesgaden . . . very clever from my perspective. He's recruited a company's worth of anti-Nazi German P-O-Ws for the operation, and they are currently planning and training at an undisclosed location south of Paris. Further, as of three days ago, they have detected no attempts by the leadership, as yet, to flee Berlin for Berchtesgaden."

"Which would be a contra-sign to the redoubt hypothesis."

"That would be my read and Donovan's, by the way, but he is still preparing for the potential. Likewise, I think you have no choice but to prepare for the possibility as well."

"I assume my orders remain the same."

"Yes . . . why would you ask?"

"The prime minister and Brookie, just a week ago, have applied considerable direct and indirect pressure to dissuade me from the pivot."

"Your orders remain as they have been for the last year. I share your apprehension regarding what the corporal and his S-S might do if they gain footing in the Alps. My read of Churchill, and thus his generals, is that his vision remains on the future. I think what you are seeing is his concerns, his worries, if you will, have shifted from the war to post-war Europe. Frankly, I think he is correct in his assessment of Stalin and the Soviet hegemonic intentions in territories they conquered."

Eisenhower nodded.

"My next topic is personal and private . . . strictly between us." Again, Ike nodded. "From here, I'm headed to Malta for a pre-conference séance between the president, the prime minister, and the combined joint chiefs. Churchill convinced Roosevelt to stop en route to agree on the negotiating strategy with the Soviets."

"Tough nut."

"Ya got that right." Marshall paused to think. "This is the sensitive part. We are all concerned about Roosevelt's health. Ever since the OCTAGON Conference, we have noticed a marked deterioration in his appearance, attention span, and . . . shall I say sharpness. Those of us who have worked with him, watched him, admired his skills, and shared his vision of things have plainly noticed the changes. A word to the wise, prepare for the day we may lose him."

"He was just inaugurated for his unprecedented fourth term," Eisenhower protested.

"Yes, he was. His health was . . . well . . . shielded from public scrutiny. But, it is what it is. My point in raising this topic with you is that many of your soldiers will have only been aware of one man as their president. You and the other commanders should be prepared to deal with the loss when it comes."

"Good point. It is not something we have discussed, and clearly, we should."

"Forewarned is forearmed."

"Indeed."

"I will say, as chief of staff, we could not have asked for a better president in the conduct of this war. He is attentive, engaged, and contributive, but he keeps his distance from operational decisions. He lets us do our work without interference."

"You would know far better than me," Eisenhower responded, "But, from what I know directly validates your observations." Ike paused. Both generals remained silent for a couple of minutes. "We'll be . . ."

"No need, Ike. I know you'll be ready. One of your strong suits . . . you see the broad view and the path forward. I trust your judgment. I've said my peace. Now, I'd love to enjoy a nice social dinner," Marshall said, "but I need to get you back to the war and the final chapter. I leave in the morning for

Malta. Thanks for coming down here for this chat. Safe journey back to Paris." Marshall smiled. "Now, skedaddle, Ike."

"Thank you, sir."

Marshall laughed. "We are both the same rank now."

"You will always be my senior."

Marshall laughed again. "Somehow, I doubt that. George is fine between us, Ike."

Eisenhower stood, followed by Marshall. "As you wish, George. Good luck in Yalta."

"We'll need all we can get." Both men shook hands, and Eisenhower departed the hotel for his waiting VIP C-54 airplane.

Captain Aaron Banks, USA, Jedburgh PACKARD team leader, had been chosen to lead the Operation IRON CROSS mission. In addition to the disruption portion of their mission, they also had a collateral mission to capture or kill Adolf Hitler.

After the war, Banks would advocate for and become the first commander of the U.S. 10ᵗʰ Special Forces Group—the next phase of American special operations organizations. He used his experience with the OSS during the Second World War to develop the body of what would become known popularly as the Green Berets.

———

Friday, 26. January. 1945
Office of the Director, Office of Strategic Services
National Institutes of Health Building
2430 E Street Northwest (E Street Complex)
Washington, District of Columbia
United States of America
15:05 hours

OSS First Assistant Director Colonel Gonzalo Edward 'Ned' Buxton Jr., USA, had been Bill Donovan's principal deputy from the early COI days and remained so into the OSS. Ned saw Donovan's Cadillac limousine arrive. He stood and waited at his office door to see if his boss was up for a quick chat after his month-long journey to China.

Donovan turned the corner, saw Buxton, smiled, and nodded. Ned went to his couch. Bill shut the door and sat in the nice leather chair across from the couch.

"How was China?" asked Ned.

"Tricky is the best word I've got. I had to play a few games with the expert assistance of Nanking Station to avoid offending Chiang Kai-shek, but I finally met with Mao Zedong."

"Excellent."

"Yes, but the alliance between Mao's Chinese Communist Party and Chang's Kuomintang is straining. After talking frankly with Mao, I am convinced that he intends to confront Chang's governance."

"Civil war?"

Donovan nodded. "I'm afraid so. I probed to find some other path short of violence, but Mao made his intentions quite clear. The alliance remains focused on the Japanese for the moment, and they are continuing to make good progress. However, once the Japanese are out, Mao will undoubtedly turn the attention of his forces to the Kuomintang. The looming civil war is going to force our hand. We will have to pick sides, and conservatives in this country will not make it easy."

"As with all things, we'll have to deal with what comes."

"Quite so. I began my debriefing on the way home, but I'll need to complete it with the China Desk fellows in the next few days. After that, we need to get the analysis to State, and of course, to the president. The post-war years are going to be very tricky . . . at least in China. The revolutionary in Indochina, Ho Chi Minh, has been doing a magnificent job against the Japanese occupation forces, but that is another nut that could cause us problems, especially if the French decide to reassert themselves in the region."

"What's your read of France?"

"De Gaulle desperately wants to cement his self-professed status as *Le Président*. He has never been easy to read, and he still isn't. I suspect he is going to push us to back his nationalistic or perhaps even hegemonic intentions to reconstitute their colonies."

"Will we?"

"Not as long as Roosevelt is president. He made that point very clearly in the Atlantic Charter negotiations with Churchill. He insists the British relinquish dominance of their colonies. He sure as hell won't support French colonial aspirations." Donovan paused to gather his thoughts. "It's been a while since I've heard anything about IRON CROSS."

"As of the first of the week, Banks reported that their training was going well. However, he believes he needs two or three more months to prepare the team fully."

"He may not have that amount of time. So, we'll need to deploy the team as soon as we get indications that Hitler is moving out of Berlin."

"I'll draft a message for your sign-off to that effect."

"Thanks, Ned. Banks can and will use whatever time we can give him to keep training his team. We'll give him as much time as we can, but the driver will be Hitler's location or signs that the government is relocating, especially to the Alps region of Southern Germany."

"I'll summarize that for you."

Donovan nodded his consent. "Have we heard anything from the White House on our post-war plan?"

"Not a peep, and now, the president is headed to Yalta. He departed four days ago."

"So, we're probably not going to hear anything at least until he returns. He's going to be very busy and have his hands full with Stalin."

"Do you want to do anything?" asked Buxton.

"Not much we can do but wait for the president's direction. We need to keep things quiet and calm until the president decides how he wants to proceed or gives us further instructions on what he wants. How are the troops doing?"

"In a word . . . restless," Ned answered. "The question that seems to be foremost is whether the O-S-S is just a wartime artifact or Roosevelt's pet project to be discarded when the work is done."

"The work is never done. The work will change at the war's end, but Stalin is not going to let us rest. And, from what I learned in China, Mao is not going to be satisfied with a piece of the pie. He wants the whole damn thing. There is going to be more intelligence demand than ever. That is the point of Roosevelt's request for the post-war transition plan. Unfortunately, our work is in the shadows, as is our plan, and rightly so. Perhaps I should put out a personal 'All O-S-S' message to tamp down some of the restlessness."

"I suggest you hold on to that thought for now."

"We need to keep everyone focused on the task at hand. This war is not done yet. The politics will sort itself out. The landscape will change, and our adversaries' nature will shift. We might be able to forge a relationship with Mao and Ho in Indochina, but I hold no hope of a constructive relationship with Stalin. The Soviet dictator is far more focused on vengeance than peace . . . on dominance than cooperation. I can't predict the future. None of us can. But, at the bottom line, I see the need for our services to be greater after the war than it is now. We know our enemies today. Those people will not be so easily seen or understood when the war is done, which to me means a greater need for intelligence."

"Gotcha! I'll have a quiet chat with the department heads to softly settle things down. We need the president's decision and direction."

"Exactly. But I know better than to poke him. He'll tell us when he's ready."

"Very well."

"Anything else for now?" Buxton shook his head in the negative. "I'm going to the office to hit some of the reading you've stacked up for me."

The two intelligence leaders parted the 20 feet between their offices.

—

Chapter 2

It would be a mistake to push a man to violence,
if violence is what he has dedicated his life to perfecting.
> -- Lieutenant Commander James Reece,
> USN [Chris Pratt]
> Terminal List
> Season 1, Episode 6 - Transience

Friday, 2.February.1945
USS Quincy
Berth 9
Grand Harbor, Valletta
Crown Colony of Malta
09:35 hours

The heavy cruiser (CA-71) had entered Grand Harbor with gun salutes and bands playing. Her predecessor of the same name had been sunk at the Battle of Savo Island in 1942. The current *Quincy* had been well into construction when her predecessor had been sunk in combat. The Baltimore-class heavy cruiser took her new name and entered service in early 1944. This morning, she moored, starboard side to, at berth 9.

President Roosevelt sat in his narrow wheelchair on the flag bridge with Admiral Leahy beside him. Prime Minister Churchill, true to his word, stood on the quay and saluted as the official gun salute was delivered. The prime minister was due to arrive aboard *Quincy* in 20 minutes.

Admiral Leahy pointed to the north. A flight of six RAF Supermarine Spitfire fighters approached at modest speed and low altitude in a perfect delta formation. The reverberating sound of six full-throated Merlin engines accentuated the flyby. The president followed the formation as they banked to the east once clear of the harbor.

"They are magnificent machines," the president commented.

"They most certainly are, Mister President . . . excellent lines and a healthy bite." Roosevelt chuckled. "Do you want to meet the prime minister on the Quarter Deck?" Leahy asked.

"We put that decision off to the very end, didn't we? I think not, Bill. I'm afraid I must pass. I don't feel up to the struggle getting down there," Roosevelt responded, even though he had four husky sailors to lift him and his chair through the passageways and hatches. It was still not easy on him. "In fact, it would probably be wise to ask the sailors to move me to the Wardroom for our first meeting."

The admiral left the president alone for a few minutes to enter the enclosed flag bridge and call the sailors for the president's transport. The four sailors secured two thick wooden poles to the sides of his chair. Then, they carried him like a triumphant emperor through the hatches, passageways, and two ladderways, two decks down to the Wardroom and Officer's Mess. Once the president was situated at the head of the table, the sailors removed their poles and retired.

President Roosevelt's chief of staff placed a tablet of lined paper and several pens in front of the president. "Do you need anything else, Mister President?" Leahy asked.

"No thanks, Bill. This first session is the welcome aboard and the only military situation discussion. We'll open the meat of it this afternoon with the diplomatic conversations."

"Would you like me to remain with you for this session?"

"United Kingdom arriving," was announced over the warship's 1MC loudspeaker system.

"Yes, please attend. Our guests and his generals have arrived."

"They'll be here shortly. The joint chiefs will accompany the prime minister and his generals to the Wardroom."

The new arrivals entered the Wardroom single file, with Prime Minister Churchill leading the group. Churchill beamed as he stepped lively to his friend and colleague. As the two leaders greeted each other warmly, the remainder of the group filed into the comparatively small compartment.

For His Majesty's Government:

-- Chief of the Imperial General Staff Field Marshal Brooke,

-- First Sea Lord Admiral of the Fleet Sir Andrew Browne 'ABC' Cunningham, Bart., GCB, DSO**, and

-- Chief of Air Staff Marshal of the Royal Air Force Sir Charles Frederick Algernon Portal, GCB, DSO & Bar, MC.

For the United States of America:

-- Chief of Staff of the Army General of the Army George Catlett Marshall, Jr., USA [VMI 1901],

-- Chief of Naval Operations Fleet Admiral Ernest Joseph King, USN [USNA 1901], and

-- Major General Laurence Sherman Kuter, USAAF [USMA 1927], representing Chief Army Air Forces General of the Army Henry Harley 'Hap' Arnold, USAAF [USMA 1907], who was seriously ill. Arnold had suffered his fourth heart attack two weeks earlier and was still convalescing. Kuter served as Arnold's chief of staff.

Bringing up the rear of the file was the supreme commander's representative, Allied Expeditionary Force (AEF) Chief of Staff Lieutenant General Beetle Smith.

With greetings fulfilled, President Roosevelt said in a firm, commanding voice, "Shall we begin, gentlemen? Welcome aboard Quincy." To Franklin's pleasant surprise, the generals did not shift to their sides. Instead, they chose to intermix with colleagues by service branch. Smith decided to sit on the periphery with Leahy. "Don't get too comfortable, General Smith. You're up first."

"Thank you, Mister President, Prime Minister. On behalf of the supreme commander, we appreciate the opportunity to update the national leadership and the combined joint chiefs.

"As of this morning, the Germans have been pushed back behind the Siegfried Line and beyond in places. Our immediate objective is to cross the Rhine across the entire front from the North Sea to Switzerland. We are not quite up to full supply levels, but we have all been impressed by the contributions of Antwerp. We have also reviewed and approved all the crossing plans. We are in good position. The Colmar Pocket is nearly collapsed, and the 6th Army Group will catch up quickly. G-2 has presented sufficient evidence that the Germans will be unable to defend the entire Rhine. We expect tough spots, but once we are across the Rhine . . . well, we are ready."

"Excellent, General Smith. Thank you. Any questions or discussion points for the Allied Expeditionary Force?"

No direct questions went to Beetle, but his report stimulated an intriguing intense debate over the post-war division of Germany. There were plenty of opinions, differing views, and objectives. One significant element yet to be confirmed was the inclusion of the French in the post-war governance of Germany. General Marshal spoke highly of the 1st French Army on the southern flank of the AEF and felt they had earned their place at the table.

First, Churchill and then Roosevelt used different words to convey similar sentiments that the French had not been given full membership at the ARGONAUT Conference but would hold observer status only. Both leaders also confirmed that the military would administer the four sectors of Germany and Berlin. None of the generals liked the potential of having to administer sectors of Berlin as an island in the expected Soviet Sector. The division of Berlin and Germany after the surrender was one of the major agenda topics at Yalta.

"If I may, Mister President, Prime Minister," Marshall began, "one item we," he gestured around the table, "have been dealing with for the last three days is a stern request by the Soviets for us to strike German lines of communications specifically affecting the Eastern Front." Churchill nodded. Franklin remained stoic but attentive. "Sir Charles," Marshall said, looking at the British chief of the air staff.

"Thank you, General Marshall. The combined air staff has examined the potential of our assistance to the Red Army. We have the collective capacity. Together, we have examined potential targets for a large demonstration in support of the Soviet request with the assistance of M-I-6 and the O-S-S. We have selected Dresden as that target. The city is a major railway, roadway, and communications crossroad that is near the Eastern Front."

"Are their military facilities or forces at Dresden?" asked Roosevelt.

"The answer depends upon how we define military," interjected Marshall.

"Are we going to play semantics with the lives of people?" Roosevelt reacted sharply.

"No Sir. I'm only reflecting on the serious concerns for the nuance of this endeavor. We," he said and gestured around the table again, "have agreed that Dresden meets the Soviet criteria."

"Then, why do you need us?" Churchill asked.

General Brooke replied, "This is a political target, not a military one."

"How so?" asked Winston.

"Dresden was not on our primary target list," Brooke answered. "The city does not meet any of our POINTBLANK requirements, and I do believe none of the A-E-F needs," he said and glanced at Beetle, who nodded his agreement. "The Red Army crossed the Oder and is roughly 70 miles from Dresden on the Elbe. So if we strike Dresden, it is to support the Soviets."

"Stalin is likely to ask," Churchill interjected.

"Exactly," replied Brooke.

"What are your thoughts, Mister President?" the prime minister asked.

"What is the proposal?" Roosevelt queried.

Portal summarized the night and day, two-day, all-out bomber offensive on the infrastructure of Dresden. The city was largely untouched by Allied bombers because it had not meant much to the Allied war effort. The mission would be an extension of Operation THUNDERCLAP—the concentrated mass bombing of German cities. As a strategic bombing target, Dresden was within the general THUNDERCLAP constraints and would serve the Red Army nicely.

"Helping the Soviet Union is a strategic purpose. As such, I am in favor of the mission," Roosevelt declared. Franklin looked directly at Winston and nodded.

"I am less generous," Churchill stated. "Yet, anything that contributes to winning the war sooner is to our purpose. I can support the mission as well."

"So be it," responded Sir Charles. "General Kuter and I will inform Bomber Command and 8th Air Force that the Dresden mission is approved."

"Not so fast," interjected Churchill. "Go ahead with the planning and allocation of forces, but the president and I should present the plan to Marshal Stalin to ensure the mission satisfies his needs. We will send a cyphered message in the next few days."

"As you wish, Sir," Portal answered and looked at Kuter.

"Agreed," Kuter responded.

Leahy stood and whispered in the president's ear. Roosevelt nodded. "The admiral reminded me that our allotted time has expired, and the Wardroom is needed to feed the ship's company. We are adjourned. I'll see you all at our dinner tonight."

They exchanged salutations and departed.

President Roosevelt disembarked from *Quincy* at 23:00 and headed by automobile to Luqa Airfield. The entire British and American delegations for the ARGONAUT Conference, 700 strong, traveled by various transport aircraft at 10-minute intervals through most of the night for Saki Airfield, Novofedorivka, Crimea. Once in Crimea, they still had a six-hour, tortuous drive by automobile to the site of the conference on the southern coast with a planned arrival around mid-day tomorrow.

———

Sunday, 4.February.1945
Livadia Palace
Livadiya, Crimea, Liberated Ukraine
Soyuz Sovetskikh Sotsialisticheskikh Respublik (USSR)
17:00 hours

Livadia Palace had been a summer retreat of the last Russian tsar, Nicholas II, and Tsarina Alexandra. The grand, white stone Palace overlooking the Black Sea would serve as the president's residence during the ARGONAUT Conference. The Palace grand ballroom would be the primary meeting room.

Prime Minister Churchill had been assigned Vorontsov Palace in Alupka, Crimea. The principal central wing of the Palace had been completed in 1837 and deeded to Russian Prince Mikhail Semyonovich Vorontsov as his summer retreat. It was the largest estate on the Crimean coast, gaining numerous additions over the following decades.

Self-proclaimed Generalissimus of the Soviet Union Joseph Vissarionovich Stalin would utilize a trio of sites for different reasons during the conference. His primary residence of record was Koreiz Villa, Koreiz, Crimea, a comparatively modest villa located six miles southwest of the conference site. He would use the Yusupov Palace when it was his turn to host an official state dinner. Stalin's summer dacha was Massandra Palace in Yalta, an impressive structure. While Stalin used his dacha when it suited him, he presumably did not want foreigners that close to his personal life, so no meetings were held there. Massandra Palace had been built by Vorontsov's son, Semyon Mikhailovich, in 1880.

During the occupation, the Germans had abused all of the properties on the Black Sea coast, and the magnificent palaces were no exception. Nevertheless, the Soviets had worked around the clock to repair and restore the various properties. The British and American advance teams gave the Soviets credit for their extraordinary efforts to make the deteriorated palaces livable. However, at the bottom line, the horror stories of dilapidation and vermin infestation shocked the western delegations accustomed to five-star accommodations.

All three delegations assembled in the Grand Ballroom for the first plenary session of the ARGONAUT Conference. Photographers jostled for position and the best angles, lens shutters clicked, and flashbulbs popped as journalists shouted unanswered questions at the leaders. After several minutes, aides began to usher the press out of the room. Once cleared and the doors closed, Stalin took the initiative. He spoke in Russian, and his interpreter offered the English words. "President Roosevelt, would you care to open our summit conference?"

Roosevelt cleared his throat and collected his thoughts. "Thank you, Generalissimo Stalin. The three superpower delegations have gathered for this historic conference as the end is near for Nazi Germany. We will cover the world map as we debate and decide the rules and guidelines for the coming peace."

The advance agenda became more contentious than anticipated as Marshal Stalin sought to impose his will on the conference. He did not feel the need to discuss Poland and Eastern Europe. The Red Army would maintain their security. Churchill was ready to jump into the governance of Eastern Europe matter. They eventually confirmed the advance agenda, which called for the current military situation as the opening item.

Chief of the Soviet General Staff General Aleksei Innokentievich Antonov spoke through an interpreter for the Soviet military delegation. "Since the 12th of January, the Red Army has advanced 300 miles across Poland and into Germany. We are across the River Oder and within 50 miles of Berlin. The Red Army has destroyed 45 enemy divisions and taken 100,000 prisoners. Lastly, as an ally, we requested air strikes on Berlin, Dresden, and Leipzig to slow or stop German troop deployments eastward. We have heard nothing, and the Germans keep coming. We are left with the impression that the West wants to enable the Germans against the tide of the Red Army."

"That is an unreasonable and illogical assumption, General Antonov," Churchill objected. "We have plenty of Germans in front of our forces. Just two days ago, President Roosevelt and I reviewed and approved the massive strategic bombing mission of Dresden to satisfy the Soviet request for assistance. Berlin has been rendered to rubble. Leipzig is not far behind. Dresden has been selected, and the mission is in the final planning stage. We do not have a mission date, but it should be in a week or so."

"Very well," Stalin jumped in, presumably to preclude a response from General Antonov. "We will assess your proposal."

"We will come back to the requested mission," announced Roosevelt. "General Marshall, you are up next."

"Thank you, Mister President, Prime Minister, and Marshal," began General Marshall, looking directly at each national leader. "Our air forces have been successful in destroying a great deal of German transport infrastructure, oil supplies, and armament and synthetic oil production. We continue to face the Germans' so-called Vengeance Two robot rockets that bombard Antwerp and London. Those rockets rain down from space daily at supersonic speeds.

"Ice and ice flows churning in the Rhine River's swift current will preclude any attempt to cross the river before the 1st of March. Nevertheless, we have pushed the Germans back beyond the starting point of their counteroffensive that began in the middle of December, and we are through the Siegfried Line defenses in several places. We expect to be on the west bank of the Rhine in four to five weeks across virtually the entire Western Front, and we are ready to cross the Rhine at multiple sites as soon as conditions permit. The opening of Antwerp port has significantly improved our supply lines, and our frontline forces are nearly back to full supply." By prior agreement in Malta, the combined joint chiefs agreed not to refer to the supreme commander's decision to pivot southeast to cut off the potential of a Nazi Redoubt in the Obersalzberg. Marshall nodded to the president.

"Thank you, General Antonov and General Marshall. That brings us to adjournment of the first plenary session. Without objection," Roosevelt paused. No objections came. "We are adjourned."

The three leaders had a private dinner planned in two and a half hours that President Roosevelt would host at Livadia Palace. They had plenty to discuss.

—

Monday, 5.February.1945
Livadia Palace
Livadiya, Crimea, Liberated Ukraine
Soyuz Sovetskikh Sotsialisticheskikh Respublik (USSR)
17:35 hours

The second plenary session had gone longer than planned and had been more contentious than expected. Roosevelt's health continued to deteriorate, and during the day, he developed a hacking cough. The president rejected the strong counsel of his physicians to rest and avoid stress. The conference was too important.

The day's meeting had been more argumentative. Several attendees observed that the closer they got to victory, the more combative the Soviets were becoming.

At noon, the combined joint chiefs of staff had met with their Soviet counterparts for the very first time since the October Revolution. They discussed a variety of matters, including the procedures for link-up on the battlefield. The British and American generals insisted upon direct communications during those critical moments of contact. General Antonov waffled with various excuses that General Marshall interpreted as deferring to Stalin. Nevertheless, the discussions among the military leaders gave the Western Allies unanimous views that the Soviet generals had very little latitude without Stalin's consent or sanction. The experience left an indelible impression.

President Roosevelt transferred from his wheelchair to an oversized, well-cushioned, leather chair and sighed audibly. He asked for and received a glass of scotch and soda. "My God, we've another week of this," he declared. "Thank God we don't have a state dinner tonight."

"Dinner can be ready in a few minutes," Anna interjected.

"I just want to enjoy the comforts of this exquisite chair and this drink," the president responded and held up his glass, "we have a couple of things to discuss. Let's try for half an hour."

"As you wish, Papa," answered Anna and then left the study of his personal suite.

Admiral Leahy and Harry Hopkins, not at peak health himself, sat quietly with the president giving him the moments he needed to decompress from the day's summit meeting. Finally, the president leaned his head back against the chair and closed his eyes. Roosevelt eventually opened his eyes, raised his head, drained his glass, and held it up for another. Hopkins tended to the president's drink.

Roosevelt looked directly at Bill Leahy. "Stalin's words and intransigence on Poland, and Eastern Europe for that matter, are bothering me. Winston has been quite insistent, but I feel the need to bring Stalin along. I want to send a personal and private letter to the marshal. Let's get the duty stenographer in here."

The president dictated the letter he wished to send. When finished, the stenographer left to type up the dictation.

"The generals had a good meeting with the Soviets this afternoon," opened Leahy, "but they were unanimously impressed by the lack of initiative or authority. They apparently defer everything to Stalin. Perhaps, it was just an artifact of this meeting environment, but none of us thought so."

Roosevelt nodded. "I was somewhat surprised we have not heard from the Soviets on the Dresden mission. I thought they would enthusiastically welcome our efforts to help them."

"They are all afraid of Stalin," Leahy added.

"An understatement," Hopkins muttered. "He purged thousands of generals and senior military officers just a few years ago."

Roosevelt ignored the comment. "When does the air force need our go consent?" he asked Leahy.

"Radio contact is not as reliable as it should be, so prior to 'bombs away' is inappropriate. I will ask Sir Charles and General Kuter. I will also see if they have established a mission target date." Roosevelt nodded. "I'll ensure they are sensitive to the situation. Further, we need to inform the intelligence guys, so they can remove any agents they might have in Dresden but ask them to establish a timeline we can attach to the go decision."

"Agreed."

Leahy glanced at his wristwatch. "I'll go check on the letter." The president nodded his agreement. Leahy went to the administrative support room.

Hopkins leaned forward in his chair. "The British did not take kindly to your statement about removing our forces from Europe after the war."

"It's a reality."

"Yes, but the British have insufficient forces to stand against the Soviets."

"Which is precisely why I am trying to keep Stalin on our side rather than become an adversary, as Winston suggests."

"Then, if I may ask, why are you against France participating in the partitioning of Germany and the Allied Control Commission?"

"I'm not as concerned about France or the post-war administration of Germany as I am about alienating the Soviets. We've got to stay together, or we're likely to become opponents on the world stage. My reading of Stalin tells me he fears consolidation of Western thought against his sense of peace. I see more cooperation in the Russians than Winston does."

"What if Winston is correct?"

"I'm trying to avoid that potential. Winston is an astute politician. He senses the pulse of things like no one else I know."

"Then, shouldn't we listen to his views? I think he deeply believes we must have France intimately involved in the post-war peace."

"Humm." Roosevelt lapsed into thought. Hopkins knew not to interfere with his thinking. The president looked at Hopkins. "Let's see how Stalin responds to my letter." Roosevelt paused for thought. "De Gaulle is a nationalist. He has remained silent on the Atlantic Charter. Winston has at least accepted reality and embraced the Charter; De Gaulle has not."

"We need to bring France along as well. They've contributed a full army and more to beat the Germans. They've earned their place at the table."

"De Gaulle . . . Harry."

Leahy returned with paper in hand. "I have the letter you wanted for Stalin."

Roosevelt took the paper and read.

```
            Koreiz, the Crimea
    My dear Marshal Stalin,
        I have been giving a great deal of thought
    to our meeting this afternoon, and I want to
    tell you in all frankness what is on my mind.
        In so far as the Polish Government is
    concerned, I am greatly disturbed that the
    three Great Powers do not have a meeting of
    minds about the political set up in Poland.
    It seems to me that it puts all of us in a
    bad light throughout the world to have you
    recognizing one government while we and the
    British are recognizing another in London. I am
    sure the state of affairs should not continue,
    and that if it does, it can only lead our
    people to think there is a breach between us,
    which is not the case. I am determined that
    there shall be no breach between ourselves and
    the Soviet Union. Surely there is a way to
    reconcile our differences.
        I was very much impressed with some of
    the things you said today, particularly
    your determination that your rear must be
    safeguarded as your army moves into Berlin. You
```

cannot, and we must not, tolerate any temporary government which will give your armed forces any trouble of this sort. I want you to know that I am fully mindful of this.

You must believe me when I tell you that our people at home look with a critical eye on what they consider a disagreement between us at this vital stage of the war. They, in effect, say that if we cannot get a meeting of minds now when our armies are converging on the common enemy, how can we get an understanding on even more vital things in the future.

I have had to make it clear to you that we cannot recognize the Lublin Government as now composed, and the world would regard it as a lamentable outcome of our work here if we parted with an open and obvious divergence between us on this issue.

You said today that you would be prepared to support any suggestions for the solution of this problem which offered a fair chance of success, and you also mentioned the possibility of bringing some members of the Lublin Government here.

Realizing that we all have the same anxiety in getting this matter settled, I would like to develop your proposal a little and suggest that we invite here to Yalta at once three representatives from the Lublin Government, the Polish government in exile, and other elements of the Polish people in the development of a new temporary government which all three of us could recognize and support. The United States Government, and I feel sure the British Government as well, would then be prepared to examine with you conditions in which they would dissociate themselves from the London government and transfer their recognition to the new provisional government.

I hope I do not have to assure you that the United States will never lend its support in any way to any provisional government in Poland that would be inimical to your interests.

```
    It goes without saying that any interim
government which could be formed as a result
of our conference with the Poles here would be
pledged to the holding of free elections in
Poland at the earliest possible date. I know
this is completely consistent with your desire
to see a new free and democratic Poland emerge
from the welter of this war.
                 Most sincerely yours,
                 Franklin D. Roosevelt
                   February 6, 1945
```

"What do you think?" asked the president.

"I think it should do nicely, and it captures your thoughts."

"I agree. Well done. The real question is, how will Uncle Joe receive it, and more importantly, respond to it?"

"My opinion, Mister President, he will say the correct things to placate you and the prime minister, and then he will do what he wants."

"Which is?"

"Install a puppet government that will deliver his bidding."

"That's rather cynical, don't you think?"

"You asked my opinion, Mister President," Leahy answered.

"Yes, I did, and I appreciate your opinion. First, however, I must find the key to convince him to go forward together."

"Great thought, Mister President, but I suspect Stalin believes he holds all the cards in Eastern Europe by virtue of occupation . . . possession and all. Just to make sure, you still want the letter delivered to the marshal's villa tomorrow morning."

"Yes."

"Very well," Leahy said.

The president initialed the letter to the right of his typed name and handed it to Leahy. "Now, let's eat," the president commanded and moved to his wheelchair.

—

Wednesday, 7.February.1945
Standing Oak Farm
Winchester, Hampshire, England
United Kingdom
15:25 hours

Farm work had significantly contributed to Charlotte's recovery from the explosion and loss of their only child and son. In addition to the milking and cheese production, she worked several aperiodic shifts at the greenhouses to cover for one worker or another who needed time off during the day or was not feeling well. Mabel had been successful in her discussions with the U.S. Army. As a result, the Basingstoke Depot agreed to double the greenhouses, and they had already begun staging the materials, surveying the layout, and laying the foundations for each new building. Charlotte also helped prepare more land beyond the new greenhouses for the open-air garden they would plant when spring arrived. She even managed a couple of afternoon horseback rides in the winter cold to Temple Manor for a social visit with Grace Palmer.

Charlotte went to the small office they built for June Sorvon Cranston, the farm's accountant. "I'm heading out to the barn to help with the afternoon milking."

"Excellent. I've got another hour or two to finish up the January balance sheet report. I'd like to stay for dinner with the crew if it's acceptable with you." June usually returned to her family in Winchester at the end of her workday.

"You are always welcome, June, anytime."

"As soon as I finish the report, I'll start dinner."

"That should do nicely. Thank you, June." Charlotte donned her winter coat and gloves. It was a fair-weather day but quite chilly. She stepped outside just in time to see the taxicab crest the far ridge. The crunch of the vehicle's tires under the wheels grew louder, but the sun glint off the car's windows precluded a preview of her arriving guest.

The first to appear was Malcolm Brian Spencer, who jumped out of the cab before it had completely stopped. He was the nearly four-year-old son of Mary and Sir John Spencer. Malcolm ran to Charlotte and leaped into her waiting arms as she knelt in the gravel. "I missed you, Sharley," he declared, using Todd's affectation of her name.

"I missed you, Malcolm."

Charlotte stood as Mary emerged from the cab. Just then, Todd burst out of the door with Edith chasing him. The two boys embraced and instantly went into their unique world. Edith did not interfere with the reunion. Mary and Charlotte embraced, kissing each other's cheeks. Grace Perkins, the Spencer's nanny, exited and assisted 15-month-old Charlotte Mary Spencer, who was now known as 'CM.'

"To what do we owe the pleasure of your company?" Charlotte asked.

"Young Master Malcolm pestered me into submission," answered Mary. "He insisted that he had to see Todd and . . . visit the farms. He loves all the animals."

"The crew is just beginning the afternoon milking if he wants to join them."

"Yes, yes, yes!" Malcolm shouted.

"I'll take them," offered Edith. She escorted the two boys to the barn.

Charlotte gestured to the front door. Grace headed to the barn with CM, who continued pointing at the retreating boys. The cab driver followed the ladies with a couple of bags. Mary paid him and added a generous gratuity. With the door closed again, the two women shed their winter coats and headed to the fireplace. Charlotte mixed two Scotch n' soda on the rocks drinks for them. After delivering the drinks, Charlotte rejuvenated the fire.

"Do I understand correctly," Mary began, "Brian has been promoted to command a squadron?"

"Yes, you are. They moved the previous commander, Lieutenant Colonel Clark, and appointed Brian as the new squadron commander—334th Fighter Squadron—the same squadron he has been with since the transfer to the U.S. Army in '42."

"Well, congratulations. I heard the news from John, but he was less than confident. According to press reports, the Allies have reached the Po Valley, but the Germans have not yet given up."

"Good news . . . not the fighting but the advances of the Allies. Brian was home for a few days a week ago. The Battle of the Bulge, as they call it, is over, and he says they see very little German air defenses these days. He would not give me an expected victory date, but I sense it is close."

"My sense as well. The prime minister and President Roosevelt are in Yalta, Crimea, for a major summit meeting. The press thinks the conference will decide the post-war peace."

"We hope."

June entered and exchanged greetings with Mary. June excused herself to start the dinner meal preparation.

"How long can you stay this time?" Charlotte asked Mary.

"A day or so if that is acceptable."

"Excellent."

"We'll see how long Malcolm lasts. He seems to prefer it here. I must also confess to a fondness for the country air and the hospitality of Standing Oak Farm."

"You are welcome to stay as long as you wish. I cannot thank you enough for all you and the ladies did to help me during the black days."

"We were all honored to be able to help. You are doing so much better than those days last year," Mary said.

"Quite so! Those days are a blur to me, but I'm well aware that I was much closer to death than I am today. So, again, thank you so much for everything you did to help me."

Mary finished her drink. "What say you . . . let us help June."

Charlotte nodded and drained the remainder of her drink. The two women joined June in the kitchen and followed her lead. They were ready ahead of the crew. The table was set, including a small adjunct table for Edith, Grace, and the children. The three women sat by the fireplace until the crew began to arrive. They waited for all the usual attendees to appear before they took to the dining room tables.

———

Friday, 9.February.1945
1637 30ʰ Street, Northwest
Georgetown, Washington, District of Columbia
United States of America
05:40 hours

Bill Donovan rose early as he commonly did. His longtime cook had prepared his usual breakfast—two eggs over easy, four strips of bacon or sausage, hashed brown potatoes, and wheat toast with coffee. The daily newspapers were laid out on the table as they were every morning he was at home—*New York Times*, *Washington Post*, and *Chicago Tribune*. He read quickly, occasionally stopping to examine the words more carefully that the author had chosen. Donovan focused on national and international articles, but he would pick up local stories when they caught his attention. He took partial notes to remind him to look more deeply once he reached the office.

Donovan savored a couple more bites of his breakfast and took another sip of his black coffee. He liked it strong. The *Tribune's* full-page headline was unavoidable—NEW SIEGFRIED OFFENSIVE! However, it was the left, multi-column title that captured his singular attention—*New Deal Plans Super Spy System*. Donovan immediately noted the byline—Walter Trohan.

"This can't be good," he muttered.

Trohan was the Washington bureau chief and an influential voice in the capital and among *Tribune* readers. He had butted heads with J. Edgar Hoover in the last decade, but since then, he had become quite friendly with the FBI director.

Donovan pushed his unfinished breakfast plate well to the side and laid the newspaper flat on the table. He read every word carefully and slowly.

"Gestapo! Jesus H. Christ!" Donovan finished his second read-through of the Trohan article. "Damn it all to hell!"

Donovan lifted the telephone handset and dialed the number he knew by heart.

"Buxton," came the familiar voice, although not quite fully awake.

"Ned, it's Bill. I need you in the office as quick as you can get there."

"What's up?"

"I don't want to talk on the phone."

"OK. I'll be there in 30 minutes."

"Please apologize to Ailine for me. I'm sorry to call so early, but it is a necessity."

"No problem. Will do. See you shortly."

Donovan hung up the handset and called out, "James!"

Only a few seconds passed until his trusted, loyal, longtime driver James Freeman appeared. "Yes sir."

"We need to go to the Complex immediately."

"No problems, Boss. The Caddie is always ready." Donovan refolded the *Chicago Tribune*, placed the newspaper in his leather briefcase, and followed James to the limousine, his private chauffeured automobile.

The two men were on their way to the E Street Complex within five minutes.

———

Friday, 9.February.1945
Office of Strategic Services
E Street Complex
Washington, District of Columbia
United States of America
06:20 hours

When James Freeman delivered his charge to the OSS headquarters complex, Director Bill Donovan headed directly to his corner office. He had barely sat at his desk when Ned Buxton entered.

"I think I know the crisis," Ned declared and held up a folded copy of the *Washington Times-Herald* with its clearly discernible headline. Donovan held up his copy of the *Tribune* with the sub-title less obvious. They exchanged papers.

Donovan read the first paragraph of the *Times-Herald* article. "It's the same Trohan article, or essentially so. Someone in a small group of people leaked a copy of the plan to Trohan, and worse, that person fed him nonsensical, highly biased opinions that he reported as fact. 'Peacetime New Deal Gestapo' . . . really? He chose those words to incite opposition."

"Any suspicions?"

"Could be anyone with access, but if I had to choose a principal, if not sole culprit, my choice would be J. Edgar Hoover. He has made no bones about his opposition to the O-S-S from before the C-O-I days. He has always been extremely territorial and aggressive in defense of his territory."

"Makes sense given his animosity toward our work. Was Hoover or the FBI on the distribution list?"

"No, but the attorney general or even the White House may have provided him with a copy. I also think Edgar felt we were making progress with the G-2 and N-2 on a mutually acceptable compromise, and he wanted to tank the deal before it had a chance to sink roots."

"How do you think the president will react?"

"Too early to tell. But when all this started last year, he was emphatic about keeping the discussion debate very close hold and beyond public scrutiny. These articles," he said pointing to the newspapers, "are precisely what he wanted to avoid. 'New Deal Gestapo' . . . that even sounds like Hoover. As I read Trohan's words, he has an unauthorized copy or has seen a copy of eleven eighty-one." JCS 1181 was the administrative document number assigned to the Donovan plan for the establishment of a central intelligence service along with associated studies and decision documents. "Every copy is numbered and recorded. I'd love to have an agent assigned to every holder to see who is missing a copy."

"We can't do that," Ned said.

"I know that, but it sure would be nice."

"What about talking to Trohan?" Buxton asked.

"In normal circumstances, a visit from a couple of FBI special agents would put the fear of God in him, but if Hoover is the leak source, there is no way we would get a proper investigation."

"What about the chiefs?"

"At this point, I'd say let's see what falls out. Our plan was for the president. We clearly have detractors, always have, which is not particularly a surprise, but the only opinion that matters is the president. He's going to be in Yalta until the 11th, and then he has several days in Egypt for meetings with regional leaders before he heads back across the ocean. We probably won't hear anything until the end of the month or early next month. Thus, to answer your query, my sense is to hunker down and weather the storm. I do not see that there is much we can do, and if we attempt to correct the record, it is more likely to make matters worse. The topic is and will probably remain secret."

"OK. Hunker down it is. Anything else?"

"No. Let's get back to our vital work."

Buxton left the director. They both turned to their inboxes to work on the constant stream of reports, documents, memoranda, letters, and messages. They also had a daily department head meeting. The morning newspaper articles occupied nearly the entire meeting. Several department heads voiced anger that Trohan appeared to know more about the transition plan than they did. The group seemed to share that view, but Donovan was not willing to take a poll. Their personnel read newspapers too. Donovan and Buxton urged the department heads to quiet concern. Bill carefully summarized the state of negotiations for the anticipated transition to a peacetime national intelligence service. He also reminded everyone in the meeting that the issue remained classified secret and thus not open to public discussion regardless of the potential press assault.

Donovan and Buxton had lunch with a couple of the department heads at their internal cafeteria. They avoided the Trohan article. Instead, sports, entertainment, and local matters occupied their conversation.

Donovan had not been able to sit down at his desk when Buxton arrived with a message.

"I just received a short message from the White House. The president will call you later this afternoon. They will link you to a secure radio-telephone connection with Livadia Palace," the president's residence in Yalta.

"No time?"

"No . . . just this afternoon."

"It'll be near midnight in Crimea."

"That's all we've got. He may have official social events this evening."

"Perhaps. Let's clear the calendar from three on."

"I'll see to it."

Both men returned to their paperwork until the red secure telephone rang.

16:30 hours [00:30, Saturday, in Yalta, Crimea]

"Donovan."

"This is White House operator 14, Mr. Donovan. I have a secure call for you. I will connect you when I get your green light."

Donovan pushed the secure button on the telephone base. He heard the expected be-bonk to signify the secure connection to the White House communications room.

"Mister Donovan, please confirm your light status."

"Green."

"Very well. My light is green as well." Another be-bonk suggested the full connection. "Mister President, you are connected with Director Donovan."

"Good afternoon, Bill."

"Thank you, Sir, and good morning to you."

"It is late here. We'll have to make this quick for a host of reasons since I do not want to discuss this topic even over the SIGSALY," the president said, referring to the encrypted communications system in use since July 1943. Donovan listened. The sound quality was scratchy and a bit echoey, but otherwise clearly understandable. "I am informed of a newspaper article published this morning that caused a bit of a stir."

"Yes Sir. True."

"I know you are prepared to discuss this matter, but I wanted to assure you that we will have a private conversation upon my return. Until then, I ask you to sweep this matter under the rug. We will assess the situation and lay out a path forward."

"Yes Sir."

"I imagine this has been rather upsetting to you, having invested so much time and effort in the negotiations toward compromise." The president paused, but Donovan did not respond. "You can continue your discussions within the closed, classified environment, but no public response. I have had a straightforward private conversation with the joint chiefs and made it clear that they were not authorized to make any public reference in any form until we establish a proper government policy position."

"As you command, Sir. I have quieted our internal rumblings, and by your direction, we will continue our classified discussions for a mutually acceptable compromise."

"Thank you, Bill. As Benjamin Franklin so eloquently stated at the signing of the Declaration, 'We must all hang together, or, most assuredly, we shall all hang separately.'"

"Indeed!"

"Good day, Bill. Now, I must be off to bed. Break it down," the president commanded the various technicians and operators facilitating the communications links. More be-bonks could be heard. Donovan's telephone light turned red.

Donovan went to Buxton's office and closed the door. He related the essence of the conversation and reinforced his earlier instructions. They returned to their work.

—

Tuesday, 13.February.1945
Dresden, Saxony
Deutsches Reich
22:13 hours

Dresden had often been called 'Florence on the Elbe' before the war. The city had been largely untouched during the war. Operation THUNDERCLAP had executed the strategic bombing of German cities and industrial centers sequentially. Today was Dresden's turn.

The operational plan called for the U.S. 8th Air Force to carry out the first wave of the three-day mission. However, weather over the target was not acceptable for visual bombing, and the first phase was canceled. As a result, the first mass attack fell to RAF Bomber Command.

The night bombing formation included 254 Lancaster heavy bombers that had taken off from airfields in England after the Mosquito Pathfinder squadron. The first bomber group, callsign Plate Rack, would drop 500 tons of high explosive bombs and 375 tons of incendiary bombs, a mixture that had been developed for just such missions. The first large-scale firebombing devastated the port city of Hamburg in July 1943.

The British Bomber Command night bombing technique worked to perfection. The Mosquito Pathfinders, callsign Seeker, used their Oboe radio navigation system in conjunction with onboard H2S ground mapping radar and surveyed templates of the Elbe River that showed up as a shaped, dark black, broad line on the radar screen to drop colored Target Indicator flares. Each Mosquito carried various colors of TI flares.

"Plate Rack, Seeker, red T-Is confirmed in place as planned. Come in and bomb the glow of the red T-Is as briefed."

The lead bombardier sighted on the red flare. He saw green, white, and new red flares appear, but he knew those late flares were decoys ignited by the Germans.

"Bombs away," came the broadcast. Bombs dropped out of the bomb bay of the lead Lancaster heavy bomber. The exact sequence was repeated on each of the 253 other heavy bombers.

The bombers turned for home without a single night fighter or flak burst to interfere with their mission.

The destruction of the first wave accomplished precisely what had been planned and intended. The high explosive bombs broke up the buildings, and the incendiary bombs ignited the exposed and broken timbers. The resultant fires became the new markers. The accumated fires induced hurrcane force winds that intensified the fires. The glow of the fires could be seen from 500 miles away at the bombers' altitude.

Bomber Command had taken the cynical decision to split the night's mission into two waves. The second wave consisted of 529 more fully loaded Lancaster bombers. Pathfinders were no longer needed. The second wave dropped their mixed bomb loads two hours after the first wave with the intent of catching the fire and rescue crews in the open. The mission plan achieved its intended objectives. The Operation THUNDERCLAP Dresden raid was not complete.

—

Wednesday, 14.February.1945
RMS Franconia
44° 37' 29" North - 33° 31' 15" East
Sevastopol Harbor, Crimea, Liberated Ukraine
Soyuz Sovetskikh Sotsialisticheskikh Respublik (USSR)
10:15 hours

Prime Minister Churchill slept late even for him. He took a handful of minutes to shake off the fog of deep sleep. Winston rang his side table bell to summon his duty private secretary; on this trip, it was Jock Colville. The trim, capable, loyal man knocked and entered the prime minister's compartment.

"Good morning, sir."

"It is indeed a good morning. That is the first decent sleep I have had in several weeks. The stress of the summit conference and those bloody dreadful conditions in Yalta simply wore me out. I could not bear another day, especially a night, in that wretched place."

"Conditions were rather grim, I must say."

"Haw!" the prime minister exclaimed loudly. "That is an understatement of the century. I would have loved to have seen those palaces in their heyday, or at least before the Bolsheviks converted them into asylums and the Nawzees denigrated them. Regrettably, that is an opportunity lost and another exigency of this bloody war." He paused for a moment. "I'll take the morning box, and would you be so kind to have Sawyers fetch my breakfast? No matter how comfortable and inviting it is, I can't spend the rest of the day in bed."

"Yes sir." Colville stepped out of the compartment for a few seconds and returned with the case that served as the prime minister's dispatch box. "I'll see to your breakfast."

Churchill nodded and jumped into his reading of messages, memoranda, letters, and documents. He wrote in the margins with a red pencil any actions he wanted, queries for further research, or opinions for designated individuals.

One message garnered particular attention. He started to ring the bell again, but he laid the paper on the duvet beside him since he knew Colville would be back soon, probably with Sawyers and his breakfast tray. He did not wait long.

The knock announced the expected arrival. Colville opened the door and held it open for Sawyers, who carried his breakfast tray. Churchill patted the bed beside him while looking at Sawyers; he wanted the tray on the bed. He was not ready to eat. While Sawyers complied, the prime minister raised the message and handed it to Colville. "Get me, Ismay. I need to see him right away."

Both Colville and Sawyers departed to their tasks. Churchill lifted the tray onto his lap and began eating his eggs on toast and fried diced potatoes with sausage links.

General Sir Hastings Lionel 'Pug' Ismay, KCB, DSO, served as Principal Assistant to the Minister of Defense (Churchill), Secretary of the Imperial Defense Chiefs of Staff Committee, and Deputy Secretary of the War Cabinet. He had been with the prime minister from the beginning of Churchill's premiership.

Pug returned in full uniform. "This," he said, holding up the message, "was the initial mission completion message. I've compiled the additional information we have as of an hour ago."

"Let's have it," Churchill said, gesturing with impatience.

"The 8th Air Force had to cancel the initial wave due to poor weather over the target, precluding visual bombing. Bomber Command had better weather, and their night-bombing procedures worked perfectly. The photo-reconnaissance bird took off at first light ahead of the American bombers, which should be taking off about now. The weather is forecast to permit visual bombing. The Americans will be taking off in a few hours."

"Results, Pug?" Churchill asked with impatience.

"Too early to tell with assurance, but the Air Ministry indicates the pilot reports confirm the fire mix worked as expected."

Churchill shook his head. "I know we had to do this, but what a bloody tragedy. Have you ever been to Dresden . . . before the war?"

"No Sir."

"It was such a gorgeous city on the Elbe, so rich in history, culture, art, music . . . It's all gone. I know we had to . . . but what a tragic waste . . . all because of that bastard corporal. What a waste!"

"Do you want to stop the rest of it?"

"The rest of it?"

"Yes Sir. Time on Target for the Americans is noon today."

The prime minister thought for several seconds. "We did what we had to do," he muttered. Ismay did not respond. "No, Pug. Let us finish this horrific task and be done with it." Churchill paused again for several seconds to grapple with his thoughts. "What else do you have?"

"We received a report from the Home Office that 14 V-2s hit London this morning."

"Dear God."

"All the rockets exploded, killing 12 civilians at Wood Green, 12 at Romford, 28 at West Ham, and three at Bexley, at least that they know of so far; many more injured, and Emergency Services are still dealing with the fires."

"Did the Home Office have any more details?"

"Not in the message, but I'm certain they are working on the trajectory analysis." Ismay paused. "I must also report that the situation in Greece is deteriorating rapidly now that the Germans are gone. The factions are near civil war. The coalition that joined to fight the Germans appears to be disintegrating into a power struggle."

"I suspected that might happen. Now, I'm afraid we must change our plans again. While accommodations aboard this ocean liner are exquisite compared to what we have endured for the last two weeks, it is far too slow in these volatile times. I want to head to Saki Aerodrome immediately. We will take Paralos to Athens as soon as we can get in the air. I must do what I can to avoid civil war in Greece and stabilize that strategic nation, and I must meet the president in Alexandria before he heads back across the Atlantic."

Paralos was the name given to the VIP configured Douglas C-54B Skymaster, serial number 43-17126. The aircraft had been gifted to him personally by President Roosevelt and was similar to the president's VIP configured C-54 code-named Sacred Cow. The Paralos aircraft was given an RAF serial number EW-999 and configured to Churchill's specifications.

The gears of travel logistics began to turn rapidly. Sawyers assisted Winston with his bath and dressing for travel. They had a three-hour drive to Saki and a five-hour flight to Athens.

—

Wednesday, 14.February.1945
Dresden, Saxony
Deutsches Reich
12:00 hours

The vast array of 316 B-17 heavy bombers was impressive enough. The 784 P-51 Mustangs, including the 4th Fighter Group, spread out above and around the bomber formation were even more imposing, especially since there were few remaining German fighters available to challenge them. Even the ugly black flak shell bursts were relatively few compared to what they encountered two years before.

But it was not the monumental display of American air power that captivated Brian and his brethren on this day and this mission. Like a powerful active volcano, the billowing columns of smoke and ash rising from the fires that continued to rage ahead of them and the knowledge of what the 8th Air Force was about to add to the misery undoubtedly playing out on the ground was the target for the bombers. The American bombers carried a similar mix of high explosive and incendiary bombs, and they added to the conflagration.

The massive fires created hurricane-force winds sucking the oxygen out of rooms, basements, and bomb shelters, suffocating people seeking protection. The fires burned so hot that soft metals melted and steel buckled. The induced firestorm was more devastating than the bombs.

The following day, the 15th, the 1st Bombardment Division with 211 B-17 heavy bombers was assigned to strike the synthetic oil production facilities at Bohlen near Leipzig. Cloud cover obscured the target. The formation diverted to their secondary target—Dresden. Smoke and clouds over the stricken city precluded visual bombing. The mission orders directed the crews to use their HSX ground mapping radar to deliver their loads of 465 tons of high explosive bombs. The Thursday mission had no incendiary bombs, but none were needed—the fires still raged throughout the city.

Over 90% of the city center was destroyed—churches, hospitals, rail stations, and museums. The bombs did not differentiate. No building was left untouched by the massive day and night bombing campaign and the subsequent fires.

The Dresden raids became a symbol of the savagery of total warfare. The city was clogged with refugees fleeing west from the advancing Red Army. Estimates varied between 22,000 to 25,000 men, women, and children who had been killed during the Dresden firebombing of February 1945.

And, "So it goes."

The catchphrase appears multiple times throughout Kurt Vonnegut's classic novel *Slaughterhouse Five*, succinctly and dramatically capturing the notion of dejected resignation. Shit happens, and we move on.

During the Allied bombing raid, Vonnegut had been a POW held in *Schlachthof Fünf* (Slaughterhouse Five), which had been converted into a detainment facility. He survived the attack. Others did not. When he saw daylight again, the city was gone.

—

Thursday, 15.February.1945
USS Quincy
31° 10' 44" North - 29° 51' 35" East
Alexandria Harbor, Alexandria
Kingdom of Egypt
14:10 hours

"A delightful luncheon, I must say, Franklin," pronounced Churchill, "and I thank you for the invitation to meet with you before your return voyage home."

The two leaders and Harry Hopkins had their private lunch in the flag conference room. The two leaders reviewed their assessments of the ARGONAUT Conference, and both agreed that the Soviet Union and Stalin would be a problem in Poland and the rest of Eastern Europe. They had all agreed to the division of Germany after the surrender, but they eventually rejected the Morgenthau Plan for the de-industrialization pasteurization of Germany. The reparations proved to be one of the more contentious issues debated by the Big Three leaders at the conference. In the end, they agreed to sector actions. Churchill and Roosevelt agreed they were far more interested in cleansing Germany of Nazis and rebuilding the country into a strong democratic nation.

"One more topic, if I may . . . ," Churchill paused to receive a nod of consent from Roosevelt, "His Majesty's Government proposes forming an atomic research facility at Harwell in Oxfordshire."

Roosevelt looked at Hopkins. "Harry, my apologies; will you excuse us." Hopkins nodded and stepped out of the compartment closing the hatch behind him. The president turned to Churchill. "Is there something wrong with Tube Alloys?"

"Not with Tube Alloys but with the Manhattan Project."

"Oh my, Winston. I thought we settled all that business last year. Henry Stimson tells me the team has resolved that last major technical hurdle, and they are now preparing for a full-scale test of the plutonium implosion design."

"You know more than me, Franklin, which is the root of the problem."

"My apologies, Winston. As I stated last year, that has never been my intent, and I'm embarrassed and disappointed that the Americans on the project team have not complied with my instructions. Nevertheless, I shall continue to press Stimson and Groves to ensure equal participation of your citizens."

"Thank you, Franklin, but my request for your consent still stands."

"You have my unequivocal and complete support for the proposed endeavor. We are so close to the end, Winston. We don't need the bomb to finish off Germany, and there is no doubt in my mind that the bomb will hasten the unconditional surrender of Japan."

"I trust your judgment, my friend."

Prime Minister Winston Churchill said goodbye to his wartime colleague.

This would be the last face-to-face meeting between Franklin Roosevelt and Winston Churchill. Their long collaboration would soon come to a sudden end.

Churchill transferred to the light cruiser HMS *Aurora* for the nautical honors tribute to the departing president. The *Quincy* and Task Group 21.5 sailed from Alexandria harbor at 16:00.

At 08:44, Tuesday, 20.February.1945, Roosevelt's longtime military aide Major General Edwin Martin 'Pa' Watson, USA [USMA 1908], passed away suddenly in his cabin from a cerebral hemorrhage, a day plus into the Atlantic beyond Gibraltar.

—

Monday, 19.February.1945
Iwo Jima, Ogasawara Subprefecture, Tokyo Metropolis Prefecture
Imperial Japan
08:59 hours

For 74 days, the surface and air forces of the U.S. Navy's 5th Fleet bombarded the eight-square-mile volcanic island with elements of the U.S. Army Air Forces 7th Air Force adding heavy bomber support.

At 06:45 this morning—D-day, the battleships and cruisers on station began saturating every foot from Mount Suribachi to Airfield No. 2. Just after 08:00, the naval guns stopped, and 120 carrier-based airplanes attacked, dropping bombs, napalm, and then rockets and strafing. As the naval aviators began their work, Operation DETACHMENT Commander-in-Chief Vice Admiral Richmond Kelly 'RK or Kelly' Turner, USN [USNA 1908], had signaled, "Land the Landing Force," to begin the crucial invasion. The first wave of Marines had begun descending into their bobbing landing craft.

The Imperial Japanese Army (IJA) had spent years preparing a vast interconnecting tunnel network across the island with retracting artillery, stocked supplies, and an underground communications system. General Tadamichi Kuribayashi, IJA, had prepared the island's defenses and his troops well. Like Admiral Isoroku Yamamoto, Kuribayashi served as an attaché in the United States and studied at Harvard University before the war.

At 08:25, as the Marines headed to the various assault beaches and the aviators pulled off, the big naval guns opened up again, firing more than 8,000 shells in less than 30 minutes.

This was H-Hour of D-Day. The initial wave of Marine infantrymen jumped into the black volcanic sand of Iwo Jima. The V Amphibious Corps under the command of Lieutenant General, Holland McTyeire 'Howlin' Mad' Smith, USMC, landed the 4th & 5th Marine Divisions that day. The brutal inch-by-inch battle began. The 3rd Marine Division served as the floating reserve and would not join the fight until the 24th.

To the Marines, they were on the island, but the Japanese defenders were in the island. As they dealt with one cave or tunnel, the Japanese popped up from other caves. Yet, the painstaking ferreting process while costly in blood and lives quickly proved its value. On Sunday, 4.March.1945, a 20th Air Force, Boeing B-29-25-MO Superfortress heavy bomber named Dinah Might, serial number 42-65280, diverted to and landed safely at South Field. Despite brutal on-going fighting not far away, the aircraft was partially repaired and refueled, and flown back to Tinian that same day. By the end of the war, 2,400 emergency landings were successfully completed on Iwo Jima.

The bloody battle lasted until 26.March.1945, At 08:00 that morning, Admiral Turner and General Smith finally declared the island secure, and the battle concluded, although a few holdouts remained in the underground maze until 1949 when they finally surrendered. The Army's 147th Infantry Regiment became the garrison force to operate the airfields as divert bases for the heavy bombers working on the Home Islands of Imperial Japan.

The extraordinary heroism of the Marines on Iwo Jima was captured in a single photograph taken by Joseph John 'Joe' Rosenthal four days after the invasion began. The image depicts six Marines assigned to E Company, 2nd Battalion, 28th Marines, 5th Marine Division, who raised the Stars & Stripes at the pinnacle of Mount Suribachi. The photograph would become the iconic image of the Second World War. Three of the six flag raisers did not survive the battle, but all six were preserved for eternity in a 32-foot three-dimensional bronze monument of the Rosenthal image that became the Marine Corps Memorial in Arlington, Virginia.

Secretary of the Navy James Vincent Forrestal with General Smith aboard the Landing Force Command Ship USS *Eldorado* (AGC-11) observed with their binoculars the flag raising atop Mount Suribachi. Forrestal turned to Smith and declared, "The raising of that flag on Suribachi means a Marine Corps for the next 500 years."

It was Commander in Chief, U.S Pacific Fleet, and Commander in Chief, Pacific Ocean Areas, Fleet Admiral Chester William Nimitz, USN [USNA 1905], who summarized the entire battle so accurately and succinctly:

Among the Americans who served on Iwo Jima,
uncommon valor was a common virtue.

The extraordinary courage and sacrifice by the Marines and Navy personnel were recognized with 27 Medals of Honor (the most for a single battle in U.S. history), 37 Navy Crosses, and 123 Silver Stars for gallantry in combat—uncommon valor indeed!

—

Chapter 3

No man ever steps in the same river twice,
for it's not the same river and he's not the same man.

-- Heraclitus

Thursday, 1.March.1945
USAAF Station F-356
Saffron Walden, Essex, England
United Kingdom
10:20 hours

Weather holds were never easy. The falling sleet and accumulating ice on the fighters did not bode well for the day's mission. The low overcast posed no obstacle for the pilots, but as long as ice adhered to the surfaces of the aircraft, it made flight too dangerous. Group held the squadron at alert standby in the distant hope the weather might break.

The squadron had briefed the mission prior to dawn despite the weather forecast. The plan called for another RODEO tasking and another fighter sweep of German airfields on both sides of the Rhine River in front of the 3rd Army. They also briefed a ground attack assignment to shoot up any German military vehicle they could find.

Into their third hour of waiting, Brian kept his attention off the waiting and the bravado chatter from the bullpen and on the stack of documents, reports, and correspondence that demanded his cognizance or action. The knock on his doorjamb brought a welcome relief.

"Excuse me, Sir. Can I ask you a question or two?" asked Second Lieutenant Morgan Samuel 'Block' Sanderson, USAAF, from Dayton, Ohio. Block had joined the squadron a week after the Dresden raid and right out of advanced training flight school. He became Rolo Stanfield's wingman in the 2nd Section, Green Flight.

The other recent replacement Captain Borman Jeremy 'Fly' Daniels, USAAF [USMA 1942] from Tulsa, Oklahoma, whom Brian assigned as the Green Flight leader, joined the day after the Dresden raid. Fly had served a tour in an air defense squadron in California before his transfer to the 334th Fighter Squadron.

In the reorganization after he assumed command, Brian had reassigned Captain Robert Charles 'Sweet' Sweeny, Jr., USAAF, an ex-patriot American from London, England, to take his place as 'B' Division and Red Flight leader. Sweet was the last of the Eagle Squadron pilots with Brian in the squadron. Arnie Clark, now the Group commanding officer, had told Brian that Sanderson was likely the last replacement pilot the squadron would receive, and as a consequence, mission limit transfers had been suspended.

Brian gestured to the chairs in front of his desk. He chose not to ask him to close the door.

"You know, Skipper, you have more combat experience than anyone I know. You are a decorated, five-time ace fighter pilot."

"I know what I've done, Block. What's your question?"

"What was it like flying in the Great Air Battle?"

Brian smiled and leaned back in his chair. "Your instigators sent you into the lion's den as a sacrificial offering to test the waters." Muffled laughter could be heard from the bullpen. The puzzled expression on Block's face coaxed Brian to continue. "What they," he said, pointing to and hearing more laughter from the bullpen, "chose not to tell you is, I'm not inclined to talk about exploits. I don't like it. My experience is my experience. You will not encounter the same conditions. You've not fired a shot in combat yet, and our job is to help you survive those first few events. That said since I hate this incessant paperwork and it's still nasty outside, I shall make an exception to my general rule and indulge your curiosity.

"To understand the experience of any one of us, you must understand the situation the British people found themselves in during the summer of 1940, but I do not have the time nor inclination to recount the history. Let it suffice to say, we flew three, four, five sorties a day, every day, for nearly two months against an overwhelming number of German bombers and fighters."

"We barely fly a sortie every other day or so. I can't imagine flying that much every day for weeks."

"We had shorter flights in Spits . . . less fuel, no tanks."

"What was it like flying Spitfires?"

Brian grinned at Morgan as if asking are you serious? "Like any other front-line fighter. Each of them has pluses and minuses. The Spit is no different."

Several other young pilots appeared at the doorway, apparently interested in listening to the conversation. Second Lieutenants John Henry 'Jack' Jarvis, USAAF, from Austin, Texas, and Stephen 'Stove' Sarron, USAAF, from Pueblo, Colorado, stood at the doorjamb. Both were wingmen in Yellow Flight.

"The stories we heard in flight school . . . you took off without your parachute or seat harnesses buckled, killed Germans attacking your airfield, and landed safely. Is all that story true?"

"They are only idle stories," Brian pronounced.

"Come on, Major," Jack said. "We've heard the stories, too."

"We just want to know if they are true," contributed Stove.

Brian pushed his chair back slightly and leaned back. "I appreciate your curiosity, guys, but I'm not particularly concerned about war stories. I'm not going to change my opinion. If you're that interested, go read the citation. I'm not going there even if the weather is nasty outside."

"Oh, come on, Skipper," protested Block.

"Nope. Sorry. You can find your entertainment elsewhere."

"It's not entertainment," Stove interjected from the doorjamb. "It's learning. We want to know what you did so that we can learn."

"Nice thought, but it won't work. Next question."

"How many times have you been shot down?" Block asked.

"Please. Enough."

"Do you want us to get shot down to learn what to avoid?" asked Block.

"No! I just don't think my experience is important."

"Trust us, Skipper, it is," Jack added.

Brian thought for a moment. *Oh heck, why the hell not?* "It's not something I've enjoyed counting." He paused to think about his answer to the query. "I've bailed out twice. My wife saved my sorry ass when I was shot up, and my Spit broke up in flight. I was thrown clear somehow, and my parachute deployed just in time. I landed in her lake, well, now our lake, and she nearly lost her life getting me out from underneath the sinking parachute. I was also shot down a couple of months later, and the impacts jammed my canopy. That time, a farmer rescued my sorry ass from my burning Spit after crashing in his field. The last one I can recall was belly landing in a field when my engine quit. I walked away from that one. I also had to make an emergency landing at Hamble after a cylinder was shot out over Cherbourg. Thankfully, that wounded Packard got me back to friendly territory."

"Damn, you were lucky," Stove commented.

"As my instructor taught me when I was a kid, you reach into your lucky bag and transfer it to your experience bag, and the objective is never to reach into your lucky bag too many times."

"Better lucky than good," Stove added.

"Another way of saying it, yes. I've reached into my lucky bag plenty, and I try not to . . ."

"Skipper," Juli Ellison interrupted, "Group on Blue."

Brian nodded his acknowledgment and lifted the Blue handset. "Drummond."

"Brian, it's Arnie. Weather guessers are forecasting the ice to persist until this afternoon. Operations for today are canceled. No word yet on tomorrow's ops. You can release your guys, but they've got to be back this evening and ready to fly in the morning, just in case. Any questions?"

"No Sir."

"Have a good rest of the day," Arnie said and hung up.

Brian stood, walked out to the bullpen, and waited for Jack, Stove, and Block to take their seats with the rest of the squadron. "We are done for the day. Ice is going to stick around until at least this afternoon. We are released for the day, but you must be back this evening since we must assume we'll fly tomorrow morning. Have fun. Watch out for the ice."

The pilots cleared out except for Block, who apparently wanted to stay for more questions. Brian shook his head and wagged his left index finger. Block got the meaning and joined the other pilots.

"You can secure too, Juli. I'll close up when I've gone through my inbox."

"Have a good day, Sir. See you in the morning." Ellison left and closed the door.

I'll call Charlotte once I get back to the O'Club. Brian returned to his desk and his paperwork.

—

Sunday, 4.March.1945
Oxford University Hospital
Headley Way
Headington, Oxford, Oxfordshire, England
United Kingdom
14:10 hours

Charlotte had received a telephone call last night that Doctor Rosemary Alice Kensington, MD, Jonathan's younger sister, was heading to the hospital with serious contractions. Charlotte called the hospital this morning and was informed that Rosemary had been admitted in childbirth. She made arrangements with June, Mabel, and Edith to take care of the farm so that she could spend a day or two in Oxford for Rose's birthing. The journey had taken most of the day, but she had finally arrived.

"May I help you?" the receptionist asked.

"I'm here to see Rosemary Kensington," answered Charlotte.

"She is in the maternity ward. I'll have one of the interns escort you."

"Thank you."

Charlotte walked at a modest pace with the young woman in a white uniform with thin red stripes. It was a longer walk than they had at Hampshire Central. The young lady, perhaps in her late teens, checked in with the ward nurse.

"Mrs. Kensington is resting now, and she needs her rest. You are welcome to use our waiting room until Mrs. Kensington can see you."

I'm not going to correct her misunderstanding of Rose's marital status. Charlotte nodded her agreement. The intern escorted her to the waiting room. Linda Kensington, née Mason, Jonathan's wife, stood when she noticed Charlotte enter the waiting room. The two women embraced and kissed cheeks.

"How is Rose?" Charlotte asked.

"It was a comparatively easy birth but still hard on Rose. Nevertheless, she birthed a beautiful, healthy boy. Rose named him George Brian Jonathan Kensington for her father. She's resting now."

"So they said at the ward desk. When did you arrive?"

"Just before young George was born. I got to talk to her after they got everything taken care of and settled down. She is excited that her pregnancy is over, and her son is here."

"Excellent."

The two women sat down and retreated to their thoughts. At a quarter past three, the assistant ward nurse entered the room to inform Linda that Rosemary was asking for her. The nurse led them back to Rose's bed with the two side curtains drawn out. Linda took the left side of the bed; Charlotte took the right side.

"Oh my . . . my cup runneth over," Rosemary declared. Linda and Charlotte embraced Rosemary gently and kissed her forehead. "They should be bringing George from the nursery shortly."

"Excellent," Charlotte said.

"We all want to see him," added Linda.

"How are you doing?" asked Charlotte.

"I'm tired and sore, but I would say fairly good, all in all."

"Excellent."

"Now that you and George are safe," Linda said. "The flame of my curiosity must be quenched. Who is the father, Rose?"

"He will be listed as unknown, and I shall never tell," Rosemary answered and then turned her head toward Charlotte and winked her left eyelid. Charlotte smiled modestly. Rosemary noticed the nurse's approach first. A broad, ear-to-ear smile bloomed on her face. Both Linda and Charlotte turned to see the source. They watched as the nurse transferred the snuggly swaddled infant to his mother's waiting arms. Rosemary took him, kissed his forehead several times, stroked his cheek softly, and then kissed him several more times. Charlotte and Linda leaned in to see a bright face and inquisitive eyes, absorbing what was hovering above him. The 'ooo's and 'ahh's kept coming as the women marveled at every slight movement on the baby's face.

"What have we here?" came the ebullient voice of Mary Spencer.

All three women looked to the foot of the bed.

"We have a healthy mother and a newborn baby boy," Charlotte declared in a louder-than-usual voice.

Mary jumped in and insisted on holding baby George. Rosemary passed the infant slowly and carefully to Mary's arms. The ladies became more animated and louder as the joyous event brought them closer together in celebration.

"The gang's all here," Rosemary declared.

"Well . . . except for Grace," added Charlotte.

"A countess cannot be expected to call upon a commoner," Mary contributed.

"What was that about a countess?" Grace Palmer said with feigned irritation. The group cheered as Countess Selborne joined the unusually boisterous women and one quiet infant boy.

Rosemary's colleagues and friends at the hospital joined the growing group of celebrants. The only men in the gathering were two doctors assigned to the hospital. The on-duty professionals did not stay long, and they cycled through to pay their respects to Rosemary and returned to their medical duties.

The ward nurses waded through the growing crowd, retrieving George to assist mother and son with lactation and feeding the infant. Rosemary was not bashful or shy.

It was late afternoon when the proud brother and new uncle arrived, which sparked another round of celebratory cheers. Jonathan kissed his wife first, kissed his sister's forehead, and then he gestured to his sister to hold his new nephew. Jonathan's attention was soon broken by the ward nurses insisting that George go to the nursery for unspecified reasons.

"I'm so glad you came through that in fine form and delivered a beautiful baby boy, Sister. I called Mum and Da once I got the call. They are both on the way but may not make it until tomorrow."

"They will get here when they get here," Rosemary replied.

"Indeed." Jonathan paused. "I'm sorry, Rose, but I can't stay long. We've a lot going on right now, and I need to get back to base to ensure everything goes well tomorrow morning." Jonathan kissed Rosemary's forehead and whispered in her ear. She nodded her head.

Linda walked out with Jonathan to say goodbye and send him off. She returned to the ladies. They stayed with Rosemary until the nurse shooed them off well past visiting hours.

They all decided to stay the night and return to see Rosemary and George when visiting hours opened in the morning.

The ladies found a hotel within walking distance of the hospital. They enjoyed a late dinner and chit-chat at a nearby public house.

—

Wednesday, 7.March.1945
Forward Supreme Headquarters Allied Expeditionary Force
Collège Moderne et Technique de Reims.
12 Rue Lesage
Reims, Grand Est
Liberated France
19:30 hours

The supreme commander invited the commanding general of the First Allied Airborne Army (FAAA) and the constituent division commanders to a social dinner. Lieutenant General Lewis Hyde Brereton, USAAF [USNA 1911], had assembled the FAAA with the British 1st and 6th Airborne Divisions; the American 17th, 82nd, and 101st Airborne Divisions; plus the 1st Polish Parachute Brigade, and SAS troops when needed. Only the SAS regiment was not represented at this commander's event.

Ike greeted each general personally with familiarity. Brereton was the last FAAA general to enter the flag dining room.

"Go Army. Beat Navy," General Eisenhower greeted General Brereton.

"Oh my gosh, General. I'm surprised you know my *alma mater*."

"We have more than a few general officers who attended Little Boys Boat and Barge School on the Severn."

"Yes Sir. There are a few of us."

"Indeed, there are, and we are grateful for your service." Eisenhower turned to the group and added, "Welcome, gentlemen. Please help yourselves to the booze of your choice. We'll eat in about half an hour."

Also in attendance, at Eisenhower's insistence, was Second Lieutenant Kathleen Helen Mary 'Kay' Summersby, BEM, née MacCarthy-Morrogh, who had been Eisenhower's assigned driver since the general's arrival in England in May 1942. She had been a trained and skilled driver in the British Mechanised Transport Corps (MTS). Her role had grown over the years of Eisenhower's generalship. Kay was now Ike's social secretary, hostess (as she was this evening), and general social assistant while still performing as the general's driver. As a measure of her importance to Eisenhower, Kay had been transferred to the U.S. Army Women's Auxiliary Corps (WAC) and promoted to second lieutenant on 3.January.1945.

As Kay saw to the drink requests, Ike noticed his chief of staff, Beetle Smith, poke his head into the room and signaled Eisenhower. Eisenhower excused himself from the conversation and went to Beetle.

"We've got General Bradley on the secure phone," Smith said.

"What about?"

"He didn't say, and I didn't ask. He just said it was urgent."

Eisenhower caught Kay's attention and gestured that he had to leave for a telephone call. She nodded and returned to her jovial efforts for their guests.

Ike lifted the handset. "Eisenhower."

"Sorry to bother you, General," said Lieutenant General Omar Nelson 'Brad' Bradley, USA [USMA 1915], Commanding General 12th Army Group.

"No problem, Brad. What have you got?"

"The 9th Armor with elements of the 9th Infantry reached the Ludendorff Bridge at Remagen this afternoon. Finding the bridge damaged but intact, troops rushed the bridge at considerable risk to themselves. We now hold both piers and stopped German attempts at demolition."

"Great news, Brad," Eisenhower shouted into the telephone. "How much have you got in that vicinity that you can throw across the river?"

"I have more than four divisions, but I called you to make sure that pushing them over would not interfere with your plans."

"Well, Brad, we expected to have that many divisions tied up around Cologne, and now those are free. Go ahead and shove over at least five divisions instantly and anything else necessary to make certain of our hold."

With surprising effervescence, Bradley said, "That's exactly what I wanted to do, but the question had been raised here about conflict with your plans, and I wanted to check with you."

"Thank you for the consideration, Brad, but we need to get across the Rhine as quickly and safely as possible. We'll adjust the plans to support your beachhead. Congratulations, Brad . . . my kudos to 9th Armor, 1st Army, and your 12th Army Group. Well done. Press this advantage as aggressively as you are able," Ike commanded. "We'll support you," he repeated. "Get the engineers on the bridge as soon as you can to safe and assess the bridge."

"Already in work. We're also setting up the deployment of an armor pontoon bridge just upriver of the Ludendorff. We got lucky. We'll press our attack to hold the initiative."

"I know you will, Brad. Go for it."

The two generals, friends, and West Point classmates wished each other good luck and signed off.

Eisenhower returned to the dinner, which was ready to be served. He chose to get folks fed first and would hold his news until they had eaten. The generals enjoyed a well-prepared steak dinner with baked potatoes and fresh green beans.

As the messmen cleared the table and shut the door behind them, the supreme commander remained seated. His guests did the same. "I don't want to keep you long," Eisenhower said, "since you all have units to command. General Bradley called to inform me that 9th Armor reached the Rhine at

Remagen and found the Ludendorff Bridge intact . . . damaged but intact. They have secured the eastern bank pier. Their hold is thin and tenuous, but they are going to exploit the bridgehead tonight and tomorrow." Eisenhower paused, and cheers from the generals filled the silence. "I say this to inform you and offer a head's up."

The supreme commander summarized the upcoming airborne operations to baseline the applicable ground situation—three major airborne operations in direct support of river crossings all along the Rhine River. In the next two weeks, the FAAA planned to carry out three major airborne assaults with parachute and glider troops: one assault group in front of the 7th Army at Worms; another in front of the 12th Army Group at Cologne; with the third group supporting the 21st Army Group at Wesel.

Eisenhower continued, "General Bradley confirmed they had secured a solid bridgehead at Cologne; Operation NAPLES II is no longer necessary and will not be executed. The same is true for Operation CHOKER II at Worms. As of this afternoon, Field Marshal Montgomery indicated he needs the jump, so Operation VARSITY remains in the active category. We are in a highly fluid phase of this campaign. I want to personally acknowledge the training and preparation of the First Airborne Army, and I want to convey my gratitude to General Brereton and his commanders for your extraordinary service. That's all the relevant news. Any questions?" Eisenhower paused to allow for queries. None came. "Thank you for taking the time to have dinner with me. Now, let's get you, gentlemen, back to your commands and your vital work."

The generals paid their respects to the supreme commander and returned to their units. The situation on the ground was progressing faster than expected, and the enemy was becoming progressively disorganized.

—

Thursday, 8.March.1945
Grand Hotel National
4 Haldenstrasse
Luzern, Luzern Kanton
Schweizerische Eidgenossenschaft (Swiss Confederation)
16:30 hours

In accordance with the prearranged instructions, OSS Bern Station Chief Allen Welsh Dulles had taken a modest room overlooking the lake in the luxury hotel on picturesque Lake Lucerne. He registered using one of his many alias names. His appointment was with and at the request of Swiss Army Intelligence officer *Major* Max Waibel. Dulles had known and worked with Waibel since his posting to Bern in 1942. He had been in the room for less than an hour, sufficient time for a cup of tea. The knock on his door came spot on time. He knew who it was.

Opening the door, Dulles found Waibel's familiar smiling face. The young intelligence officer was dressed in a simple business suit rather than his Army uniform. "Good afternoon, Max."

"And to you, Mister Dulles." They spoke English.

Waibel declined the proffered tea. The two men sat in comfortable upholstered chairs opposite each other with a small coffee table between them.

"You said you had news," Allen opened.

"Yes, I do. I am authorized to speak for and act on behalf of *SS-Obergruppenführer* Wolff."

SS-Obergruppenführer Karl Friedrich Otto Wolff had been the Supreme SS and SD Leader in Italy since September 1943. Prior to his current assignment, Wolff had been on Himmler's personal staff. He was a very well-connected Nazi.

"The head of the S-S in Italy."

"Yes."

"But not Kesselring?" Dulles asked.

Generalfeldmarschall Albert Kesselring had been the commanding general of Army Group C—all German forces in Italy, since 1943.

"No. General Wolff has indicated that leadership is in turmoil. The professional military knows the war has been lost since Stalingrad, and the last holdouts were finally convinced after the Falaise Pocket collapsed. According to Wolff, Hitler himself has reassigned Kesselring to relieve von Rundstedt as O-B West."

"So, who is relieving Kesselring?"

"Wolff does not know, but his guess is von Vietinghoff."

"Ah, yes, the consummate Prussian. So, now, to the brass tacks. What does Wolff want?

"He wants to negotiate the surrender of German forces in Italy . . . all of Army Group C and the S-S in Italy."

"That's a rather bold and dangerous move for one of Himmler's disciples. Does he have the authority to do such a thing without the apparent consent of the Army?"

"When I talked to him in Lugano three days ago, he seemed pretty confident and sure of himself. I did ask that specific question, but he avoided answering."

Dulles thought for a few moments. "I am certain Wolff knows the Allied terms."

"Yes, he does. I can assure you of that."

"Then, he also knows I am not authorized to negotiate surrender terms other than unconditional. The best I can do is to inform Washington and London."

"He knows that, but he wants to start the dialogue."

"Doesn't he think he should confer with Kesselring's successor before taking such a huge step?"

"I do not know, but my read of the man is he's fairly sure that whoever assumes command of Army Group C will recognize reality."

Again, Dulles considered Waibel's information. "Very well, Max. I shall notify Washington and London first thing tomorrow morning. Any other business?"

"No Sir."

"Then, what do you say we enjoy an exquisite early supper in the dining room and then perhaps take a stroll on the famous promenade."

"That would be delightful, Allen. Thank you."

The two intelligence officers did just that. They enjoyed an excellent meal and a pleasant walk along the famous lakeside promenade, with the rest of the war-torn world oblivious to what had just happened that afternoon.

—

Thursday, 15.March.1945
Oval Office
The White House
Washington, District of Columbia
United States of America
15:00 hours

Admiral Leahy entered the president's office as Treasury Secretary Morgenthau departed. "Secretary Stimson is here for your three o'clock." Roosevelt nodded his head barely and did not respond otherwise. "Would you like me to attend this one?"

Henry Lewis Stimson had a long history of government service and remained a staunch Republican politically. He had been Secretary of War in the Taft administration and Secretary of State in the Hoover administration. As the clouds of war darkened, President Roosevelt asked Stimson to serve as his Secretary of War. Stimson accepted the challenge and joined the Roosevelt administration in July 1940. When the president transferred leadership of the atomic weapons development program in June 1942 to the Army, Stimson was the designated Cabinet minister supervisor.

"No, thank you," murmured Roosevelt. "That won't be necessary."

"Very well." Leahy answered and went to the door. "Mister Secretary, the president can see you now." He closed the door.

President Roosevelt had not moved from the Hoover Desk. Instead, he gestured to the wooden, arm chair to the right of his desk. The two exchanged their cordialities before Stimson sat.

"So, you have news on our special project?" the president asked, jumping into the topic for the private meeting.

"Yes Sir. The team believes they have resolved the technical issues with the implosion concept through all the elemental experimentation they can devise."

Roosevelt raised his left hand, palm out. "Sorry, Henry. Please remind me what the implosion concept is?"

"Early on, they considered numerous techniques to achieve critical mass, which is the threshold of sustained reaction—the fissile material divides rapidly with an explosive release of energy. The team has been confident in the gun system, which will work for the uranium device, but it was insufficient for the plutonium weapon. They developed a set of conventional explosive lenses to instantaneously compress a plutonium sphere from the size of a softball to a tennis ball diameter to achieve critical mass."

"The implosion technique seems far more complicated than the gun technique."

"It is. However, contributing factors—the production process and volume, material stability, and conversion efficiency—make the plutonium device significantly more attractive operationally."

"I see."

Stimson nodded. "The team has arrived at several conclusions that I needed to brief you on and seek your consent." Roosevelt nodded his agreement. "We have transitioned from Germany to Japan as the situation in Germany continues to progress swiftly."

"Agreed. We are closer to victory in Europe than in the Pacific."

"To that end, we've begun developing our target list." Again, Roosevelt nodded. "We have sufficient fissile uranium material for a viable weapon in the final stages of assembly and preparation. We currently have sufficient fissile plutonium for two implosion devices, and our production rate is roughly eight times greater than enriched uranium. Nevertheless, because of the detonation technology and more difficult science involved, the team has requested a full-scale test of the implosion device. A group of dissenting physicists on or associated with the development team have put forward an aggressive argument against the use of any atomic weapon against populous targets and press for a demonstration that is observable by the Japanese."

"Let them see the power before they feel the effects?"

"Yes, precisely."

"Interesting moral conundrum."

"Which is why I am here. While we have this dissent counterproposal, the team's collective opinion is and remains the risks of such exposure may be counter-productive to achieving our goal of the unconditional surrender of our adversaries."

"How so?"

"The collective body of physicists maintain that there is a substantial risk of a complete dud—a failure to detonate—or worse, a partial 'dirty' explosion, a detonation of the conventional explosives but a failure to achieve critical mass. The result would likely be the spreading of radioactive material over a large area. It might look like a large conventional bomb with the damage effects being less visible or detectable until the effects on living creatures, including human beings become medically obvious. To achieve the desired results within the Japanese government, we need an irrefutable event to show them the hopelessness of their situation." Stimson paused to give the president time to process the information and his response.

"That is quite the question . . . or rather set of questions," Roosevelt replied. "First, my inclination is to accept and agree with the scientists that a full-scale test would answer the question of function. We will all know whether the design actually works as intended. In that context, I favor a test with the proviso that we have sufficient core material for more than one weapon at the time. If the test is good, we must use those additional devices toward the end objective.

"Second, my reading of the Japanese tells me they aren't likely to respond positively to a demonstration that does not extract a cost. They view demonstrations as weakness. I understand and appreciate the reluctance of some to use such a potentially devastating weapon. Nevertheless, they have demonstrated their willingness to sacrifice whole blocks of their population and take as many of our soldiers as possible in the hope that we will give up before they do.

"Third, a question from me: where is the team proposing we perform this verification test?"

"The team recommends a secluded portion of the Alamogordo Bombing Range in New Mexico. It is not far from the Los Alamos research center and meets all test requirements with minimal outside impact."

"That is a big statement to make, Henry."

"Yes, it is. I have reviewed the survey and estimates of thermal, pressure, and radiation as a consequence of a full-scale detonation. The surrounding mountains offer substantial protection, not complete, but sufficient safeguards."

"Some folks speculate this thing will ignite the atmosphere and wipe out life as we know it," the president observed.

"You've heard that?" Roosevelt nodded and added a wiry grin. "The scientists can find no justification for such a hypothesis in physics. The team has gone over and over the process from complete success to total failure and everything in between. Nevertheless, the team is confident they have bracketed the potential outcomes."

"Very well. Does the plan call for briefing the governor and local law enforcement?"

"Mister President, part of the plan is to issue a broad spectrum press release that the government, without indicating who or what would be conducting a pre-dawn test in the desert. We don't want to provide likely noticeable effects because we don't want to stimulate anyone's curiosity. Therefore, we recommend avoiding any details and sticking with the press notice. Then, if the test device fully functions, we will follow up with a partially truthful explanation that we conducted a test of a new explosive, explain the obvious phenomena—flash, shock wave, sound, and such—and pass off the event as a normal developmental effort."

President Roosevelt looked across the room's long axis at the far wall and the inactive fireplace. He considered Stimson's words and recommendations. "I agree with the need for a full-scale test. The science is pretty far out there. I think we would all like to know if this thing works before we confront the enemy . . . or use it on his land and people." Roosevelt withdrew into thought. When he returned, the president looked at Stimson. "I approve the test, Henry. When will they perform this test?"

"Part of the setup for the test will entail a pre-test event to calibrate the instrumentation array and procedures. The calibration test itself will be a major event in that it will be the largest man-made explosion in history and will involve a raised pile of one hundred tons of conventional explosives. The team is pushing for mid-May, but General Groves and I think it will be closer to June or July."

After thinking for several seconds, Roosevelt nodded. "The sooner, the better, but the project team must be satisfied they have everything set as they need it to gather the most data they can from such an event."

"Thank you very much, Mister President."

Again, Roosevelt nodded. "Good luck, Henry. Good day."

Stimson stood and departed. Leahy returned, and they were on to the next appointment.

—

Sunday, 18.March.1945
Trollenhagen, Mecklenburg
Deutsches Reich
13:40 hours.

"I'm hit," came the shouted radio broadcast.

Hunter diverted his attention from scanning for the enemy to checking on his squadron. Corn was where he should be. Hole and Horn were off his left wing. Fly was in a tight reversal with Rolo and Block swinging outside.

"We've got you," Fly radioed.

As Hunter rolled to scan behind him, he saw the black smoke and followed it to the engine flames.

"Jump, Antler," commanded Fly. "Get out."

Antler pulled up sharply, as marked by the black smoke trail. He rolled inverted. The aircraft popped up, and Antler flew out of the cockpit through the open canopy. Antler pulled the ripcord as soon as he was clear of the fatally wounded airplane.

Hunter held a wide orbit as Antler descended under a full canopy. He was going to land in a dry plowed field north of the village. Brian scanned the sky around them and then the ground around Antler's expected touchdown location.

"Cobweb Six, Cobweb Red. German troops deploying on the other side of the tree line and moving toward Antler."

"If you have position, hose 'em down. Slow 'em up."

"Wilco."

Brian saw Sweet's 'B' Division rolling in sequence to carry out their orders. Brian returned his attention to Antler and then saw Fly with his landing gear and flaps down in a descending base leg approach turn to land with the furrows. *Damn! That's a ballsy move. Should I stop him? Naw!*

"Sweet, take top cover. Able, let's protect 'em," Hunter commanded.

Fly landed safely in a cloud of dust. Brian saw small dirty geysers near Fly and Antler. *Bullets.* He dove to a spot south of Fly's aircraft. Antler ran toward the Mustang with its large diameter propeller still turning. Fly stood in the cockpit against the prop wash and shucked his parachute to make as much room as he could.

Brian pushed his throttle to full power and leveled off just above the ground. Muzzle flashes dotted the tree line to the north. *This is going to be too close.* He adjusted to clear Fly's Mustang and put his sight pipper on the concentration of dots in the trees. Brian squeezed the trigger on his stick. All the guns erupted. The bullet impacts began to chew up the trees. Brian smoothly pushed his rudder pedals and countered with opposite aileron to spread his bullet streams as wide along the tree line as possible. He pulled up sharply to avoid getting too close, although no Germans appeared to be firing at him, or anyone else for that matter. The spacing with the rest of his division displayed his place. He adjusted his climb to that place.

As Hunter rolled onto his back and scanned the area below him, Corn duplicated his low pass and pulled up. Hole and Horn took a more conventional diving attack on the tree line. Hunter could not detect anyone or anything moving on the ground other than Fly's Mustang. He was turning for takeoff. Rolo and Block also chose diving attacks.

The large dust cloud behind Fly signified his takeoff run. *Another pass won't be necessary.* Hunter watched as he scanned for possible targets. Puffs of additional dirt probably indicated that the massive propellor at full power was nipping the mounds of furrowed dirt. Fly had the canopy open. Good move. Fly's takeoff run took longer than expected, but he eventually got the Mustang into the air and quickly cleaned up the aircraft configuration. He barely cleared the tree line, but Fly with his passenger was flying. Hunter scanned the sky. *We're clear.*

"Cobweb, Cobweb Six. We're bingo. Cobweb Red, we're climbing to you."

As they joined up for the transit home, Brian counted his aircraft. 15. *All accounted for except for Antler's destroyed fighter.* Antler was sitting on Fly's lap in the very crowded cockpit of Fly's QP-P Mustang. It was probably not comfortable for the doubled-up crew, but the flight back to Debden was uneventful. Even the weather cooperated.

Brian reviewed the mission in his head during the routine return flight. The fighter sweep of a handful of Northern German airfields. He had not seen what got Antler's aircraft, but he remembered that he had said it had been hit, which meant ground fire. They had not seen a German fighter in the air for several weeks. They caught many on the ground with no detectable attempt to takeoff. *Had German crews abandoned their country's hopeless defense? Or were they out of fuel, ammunition, or both?*

The landing back at Debden was easy and without incident. As they secured and jumped out of their fighters, they gathered around Fly's fighter. They all congratulated Antler for making it home and Fly for his courage in recovering a downed mate, saving him from capture and imprisonment.

"You dropped hot brass on us, Skipper," protested Antler.

"Not my intent."

"That was a helluva pass, Hunter," Sweet added.

"Yeah!" several of the pilots confirmed.

"Why did you go in so low?" asked Sweet.

"I wanted the Krauts to see me coming!"

The pilots shouted, cheered, and pumped their fists.

"It worked," Sweet confirmed.

"It sure did," contributed Fly. "They didn't shoot a single round at us after that pass."

"All right, lads, enough bravado. Let's get our debriefings done, so we can get dinner and celebrate Antler's escape from capture." Brian chose to debrief last. Hunter's young corporal debriefer kept his questions simple and straightforward. Once complete, the squadron was released.

Dinner was louder and more raucous than usual. It had been a very good day for all three of the Group squadrons. The evening became even rowdier in the bar as the pilots embellished the details of Fly's rescue of Antler inside Germany. They all noted the lack of German adversaries. The end felt near.

Before retiring to his room for the night, and even though it was comparatively late, Brian called Charlotte to hear her voice and let her hear his voice. Then, after a short conversation, they hung up. *A good day!*

—

Thursday, 22.March.1945
Oval Office
The White House
Washington, District of Columbia
United States of America
16:00 hours

"Welcome back, Bill."

"Thank you, Mister President," responded OSS Director Major General Donovan.

"Where were you off to this time?"

"South America, again, although I do not publicize that fact to avoid stimulating Director Hoover."

Roosevelt smiled, recognizing the difficulty working with FBI Director J. Edgar Hoover. "What did you learn?"

"We can confirm our suspicions. The Germans, or more specifically the Nazis and precisely the S-S, are fleeing *en masse* to South America. All of the southern countries, Brazil, Peru, Ecuador, and south are involved. The number of them is too vast to deal with, and many, if not most or all, have local government connections and protection. Our agents are working to identify, record, and catalog their findings for future use. Our field agents are also trying to do the same thing with governmental officials to illuminate the believers, the supporters, the incidental facilitators, and those who are offended by or opposed to the influx of Germans into their country. The Nazis are moving considerable fungible assets from artwork to gold so that they can buy a lot of support."

"Disappointing, but well done, Bill. Keep up the great work. I suspect we will need that information for the criminal prosecutions that are sure to come."

"Yes Sir."

"We received a missive from Stalin," Roosevelt said, changing the subject, "to convey his ire over the Wolff initiative we are negotiating."

"I'm not surprised."

"He accuses us of violating our agreement regarding unconditional surrender and no separate peace negotiations."

"Wolff only represents Army Group C, not the German Armed Forces or the government. M-I-6 confirmed that Kesselring was reassigned to O-B West, and General von Vietinghoff assumed command of Army Group C. Bern Station also confirmed that von Vietinghoff consented to the Wolff negotiation. They are ready to surrender."

"Apparently, Stalin does not agree. He fears they will be left to fight the Germans alone."

"Perhaps, he does not realize Army Group C is not O-B West, and the Germans are still fighting as best they can on the Western Front."

"There is that. I intend to respond to his message with pronounced disappointment in his distrust of us. I will also note for you and a few others that I find his outrageous distrust of us extraordinarily ironic given his conduct and actions, especially in Poland. I will also tell him emphatically that we will not alter our strategy, policy, or efforts to secure the surrender of Army Group C."

"I concur, Mister President. He is trying to intimidate us into deferring to him."

Roosevelt nodded. "That is my impression, and that is not going to happen. I have given far too much already in my unsuccessful efforts to build a relationship with him. I do not want the Soviets as adversaries after the war, but I cannot allow him to dictate Allied policy. Their bellicosity will not cow us."

"I can say, Mister President, we are finding quiet dissidents within the Red Army and Foreign Ministry. We are working aggressively to cultivate their dissatisfaction with Stalin's confrontational position, but they are also quite fearful of the N-K-V-D and N-K-G-B, and rightly so.'

"Press on, Bill. Great work. We are really going to need your services in what will undoubtedly be a tumultuous time in the post-war world, given what we know of Stalin's and Mao's ambitions. To that end, I also want to say to you directly that I appreciate your discretion and perseverance in resisting Edgar's antagonism. Frankly, I agree with your assessment. I think it was Edgar who leaked your central intelligence service proposal to the press and colored their view of the proposal. We must not chase him down that rabbit hole. I have left you hanging far too long, but I ask you to hold your tongue and words until at least the war in Europe is won. Within a week or two of victory in Europe, I will present your proposal, our proposal, to the Cabinet and Congress. I like it, Bill. You've done a magnificent job . . . exactly as we discussed. I do have one question." Without expression, Donovan nodded. "I like the potential of this air service you mentioned. I am curious whom you have in mind to run this air service?"

Donovan chuckled softly with his head bowed and left fist in front of his mouth. He looked up and then into the president's eyes. A slight grin grew. "Please allow me a slight prologue, Mister President." Roosevelt nodded his consent. "The model for the new air service comes from the experience we have gained during the war with Bainbridge Air Services, the airline owned and operated by Major Brian Drummond. We owe him and his company an exemplary debt of gratitude. B-A-S is the model. As such, my first choice is Brian Drummond."

"Will he take the job?"

"I have not asked him and will not until we actually have a job to offer him."

"Good point. I've met Major Drummond several times . . . a very impressive and accomplished young man."

"And very wealthy, I might add."

"How can an Army major be wealthy?"

"His parents deceased several years ago, and he inherited the estate his parents had quietly built. I don't know his net worth, but it is probably well into eight or nine figures in rough measure."

"So he doesn't need a job."

"No, he doesn't. He just loves flying, so any job offer would probably have to be a hybrid, a working manager."

"Flying?"

"Yes."

"What if we keep him on active duty and assign him to the position?" asked President Roosevelt.

"I had not considered that option, I am embarrassed to say."

"Keep the arrow in your quiver until you need it. One last item before I must go on to my next appointment. What is your biggest obstacle to achieving our central intelligence service?"

"The Joint Intelligence Committee has agreed on virtually everything except organizational position. The Army and Navy Intelligence see an elevation of the new service above them as a direct threat to their position of influence."

"Which is precisely why the Office of the President needs a presidential-level strategic intelligence service. So, besides dealing with Edgar's offended sensitivities, we must tamp down the G-2, N-2, and their supporters in Congress."

"That is exactly as I see it, Mister President."

Roosevelt nodded his acknowledgment. "We'll deal with it when the time comes, but for now, let's do our part to keep things quiet. Now, I must be on to my next appointment. Thank you very much for the discussion, Bill. Keep up the great work."

"Thank you, Mister President."

As Bill Donovan departed via the anteroom door, Admiral Leahy pushed President Roosevelt out the exterior door for an official state welcome of Governor General of Canada, the Earl of Athlone, and his wife, Princess Alice.

———

Saturday, 24.March.1945
Okinawa, Okinawa Prefecture
Imperial Japan
16:30 hours

Operation ICEBERG—the invasion of Okinawa—brought the 5th Fleet with 40 aircraft carriers of various sizes, 18 battleships, and assault and supply ships with the 10th Army embarked and composed of the III Amphibious Corps, and the XXIV Corps. The Landing Force Commander Lieutenant General Simon Bolivar Buckner, Jr., USA [USMA 1908], commanding the 10th Army, would report to Amphibious Task Force Commander Vice Admiral Kelly Turner until they completed the landing process and then to Commander 5th Fleet, Admiral Raymond Ames Spruance, USN [USNA 1906].

ICEBERG was the largest amphibious assault in the Pacific region. The III Amphibious Corps was commanded by Major General Roy Stanley Geiger, USMC, a renowned Marine aviator and former assistant naval attaché in London. The XXIV Corps was commanded by Major General John Reed Hodge, USA.

Lieutenant General Mitsuru Ushijima, IJA, commanded the Japanese 32nd Army and decided to focus on a series of defensive lines on the southern end of the island. He had prepared his limited forces well.

Beyond the coming bloody ground combat to dislodge the Japanese defenders, the battle would be known for the desperate *kamikaze* suicide bombers and *Ohka* rocket-assisted suicide flying bombs that relentlessly attacked the 5th Fleet with successes but at a terrible cost. The Japanese also committed their largest battleship, IJNS *Yamato*, to a naval suicide mission and quickly met her ignominious fate under relentless bombardment by unopposed American naval aviation aircraft before reaching the American Fleet.

———

Saturday, 24.March.1945
Xanten, Nordrhein-Westfalen
Deutsches Reich
10:00 hours

Prime Minister Churchill stood boldly, fists on his hips, on the crest of a small knoll within sight of the Rhine River. With the prime minister were Field Marshals Brooke and Montgomery, and Supreme Commander General of the Army Eisenhower. The drone of multitudinous aircraft engines grew progressively louder. Several squadrons of Spitfire and Mustang fighters raced across the scene in front of them. Some fired rockets at unseen targets. More fired their wing guns and cannons.

The leaders had gathered to witness the beginning of Operation VARSITY and the 21st Army Group's second crossing of the Rhine River after the less-than-successful Operation MARKET GARDEN in September of last year.

A vast array of transport planes, 1,625 in all, along with 1,348 gliders pulled behind their tractor aircraft, appeared to the southwest. Once across the river, they turned north, heading to their drop zones. They could easily see the battered remains of the village of Wesel on the far side of the river and, more importantly, *Dierfordterwald*. In direct support, the XVIII Airborne Corps planned to parachute into landing zones on the east side of the forest between the woods and the Issel River. The British 6th Airborne Division would jump into the north end, and the American 17th Airborne Division would take the south end.

As the transport air fleet approached, swirls of fighters kept watch above the transport aircraft. The array and sound of the massed aircraft were impressive enough, but then, the twin-engine transports began to disgorge their paratrooper passengers.

"Magnificent!" exclaimed Churchill.

"It is quite the sight," Eisenhower added.

"Sixteen thousand men and their combat equipment will be on the ground in an hour," Montgomery said. He pointed to the left. "The boat crossing is underway in conjunction with parachute assault."

"There are fewer German troops in the area of Wesel. The combined air forces have done their task in fine fashion."

"We shall make quick work of this crossing," Montgomery commented.

"We are crossing all along the Rhine," Eisenhower added, "this weekend and the coming week. Then, by the first of next month, we will have our armies across the Rhine and moving into the heart of Germany."

Churchill turned to face Eisenhower. "Well done, Ike. We eagerly await the rapid advance of your forces to the east."

"We are ready, Prime Minister."

"I know you are. Now, I must be off to the aerodrome. I must get back to London this afternoon. First, I shall brief the War Cabinet on what I witnessed this morning. Thank you very much. Good show!"

Prime Minister Churchill and Field Marshal Brooke went to the airfield. The prime minister's C-54 Paralos waited in readiness. They would land back at Northolt in two hours.

———

Sunday, 25.March.1945
Chequers Court
Ellesborough, Buckinghamshire, England
United Kingdom
16.20 hours

Prime Minister Churchill had recently risen from a most restful and rejuvenating nap and returned to his study, working with his Principal Private Secretary John Miller Martin, CVO. The 41-year-old Martin had been with Churchill since the beginning of Winston's premiership. They had made good progress through the afternoon's correspondence. Thirty-five minutes into the afternoon session, Martin saw the red alert light illuminate.

"Excuse me, Sir. I need to check on something."

Churchill nodded. He continued to write his thoughts, notes, comments, and actions in the margins of the various documents. Several uncounted minutes passed when a single knock preceded Martin's return.

"Excuse me, Prime Minister, Ambassador Winant has arrived unannounced with an urgent for you."

U.S. Ambassador of the Court of St. James's John Gilbert 'Gil' Winant had been a familiar and regular guest at Chequers and in the Churchill household. Gil and the Churchills' second daughter Sarah Millicent Hermione Churchill had maintained a multi-year, not-so-well-hidden intimate affair. However, despite Winant's familiarity with the Churchill family, this weekend was not one of the weekends the ambassador was expected at Chequers.

"Let us not keep the ambassador waiting."

Martin opened the door and announced, "United States Ambassador Winant to see you, Sir."

Churchill stood and stepped toward the door, meeting Gill halfway. The two men shook hands. "This is rather unusual, Gil. To what do we owe the pleasure of your company?"

Winant opened his leather briefcase and extracted a document. "I just received this letter from the president to Marshal Stalin. He specifically asked me to show you."

"That's odd. Why didn't he send it to me? We have been communicating directly and privately for many years." The prime minister took the proffered document.

"I don't know, Prime Minister. All I know is what the president had asked me to do."

Churchill nodded his understanding and began reading.

TOP SECRET

No. 281

PERSONAL AND TOP SECRET

FOR MARSHAL STALIN

FROM PRESIDENT ROOSEVELT

Ambassador Harriman has communicated to me a letter which he has received from Mr. Molotov regarding an investigation being made by Field Marshal Alexander into a reported possibility of obtaining the surrender of part or all of the German army in Italy. In this letter, Mr. Molotov demands that, because of the non-participation therein of Soviet officers, this investigation to be undertaken in Switzerland should be stopped forthwith.

The facts of this matter I am sure have, through a misunderstanding, not been correctly presented to you. The following are the facts:

Unconfirmed information was received some days ago in Switzerland that some German officers were considering the possibility of arranging for the surrender of German troops that are opposed to Field Marshal Alexander's British-American Armies in Italy.

Upon the receipt of this information in Washington, Field Marshal Alexander was authorized to send to Switzerland an officer or officers of his staff to ascertain the accuracy of the report and if it appeared to be of sufficient promise to arrange with any competent German officers for a conference to discuss details of the surrender with Field

Marshal Alexander at his headquarters in Italy. If such a meeting could be arranged Soviet representatives would, of course, be welcome.

Information concerning this investigation to be made in Switzerland was immediately communicated to the Soviet Government. Your Government was later informed that it will be agreeable for Soviet officers to be present at Field Marshal Alexander's meetings with German officers if and when arrangements are finally made in Berne for such a meeting at Caserta to discuss details of a surrender.

Up to the present time the attempts by our representatives to arrange a meeting with German officers have met with no success, but it still appears that such a meeting is a possibility.

My Government, as you will of course understand, must give every assistance to all officers in the field in command of Allied forces who believe there is a possibility of forcing the surrender of enemy troops in their area. For me to take any other attitude or to permit any delay which must cause additional and avoidable loss of life in the American forces would be completely unreasonable. As a military man you will understand the necessity for prompt action to avoid losing an opportunity. The sending of a flag of truce to your General at Konigsberg or Danzig would be in the same category.

There can be in such a surrender of enemy forces in the field no violation of our agreed principle of unconditional surrender and no political implications whatever.

I will be pleased to have at any discussion of the details of surrender by our commander of American forces in the field the benefit of the experience and advice of any of your officers who can be present, but I cannot agree

to suspend investigation of the possibility
because of objection by Mr. Molotov for some
reason completely beyond my comprehension.

Not much is expected from the reported
possibility, but for the purpose of preventing
misunderstanding between our officers, I hope
you will point out to the Soviet officials
concerned the desirability and necessity of
our taking prompt and effective action without
any delay to effect the surrender of any enemy
military forces that are opposed to American
forces in the field.

I feel certain that you will have the same
attitude and will take the same action when a
similar opportunity comes on the Soviet front.

Franklin D. Roosevelt

FDR

TOP SECRET

"This is more like it," Churchill said, waving the letter in the air and displaying a broad smile across his face. "I have held concerns about the president apparently being spellbound by Uncle Joe's affability since Tehran."

President Roosevelt appointed, and the Senate confirmed Harriman as U.S. Ambassador to the Soviet Union. He assumed his post in October 1943. William Averell 'Ave' Harriman, son of railroad tycoon Edward Henry 'E.H.' Harriman, had been the president's representative as the Lend-Lease liaison in London since the program took effect in the spring of 1941 until his ambassadorship. While the relationship between Sarah and Gil was more apparent within the family and less so to the public, the opposite was true for the relationship between their son Randolph's wife, Pamela Beryl Churchill, née Digby, and Ave Harriman while he was stationed in London.

"The initial contact with Bern Station Chief Dulles must be explored as deeply as possible in the shortest possible time to save lives."

"Precisely! The surrender of Army Group C would be a far greater impact than the surrender of the German 6th Army at Stalingrad two years ago. The Soviets did not engage us in the surrender of the 6th Army and were never involved in the Italy campaign, just as they are not involved in the Pacific war. This action," Churchill said, holding up the letter again, "is exactly what is needed. The Soviets are not excluded, but they are also not relevant to Army Group C. Please convey my gratitude to the president."

"I will."

"I have no guests for supper. Can you stay? Neither Clementine nor Sarah is here, but I would enjoy your company."

"Thank you so much, Winston, but I really must get back to the embassy."

Churchill knew that Sarah was in London, but he was not going to raise that fact with Winant. "Very well. Anything I should know?"

"No . . . nothing dramatic . . . just time critical, and we are behind."

"Safe journey."

"Thank you, Sir." Winant returned the letter to his briefcase and said goodbye.

When Martin returned, the prime minister and his duty private secretary picked up their communications processing where they had left off.

———

Thursday, 29.March.1945
Bureau of Engraving and Printing
14th and C Streets, Southwest
Washington, District of Columbia
United States of America
16:00 hours

President Roosevelt settled into his favorite cushioned leather chair in the presidential railcar—U.S. Car One, Ferdinand Magellan. He looked forward to several weeks of no appointments, no meetings, and no problems. Admiral Leahy would run interference. The president's supporters, from Leahy and Hopkins to Daisy and Polly, would do their best to insulate the president from the stress of the world for a few weeks. Rest and relaxation were what the doctors prescribed, and that was what he was going to do. With the president for the overnight journey south to the relief he always enjoyed at Warm Springs, Georgia, Franklin had Anna and family friends Daisy Suckley and Polly Delano.

Margaret Lynch 'Daisy' Suckley was Franklin's sixth cousin once removed and a consistent confidante of the president. She had been close to Franklin going back to her childhood and was nine years younger than Franklin.

Laura Franklin 'Polly' Delano possessed a dominant, often overwhelming personality. She was also another cousin of Franklin, who was three years younger than the president. Franklin enjoyed Polly's eccentricities and her penchant for gossip.

Both women had been Franklin's frequent travel companions, especially during his political campaigning, and that part of their relationship with the president had not changed during his presidency. Franklin valued their insights, especially with personal contacts, and relied upon their opinions about all sorts of things. This journey was no different from many earlier trips over a couple of decades.

"I'm going to check on the loading, Papa. I'll be right back. We should be departing soon," Anna declared and departed the presidential salon car.

"Would you care for some tea, Franklin?" said Daisy.

"Thank you, no, but I'll take a scotch & soda with a twist of lime as I like it."

"You really shouldn't, Franklin," Polly protested. "The doctors told you to rest, relax, AND enjoy healthy living."

"A nice cocktail is relaxation."

"Well, you got me there, but I'm quite mindful of what the doctors told all of us. You're still a young man, Franklin, and we must all help you strengthen yourself. Yalta took a heavy toll on your body. The war is approaching its end. You have seen us through the Great Depression and now the war. You deserve to enjoy the accolades of victory."

The president nodded and waved his left hand dismissively. He started to shift himself toward his wheelchair.

"What are you doing?"

"I'll make my drink myself. I'm not an invalid."

"Oh, stop, Franklin. You're such a stubborn sod," Polly said, standing from her chair and stepping to the small bar. She began mixing drinks for each of them. The trained lurched forward. The president's expression immediately flashed to worry until a breathless Anna burst into the railcar.

"We're . . . moving," Anna announced as she struggled to catch her breath.

"I thought we might have left you," Roosevelt said.

"Would you care for a cocktail, Anna dear?" Polly asked.

"Papa's not supposed to have alcohol on this trip."

"Then, you talk him out of it. He won't listen to me."

Anna turned to face her father but stopped when she saw his raised left hand, palm out. Franklin shook his head slightly to convey his rejection of any confrontation between the women around him.

With drinks served and the train moving, the president and his three female companions settled into the latest social gossip from New York City, Chicago, and Hollywood. This was relaxation for Franklin Roosevelt, and his guardians were content with their role in his life.

—

Chapter 4

When the people of the world all know beauty as beauty,
There arises the recognition of ugliness.
When they all know the good as good,
There arises the recognition of evil.

-- Lao Tzu

Sunday, 1.April.1945
Okinawa, Okinawa Prefecture
Imperial Japan
08:30 hours

This was L-Day and H-Hour. Operation ICEBERG and the invasion of Okinawa had begun. The 2nd Marine Division performed a feint landing at the island's southeast tip before the division became the 10th Army's reserve. The 1st and 6th Marine Divisions of the III Amphibious Corps landed on the west coast, north of Hagushi, and the 7th and 96th Infantry Divisions of the XXIV Corps landed on beaches to the south of Hagushi.

The landing force split the island in the first few days of the battle. The Marines turned left and headed north. The Army turned right and headed south. By L+10, the Marines were north of Ishikawa, and the Army was south of Futema. They had taken two significant airfields at Yontan and Kadena that would soon be turned into Allied airbases for the rest of the war. By the end of April, the Marines had reached the northern tip of the island and secured the northern two-thirds of the island. From that point, the majority of the III Amphibious Corps was redeployed as part of the 10th Army to the south when the XXIV Corps hit the Japanese first major defensive line anchored at Shuri Castle.

The early days were virtually unopposed, but the brutal battle would rage on the southern third of the island for nearly three months at a terrible cost, both on land and at sea.

The author's father, Charles Fredrick Parlier, had been a member of the 96th Infantry Division until he was seriously wounded and nearly killed on Leyte Island, Philippines, in the previous November. He would have been engaged in the brutal, meat-grinder combat on Southern Okinawa had he not been medically evacuated from the Philippines.

———

Monday, 2.April.1945
No.10 Downing Street
Whitehall, London, England
United Kingdom
11:10 hours

Chancellor of the Exchequer Sir John Anderson, GCB, GCSI, GCIE, PC, requested an urgent private meeting with the prime minister. He joined the Civil Service once he had graduated from university and served various administrations from Campbell-Bannerman to the present. Sir John had held different ministerial positions since the beginning of the Churchill premiership.

"Good morning, Sir John."

"And a very good morning to you, Prime Minister."

"Your message said urgent. Are you here to tell me we've finally run the Treasury dry?"

"No Sir. In a form, far worse from my perspective."

"Do tell."

"I have from a confidential source that B-I-S has recently transferred German gold on deposit with the bank to the Central Bank of Argentina."

"I'll be damned!" exclaimed Churchill.

The Bank of International Settlements (BIS) was established in 1930 in Basel, Switzerland, by 63 constituent national central banks. The bank's purpose was to facilitate German war reparations after the Great War. BIS transformed into a medium of secure communications between the world's largest central banks.

"ODESSA?" Winston added.

"That is my guess as well."

"We must stop that transfer," Churchill declared.

"We cannot, Winston. We need the banking network more than we need to stop the German gold. We cannot pursue the gold without sacrificing our relations with the Bank of England and the bank's standing with BIS."

"Have you talked to Norman?" Churchill asked.

"He is retired," responded Sir John.

Montagu Collet Norman, DSO, PC, had been governor of the Bank of England, the central bank of the United Kingdom, since 1920 until he retired last year. King George VI created him 1st Baron Norman of St. Clere, County Kent. Lord Norman had been replaced by Lord Catto—Thomas Sivewright Catto, CBE PC, 1st Baron Catto, but Lord Norman had been instrumental in the formation of BIS and knew the operations of BIS better than nearly all people inside Great Britain.

"I think you know the answer we're going to get," Sir John continued.

Prime Minister Churchill thought for a moment. "Yes, I do. Damn bankers are only interested in money, not patriotism."

"That's not fair, Winston, and you know it."

Churchill's chin lowered like a bull preparing to charge. "I have seen those damn Nawzess for what they are from long before that bastard corporal became *der Führer*. They have raped Europe and now raping what is left of Germany. They care about no one but themselves and their disgusting religion . . . no wait . . . that is an insult to other respectable religions . . . cultists, that is what they are. The Nawzees are fleeing like rats from a sinking ship to South America, to friendly states, for the resurrection. What do you propose we do with this information?"

Sir John thought for a moment. "I brought you the information because it is relevant to the current situation. I was not and I am not seeking action. I think any action on our part would be counterproductive to the war effort."

"I'm sorry you feel that way, John. Men are dying every day that this war goes on. Women and children have been dying from the Nawzees' damnable vengeance weapons. This gold transfer will extend the killing and enable the perpetrators of this horror we witness." The prime minister lapsed into thought, and Anderson was unwilling to disturb his contemplation. "I suppose your sources are no different from other highly sensitive sources," he said, reluctant to say the name Boniface or ULTRA. "Very well, we won't interfere with the operations of B-I-S. However, I direct you to meet with 'C' and the chief of O-S-S London Station, and I want you to tell them what you have told me. If you have more detailed information, you will convey that to both intelligence chiefs. The object here is the transmission of essential information to allow the field agents to track the gold, the transfer of the gold."

"What do you expect the shadow warriors to do with the information?"

"That is not for me to determine. Menzies and Bruce will know what to do with the intelligence. I surmise they'll use the data as clues to track the movement, use, and access to identify individuals or groups."

Sir John considered the prime minister's direction. "As you wish. I'll see to it as quickly as I can arrange the meetings."

"I would suggest separate meetings to allow for unique queries. Plus, we need the services to develop their own approaches." Sir John nodded his agreement. "Thank you for bringing this to me . . . no matter how disturbing the news may be."

"You are most welcome, Winston."

His Majesty's Government financial minister departed. Churchill considered calling Menzies and Bruce, but he soon decided to leave it to the Chancellor who had acquired the information. Nevertheless, BIS serving as an unwitting agent for the Nazi regime, even in the guise of neutrality, left him with a very disquieting sensation.

—

Tuesday, 3.April.1945
Headquarters, 1ˢᵗ Army
Bad Godesberg, Nordrhein-Westfalen
Liberated Germany
14:15 hours

Elements of the 1ˢᵗ Army had just completed the encirclement of German Army Group B, defending the Ruhr industrial complex of Duisburg, Düsseldorf, Essen, Dortmund, and Hamm. The 1ˢᵗ Army made quick work of the bridgehead at Remagen. They joined up with the U.S. 9ᵗʰ Army, part of the 21ˢᵗ Army Group, completing the encirclement two days ago.

Commanding General 1ˢᵗ Army Lieutenant General Courtney Hicks 'Court' Hodges, USA, welcomed his guests to his mobile headquarters. General Eisenhower had notified him yesterday that he was sending the SHAEF G-2 and G-3 for a private conference, and he was ready.

Assistant Chief of Staff for Operations (G-3) SHAEF Major General Harold Roe 'Pink' Bull, USA [USMA 1914] and Assistant Chief of Staff for Intelligence (G-2) SHAEF Major General Kenneth William Dobson 'Ken' Strong, OBE, LM, arrived a little late due to an unspecified aircraft problem.

After the common cordialities between flag officers, the three generals sat at the Map Room conference table.

Hodges began, "There was no notice of subject, so I assume y'all are here to discuss our plan for the encirclement."

"Well done, I must say," Bull responded, "but no. The Supreme Commander sent us here to discuss a more sensitive issue."

A puzzled expression bloomed on Hodges' face. "More sensitive than the Army Group B?"

"Yes Sir. It is our understanding that the 3ʳᵈ Armor has reached Paderborn."

"Correct. They're facing modest resistance."

"We also understand they have captured and occupied Wewelsburg Castle."

Again, a more puzzled expression painted Hodges' face. "What is going on here? Why such interest in a damn German castle. We've captured dozens so far and take more as we go."

"Before we get to that," said Bull, "the supreme commander wants you to issue immediate orders to secure the site and prohibit entry except to secure the castle and its environs. Looting or damage will be prosecuted very seriously." Bull glanced at Strong to pick up the discussion.

"Wewelsburg holds a unique place in the Nazi community. Himmler obtained and transformed the castle and its outbuildings into the spiritual center of the S-S. They routinely held initiation ceremonies and meetings for senior S-S leadership at that castle. We believe that place holds secrets that we will need for prosecution of the Nazis for their crimes against humanity."

"Is this a joke?"

"I'm afraid not, General. M-I-6 has developed quite the dossier on Himmler's activities since the 20s to create a spiritual basis and foundation for the S-S, a Nazi religion if you will."

"This has to be a joke. The S-S are common thugs."

"We understand your skepticism," Bull said, picking up the dialogue, "but this is no joke. It is very real, and we must preserve that site . . . at least for now. Once it is secure, we have several joint exploitation teams that will sift through every inch of that place to collect as much information and evidence as we can. If you captured any Germans at that place, we want them segregated from all other prisoners and protected until the intelligence and counter-intelligence folks are done with them."

"We believe that castle," Strong interjected, "is a key S-S facility. We have begun to liberate concentration camps operated by the S-S, which are centers for the horrific treatment of dissidents, political and military prisoners, and others the S-S deemed unworthy. The Allied leaders have agreed that we will capture, detain, try, convict, and punish the perpetrators of these crimes against humanity."

"That's what they're calling it?"

"Yes."

"Fighting the Germans on the battlefield has been bad enough. Now, you're adding this . . . this disgusting dimension."

"We're not adding anything, General. We're only trying to do our part to ensure justice is served for what the Nazis have done to their own citizens and so many others in the occupied countries."

Hodges thought about what he had just been told. "You said immediately, so I'd better get those orders issued pronto."

"Yes Sir," said Bull. "I should have added at the outset that General Bradley has been informed of and supports our mission. Your battlefield orders have not changed. We've only added this additional task to secure and protect Wewelsburg Castle."

"I'll see to it. How much should I disclose to my line commanders?"

"What we know about Wewelsburg suggests that anyone who enters will quickly discern the purpose," Strong answered. "We would prefer you avoid any reference to the Nazis or the S-S. Our purpose in protecting that site is for war crimes prosecutions." Bull nodded in agreement.

"Very well. We will do our best to comply, but my focus remains on the offensive and moving east as quickly and safely as possible."

"This task should not interfere with those orders, Sir," Bull responded. "If you have any difficulties in securing that site, please let us know immediately."

"We need a couple of weeks," added Strong, "to get the exploitation teams in place, and we are informed that those teams will add their own security, which should relieve your units."

"Thank you, gentlemen."

Bull and Strong departed and left Hodges to see to his new orders.

The 1ˢᵗ and 9ᵗʰ Armies met up at the Ruhr River, splitting the Ruhr Pocket and hastening the surrender. The Germans, cut off from resupply or reinforcement in the Ruhr Pocket, would fight for nearly three more weeks. In the end, more than 300,000 German troops surrendered their arms.

In an attempt to penetrate the encirclement and escape capture in the Pocket, *Generalfeldmarschall* Otto Moritz Walter Model committed suicide and thus ended *Wehrmacht Heeresgruppe B.*

———

Wednesday, 4.April.1945
Konzentrationslager und Zwangsarbeitslager Ohrdruf
Ohrdruf, Gotha, Thuringia
Liberated Germany
09:05 hours

The combination forced labor and concentration camp was located 86 miles south-southwest of Leipzig. The camp was operated as a sub-camp of the Buchenwald complex. Elements of the 4ᵗʰ Armor and 89ᵗʰ Infantry Divisions liberated what was left of the camps.

The SS had evacuated as many of the prisoners as they could in front of the rapidly advancing American 3ʳᵈ Army. The Americans found emaciated human beings still alive but just barely. Many were dead; a good portion of those had been murdered by gunshot and were in various stages of decomposing. The dead who could not be disposed of were stacked like cordwood. Some had been doused with lye. Others had been burned in makeshift pyres.

The unit commanders promptly reported what they found and continued to discover as their troops investigated the horrors of the camps. General Patton listened to the reports with keen interest and cogent, incisive questions. The field commanders soon had orders directly from General Patton to photograph and document everything they found and preserve as much as they could while they helped the survivors.

As soon as Patton had sufficient information, he called his boss, General Bradley, to inform him what the lead troops had uncovered. The notification of the chain of command progressed rapidly all the way to the president in Warm Springs, Georgia. General Eisenhower notified his commanders that he would visit the Ohrdruf camp on the 12th to see for himself. Generals Bradley and Patton would join him.

—

Thursday, 5.April.1945
Flugplatz Einsatzhafen I
Unterschlauersbach, Fürth, Mittelfranken, Bavaria
Deutsches Reich
09:00 hours

Hunter had briefed the squadron for the day's RODEO 391 mission. Their target was a grass landing area airfield near Unterschlauersbach, Germany, 14 miles west-southwest of Nürnberg. The airfield had been a twin-engine flight training facility throughout most of the war and transitioned to a regional fighter base in mid-1944. The whole squadron would hit the airbase 30 minutes before an 8th Air Force B-17 bomber group would drop their high explosive bomb loads to saturate the airfield. Hunter and the 'A' Division would spread out in a line abreast at low altitude to sweep the entire airfield complex. Sweet's 'B' Division would be a second wave two minutes behind 'A' Division. Then, each of the divisions would pull off by section and circle to hit the airfield again with each section diving from a different direction. After the second pass, 'A' Division would go higher to provide a flying reserve for 'B' Division's second pass. Once the squadron completed their attack, they would climb to Angels 20 to provide precautionary cover for the bomber group during their attack. They did not expect German fighters since they had become few and far between, but they would also try to suppress any remaining antiaircraft fire should any develop before the bombers arrived.

Lead elements of the XXI Corps, 7th Army, 6th Army Group were just 22 miles west of Unterschlauersbach and advancing rapidly. Hunter cautioned his pilots not to get too close. They did not need any friendly fire incidents. The 6th Army Group had been notified of the raid on Unterschlauersbach, but mistakes did occur in such swiftly changing ground situations.

The bombers were airborne and headed to the target when the 334FS readied their fighters for flight and combat. The other two Group squadrons, 335FS and 336FS, had similar missions but farther into Germany, so they took off first. When cleared, Hunter led the squadron onto Runway 10. They took off by section, joined up en route, and climbed to Angels 10. The squadron overtook and underflew past the bombers prior to the German border. They held the cruise altitude until they reached the Rhine River, and then they descended to their treetop penetration altitude. Since they were over friendly territory, each fighter held their drop tanks until they were empty. Hunter was nearly the last to jettison his aux tanks.

Germany is a beautiful country . . . except for the pockmarks of bomb craters and battle damage. They used the valleys around mountains. *It's almost like we're on a flying tour.* Hunter kept up with the navigation task marking their progress. As they overflew Army units, they saw soldiers wave and appeared to be cheering, although each of them could only hear the melodic hum of his big Packard engine and the whistle of the aerodynamic noise of their airspeed. *We're tracking on time. We should hit our time on target.*

At 100 miles west-northwest of their target, Hunter broadcast to the squadron, "Cobweb, Cobweb Six. We passed our I-P. Attack positions." As Brian scanned the sky around them and the ground passing below them, he watched the 'A' Division move up into the line abreast formation, and the 'B' Division drop back. Hunter rechecked his switches. *The guns are armed and alive. Sight lit and alive as well. Ready.* Hunter refined their track for their approach to the target.

"Cobweb, Cobweb Six. Tally Ho! 12 o'clock. It's showtime. Let's go to work."

German fighter aircraft—Bf109s and Fw190s—were scattered across the far side of the grass landing area. *No troops. No pilots. They're making no effort to defend themselves.* Hunter picked his targets and adjusted his alignment. *This is too easy . . . fish in a barrel. Where are the pilots? Are they out of fuel?' Are they out of ammunition or both?*

Tracers began to fly left and right. Hunter concentrated on his targets and squeezed his trigger. All the guns fired. Impacts danced all over the nearest Fw190. The left main landing gear collapsed. The canopy shattered. He let up on the trigger, walked the fixed reticle to the next aircraft, a Bf109. Hunter squeezed the trigger again. Like the previous target, impacts danced all over the fighter's center. Chunks of the static German fighter flew off. Hunter shifted his reticle to the aircraft hangar beyond and opened fire. Sparks flew around each impact on the partially open hangar doors and chipped off puffs of concrete of the building and floor. He could not see what might have been damaged inside the hangar, but again, no fires.

Hunter pulled and rolled to his assigned heading. As he turned, he looked over his shoulder. Corn was turning wide on his wing. Hole was turning harder with Horn on his wing. *No fires or explosions. No petrol or ammunition.* Hunter saw the line of Sweet's 'B' Division on their approach. Hunter adjusted their loop to turn back into the target. He and Corn would be the first 'A' Division section back on the target. They were assigned what intelligence guys believed was the ammunition storage bunker and fuel storage farm. As Hunter began their dive toward their next target, 'B' Division pulled up and split. He placed the sight reticle just short of the bunker and depressed the trigger. Dust and concrete powder kicked up into a cloud. Corn added his bullets as Hunter released the trigger, modified his flight path, and took a flatter trajectory to the fuel storage tanks. He danced rounds off as many tanks as he could before he had to pull off and up, climbing to their perch altitude at Angels 20. Brian noted small flashes of flame with some of the impacts, but there were no eruptions of flame and black petroleum smoke. *They're empty.*

Brian scanned the sky around him. Corn was in position. He saw the bomber formation inbound from the west. *No bogies.* 'A' Division was climbing to join up. Hunter watched Sweet's 'B' Division make their second pass. He was too high to see their bullet impacts. *There's still no smoke. No fires. No explosions. That's just metal and concrete down there. Not one human being is anywhere to be seen. They've abandoned the base.* Hunter scanned the climbing fighters and the approaching bombers. The fighters were clear but would not all make it to their perch altitude by the time the bombers reached their target and dropped their bombloads, but they would be clear.

The 334FS held a wide orbit around the target area, with flights in trail spread a quarter of the orbit circle apart. They had front-row balcony seats to observe the effects of a Bomb Group's deposit of high-explosive bombs. The flashes of bomb explosions covered the entire area that had been a German Air Force base. Clouds of dust soon obscured the one-time fighter base. *I can't imagine what it must be like under that barrage.*

The bomber formation turned for home. Hunter kept the 334FS orbiting over the airfield until the dust began to blow away. *Damn! Craters replaced what had been a fighter base. That base is no longer capable of flight operations.* Several of the hangers had partially collapsed. *Still, no smoke, just dust.*

"Cobweb, Cobweb Six. We're done here. Flight leads, let's take the corners over the bombers."

Hunter led the 334FS to catch up to the bomber formation. They had no other mission. So Brian figured they might as well cover the bombers, although the bombers had been unopposed in any form, and enemy action was no longer anticipated.

During the slow transit back to England, Brian kept his scan for enemy fighters while his mind wandered to less current matters. *Germany is no longer what it was five years ago. The British were so alone in August 1940, and the Germans were so strong. We were nearly spent and look at how far we've come. The end has to be very close. I need to call Charlotte tonight when things settle down.*

With the green of Southeast England in sight, Hunter broadcast, "Cobweb, Cobweb Six, join up." Then, he turned left to pick up a heading direct to Debden and began a descent. With all four flights in formation, Hunter radioed, "Cobweb, Cobweb Six, switch button Baker." Brian pushed the 'B' button on the aircraft's SCR-522-A VHF radio. A handful of seconds later, he broadcast, "Garter, Cobweb, flight of 16, 25 miles east for penetration to Carmen."

"Cobweb, Garter, you are cleared to enter. You can switch to Carmen when ready."

"Roger, Garter. Cobweb, switch button 'A.'" Again, he waited a handful of seconds. "Carmen, Cobweb, flight of 16 for landing."

"Roger, Cobweb, in sight. Pattern clear. Winds light and variable. Altimeter nine nine seven. You're cleared to land runway two eight. Welcome home."

"Roger, Carmen. Clear to land. Break, Cobweb, sections in trail for straight in."

They landed by sections back at Debden.

As he always was, Sergeant Tomlinson was waiting for him at Hunter's parking spot. Larson was on the left wing root when the prop stopped. Brian secured his cockpit. Larson assisted Brian in disconnecting from the Mustang. When he removed his flight helmet with oxygen mask and goggles attached, Brian looked at Tomlinson and announced, "No holes. No impacts. Only petrol and bullets."

"Yes Sir. We'll give her a good look-see and turn her around pronto."

"No rush. I think we're done for the day."

Brian checked in with Juli. Nothing. As it had become his practice, Brian chose to go last for the intelligence debriefing. He dutifully reported what they had done on the mission and what they saw during their attack and the bomber raid.

When he returned to the Ops Shack, he told his pilots, "Let me check in with Group and see where we're at." After a five-minute conversation with Arnie Clark, Brian returned to his pilots. "OK, lads, listen up. We're done for the day, and we're released. Tomorrow, we will revert to reserve status, and each flight will be given a 24-hour pass. We'll report in here at zero seven hundred for muster. Then, each flight will go on leave in sequence. Yellow Flight will be first up. Make sure you're back here for muster. Dismissed."

The cacophony of chairs, desks, flight equipment, and excited conversation filled the room as the pilots departed to the waiting truck. As the last pilots filed out, Brian looked at Ellison. "You can secure too, Juli. I'm going to get some paperwork done. I'll close up when I'm done."

"Do you want me to order you a car?"

"No, thanks. I'll walk. Also, you can take your pass tomorrow. I'll get one of the other lads to watch the desk."

"Thank you, Sir. See you in the morning."

Brian left the main door and his office door open. He sat at his desk and jumped into his Inbox. Clearing the Inbox took several hours. Brian reached for the telephone, held short, and then withdrew his hand. *I'll wait to use the call box at the Mess after dinner.* Brian straightened his desk and lined up the desks and chairs in the bullpen into four rows and columns. He switched off the lights and closed the main door. He walked back to the Mess in the cool, crisp, early spring afternoon air. Brian went to his room and read until it was time for dinner.

—

Monday, 9.April.1945
Konzentrationslager Flossenbürg
Flossenbürg, Bavaria
Deutsches Reich
15:20 hours

The camp had been built by the SS and gone into operation in 1938. Initially, the camp specialized in criminal and asocial prisoners. However, once the war began, the camp spread out into smaller sub-camps and transitioned to forced labor, building components for Bf109 fighters and working a quarry for granite and the glory for the Third Reich. The camp was located 62 miles east-northeast of Nürnberg and less than two miles from the Czech border.

On 14.February.1944, Empire Chancellor Hitler dissolved German Military Intelligence—*der Abwehr*—and dismissed its chief, Admiral Wilhelm Franz Canaris. The admiral remained under house arrest until the failed assassination of Hitler on 20.July.1944. Canaris had been taken into Gestapo custody on 23.July.1944 on suspicion that he had been involved in the plot. The admiral had been confined at *No.8 Prinz-Albrecht-Straße* – the Gestapo jail in Berlin. Despite months of unsuccessful investigation, Canaris and others had been transferred from Berlin to *Flossenbürg KZ* on 7.February.1945, where he was humiliated and abused daily by the SS.

The gray overcast and early morning hours provided the appropriate gloom. Gallows had been erected hastily in the courtyard of the prison. Admiral Canaris, Major General Hans Paul Oster, Lutheran pastor and theologian Dietrich Bonhoeffer, Judge Advocate General Karl Sack, and Captain Ludwig Gehre were ordered to remove every stitch of their clothing. They shivered in the early spring chill. The condemned prisoners were paraded in front of many witnesses down the steps into the courtyard. They were taunted, slapped, poked, spit on, and abused by the SS guards. Finally, all five naked men knelt to pray for the last time. The five men were hanged naked and left to decompose, where they were found when the camp was liberated two weeks later.

Circa 10:30 hours on 23.April.1945, the U.S. 90th Infantry Division of the 3rd Army liberated the main camp and took it without any fighting.

After the war, the Allies learned from a Flossenbürg survivor of Canaris' last words. Danish Colonel Hans Mathiesen Lunding, former Director of Danish Military Intelligence, had been imprisoned in the cell next to Canaris in Berlin and Flossenbürg. Using Morse code tapping on the cell wall between them, Canaris had told Lunding:

> "This is the end. Was not a traitor. Badly mishandled. My nose broken. I have done nothing against Germany. If you survive, please tell my wife."

Colonel Lunding dutifully delivered the admiral's final message to his family after the war.

—

Monday, 9.April.1945
Little White House
401 Little White House Road
Warm Springs, Meriwether County, Georgia
United States of America
13:10 hours

President Roosevelt had enjoyed a refreshing and rejuvenating dip in the warm mineral waters in the morning and a simple but nice lunch with Anna, Polly, and Daisy. He had found considerable comfort in the facilities and therapists. He truly loved Warm Springs since his affliction with poliomyelitis in 1921 at age 39. After lunch, Daisy and Polly left to tend to unspecified tasks.

The telephone rang. Anna lifted the handset. "Little White House." "Yes." "Thank you." She hung up the handset and turned to her father. "Our guests are here." Anna could see her father's eyes brighten. "I'll go get them settled in Cottage 4 and 5."

"Thank you, dear."

Anna departed the house. Franklin returned to his reading—Fyodor Dostoevsky's *Crime and Punishment*. He had only confessed to Anna that he distantly hoped to gain some sliver of insight into the Russian psyche. Franklin read a dozen pages when Anna returned with her father's one-time mistress and long-term friend, Lucy Page Mercer Rutherfurd, who went directly to Franklin and kissed his cheek.

"May I introduce Elizabeth Shoumatoff, the artist and portraitist I told you about."

Roosevelt shook Shoumatoff's hand.

"A pleasure to meet you, Mister President."

"I commissioned Elizabeth to paint your portrait, Franklin."

Roosevelt smiled weakly. "I'm not so sure I'm in acceptable form for a portrait. Do I detect a Russian accent?"

"Ukrainian. I was born in Kharkiv, Mister President. We immigrated to this country in 1917. The Bolshevik Revolution and Stalin were not kind or respectful to my family."

"I am sorry to hear that, but we are better for your citizenship."

"Thank you, Mister President."

"Elizabeth is the best, Franklin. She will paint a glorious portrait worthy of your stature and contributions to the nation."

"Knock, knock," Polly said loudly as she and Daisy entered the house.

All the women, except Shoumatoff, knew each other from previous meetings. Elizabeth's introduction was completed in joyous fashion. Both Daisy and Polly had seen Shoumatoff's work and eagerly anticipated her portrait of the president.

"How would you like to proceed?" Franklin asked.

Elizabeth surveyed the living room, especially the windows, and evaluated the lighting since she had no artificial lights. "Actually, Mister President, I think the natural light is best at your desk," she answered with a pronounced Ukrainian accent. "I can start now if you wish." Roosevelt nodded his consent. "Excellent. Please allow me a few minutes to retrieve a canvas and my materials." Again, the president nodded his approval. Elizabeth left to collect what she needed.

"Should I change my suit?" he asked the other ladies.

"No," replied Lucy promptly. "You're dressed exquisitely . . . very presidential." She straightened his tie and smoothed his suit jacket.

"I agree," Anna added.

Franklin looked at Polly and Daisy. "Let's have a complete vote."

"Lucy could not have said it better," Polly added.

"I will make it unanimous," said Daisy.

"Very well, then, the grey suit and red tie it is. Thank you, Lucy, for doing this. I'm not too keen on sitting still for that long, but that is better than this incessant paperwork." They all giggled at Franklin's declaration.

Elizabeth returned with an easel, her fishing box of paints and brushes, and a fresh canvas. The setup process took several minutes until she was satisfied with Franklin's position in the light. The president patiently tolerated the minute adjustments of his chair, body position, arms, and even his head. When she was satisfied, Elizabeth began by sketching the general, broad shapes of what she saw.

The other ladies watched for 20 minutes and then started to turn to other activities and their ever-present social gossip. Lucy fit in with the group in fine form.

Elizabeth used the distraction of the other women as an opportunity to converse with President Roosevelt about non-war, non-presidency, personal topics like childhood interests, dreams, nightmares, favorite foods, movies, music, and such. Their conversation as she worked remained calm, quiet, and unperturbed.

—

Tuesday, 10.April.1945
Standing Oak Farm
Winchester, Hampshire, England
United Kingdom
14:15 hours

Brian made a small fire in the pit under the giant oak tree. He sat next to Charlotte on the broad oak bench and grasped her cool right hand.

"Thank you, my darling," Charlotte said. "It is always a pleasure having you home . . . even if for only a day."

"Maybe for a lot longer soon."

"I don't want to get my hopes up, but do you really think so."

"The last mission we flew a few days ago was a unilateral affair. We hit a German fighter base near Nürnberg before the bombers leveled the place. They couldn't get a single fighter into the air, and there was no antiaircraft fire. They have no fuel and little ammunition. The end for Germany cannot be far away."

"Good, we need to be done with this sordid affair. From our perspective of the farm, something major has changed. Mabel and I met with Major General

Jensen of the American Army Logistics Command Europe at Basingstoke and two of his staff officers. As you know, the Army finished the second build of greenhouses several weeks ago, doubling our capacity. Mabel has them all in operation today. The general said the Army would build as many greenhouses as our land could accommodate. They also agreed to provide all necessary supplies other than water, including seed and fertilizer, and they even agreed to subsidize our recruitment of workers. He also told us the Army's demand would last for several years after the war until local farm production can be stabilized in the war-damaged areas. The general would not say what the urgency is, but my guess is the number of captured German soldiers, the people of Germany who cannot find food, and the survivors of those dreadful concentration camps the newspapers have been telling us about. They have also asked us to consider a powdered milk production facility they would provide and we would operate. They also want all our cheese production. I could not agree with that. The general offered to increase our production capacity if they could have the additional products. They want everything they can obtain."

"How big are we talking?"

"Mabel is doing the water assessment to see how much water we can draw off the river, and the Army is sending an engineer survey team tomorrow to assess the layout and capacity of our land. I've also visited adjoining landowners that would be compatible with our land and plans. The general said they will buy as much as we can produce year around."

"Amazing, sweetheart. You've done so well." Brian refreshed the fire. "Have you heard anything from Bobby?"

Bobby Joe Sales had been the general manager of Bainbridge Air Services, Inc. (BAS) from the beginning of the Drummond's airline company. BAS also provided a secret air transportation service to the OSS.

"He sent an update a couple of weeks ago that profits remain healthy, and he had not heard a peep from the government."

OSS Director Major General Bill Donovan had requested BAS submit an air support plan as part of his post-war intelligence service proposal to President Roosevelt. BAS complied last fall.

"Let's tell Bobby to plan on no contract and transition the company to straight commercial operations. The government contracts will likely terminate abruptly, and we have no guarantees from Donovan."

"I'll take care of it tomorrow, which brings me to your plans. What are you going to do?" asked Charlotte.

"The honest answer is I don't know. They have told us to prepare for transfer to the Pacific to finish off Japan, but no orders have been issued. No one wants to talk about the next step until Germany has surrendered and capitulated. We don't know what to expect."

"Will you really go to the Pacific?"

"I don't know, Charlotte. I just don't know. Like the uncertainty with the future of B-A-S, what lays ahead from me is equally unknown."

Charlotte walked to the fire, extended her hands to warm them, and then walked to the pond's edge. She stared out across the water to the hills beyond. Brian refused to disturb her thoughts. Finally, after perhaps five or six minutes, Charlotte turned back to the fire to warm her hands again. Eventually, she looked up directly into Brian's eyes with tears streaming down her cheeks. Brian wanted to go to her, to hold her, but he knew she needed space.

"We have lost so much, Brian. It has been hard enough with long periods of missing you, not knowing if you are even alive, and fearing the visit of some Army officer to tell me you had been killed in combat. Yet, it was reassuring to know that you were not far away. The thought of you doing all this on the other side of the world takes away the only sliver of reassurance that has sustained me all these tragic years. You have done your duty, Brian. They can get along without you. I cannot!" Brian held her eyes and smiled meekly, but he did not speak. It did not feel like she was finished. "You were a volunteer, an American volunteer, during those very dark days of 1939 and 1940. You have amply done your duty, Brian. I need you. It is time for you to come home." Charlotte stared at her husband, who simply held her eyes. "Aren't you going to say anything?"

"What do you want me to say?" Brian responded.

"The truth, Brian. Be honest with me. I've told you what I'm thinking. So let's hear your view."

Brian stood, went to Charlotte, and enveloped her in his arms. He kissed her several times, with the last version more passionately. Brian relaxed his embrace and held her shoulders. Looking deeply into her gorgeous eyes, he said, "I've loved you from the very first moment I met you. You were a bit cantankerous, but that was part of your attraction to me.

"I left the United States on my own when I was 18 years old. I did that because I love freedom and believed I had the skills and abilities to defend freedom. I could fly. I wanted to fly. I traveled across the Atlantic and joined the R-A-F before the war began.

"As you know, I had the opportunity to leave the cockpit and take some staff job in Washington, but I chose to stay in fighter cockpits. I knew I was good at what I do. We're still at war with the forces of fascism. We're nearly victorious in Europe, but Japan is no different from Germany and Italy. They took the world to war. I have always felt an obligation, my part, to win this war and be done with fascism.

"I want to be here with you. I've always wanted to be here with you, but I believe the best way to do that is to be done with this war. It's not fair. If that means going to the Pacific to end the war, then that is what I must do." Brian hugged and kissed Charlotte, but she stiffened and did not reciprocate. "I know this is difficult. I recognize and acknowledge that your sacrifice has been excessive. I don't want to ask you to endure more, but I must. It's my duty, Charlotte."

Mrs. Drummond turned away, walked to the pond's edge, and this time, she began to pace, looking at her feet. Brian refreshed the fire again and waited for Charlotte to return. Horace, Lionel, and Jacob completed the afternoon chores. They waved as they entered the main house. Brian returned their gesture. *It's nearly dusk. Dinner's close, and we're not done.*

Charlotte turned with a serious expression and walked to the bench without looking at Brian. She sat and patted the bench next to her. Brian joined her. "I don't know how long I can endure, Brian. When we lost Ian, I was sure I was done. I gave up. You saved me."

"The ladies did much more than me. They were here every day. I wasn't."

"Don't quibble with me. I'm grateful for the support of our friends, but I also know I did not feel life again until you brought me out here."

"I'm just glad I could help."

"I can't imagine going through that pain and grief with you on the other side of the world. You always know how to buttress my sagging walls. You can't do that in the Far East."

"We'll do what we must do to live, Charlotte. I have faith in you. You are far stronger than you give yourself credit for. We've faced many challenges. We'll face many more ahead. And, we'll deal with whatever comes our way . . . together . . . as we always will."

Charlotte smiled broadly. "You have always had more faith in me than I've had in myself. Yes, we'll do what we have to do. You may not be here, but I know you'll be with me." Charlotte looked beyond Brian. "We're being signaled." Brian turned to see Edith waving to them from the front door. Charlotte added, "It must be dinnertime, and they're waiting on us."

Brian and Charlotte hugged and kissed. He doused the fire and spread the coals. They walked hand-in-hand to the main house and joined their extended family for a simple but delicious dinner.

———

Wednesday, 11.April.1945
Headquarters, 12th Army Group
Verdun, Meuse, Grand Est
Liberated France
09:35 hours

"Welcome back, Ike," Bradley greeted the supreme commander.

"Thanks, Brad. I'm making the rounds . . . just routine."

"Although there is nothing routine about how fast things are moving."

Eisenhower smiled. "Quite so, and quite the change from a year ago."

"Indeed!"

The two generals sat in comfortable chairs across from each other for their private chat in Bradley's small but separate office.

"The situation is changing rapidly, so I decided to make a command tour. I was with Montgomery yesterday. You're next. Let's start at the quick summary level."

"Yes Sir. The 3rd Army is roughly 70 miles from Leipzig with limited pockets of modest resistance. Our biggest problem at present is dealing with the flood of P-O-Ws. Georgie has actually asked for help to handle the quantity of P-O-Ws so that he can keep his divisions on the move. He does not want to slow up for any reason."

"That's Georgie. God bless him."

"The 1st Army continues to work on the Ruhr Pocket, but Court is pressing his advance aggressively. His XIII Corps has nearly encircled Hanover and is about 140 miles from Berlin.

"All of my Group are liberating these dastardly concentration and labor camps. The 104th Infantry with 3rd Armor reached the Nordhausen-Dora complex at the base of the Hartz Mountains. The 104th has entered the labor tunnels where they assembled V-2 and V-1 weapons. Like the other camps, they are finding terribly emaciated men. I've issued orders to treat the prisoners as best they can while getting a medical hospital unit out there to help. I also ordered them to preserve all the articles and equipment they find to protect the tools and the assembled weapons. The exploitation teams are en route. Most of the Germans, especially the leadership, ran a few days ago. The few lower enlisted left behind will be interrogated by the intelligence experts.

"The 3rd Army completed their liberation of the Buchenwald complex, well, at least the outlying camps they are aware of. Given our experience from Ohrdruf on, we all suspect they will find more as they advance. I must say, Ike, my wildest imagination could've never constructed such brutality perpetrated by the Nazis at these camps. We need medical assistance on a major scale to treat these wretched prisoners. Just food, basic necessities, and tents are more than we have the capacity to handle."

"It is a terrible situation. I think you are going with me tomorrow to meet Georgie and tour the Ohrdruf camp."

"Yes, I am. I must say, Ike, I'm not eager to witness this level of inhumanity."

"But, we must, Brad."

"I know. Just the descriptions from the line commanders leave me nauseated and angry beyond words."

"Which is precisely why we must all bear witness to what the Nazis have done."

"Nordhausen seems to be primarily a forced labor camp with men from the occupied countries, but Buchenwald has more Jews, gypsies, homosexuals, and political prisoners of all types. They are all malnourished and mistreated. We have also not found any evidence that the military was involved. Unique units of the S-S ran all the camps we've reached so far."

"Monty has reported the same. These camps are the Nazis' doing, not the Germans, but we are going to compel the local town's people to go through those camps. We're not going to allow them to claim—we didn't know. Where appropriate, we will order them to bury the dead in a respectful manner."

"We never planned for this overwhelming flood of human beings, from P-O-Ws to concentration camps, that need to be protected from the elements, fed, in some cases clothed, and treated for a plethora of diseases, injuries, and illness. We need help, Ike."

"We are moving all our medical units forward to assist. The War Department has also issued urgent orders for medical units to deploy from the States. We are going to have to do the best we can with the resources we have until the proper units arrive. If we must prioritize who gets the resources we have, first priority should be the concentration and labor camp survivors. Let the German P-O-Ws sleep outside. Don't withhold treatment, but the survivors must get the best we have."

"Understood. I'll get the orders out to the line commanders."

"I haven't had the chance, Brad, to thank you and Court for the extra effort to secure and protect the Wewelsburg Castle affair. The intelligence exploitation teams are still working on their discovery process. So far, they've not found what they were looking for. Their opinion is Himmler directed the S-S to remove everything they could once we crossed the Rhine."

"Court was a bit perturbed that he had to sit on that castle when he had a war to fight, but he got it done. If I may ask, Ike, what is so special about that place."

"According to Ken Strong, M-I-6 is collecting as much evidence as they can about Himmler's actions to build the S-S as some absurd religion. I only know what Ken, Bill Donovan, and other intel guys have told me, but it sure sounds like a cult with more than a little pseudo-spiritualism. They are trying to understand why. What led these educated men to adopt this cult mentality and abandon any semblance of humanity, as we have heard at those concentration camps? We must do our part as we uncover more evidence. I know all these additional demands are a serious distraction from our mission, but the world must know. They must remember what these Nazis have done to so many people. We will show the flag and our stars tomorrow, and I've directed ample photographers and journalists to join us."

"We need more troops, more supplies, more of everything. I know it is poor form, Ike, but do you think the president and secretary know what we are dealing with here."

"I have not talked to the president or the secretary, but the chief has, and he has assured me the leadership is well aware."

"It would be nice if they send troops rather than close the tap."

"Understood, Brad. If it's any comfort, Prime Minister Churchill has organized M-Ps and Lords as well as the British Press to tour the camps. We've agreed that Buchenwald is the best example we've found so far. He told me yesterday that the parliamentary delegation will visit Buchenwald on the 27th. I will continue to press Washington. The humanitarian aspects of what our troops are turning up has vastly exceeded all our estimates."

The supreme commander would spend the remainder of the day with the 12th Army Group staff and various social and official events. Eisenhower and Bradley planned to travel to the 3rd Army headquarters in the early morning. They would join General Patton for the planned tour of the *Ohrdruf KZ*.

—

Chapter 5

O to be self-balanced for contingencies,
To confront night, storms, hunger, ridicule,
accidents, rebuffs, as the trees and animals do.

-- Walt Whitman

Thursday, 12.April.1945
Headquarters, 3rd Army
I.G. Farben Building
Grüneburgweg 1
Frankfurt am Main, Hessen
Liberated Germany
10:15 hours

General Eisenhower arrived before General Bradley and their pending tour of *Ohrdruf KZ*. General Patton greeted his guest and his boss's boss. They sat at the four-place table with a cup of coffee each.

"I must tell you, Ike, I'm not looking forward to the tour this afternoon."

"Me either."

"I've seen ravaged men for too many years. I've seen good men with legs blown off, and their guts sliced open with their entrails hanging out. But, I've always rationalized those damaged soldiers that it's just part of combat. What those damn bloody fucking Nazis have done to innocent, unarmed, restrained, civilian human beings is an outrage to all decent people and especially the professional military."

"I share your sentiment, Georgie. From everything we have heard so far, we know it's not going to be a pleasant affair, but we must see. It is also essential that the world sees us there. Those Nazis need to realize we know and we're not going to forget. This public tour is far more about the future than the past and what those animals have done. The worst of it is, we are only seeing part of the whole picture. The Soviets are reporting outright death camps. Some camps exist only to murder innocent people on a mass industrial scale." Eisenhower paused for a few moments. "Anyway, we'll do our part in this dreadful affair.

"Now, Brad should be here any minute; how about a quick summary of your situation."

"Court's 9th Armor and 3rd Army's 6th Armor are 20 miles west-southwest of Leipzig. We just passed Naumburg. The town was abandoned by the German 26th Infantry Division. The 4th Armor is moving nicely down the road to Chemnitz. At our rate of advance in the last couple of weeks, we should take the cities next week and be on our way to Dresden. My coordination with

Court's 1ˢᵗ Army suggests we may have to surround and bypass Leipzig rather than get bogged down in urban combat."

"Excellent, George. Keep up the pressure. I will add that Devers' guys are on track to take Nürnberg in the next few days. Unfortunately, the 1ˢᵗ French Army is less mobile than the 6ᵗʰ Army Group. They are lagging behind and stretching the 7ᵗʰ Army."

Patton nodded and then continued, "I must acknowledge that our fuel and ammo supplies are and remain ahead of our consumption," Patton said proudly. "Our logistics are a whole lot different from what we faced last fall. Antwerp is a godsend in our warfighting capacity. Once we vanquished the German counterattack and crossed the Rhine, we encountered pockets of German resistance, but frankly, they are a shell of what they were a year ago."

"Have any of your units encountered any S-S men trying to make their way south to the mountains?"

"Not a one that we have been able to identify,"

"So, perhaps the Nazi Redoubt was a pipe dream," Eisenhower mused.

"Or, a plan unrealized because of your vision to thwart their intention."

"We may never know."

Patton nodded his head again. "Which reminds me, we continue to come across abandoned mines and caves with looted material. One mine we discovered with stolen artwork—paintings, sculptures, religious icons, and original music scores. They've also counted US$250 million in gold bars, coins, and artifacts. We've even found some of the Nazis' documents, like those they were looking for at Wewelsburg Castle. These damnable Nazis have looted Europe, Ike . . . looted the bloody place—all the heritage."

"We have a special team assigned to the G-9. More precisely, the Monuments Section stands within the Civil-Military Affairs Department. We call 'em the Monuments Men. After your initial report, we mobilized several of their teams. They will document and catalog everything that is in those caves. They will also take custody of the items and ensure the return to the rightful owners."

On 23.June.1943, President Roosevelt created the American Commission for the Protection and Salvage of Artistic and Historic Monuments in War Areas, also known as the Roberts Commission, for its presidential-appointed chairman, Associate Justice Owen Josephus Roberts. The Commission recruited and engaged a wide variety of investigators, art historians and scholars, artists, archeologists, architects, librarians, and archivists from 14 nations. Teams were assigned to every theater of operations, including the ETO and SHAEF. The Monuments, Fine Arts, and Archives (MFAA) Section was assigned to the SHAEF G-9 Civil-Military Affairs Department. The MFAA was a mobile group of experts needed to research, assess, catalog, and take custody of the looted works.

"The Nazis have given us plenty to deal with," Patton added.

"Quite the understatement, Georgie. We need to remain attentive, even well after their surrender. The S-S fanatics will disappear into the populous in their effort to escape. They will likely shuck their black uniforms, but it won't be so easy to obscure their blood group tattoos."

"We're watching all of it."

"Thanks, George. I wonder what's happened to Brad?"

Almost as if on cue, the knock at the door preceded Bradley's arrival.

"Welcome, Brad," Ike said.

"Thanks, Ike, Georgie. My apologies . . . aircraft problem and no backup."

"Happens to all of us." Eisenhower stood and straightened his signature waistcoat uniform jacket. "We'd better get going."

The three generals were a contrast in uniform attire. Eisenhower wore his signature waistcoat and a framed hat. Bradley chose his combat fatigues with an overcoat and helmet. He also had an M1911 semi-automatic pistol in a tanker's shoulder holster outside his overcoat. Patton was Patton; he was dressed to the nines in his cavalry riding breeches, riding boots, helmet, and his signature silver plated, ivory gripped revolvers—a Colt M1873 Peacemaker on his right hip and a Smith & Wesson Model 27 0.357 Magnum revolver on his left hip. The ivory grips on both pistols were engraved with his monogram—GSP.

The day's tour of the *Ohrdruf KZ* camp would show the stars to the frontline American combat troops who faced these abysmal camps and to the world through the bountiful photographs that would be taken during the visit. The generals would do their part.

———

Thursday, 12.April.1945
Little White House
401 Little White House Road
Warm Springs, Meriwether County, Georgia
United States of America
12:45 hours

The clear, warm, spring day brought the melodious sounds of birds chirping on the gentle breeze, carrying the scent of pine. President Roosevelt had arrived not quite a fortnight earlier for an extended rest and recuperation stay at his favorite spa. He had been visiting Warm Springs since 1924, shortly after the permanence of his polio affliction had become apparent. The cottage had been completed in 1932 before he became president. On this particular visit, Roosevelt had reluctantly agreed, after the persistent insistence of his long-term, intimate friend and confidante Lucy Page Mercer Rutherfurd, to sit for a portrait by the renowned American painter of Russian heritage Elizabeth Shoumatoff. Lucy gushed effusively about Shoumatoff's talent as a portraitist and actually commissioned the artwork. The artist had positioned her easel and palette table, as she had done for the last week so that the President had to only swivel his leather chair slightly from his desk in the living room. On the other side of the living room, Lucy sat with Franklin's cousins Margaret Lynch 'Daisy' Suckley and Laura Franklin 'Polly' Delano. The ladies had been talking about nothing in particular beyond the upcoming barbeque and following music recital by polio patients planned for that evening and the delightful spring weather in Georgia.

13:00 hours

The president had just completed signing several documents that needed attention that day. He turned back to Shoumatoff and said, "We have only fifteen minutes remaining in this session."

"Yes, Mister President. That should be sufficient for this session," answered Elizabeth. She had been working on the portrait for several days. Shoumatoff expertly worked with her brushes, paints, and the canvas. She had nearly completed his face and was working outward from there. No one mentioned and even remotely hinted at the generous regressive rendition of Roosevelt's decidedly ashen and tired appearance everyone had noticed since before the Yalta Conference. Franklin Roosevelt's health had clearly deteriorated, and his friends hoped a pleasant long stay at Warm Springs would help him recover some strength. The end of the war was in sight, and they all wanted Franklin to enjoy the fruits of sacrifices and the accolades of victory.

13:15 hours

"I have a terrific pain in the back of my head," the president said and grabbed the back of his skull. Then, before anyone could react, Roosevelt's head fell back on the chair, his lower jaw slacked, and his arms went limp.

Lucy exhaled sharply in what sounded like a muffled scream.

'Polly' sprang to her feet and commanded in a robust and firm voice, "Arthur, fetch Doctor Breunn now!"

From the kitchen, Roosevelt's long-term valet and retired Navy chief petty officer Arthur Prettyman knocked over the chair he had been sitting on and sprang out of the house to the nearby cottage of Commander Howard Gerald Breunn, USN MC, the Navy cardiologist assigned to the president's medical service from Bethesda Naval Hospital.

Breunn and Prettyman returned in what seemed like seconds, followed shortly after that by the president's Private Secretary Grace Tully. The doctor placed his black bag on the desk beside the president. Lucy was standing over Roosevelt patting his left cheek and crying his given name. 'Daisy' and 'Polly' were beside the president. Breunn ordered, "Back off, please." The ladies did as they were requested. Breunn applied his stethoscope inside the president's jacket and over his shirt, and then shined a small light in Roosevelt's eyes after raising each eyelid. "Let's get him to his bed."

Prettyman and the duty steward lifted Roosevelt from his chair, cradled and carried the president to his bedroom.

"Be careful," 'Polly' again commanded as the men diligently moved the president's limp body and maneuvered into the president's bedroom.

They laid the president on his bed. Prettyman helped Breunn remove Roosevelt's jacket, necktie, shirt, and undershirt. The doctor checked his vital signs, this time including blood pressure. Breunn offered no indication of what he was finding.

"What happened?" asked Breunn, as he continued his examination of the president.

"He complained of pain at the back of his head," answered Polly, "just before he collapsed."

Breunn checked the back of the president's head and neck. He looked for and saw Grace Tully. "Please get Doctor McIntire on the telephone, quickly, please." Tully jumped to her task.

Shoumatoff gently grasped Mercer's arm and pulled her away from the bedroom door. "Lucy, this is serious. We need to go. Family members will surely arrive soon, and I'm sure you recognize that it would not be wise for us to be here when they arrive . . . too many questions."

Mercer initially shook her head, not wanting to go, but then nodded her head in agreement. Lucy went to the adjacent bedroom and swiftly gathered up her belongings and removed any evidence of her presence. Before departing, Lucy whispered to Polly, "I have to go. I will pray for Franklin. Please, please, call me as soon as you know something." Delano nodded her head and did not speak.

Elizabeth packed up her painting kit, placed the unfinished portrait in a carrying case, and went to her cottage to pack her personal things. Mercer and Shoumatoff left Warm Springs, initially for Atlanta and then for New York City.

Doctor Breunn talked on the telephone to Vice Admiral Ross T. McIntire, USN, MC, MD, the president's physician at the White House, to report his preliminary findings. He said, "The signs point to a stroke or cerebral hemorrhage. He is non-responsive." They agreed on the immediate efforts to resuscitate the president, while McIntire worked on getting further medical assistance headed toward Warm Springs as quickly as possible. Breunn administered a shot of adrenaline directly into the president's heart, trying in vain to revive him.

15:35 hours

"He's dead," pronounced Doctor Breunn. He looked at his watch. "Time of death, fifteen thirty-five." He reported the reality to Doctor McIntire, who had been listening to the final proceedings with Prettyman holding the telephone handset near the bed. It was over. The term of the longest-serving U.S. president in history had come to an end. To those present, Franklin Roosevelt's passing came in a nauseating flash.

—

Thursday, 12.April.1945
Room 5E766
Pentagon Building
Arlington, Arlington County, Virginia
United States of America
16:20 hours

The gathering of eagles had been scheduled for several weeks. President Roosevelt had tasked them three weeks ago to come to a unanimous conclusion preferably, but a decision, nonetheless. The singular object of the president's charge was the OSS proposal for a central intelligence service to replace the OSS in the post-war government.

The cognizant group of four Cabinet ministers included Secretary of State Edward Reilly 'Ed' Stettinius, Jr.; Secretary of War Henry Lewis Stimson; Secretary of the Navy James Vincent 'Jim' Forrestal; and Attorney General Francis Beverley 'Frank' Biddle. Since Bill Donovan submitted the proposal last November, their respective departments had been secretly chewing on the OSS proposal as part of the Joint Intelligence Committee (JIC) tasking.

"Well," began Stettinius, "I suppose I should kick off this meeting as the senior minister. When the C-O-I was created four years ago, my guys were not too keen on a national intelligence agency. They laud Donovan's cool, calm manner in dealing with this matter. We think Donovan has framed an intelligence agency that is respectful of our departmental intelligence initiatives and needs. State is in favor of the Donovan proposal as modified by the JIC."

"I think y'all know the problem I'm dealing with. Director Hoover has made his resistance to and disapproval of Donovan's national intelligence service quite clear. He is convinced such an organization will compromise criminal and counter-intelligence investigations."

"We're all on the same team, Frank," interjected Stettinius.

"We know that Ed, but Edgar has developed his own little fiefdom at the F-B-I. I cannot ignore him. We . . . cannot ignore him."

"What do you suggest we do about Edgar's objections?" Stimson asked. "If I have been informed properly by the G-2, Hoover's objections were addressed in the JIC deliberations. The F-B-I's position is nothing short of no national intelligence service, which in turn does not meet the president's requirements. So, back to my question."

"I mentioned the F-B-I objections because we need to acknowledge those objections. However, from the broader perspective, I agree with Ed's earlier assessment. Bill Donovan has done a magnificent job. He has shared intelligence with all of us. He has done precisely what he said he would do four years ago. Therefore, for Justice, my recommendation is approval as amended and supported."

"State concurs."

"Well, Jim," Stimson said, looking at Forrestal, "I guess it comes down to us. I will confess that the G-2's initial reaction to the proposal was not positive. However, the G-2 acknowledges the good faith efforts the O-S-S fellows have made. The G-2 has moved to the neutral position. They have concerns and reservations but no longer oppose the Donovan proposal. We think Bill has done a good job of dealing with our issues, which there will inevitably be. The JIC adjustments offer a good way to reconcile and adjudicate issues. With that said, the Army supports the national intelligence service."

"Uh-huh," Forrestal reacted. "Henry and I have discussed this matter numerous times in the last few weeks. While the N-2 and G-2 have moved away from outright rejection toward acquiescence, Navy Intelligence has not come as far as the G-2. C-N-O and I have met several times with the N-2 and his staff. They are convinced the new service will be more work than it's worth. After several heated discussions, they confessed that the O-S-S had not interfered in naval intelligence matters as much as they had anticipated at the outset, and they admitted that the O-S-S had provided valuable warfighting intelligence. I think Henry and I agree that the reactions of our respective intelligence branches have been more emotional than factual." Stimson nodded in agreement. "As Henry said, the Navy Department will support the Donovan proposal for a national intelligence service."

"Well then," said Stettinius, "if I understand everyone's position, we are in agreement, and our unanimous recommendation to the president is to accept and support the Donovan plan." The others nodded their heads in agreement.

"So be it. I'll send him a simple message statement. I will schedule a briefing meeting when he returns to Washington."

"There are going to be disagreements," Stimson added, "but Bill has gone the extra mile to provide a mechanism for reconciliation. We need a permanent O-S-S. We can work with . . ."

The knock at the door halted the discussion. A young man dressed in a light grey business suit partially opened the door and stepped one foot into the room. "Excuse me, Mister Secretary," he said, looking directly at Stimson, "you have an urgent holding for you."

"Who is it?"

"May I speak to you privately?"

"Humpf!" Stimson looked at the other officials. "Excuse me, gentlemen. I'll see what this is."

Once outside the conference room, the aide glanced over both shoulders to ensure he had space, and then he whispered to the secretary. "National one four one four operator says she has a most urgent call for you." Most of the government leadership knew that telephone number was the White House switchboard.

"Where?"

"Your office, Sir."

Stimson emerged several minutes later with a grim, stern expression and only shook his head to his aide. He returned to the conference room and closed the door behind him. "That was the White House. The president is dead." Stimson paused, but the room remained silent. "He was declared dead by the medical staff an hour ago. The V-P will be sworn in at the White House this evening, and all of us are required to witness. Given this news, I think we're done here until we can get new instructions and guidance from the new president."

They disbanded and went their separate ways to reassemble at the White House in a few hours.

—

Thursday, 12.April.1945
Headquarters, 3rd Army
I.G. Farben Building
Grüneburgweg 1
Frankfurt am Main, Hessen
Liberated Germany
21:25 hours

Bradley had headed back to his headquarters three hours ago. The supreme commander had decided to spend the night in Frankfurt.

The three generals talked before and during dinner before Bradley departed. None of them wanted to talk about the horror they saw at Ohrdruf. Instead, their conversations focused on the objectives ahead.

The political leaders had agreed to divide Germany into sectors. They had also decided to add a French sector that was essentially the Rhineland of West Germany.

Eisenhower and Patton had also talked about the Farben building. Ike had decided to move the SHAEF headquarters to Frankfurt and the Farben Building when the war concluded. The massive building had plenty of room for SHAEF, the 12th Army Group, and the 3rd Army.

A diminutive first lieutenant from the 3rd Army communication center entered. He looked directly at General Eisenhower. "Sir, I have your Sent copy."

Eisenhower read the message and handed it to Patton. "Thank you, Lieutenant. That will be all."

SECRET

```
SECRET
DATE 121915Z APRIL 1945
TO COS ARMY ONLY
FROM SUPCMDR SHAEF
E Y E S   O N L Y   P E R S O N A L
URGENT
BREAK
WE CONTINUE TO UNCOVER GERMAN CONCENTRATION
CAMPS FOR POLITICAL PRISONERS IN WHICH
CONDITIONS OF INDESCRIBABLE HORROR PREVAIL X
I HAVE VISITED ONE OF THESE CAMPS MYSELF AND
I ASSURE YOU THAT WHATEVER HAS BEEN PRINTED
ON THEM TO DATE HAS BEEN UNDERSTATEMENT X IF
YOU WOULD SEE ANY ADVANTAGE IN ASKING ABOUT A
DOZEN LEADERS OF CONGRESS AND A DOZEN PROMINENT
EDITORS TO MAKE A SHORT VISIT TO THIS THEATER
IN A COUPLE OF C54S I WILL ARRANGE TO HAVE
THEM CONDUCTED TO ONE OF THESE PLACES WHERE
THE EVIDENCE OF BESTIALITY AND CRUELTY IS SO
OVERPOWERING AS TO LEAVE NO DOUBT IN THEIR
MINDS ABOUT THE EVIL PRACTICES OF THE NAZIS
IN THESE CAMPS X THE WORLD MUST KNOW WHAT THE
NAZIS HAVE DONE AT THESE CAMPS X I AM HOPEFUL
```

```
THAT SOME BRITISH INDIVIDUALS IN SIMILAR
CATEGORIES WILL VISIT THE NORTHERN AREA TO
WITNESS SIMILAR EVIDENCE OF ATROCITY END
SECRET
```

SECRET

"Good summary, Ike. Do you think the chief will take you up on your suggestion?"

"I have no idea, but I felt compelled to make the offer after what we saw today."

"You know, Ike, the warrior in me cannot believe the professional military was involved in these outrageous camps. But, to my knowledge, we have seen no evidence that the soldiers did anything to stop it, which makes them complicit. I respected them as adversaries. They were worthy. I don't think so after seeing that bloody camp for myself."

"That says a lot coming from you, Georgie."

The communications center lieutenant returned and handed another message folder to the supreme commander without expression.

```
DATE 122103Z APRIL 1945
TO SUPCMDR SHAEF
FROM SECWAR
UNCLAS
URGENT
BREAK
WITH PROFOUND SADNESS I INFORM YOU THAT PRESIDENT
ROOSEVELT HAS DIED X VICE PRESIDENT TRUMAN WILL
BE SWORN IN AS PRESIDENT THIS EVENING X INFORM
ALL CMDS ASAP END
BT
```

Eisenhower handed the unclassified message to Patton and dismissed the lieutenant.

"I'll be damned . . . so close to victory," Patton said.

"Yeah, quite sad. I didn't agree with everything he did, but he was an exceptional commander-in-chief. He had just the right touch—interested, engaged, and respectful. He asked the right questions but didn't get involved in our work. He trusted us, and we trusted him."

"I always saw him as a softie."

"Far from it, Georgie. History will eventually record that he was tough as nails when the country was possessed by that blind isolationist bent before the war. He kept his cool, and he kept his eye on the ball."

"I don't know anything about Truman. So I don't know how this will affect our operations?"

"I've only met Truman twice. I don't have a read on him. Until or if we hear otherwise, we'll press on with our operations plan."

"By your command. I'm not going to let any grass grow under my feet."

"Great, Georgie. Press on."

"You know I will," Patton said and grinned.

The two generals retired for the evening.

—

Thursday, 12.April.1945
Office of the Speaker of the House
House of Representatives
Capitol Building
Washington, District of Columbia
United States of America
17:00 hours

"Good afternoon, Sam," said Vice President Truman as he entered Speaker Rayburn's Capitol office.

Harry S Truman had been the senior senator from Missouri when he became Vice President of the United States in the Roosevelt administration three months earlier.

Samuel Taliaferro 'Sam' Rayburn had been the representative for the 4th District of Texas since 1913 and Speaker of the House of Representatives since 1940.

"And, a delightful afternoon to you, Mister Vice President," Rayburn responded. "I have a nice bourbon and branch waiting for you." The Speaker gestured to his inner office.

The telephone on the desk of his secretary-receptionist rang. Before the two senior politicians could reach the inner office door, his secretary announced, "Excuse me, Mister Vice President, I just received a message for you to call National One Four One Four." They all recognized the number as the White House. "Would you like me to connect you?"

"Yes, please," Truman said and moved to her desk. He took the handset proffered to him. He listened for several seconds. Truman asked, "Why?" He then exclaimed, "Jesus Christ and General Jackson!" He handed the handset back to her and turned to Rayburn. "I've been summoned to the White House immediately."

"Sounds ominous."

"Yes, but the office did not say the topic. I'm sorry, Sam. I shall have to beg your forgiveness and pass on your bourbon. Perhaps we can pick up here tomorrow afternoon."

"I'll have the bourbon ready whenever you are available."

Truman nodded and departed the Capitol Building.

—

Thursday, 12.April.1945
The White House
Washington, District of Columbia
United States of America
17:30 hours

Several staff members waited at the West Wing entrance. They ushered the vice president to the second-floor residence, expecting a private dressing down by the president for some unknown transgression or oversight. When he entered the residence, the First Lady stood and walked toward Truman. She was dressed in all black – not a good sign.

"Harry, the president is dead," announced Eleanor Roosevelt directly.

"Dear God above us all. May God rest his immortal soul." They stood in awkward silence for several moments. "Is there anything I can do for you?"

Eleanor Roosevelt actually chuckled softly. "Is there anything we," she said emphasizing the pronoun, "can do for you, for you are in trouble now?"

Truman swallowed hard as the weight of what had just happened enveloped him. "You are such a dear."

"As I understand events, you became President of the United States at three thirty-five this afternoon, in accordance with the Constitution. You are to take the oath of office at seven in the Cabinet Room. Franklin's Cabinet has been informed and recalled for the ceremony. Your life has now changed dramatically by fate."

"Yes, well, I suppose that may be an understatement. Nonetheless, please do not hesitate to call me at any time, especially if there is anything I can do for you."

"Thank you, Harry. I would like to have a few days to bury Franklin. I will ensure we vacate the residence for you and 'Bess' as soon thereafter as possible."

"Yes, of course. Please take all the time you need. 'Bess' and I are just fine and in no hurry."

"Thank you, Harry."

"You are most welcome, Eleanor. My deepest and sincerest condolences for your tragic loss."

Eleanor Roosevelt nodded her head. President Truman departed the residence for the Oval Office in the West Wing. He had been vice president for only three months. Now, he was President of the United States of America. His mind swirled in a vortex of conflicted thoughts, images, and concerns for the future. Eleanor's prophetic words gave him a chill.

—

Thursday, 12.April.1945
No.10 Downing Street
Whitehall, London, England
United Kingdom
22:45 hours

"Prime Minister," said duty Private Secretary John Martin somewhat breathlessly, "we were just notified by the Foreign Office that President Roosevelt died this afternoon . . . at half past nine our time."

"Dear God, no," Winston answered, "surely you are joking."

"No, I'm afraid not. The Foreign Office confirmed the information with the U.S. Embassy before notifying us. According to the message, Ambassador Winant was notified at the same time we were."

Churchill thought for a moment. "Please get Anthony Eden on the telephone immediately."

"He is in San Francisco for the United Nations conference."

Winston thought for a moment. "Fine. He is eight hours behind us, so it is afternoon for him."

"Yes Sir. I will see to it immediately."

Churchill went to his office window and stared at the still churned-up earth of the once beautiful garden. Tears descended his cheeks as he remembered the more than three decades he had known his friend since Franklin had been an assistant secretary of the Navy and he had been in his first tenure as first lord of the Admiralty. Franklin was a kindred spirit on the long, arduous, and the tortuous journey they both found themselves in by fate, not by choice. They had been through so much, and they were so close to the finish line. "What a shame . . . a tragic shame," Winston said aloud to no one.

This time, Martin knocked twice before entering the prime minister's office. "Sir, Foreign Minister Eden is waiting for you on the blue telephone.

"Thank you, John." Churchill went to his desk, sat, and picked up the blue phone. "Anthony, how is San Francisco?"

"Rather cool and foggy, not the foggy season they tell me, but foggy nonetheless – a bit like London."

"Good luck at the conference. I called first to make sure you have heard the news."

"I presume you are referring to the president's passing."

"Yes, tragic news. He was such a good friend and companion. Do you have additional information?"

"I was informed first by Lord Halifax and then by Secretary of State Stettinius. Vice President Truman became president on Roosevelt's death. I am informed that the new president has been primed. Ed indicated the official oath of office would be administered later this evening."

"Will the conference proceed since the host country will be in mourning?"

"I asked exactly the same question in my conversation with Ed. He does not know and hopes to gain the president's guidance after the ceremony. Ed asked me not to assume the worst or expect an immediate answer. He favors proceeding, but it is the president's decision. The official conference begins in a fortnight. There is plenty of work. I met with our team shortly after we received the news. We will press on with negotiating the details of the charter. We should know the American intentions before the conference convenes."

"The emotions are still rather raw. My urge is to attend the president's funeral. However, we won't be able to finalize the plans until we know the details. Unless you have a reason for me not to attend, I will continue planning as details become known. I will confer with the King as soon as possible."

"That sounds reasonable to me."

"Very well. On a personal note, I am devastated, Anthony. This is a terrible loss . . . to me personally, to the nation and the empire. He has been such a major force in American politics and in international relations, for that matter. He was a genuine and true friend."

"My condolences for your loss, Winston," Eden interjected. "From the very first time I had the privilege of seeing the interaction between Franklin and you, I have been and remain deeply impressed by the friendship the two of you were able to forge in such troubled times."

"Thank you, Anthony. Yes, he was a good friend. Now, he is gone. Have you met the new president?"

"No."

"Has Lord Halifax?"

"No, not to my knowledge."

"Well, that is the first order of business of the highest priority. We must develop an impression of the new president and find our path to compatible relations. We need to look for an opportunity for me to meet with Truman as soon as possible . . . while I am in the U.S. for Franklin's funeral."

"We'll see what can be arranged."

"Thank you. Now, I'm sure you have work to do. Please keep me apprised of your progress. I look forward to having you back in London."

The two men traded familiar cordialities before they terminated the telephonic conversation. They were both grateful for the dramatic improvements in communications.

Churchill took a moment to look out the window and then lifted the black telephone. "John, I have a task for tomorrow."

Martin appeared at the door. "Yes Sir."

"Tomorrow, we must quickly plan for me to attend President Roosevelt's funeral and hold an option of meeting with President Truman."

"Yes Sir. We will jump on it first thing in the morning."

"Thank you. How are we standing on the Dispatch Box?"

"We are in fine shape until the morning."

"Very well. Then, I think I shall retire and do some reading."

———

Thursday, 12.April.1945
USAAF Station F-356
Saffron Walden, Essex, England
United Kingdom
23:05 hours

Brian was rapidly approaching his tolerance limit for tobacco smoke and alcohol consumption in the O'Club bar. The stories got wilder and more detached from reality. As the night wore on, as usual, the noise level continued to ratchet up until the final burst at last call. He saw no reasons for waiting for the bar to close.

The squadron had another successful, near perfect, fighter sweep mission. Other groups still encountered German fighters, but it had been several weeks since the 4FG engaged in aerial combat. Nevertheless, they could still find ground targets between the constricting Allied lines—troops in the open, tanks, trucks, and today a moving train.

"Whoa!" shouted the lead steward. "Listen up, gentlemen." Not satisfied with the response of the pilots, he shouted as loudly as he could, "Shut the fuck up!"

The admonition worked. The pilots went quiet, and the radio announcer's voice came through.

". . . confirmed the information. To repeat, President Roosevelt died this afternoon . . ."

"Damn!" "What the hell!" "That can't be true."

". . . the U.S. Embassy in London has validated the earlier announcement. To repeat our main story, President Roosevelt has died, and Vice President Truman will be sworn in as the new President of the United States of America. May God bless the United States and President Truman.

"Now, to our next news story . . ." The volume on the radio diminished to a less than audible level.

"Pardon me, Sirs," the chief steward apologized. "I thought you would want to hear the news for yourself."

More than a few pilots offered words of thanks, gratitude, and acceptance. Many pilots called it quits and went to their rooms. Brian finished his beer and left as well. He stopped at the telephone booths and considered calling Charlotte, but his wristwatch told him it was too late. It's already well passed her bedtime . . . and mine, for that matter.

Brian undressed and readied himself for bed. He thought about reading, but he realized he would not last long. He thought of the president's passing as sleep promptly claimed his consciousness.

—

Thursday, 12.April.1945
Hôtel Ritz Paris
15 Place Vendôme
Paris, Île-de-France
Liberated France
23:15 hours

Bill Donovan found himself dozing off with the latest budget report from his financial director on his lap. The service was in a good position financially. Nevertheless, he had to review the reports, although it had been several years since the service had a budget issue. Donovan did not like budget reports, but they were a necessary evil and part of the job.

The day had gone well. His primary purpose had been discussions with Paris Station chief Emil Forgan. Donovan's immediate question to Paris Station was about the quickly evolving political situation in France. De Gaulle implicitly declared himself president of liberated France, and he undoubtedly believed in his feelings of supremacy in France. Donovan had also invited London Station chief David Bruce to join the discussion as he suspected the question would require a more extensive answer.

Just as the warm blanket of sleep descended around Bill Donovan, his room door burst open, and the lights were switched on, giving Donovan a shot of pain as his eyes tried to adapt to the sudden light rapidly. A few seconds revealed both Bruce and Forgan. Emil held a single piece of white paper.

"Sorry, Bill. Paris Station just received this Unclas, and I knew you would want to see it immediately."

"Unclas, you say," Bill replied as he blinked and rubbed his eyes. "What could be that important?"

Emil handed the message to Donovan.

```
OS
HQ OSS NR 193
U 122103Z APRIL 1945 ROUTINE
FM 106
TO 109
UNCLAS
BT
WITH WHITE HOUSE NOTIFICATION AND PROFOUND
SADNESS I MUST INFORM YOU THAT PRESIDENT
ROOSEVELT HAS DIED IN WARM SPRINGS GEORGIA OF
AS YET UNKNOWN CAUSES X VICE PRESIDENT TRUMAN
WILL BE SWORN IN AS PRESIDENT THIS EVENING END
BT
```

"Well, damn! That throws a clot in the churn, doesn't it?"

"I would say so," Bruce added.

"What do you need us to do, Chief?" Forgan asked.

"What does this do to your transition plan?" added Bruce.

"I do not have answers, fellas. I have the same questions as you. It's too late to get back to Washington. Alert the aircraft crew; I'd like to take off as soon as possible to get back to DC. We'll drop you off in London on the way."

"Not necessary, Bill. I'll stay here to discuss a few more things with Emil, which is what we were doing when the message arrived, and then I'll make my way back. Thank you for the offer."

"If you change your mind before they close the airplane hatch, you're welcome to a seat. We've plenty of room on the Connie, and it's a very comfortable mode of travel . . . fast too I might add. We needed that aircraft years ago, but at least we have it now."

"Good to know."

"I guess we don't have a secure phone," Bill said.

"The only ones I know of are the Station unit and General Eisenhower's device at Versailles, nothing close by."

"As I figured, but we never know unless we ask. So, it will have to wait. Please send a message in the morning to Colonel Buxton and tell him I'm on the way home. One more thing, the president's passing does throw an obvious question mark on the transition plan. It serves no purpose to speculate. I've not discussed the transition plan with President Truman, so I've no idea what his position is. I'll talk to him as soon as possible. I'll let you both know as soon as I have something to report. I urge you both to calm all your people. Let's keep doing our great work until the president decides. We'll deal with whatever comes."

"We'll take care of it right away," Forgan replied.

"I'll jump on it as soon as I return to London."

"There's nothing more we can do tonight, so get the hell out and switch off the lights."

They all laughed. The two station chiefs did as they were directed.

Donovan had been so close to sleep before the intrusion. Sleep was farther away now. Bill picked up the service budget report since he knew that was his best shot at sleep.

———

Thursday, 12.April.1945
Headquarters, 3rd Army
I.G. Farben Building
Grüneburgweg 1
Frankfurt am Main, Hessen
Liberated Germany
23:55 hours

George Patton finished his latest reading of von Clausewitz's *opus magnum, On War*. He had tried several times to read the original German version but eventually abandoned the effort. The English translation of a von Clausewitz pronouncement dominated his thoughts. 'War is the continuation of politics by other means.'

"Wise words," Patton said aloud as he placed the book on the side table.

The general looked at his wristwatch. "Damn." The little hand was just passed the nine, and the big hand was on the 17.

Patton switched on the radio in his quarters. He knew the time had to be approaching midnight and the BBC World Service always had a time tone on the hour. The broadcaster was into their regular end-of-the-hour disjointed coded phrases to pass simple messages to field agents, resistance fighters, and other supportive individuals in the occupied countries.

"That concludes our 11 o'clock hour program," the broadcaster said in clearly enunciated words. Another voice came over the radio, "At the tone, it will be midnight, Double Summer Time." A series of beeps counted down the last five seconds to a pronounced distinctive tone.

Patton set his watch to midnight and wound the watch stem until it was tight.

"Ladies and gentlemen, this is Hugo Andergrif. At the top of our midnight program, I must repeat our earlier news. It is my sad duty to inform our listeners that we were notified earlier this evening by the American ambassador and our ambassador in Washington that President Roosevelt has died. May God bless President Roosevelt's immortal soul. Vice President Truman will be sworn in shortly as the new president . . ."

Patton switched off the radio and said to himself, "Well, I guess that makes it official."

The general switched off the light, laid down, covered himself with a blanket, and was soon fast asleep.

—

Thursday, 12.April.1945
Cabinet Room
The White House
Washington, District of Columbia
United States of America
19:10 hours

Surrounded by Roosevelt's Cabinet ministers at the far end of the large conference table, Harry S Truman stood in front of his wife Elizabeth Virginia 'Bess' Truman, née Wallace, below the portrait of Woodrow Wilson that Roosevelt favored, and facing Chief Justice of the Supreme Court Harlan Fiske Stone. The Truman's daughter and only child, 21-year-old Margaret stood to 'Bess's left and to the right of Stone. Eleanor Roosevelt stood at the other end of the table with the photographer and several staff members.

"Are you prepared to take the oath of office, Mister President?" asked Chief Justice Stone.

"Yes, Mister Chief Justice."

"Please raise your right hand." Truman placed his right hand on a Gideon Bible retrieved by the White House Head Usher, and Harry held it in his left hand, as if in a brief moment of prayer, and then raised his hand to his shoulder.

"Repeat after me. I, Harry Shipp Truman . . . ," Stone began, incorrectly inserting a name for Truman's single-letter middle name.

Truman confidently spoke his oath of office and ignored the Chief Justice's mistake. "I, Harry S Truman, do solemnly swear that I will faithfully execute the Office of President of the United States and will to the best of my ability, preserve, protect and defend the Constitution of the United States, so help me God." Truman kissed the Bible, as previous presidents had done, and then he shook Stone's proffered hand.

"Congratulations, Mister President," the Chief Justice announced.

After more photographs, congratulatory words, and handshakes, the observers and witnesses were ushered out, and the Cabinet took their usual seats around the table. It took several minutes for the shuffling to quiet.

19:18 hours

"First," began President Truman, "we shall have our time to grieve. Tonight, we have an army in the field and a navy on the seas that are depending upon us to do our part in bringing victory as quickly as possible. We must all reassure the nation and the world that we shall not blink before our duty.

"Second, the Secretary of State is concerned about the inaugural United Nations conference set to begin in San Francisco. I want there to be no doubt, confusion, or hesitation; the conference must proceed as planned. I have an awful lot to learn and no time to learn it. So, for now, Secretary Stettinius, please proceed as President Roosevelt instructed you. In fact, the same charge goes to all of you. I insist that the business of governance proceed as approved by President Roosevelt. We will have time to adjust, as I come up to speed."

Truman's first Cabinet meeting continued for nearly an hour as each minister offered a brief summary of their department's situation and any pressing matters that he needed to move up on the priority list. The meeting concluded and the Executive Branch department heads made their way out of the room. Secretary of War Stimson lingered and waited until he and the president were alone and within arm's reach.

Stimson said in a low voice, "Mister President, I have a matter of utmost urgency to discuss with you that I could not raise in the Cabinet meeting."

"OK," the president responded with some confusion and gestured for the War Secretary to proceed.

"I need the project director here. I would like to schedule a private, closed, classified meeting to brief you thoroughly on a very important project that has been underway for several years and is approaching its conclusion."

"And, we can't talk about it now?" asked Truman.

"I would prefer not. You deserve the experts to brief you. I am knowledgeable, but I am not that expert."

"Very well. Please schedule this briefing with Admiral Leahy or Miss Tully." Truman started to leave and then turned back to Stimson. "Who is this expert, if I may ask? So, I will recognize his name when it appears on the calendar."

"General Groves . . . Major General Leslie 'Dick' Groves. He's the project director and has been since the military assumed supervision of the project."

"Very well. I will look for this meeting as soon as you are ready."

"Thank you, Mister President."

The two men left the room and went their separate ways for the evening. 'Bess' and Margaret were waiting for him in the anteroom of the Oval Office. They entered the distinct room, and Harry brought his wife and daughter up to date with what he knew. They talked for 30 minutes, then departed with a Secret Service protection detail to the Vice President's residence at the Naval Observatory.

—

Chapter 6

Finality is death. Perfection is finality.
Nothing is perfect. There are lumps in it.

-- James Stephens

Friday, 13.April.1945
No.10 Downing Street
Whitehall, London, England
United Kingdom
19:30 hours

"I've got dinner guests in 30 minutes, Pug. What have you?" asked Prime Minister Churchill.

"Yes Sir. I just received confirmation from Beetle that the Red Army has taken Vienna."

"Well, that is not good news. The Soviets have nearly surrounded Berlin and are far deeper into Europe than I had hoped. They are not going to let them be free. Listening to Stalin, they are going to turn Eastern Germany into a desert. They will bleed them of everything of value and leave them with nothing but scorched earth. Now, with the loss of Austria, they will do the same in that ancient land."

"Are you still going to America for the president's funeral?"

"No. I've decided against it. Too many members of the War Cabinet and ministers, in general, are out of the country. I must mind the fort. I will pay my respects to Eleanor, the family . . . and, I will meet with President Truman in due course."

"Quite understandable, Sir. Now, I do not want to leave you on a sour note. On the positive side of the ledger, Beetle also confirmed that the American 1st Infantry Division, part of the VII Corps, 1st Army, the left flank of Bradley's 12th Army Group, has taken Hermann Göring Aeronautical Research Center at Völkenrode, near Braunschweig."

The *Luftfahrtforschungsanstalt* (Aeronautical Research Institute, LFA) was the most advanced aeronautical research organization in the world at the time. Scientists and engineers at LFA provided critical developmental data for many of Germany's most advanced aircraft designs. Some reached production. Others were in various stages of development, from modeling to prototypes.

"The initial impression from the line troops is that the files appear to be intact. From Beetle's report, the Germans appear to have left everything 'as-is.' The supreme commander issued orders to secure the whole facility and everything in—no souvenir hunting."

"Excellent. Have we sent a Farnborough exploitation team?" the prime minister asked.

"Beetle said the SHAEF G-9 would handle coordination with R-A-E and A-F-R-L."

Both countries had aeronautical research organizations equivalent to LFA. Royal Aeronautical Establishment (RAE) at Farnborough in Hampshire provided advanced aeronautical research and development support. RAE also maintained and operated captured German aircraft to learn the capabilities and limitations of each design. The U.S. Army Air Forces Research Laboratory (AFRL) at Dayton, Ohio, provided similar services at RAE to the Army Air Forces.

"It sounds like things are well in hand. I'll be leaving right after dinner tonight for the weekend at Chequers. Would you be so kind to brief the Professor and ask him to follow up on the L-F-A exploitation? We need to get as much as possible out of the German find."

"It's a little late tonight. I'll contact Doctor Lindemann tomorrow morning. I will try to get him connected with the exploitation team leader as soon as possible."

"Thank you, Pug. Now, if you will excuse me, I must see to my guests."

"Certainly, Prime Minister. Have a good evening and a relaxing weekend." General Ismay went right and departed Number 10, while Churchill went left to join his guests.

One of the captured German aircraft transferred to AFRL for exploitation was a Ju88D-1 medium bomber configured as a high-altitude, photo reconnaissance airplane. The machine was flown from Egypt across Africa, the Atlantic Ocean to Brazil, and then north to Dayton, Ohio, in October 1943. The pilot was Major Warner Eugene Newby, USAAF—the author's maternal uncle, his mother's older brother. Major Newby would rise to the rank of major general before retiring from the U.S. Air Force as the base commander of Vandenberg Air Force Base.

———

Saturday, 14.April.1945
Waischenfeld, Bayreuth, Bavaria
Liberated Germany
10:45 hours

Sherman tanks of the 14th Armor Division entered the outskirts of the village with the caution and suspiciousness of seasoned warriors. The town had no observable war damage. It appeared to be a pristine, Bavarian, mountain village. What raised the caution and wariness of the point tank platoon was the paucity of any living creature—no animals, no human beings, nothing was moving.

The tank platoon commander, First Lieutenant Robert 'Bob' Lourdes, signaled the column to halt and deployed the mounted infantry for possible urban combat. Before the infantrymen could move forward to clear the buildings and side streets, A boy, perhaps 12 years old, dressed in traditional *lederhosen* with an open jacket, appeared from a side street. He stood in the middle of the roadway and held up his left hand to stop like a traffic cop.

"Freeze," commanded Lourdes. "Kurt, get up here," he added as he lifted himself out of the turret hatch and stood at the rear of the tank's main battery turret.

Kurt Schmidt was the tank crew's loader and a fluent German speaker. He lifted himself out and stood in front of the turret. "*Sprechen!*" he shouted to the boy.

"*Amerikaner?*" the boy asked.

"*Ja.*"

"*Sind Sie wegen der S-S-Männer hier?*"

"I got the gist of that, Schmidt, but what did he ask precisely?" Lourdes asked from behind Kurt.

Without taking his eyes off the boy, Schmidt answered, "He's asking if we are here for the S-S men?"

The lieutenant jumped to the hatch and plugged in his headset and throat microphone. "S-S in the area," he radioed his platoon. "Keep your eyes out and stay on your toes. Lock and load . . . ready for combat." Then, satisfied he had prepared his platoon and warned his company and battalion commanders, the lieutenant softly spoke to Schmidt, who was still not looking at him. "Tell the boy yes, and ask him where they are?"

"*Ja. Wo sind sie?*"

The boy turned and pointed behind him to the forested mountains southeast of the village.

"*Wo?*" asked Schmidt.

"*Kleines Teufelsloch,*" the boy answered, "*Das Kleine Teufelsloch.*"

Schmidt turned to the lieutenant. "He says they are at a place called Little Devil's Hole."

The lieutenant grabbed his map from his station in the tank. He studied the town's layout. It was long and narrow. They were on the main road through the village.

The infantry platoon commander, Second Lieutenant John Singleton, USA, assigned to Lourdes' tank platoon climbed up on the tank. "Whacha got, Bob?" he asked.

"The boy out there," he answered, pointing to the boy still standing in the middle of the road, "says the S-S are located at a place near here called Little Devil's Hole."

"Could be a trap . . . an ambush."

"Yep, it sure could be . . . but it could also be one of those Nazi caves with God only knows what stolen stuff the Nazis looted." Lourdes scanned the terrain and the map. Nothing on the map indicated any site labeled Little Devil's Hole or any combination of those words. However, he did find a noted dirt road that ended in the forested, steep terrain. A white waft of smoke rose from the forest in the area of the road terminus he saw on the map. Bob put his right fingertip on the end of the road. Both lieutenants nodded. "But I'd better get on the horn to the boss."

"Yeah. I'll let you handle that one. We're here to scrub your back."

Lourdes held up his left index finger. He keyed the radio. "Jacko Six, Jacko Two." "Jacko Two is at Dog Four. A local says there may be one of those S-S caves close by." "Yes Sir" Lourdes nodded, listened, and nodded again. He turned to Singleton. "The company is a half mile behind and will handle the village. My Six wants us to recon the information we have." Lourdes held up his left index finger again and keyed his mic with his right hand. "I'm going to be off the box for a few minutes. I'm going to have Schmidt with me. Jonesy, replace Schmidt as loader. Shoot at anything that looks like it might shoot and get the beast to cover in the village. Radio the captain if anything suspicious turns up."

"Gotcha, boss," came the crew response in his headset.

Lourdes looked at Singleton. "Let's go talk to the boy. You're coming with us, Schmidt."

The three men jumped off the tank hull and walked up to the boy. Lourdes held his map flat. "Tell the boy to show us where the S-S men are on the map."

"Zeigen Sie uns, wo die S-S-Männer auf der Karte sind?"

The boy stared at the map and ran his right index finger over the paper. He tapped his finger on the map to identify the village and said, *"Wir sind hier?"*

"Ja," answered Schmidt.

The boy tapped the map as he counted the roads off the main road going east. On the third one, he said, *"Dieses hier."* The boy ran his finger along the road to the end, tapped it three times, and pronounced, *"Das Kleine Teufelsloch."*

"Danke," Lieutenant Lourdes said.

"Ich will mit dir gehen. Ich will dir zeigen."

"He wants to go with us and show us the hole."

"Nope. If there are S-S men up there, we're likely going to get in a fight, and I don't want him in the middle of it. Plus, if the S-S see him with us, they'll likely take vengeance out on him and his family and friend, and we can't have that."

Schmidt turned back at the boy. "*Nein. Zu gefährlich.*"

The boy started to react, shook his head, and then nodded. He came to a smart position of attention and saluted in sharp American style. Lieutenant Lourdes returned the salute and smiled. The boy moved off to the side of the road.

Lourdes looked at Singleton. "Let's mount up and get this done."

"Let me brief my squad leaders. This could get dicey, and I want everyone on their toes."

"Sure. Give me a pump when you're ready. I'll be in my turret."

"Will do." Singleton circled his right hand above his head to signal his squad leaders to gather around him. He headed back to the third tank.

Lourdes nodded to the boy and then climbed up on the tank. Schmidt dropped into the turret first. Each of the crew took their normal positions. Lourdes keyed his mic. "OK, guys. We're going up to recon the cave. This could be an ambush. We've all got to be sharp. Anything moves, let the platoon know pronto. We'll move out as soon as the straight legs are ready to kick off."

The infantrymen mounted up on the tanks. Lieutenant Lourdes signaled for the platoon to move out. As they neared the road of interest—it was more like a worn path—a flight of four P-51 Mustangs with red noses flew low and fast overhead. Spontaneous cheers could be heard inside and outside the noisy tanks. Everyone to a man liked the sound of those sleek machines in proximity. That brief low pass was a positive sign.

The tank platoon made its way up the road cautiously but steadily. The cave entrance was indeed at the end of the road. A rusty 55-gallon drum was still smoking outside the cave. Lourdes signaled for the infantry to deploy to clear the area. They did not need prompting. The platoon spread out swiftly and professionally to clear the forest around the cave entrance.

When they were satisfied the forest was clear, one squad took up overwatch positions. Another squad fanned out around the open area at the entrance while the third squad began the process of searching the cave. A steel wall and locked steel door filled the cave passageway—a couple of small explosive charges made quick work of the locks.

The initial clearing process took just under two hours. Then, the squad leader reported to the lieutenants. They found rows and rows of metal file cabinets filled with documents, various artifacts, and even a cache of gold, silver, and jewels in myriad forms. There was some artwork, but most of what they found appeared to be Nazi memorabilia.

Lieutenant Lourdes radioed their findings and received orders to secure the site. Various exploitation teams were ordered to the cave—counterintelligence, Monuments, and engineering teams, along with a Military Police unit to take over security for the site. The lieutenants agreed on a watch schedule to protect the cave, rotate running the tanks to keep one operational, save fuel, and allow the troops to eat and sleep until they were relieved.

What the armor and infantry officers and soldiers did not know at the time but would eventually learn, they came upon, discovered, and secured the largest cache of *SS-Ahnenerbe* repository documents in that cave network. Deutsches Ahnenerbe (German Ancestral Heritage) formed by order of *Reichsführer-SS* Heinrich Luitpold Himmler on 1.July.1935. Himmler and the Nazis sought the spiritual basis for what the SS had become in all its dimensions and manifestation. A goodly portion of the material recovered at Little Devil's Hole had been transported from Wewelsburg Castle and would provide valuable evidence for the post-war Nürnberg Trials.

—

Monday, 16.April.1945
USAAF Station F-356
Saffron Walden, Essex, England
United Kingdom
07:55 hours

The 334th Fighter Squadron took to the air with full internal and auxiliary wing tank fuel. The RODEO 397 mission plan called for the squadron to hit two auxiliary airfields in Southeastern Germany on their way to two primary airfields used by the German Air Force in Czechoslovakia. The fighter squadron had assigned air base targets in Eastern Germany ahead of the U.S. front lines, which were on the outskirts of Chemnitz, halfway to encircling Leipzig, and 20 miles from what was left of Dresden. The Mustangs emptied their wing tanks before reaching the front lines and pickled them for combat.

They found virtually nothing to shoot at either of the German airfields. Yellow Flight had the line and destroyed two Fieseler Fi156 *Störche,* the last two aircraft not already destroyed at either airfield. Both German aircraft joined the rest of the wreckage.

The squadron knew from the intelligence information at the mission briefing that the German aircraft in Czechoslovakia were likely to be more active. German-occupied Czechoslovakia had not been subjected to the bomber and fighter attacks that the airfields in Germany had suffered. The question the intelligence blokes could not answer was whether the aircraft in Czechoslovakia had the fuel to fly and the ammunition to fight.

Hunter wheeled the squadron south-southeast. "Cobweb, Cobweb Six. Peter One."

The Primary One target was Prague-Kbely airfield, six miles northeast of Prague Center. As they had done for the last few months, they approached their target at high speed and low-level tree top height. The squadron spread to hit the entire airfield at the same time. Each pilot had his assigned lane. With Allied lines so close, the intelligence analysts suspected but did not know whether the Czech-based German Air Force would have any early warning of the planned attack. They had to assume the Germans would receive warning and would respond.

Five miles prior to their target, Brian checked the deployment of his squadron. *Perfect!* He scanned the sky. *No fighters yet.* They were boresighted on their target.

As they burst across the last tree line and saw the whole of the grass airfield before them, they were surprised. *Look at all those aircraft.* There were several squadrons worth of Bf109 and Fw190 fighters, a couple of squadrons of Ju88 bombers, several Ju52 transports, and at least one Me262 jet fighter. None of them were moving. Pilots and ground crew could be seen running to the aircraft. *We caught 'em with their pants down.* Brian concentrated on the targets in his lane. The Ju52s and a portion of the Ju88s were laid out before him. He opened fire early. The tracers arced to the static aircraft. Brian kept his trigger down and kicked his rudder to spread his bullet streams over the largest area of his lane. Flashes dotted many of the aircraft. The Ju52s burst into flame. Hunter adjusted his attack run to avoid the fireballs and developing smoke plumes. Explosions to the left and right of Brian appeared in his peripheral vision. Brian moved his sight reticle to the open hangar door and unleashed his guns. Explosions and fire blossomed in the dark interior. They crossed the far boundary.

"Cobweb, Cobweb Six. Peter Two." Brian turned southwest. *They know we're here now.* The two sides swapped positions swiftly and precisely. They settled into position before they reached Prague.

The squadron stayed at rooftop level, dodging church steeples and other obstacles. Tracers flashed up from the ground but hit nothing. The mission plan required them to avoid firing at targets of opportunity, of which there were many, as they transited to their Primary Two target—Pilsen-Slowan airfield. The squadron needed to conserve their ammunition for the next target. *We achieved surprise at Prague. We won't enjoy surprise at Pilsen.* Brian scanned the sky. *Still no fighters.* Hunter took a quick inventory of his aircraft. *All present.* He adjusted their flight path slightly to the right for a direct line to their next target.

Pilsen-Slowan was another large grass landing area airfield and located three miles southwest of Pilsen. The buildings of Pilsen appeared first. Hunter adjusted their flight path again.

"Bandits climbing out," radioed Hunter. "Cobweb Baker press the attack. Cobweb Able deploy for air combat. Fly, take the low ones. Blue will take the high ones. Hole, take the right. We'll take the left."

Two Fw190s were turning to engage the approaching Mustangs. Hunter maneuvered to intercept the lead German. As he closed, he scanned the sky to ensure he had not missed anyone. Good. Hunter fired a burst before his adversary could get his nose on him. Corn made a similar shot at the German's wingman. Brian's tracers caused the German to flinch and roll right away from Hunter. He had the speed advantage but a larger turn radius. Brian did not want to give the German the turn advantage. He traded his speed into a high-g climbing reversal to gain height for potential energy and kept his nose coming around. The German had not anticipated Hunter's move. As he reached the apogee of his turn and in the inverted attitude, Brian picked up the German and saw him react to Hunter's superior position, but it was too late. The 190 rolled sharply into Hunter's rapidly closing attack to increase his attacker's diving angle, but that move was too late as well. Hunter led his adversary and opened fire. Impacts flashed all over the 190 until he exploded and disintegrated. The wingman had taken a bad position on his leader. Hunter pulled his throttle back, pressed his dive, quickly adjusted to the wingman, and squeezed his trigger. Again, flashes danced across the wingman. Fire burst from the engine cowling. The ground was coming up too quickly. Hunter rolled left and pulled up hard, feeling his Mustang shudder near stall. He released a little of his back stick pressure. Corn pressed the attack and finished the second German off in the same fashion.

Brian rolled back to the right and scanned the sky around him. The other sections of his division were engaged in separate dogfights. Numerous fires and smoking wrecks littered the airfield. Sweet took his 'B' Division into re-attacks to finish off as many intact aircraft as they could with their ammunition remaining. Brian focused on the flying Germans. With Corn on his wing in combat spread, Hunter circled overhead, looking for an opening or opportunity. He continually scanned the sky expecting reinforcement to arrive for the beleaguered Germans, but the sky remained clear except for the fights below him. All the Germans who made it to flight were in the air and in the fights.

Sweet and his 'B' Division continued to crisscross the airfield shooting up anything that even remotely looked like it might fly. Explosions and fires continued to pop up, by now mostly in the dispersal areas and hangars. One of Sweet's guys hit the camouflaged fuel storage tanks with huge white, red, orange, and massive plumes of black billowing smoke laced with red streaks.

One by one, the airborne Germans were shot down. No parachutes appeared. None of the Germans survived.

Brian checked his remaining fuel. They were past their bingo fuel for Debden. They would have to take their divert field.

With no more airborne Germans, Fly, Rolo, and Hole climbed their sections to rejoin Hunter. The 'B' Division was managing the ground attack quite well, and Brian did not feel the 'A' Division needed to join that part of the fight.

"Swede is Winchester and past bingo fuel."

"Pile Winchester."

"Cobweb, Cobweb Six. That's it, lads. We'll head to 'A' 96." Brian turned to two five three magnetic and climbed to Angels 15 to avoid any artillery fire near the front lines. The transit across Southern Germany was smooth and uneventful, with scattered clouds that were overflown or circumvented. Radio calls cleared the squadron to land at Nancy.

USAAF Station A-96 (Toul/Ochey Airfield)
Nancy, Meurthe-et-Moselle, Grand Est
Liberated France
14:25 hours

The squadron landed safely in order by section. A sergeant crewman in overalls waited for Hunter to reach the ground.

"We need fuel. Do you have a radio back to England?"

"Better yet, Major, the C-O has a secure phone in his office," the sergeant said, pointing to a small, wooden, clapboard building.

"Thanks, Sergeant. What about food for my pilots?"

"The cooks can handle that in the mess hall," he added, pointing at a larger version of the commander's building on the other side of two concrete hangars.

"Thanks."

Hunter removed his flight helmet, goggles, and oxygen mask. Then, he walked around his aircraft's tail to talk to Corn.

Corn removed his helmet as he jumped to the ground. "I'm going to try to call Group. Gather up the lads. We'll take fuel only for now. Hold on the ammo load until I figure out what Group wants us to do. Get everyone fed. The mess hall is that building over there," Brian said, pointing to the mess hall building.

"Count on it, Boss. We'll get the guys fed and ready to go."

"Thanks."

Brian went to the commander's building, asked to see the CO, and waited for a few minutes. Finally, an Army major came out. "Major Stressor," he said and extended his right hand.

"Brian Drummond. My squadron diverted here for fuel. I understand you've got a secure telephone back to England."

"What is your rank, Mister Drummond."

Brian pulled his flight vest back to display his gold oak leaf insignia.

"Yes, there is a secure phone in my office, but it's for official use only."

"Well, Major Stressor. I need to call the Fourth Fighter Group to clarify my orders."

"Sounds official to me."

"It is."

"The phone can be rather tricky. If you don't object, allow me to make the connection."

"Sure."

Brian followed Stressor into the office. Just listening to one side of the various conversations, the secure phone was not a simple telephone. Stressor eventually held the handset out to Brian and said, "Colonel Clark."

"Arnie, Hunter."

"Everything OK?"

"Yeah, fine. We extended over the target. I'll explain later. We diverted to 'A' 96 for fuel. Do you have anything else for us since we're in Eastern France?"

"Great initiative, Hunter. Nope. Nothing more. Head home."

"Wilco. We're about two hours out. We'll take off as soon as we're fueled and the guys are fed."

"Get 'em home safe."

"Wilco." The connection was broken down. Brian returned the handset to the cradle. "Thank you, Major. We'll be returning to England as soon as our aircraft are fueled and my pilots fed."

"You are welcome, Major. That's why we're here."

Brian nodded and departed. He went first to the sergeant, who was finishing up fueling his aircraft. "Fuel only, Sergeant. We're headed home once we're fueled."

"Should be another hour for all of your aircraft . . . unless you ask for a war scramble."

"Not necessary."

Brian joined his pilots in the mess hall. Corn got a ham & cheese sandwich for him, along with a couple of cookies, and a glass of iced tea, to his surprise. In between bites, Brian briefed the pilots on his fuel-only order. They did not need ammunition since they were a long way from the front, and there was no air threat. The guys were already regaling in their accomplishments on the day's mission. Brian had not seen it, but Sweet's Division caught several 190s and 109s in their takeoff runs. They believed they had shot up or destroyed every observable aircraft.

As he usually did, Brian listened to the storytelling. The squadron was definitely in high spirits. These guys were good, and they knew they were good.

The sergeant stepped into the mess hall, waited until he caught Brian's attention, and gave him a thumb's up. Brian nodded. "OK, fellas. We're fueled. Let's mount up and get home."

15:45 hours

The squadron took off by section. Once the join-up was completed, Brian increased power for a fast cruise. He stayed at Angels 8. The transit along the French-Belgian border and the clear, nearly cloudless sky gave each pilot a glorious aerial view of the historic region. They landed safely back at Debden without incident.

On the ground, they turned over their aircraft to the crew chiefs for refueling and rearming. By the time the pilots completed their debriefings, which took longer than usual, the evening meal was being served in the Officer's Mess. It was an unusually noisy meal. The other two Group squadrons had their own extraordinary missions on the day. Brian just listened despite repeated attempts to coax him into participation. Corn managed a decent presentation of their aerial engagement. Brian finished his meal and excused himself, inducing hoots and hollers.

A telephone call to Charlotte seemed and proved more important than war stories. The farm was doing well. Mabel had been able to find experienced young women to work the rapidly expanded greenhouse production. The farm was delivering. Charlotte also reported on their U.S. business operations. Bobby Joe Sales had a working plan, with or without an OSS contract, for post-war operations. He had intriguing ideas for expanding their ridership in an environment of much larger, more established airlines. Bobby also reported on Gertrude Bainbridge's discovery of Malcolm's notes on air freight operations. He had no news from anyone in the government and had not initiated any attempt to contact their project manager. The taskings from the OSS had declined but still occurred. Bobby was proceeding with the worst-case assumption, i.e., no government contract or business. Brian found himself thinking about jumping into Charlotte's world. By the end of the conversation, Brian was most impressed by the lightness, enthusiasm, and upbeat tone of Charlotte's words, a marked difference from what they faced last fall, with Charlotte deep into her grief for the loss of Ian. Her rebirth refreshed him.

Brian considered heading to bed but decided to join his brethren for a beer or two to celebrate the day's accomplishments. More so than usual, the

O'Club bar was more crowded, louder, and smokey'er than usual, which was in itself a measure of the Group's success on the day's missions. The cigarette, cigar, and pipe tobacco smoke proved too much and forced him out after just one beer. Brian took a quick shower to wash off the smoke that saturated his body. Sleep claimed him swiftly.

The debriefings, along with the processing and analysis of the gun camera film, would take several days to complete. The command intelligence units worked hard to complete their work. When the final assessment of the RODEO 397 mission was completed, the 334FS had a very good day. At Prague-Kbely, they destroyed 26 fighters (Bf109s & Fw190s), 19 Ju88 bombers, two Ju52 transports, and one Me262 fighter. At Pilsen-Slowan, they destroyed 20 Bf109 and Fw190 fighters, including one and a half victories added to Hunter's tally. Most were destroyed on the ground. Worse for the Germans was the destruction of their entire fuel supply at Pilsen.

The 8th Fighter Command took full advantage of the vastly diminished *Luftwaffe*, and the missions of mid-April would prove to be the *coup de grâce* for what was left of the *Luftwaffe*.

——

Wednesday, 18.April.1945
House of Commons
Westminster, London, England
United Kingdom
16:30 hours

"The House will come to order," the speaker announced. He waited for members to quiet and sit. "Prime Minister, you have the floor."

"Thank you, Mister Speaker," Churchill said and stood to the podium. "I am pleased to report on my telephonic conversation with Supreme Commander General of the Army Dwight Eisenhower earlier this afternoon. He is satisfied with the A-E-F's progress. Victory is near. They are at the Elbe in the north and south of Berlin, and on the outskirts of Wittenberge in the north. The A-E-F is approaching Dresden and the Czechoslovak and Polish borders. He was quite emphatic that they have yet to see any significant S-S resistance in Bavaria. General Eisenhower was not ready to declare success in thwarting the Nazi Redoubt in Obersalzburg, but so far, so good. The A-E-F expects to link up with the Red Army near the Elbe in the south next week.

"The 8th Air Force indicates that *Luftwaffe* resistance has effectively ended. They believe the Germans have run out of fuel and/or ammunition. As a result, their viable targets are rapidly dwindling to insignificance.

"Lead troops continue to uncover mines and caves filled with stolen artworks of all forms from all over Europe, including precious religious icons, large caches of gold, other precious metals, jewels, and jewelry. I offer tribute to President Roosevelt, may God rest his immortal soul, and Supreme Commander Eisenhower for the formation of the joint Allied commission for the recovery of stolen artworks. There are numerous joint exploitation groups to safeguard as much of the German research as possible—aircraft and rocket engineering, medical, physics, construction, and so many others. The free world will benefit from this exemplary work.

"This brings me to the worst of it from what we know so far. As honorable members know all too well, the A-E-F has liberated numerous camps in Western and Central Germany. We have reports of what the Red Army has discovered in Eastern and Central Poland. For several years, we received reports, difficult to corroborate, I must say, of special units operating in Eastern Europe carrying out wanton killings of special Jewish people. What we have now seen with our own eyes is the corroboration of those reports. The Nawzees, and I say them precisely, although other Germans have some culpability, have carried out bestial murders on an industrial scale. The inhumanity represented by all these dreadful camps is so far beyond the worst of nightmares and imagination. There is nothing even remotely or distantly comparable in the animal kingdom. What the Nawzees have done will be recorded by history as the worst in all human history.

"Units of the American 3rd Army recently liberated another concentration camp near Buchenwald in Thuringia. General Eisenhower and I discussed what we should do for posterity . . . to ensure no one can cast doubt or feign ignorance of what the Nawzees have done. We seek a high-level governmental delegation to bear direct, intimate, and recorded witness to what has occurred at these camps and specifically Buchenwald.

"I stand before the House to encourage a parliamentary, cross-party delegation to visit the Buchenwald camp as guests of the supreme commander. I have conferred with Lord Cranborne. Lords Stanhope and Addison have volunteered to represent the House of Lords for this delegation. On behalf of His Majesty's Coalition Government, I ask members to volunteer for this delegation. Submit your name to the Privy Seal. We shall select eight members of Commons to join the Lords. We have provisionally set this coming Saturday for the visit. We will coordinate all travel arrangements."

"Hear, hear," shouted many voices.

The House of Commons moved onto other domestic matters. Of the ample volunteers, the War Cabinet selected members from all the major political parties and included two doctors, a woman, and a journalist.

—

Saturday, 21.April.1945
Buchenwald Konzentrationslager
Buchenwald, Weimar, Thüringen
Liberated Germany
10:15 hours

At the insistence of Prime Minister Churchill, eight members of House of Commons and two Lords traveled to Buchenwald, the largest of the concentration camps on German soil. The camp had been established in 1937 and continuously operated by the SS until the camp was liberated by the U.S. 6th Armor Division ten days earlier.

The parliamentary delegation endured the entire tour, every disgusting scene from the unclean, emaciated survivors in tattered, thread-bare, striped uniforms to skeletal bodies stacked five deep. They saw the burn pits with loose and skeletal bones among partially burnt bodies.

They listened to the impromptu statements of the survivors about their treatment at the whim and brutality of the *SS-Totenkopfverbände*--elements known as Death's-Head Units. The *Totenkopfverbände* were trained and conditioned to operate the labor, concentration, and death camps throughout the occupied lands to kill innocent, unarmed people in an instant. The survivors displayed their identification arm tattoos and explained the symbols each prisoner was compelled to wear on their striped uniforms. An inverted, equilateral triangle was the base symbol with red for political, green for criminal, black for asocial, pink for homosexual, yellow for Jew, purple for Jehovah, and blue for emigrant. Jews with other factors might have an upright yellow triangle and another colored triangle on top to form a six-pointed star of David.

Buchenwald held prisoners from all over Europe and the Soviet Union. Political prisoners who resisted or did not conform to Nazi dicta were among the earliest captives. There were Jews, Jehovah Witnesses, Freemasons, gypsies, and Romani. Those mentally ill and physically disabled people who survived the Nazis' *Aktion T4* (Action T4) euthanasia program were sent to Buchenwald as well. Ordinary criminals and sexual 'deviants' became prisoners. In essence, anyone whom a Nazi official of one form or another did not like for any reason found themselves confined at Buchenwald. All prisoners worked primarily as forced laborers in local, peripheral, armaments factories. If a person was unable to work, they were summarily executed by the SS guards.

The MPs and Lords were shaken by what they saw, heard, and learned. Some took notes. They unanimously agreed that the perpetrators had to be held to account and appropriately punished. They also vowed to sponsor and support legislative measures to prevent future abuses like those they witnessed during their day tour of the concentration camp. They promised to do their best to support and repatriate the survivors to their pre-war countries and communities. The delegation would report to Parliament what they had been exposed to at Buchenwald.

The leader of HMG's delegation was James Richard Stanhope, 7th Earl Stanhope, KG, DSO, MC, PC. Thomas Edward Neil Driberg, Member of Parliament for Maldon, a Labour Party member, and former journalist, served as the delegation's recorder. Driberg wrote the delegation's final report titled: "BUCHENWALD CAMP – The Report of a Parliamentary Delegation." The delegation members approved, and Lord Stanhope presented the report to His Majesty's Government six days after the delegation witnessed the atrocities of Buchenwald.

Driberg wrote, "Our objective was to 'find out the truth,' while the evidence was still fresh." He concluded the delegation's report, "Such camps as this mark the lowest point of degradation to which humanity has yet descended. The memory of what we saw at Buchenwald will haunt us ineffaceably for many years."

—

Wednesday, 25.April.1945
USAAF Station F-356
Saffron Walden, Essex, England
United Kingdom
16:10 hours

Brian had experienced a milk run mission or two in the last six years of his contribution to winning the war in Europe, but the day's RODEO mission had an entirely different feel to it. They literally ran out of targets in their assigned sector. None of them fired a shot as they roamed over their sector—no enemy aircraft, no vehicles, not even a train to shoot up.

They met the Red Air Force in the air over Eastern Germany. Fortunately, the coordination procedures they had briefed for every mission in the last three weeks worked as intended and expected. Neither group acted aggressively toward the other. They said hello in aviator fashion, and then the Reds peeled off heading east, while the 334FS headed west.

Brian tried several different tactics to see what they might be able to flush out. They continued to innovate and prowl, but nothing turned up before they reached their bingo fuel and took a beeline back to Debden to preclude a divert short to an auxiliary airfield for fuel. Brian had considered some precision formation flying just to change things up, but using the extra fuel for maneuvering was not worth a diversion.

The squadron landed safely by section. A captain from the Group staff waited with an Army photographer and three men in civilian clothes, with one also carrying a camera. *Journalists.* Brian was the first to shut down.

"How'd it go, Skipper?" asked Larson once the powerful Packard engine stopped.

Brian secured the Mustang. "Not a single shot fired by any of us. Just petrol, Larson. Bird's in great shape."

"We'll get her fed, fully checked, and put to bed."

"Thanks, Larson." As Brian unstrapped, he added, "What's going on with our guests?" He gestured with his left thumb over his left shoulder.

"Don't know, Sir. They didn't tell me, but they are waiting on you."

"I guess I should not keep them waiting."

Brian stepped out of his cockpit and jumped off. The captain stepped forward.

"Captain Simmons, Sir. I'm on the Group staff. I have orders from Colonel Clark to get some photographs of the squadron pilots in front of your Mustang."

"What's the occasion?"

"According to the colonel, that may be the squadron's last mission. He wants a historical record photograph of you and your pilots."

"You really should photograph the crew chiefs, armorers, and mechanics. Without them, the rest of us don't matter a twit."

"We'll get them too, Sir. But, we'll start with the pilots."

Brian nodded his head. He shouted commands for his pilots to gather for a photograph.

The Army photographer directed the repositioning of Brian's QP-G Mustang as the photographers checked the natural lighting.

Simmons said to Brian, "The Press wants to interview you, Major."

"Why?"

"Well, it could be you are one of the highest scoring fighter aces in this war, and you're highly decorated for that accomplishment."

"Nonsense."

"Major, Colonel Clark approved the interview."

Brian stared at the captain, did not speak, and only nodded.

The photographs were taken. When satisfied, the pilots were instructed to complete their intelligence debriefings and stand by. Captain Simmons asked Brian to remain for several additional solo photographs by his fighter aircraft, and Brian was insistent that Larson Tomlinson stand with him for the last few.

The two male journalists did not wait for permission or encouragement and pressed Brian with their questions.

"You are quite the hero, Major," stated the younger reporter.

"No, I am not," barked Brian, perhaps a little more harshly than he intended. "I am just a fellow who loves flying these magnificent machines," he added, gesturing to the Mustang, and patting the airplane like a prized racehorse.

"You are five times an ace, Major. Very few Americans have achieved that status. You've been decorated by King George and the U-S Army." Brian refused to react since no question had been asked. "To our knowledge, you have served in combat airplanes more than any other American—nearly six straight years." Again, no questions and no responses. "Why did you do it?"

"As I said before, I love to fly."

"But," the older reporter jumped in, "you could have flown back in the states training other pilots, flying transports, and any number of other flying jobs. Why stay in a combat post when you didn't have to?"

"I set out six years ago to defend freedom. We are not yet done with that task."

"You're reportedly a very wealthy man, Major. You don't have to take these risks, which makes us curious to inform our readers. Why? What drives you to fly these things?" he asked, pointing over Brian's shoulder at the fighter.

"You are unique, Major," joined in the younger reporter. "What about your wealth?"

Brian stiffened. "First, that is none of your business. I get paid the same as everyone else in the Army. Second, my private life is my business, not yours nor your readers. Third, I've answered the question. That's all you're going to get from me."

The older reporter nodded and asked, "Do you have a government contract for air transport services?"

"No comment."

"Come on, Major! You're a *bona fide* hero. You gotta give us more."

Brian stared at the man as expressionless as he could manage. "No, I'm not, and no, I don't. Now, if you will excuse me, I've got a squadron to run." Brian turned and brushed past the two reporters and sneered at Captain Simmons.

"Wait, Major. We've got more questions. We're not done."

"I am," Brian said as he rounded the wing. He heard unintelligible words between the three men, but he did not look back. Brian felt demonstrable anger with the reporters' questioning, but he refused to give them the satisfaction of the adverse reaction he felt.

As Brian passed the Ops Desk, Sergeant Ellison announced, "Colonel Clark on black, Sir."

Brian only grunted, went to his office, and closed the door. He inhaled and exhaled a deep, cleansing breath. "Drummond."

"Hey, Hunter, Arnie here. How was the mission?"

"In a word, worthless. We couldn't find even a marginal target, and not a single bullet was fired."

"Likely your last combat mission. We have no orders or pending orders from headquarters. The heavies are still sorting out what happens next. They expect the Germans to surrender any day now. They've already issued the warning order for the transfer to the Pacific." Clark paused. Brian listened. "How did the interview go?"

"Also worthless. They only want sensation."

"Thank you for doing it, Hunter. I know you don't like the attention or limelight, but you are among a very rare group of aviators, and the Press has a very genuine interest in telling your story. Anyway, once your guys have completed their mission debriefings, the squadron is released for the evening. No day passes yet. And everyone will be at muster in the morning. Have a good night. Say hello to Charlotte for me."

"Thanks, Boss. Will do."

—

Wednesday, 25.April.1945
Oval Office
The White House
Washington, District of Columbia
United States of America
10:30 hours

"Thank you for taking the time for us, Mister President," Stimson said as he and General Groves entered the president's official office. "It is my honor to introduce Major General Dick Groves. General Groves, the President of the United States."

"Pleasure to meet you, Mister President," Groves said as he accepted the president's proffered right hand.

Truman gestured to the facing couches. Stimson and Groves sat together on the matching couch opposite the president.

President Truman held the two-page preparatory memorandum from Secretary Stimson. "I appreciate the primer, Mister Secretary, but the opening sentence seems rather ominous." The president lifted the memorandum and read, "'Within four months, we shall in all probability have completed the most terrible weapon ever known in human history, one bomb of which could destroy a whole city.' And that was only the first sentence. Those words worked as you probably intended them . . . got my attention. So, pray tell me, what is this secret project of which I'm only hearing about today."

"Mister President, to be direct, President Roosevelt directed who would be read into the Manhattan Project and the PARAMOUNT T-S-S-C-I compartment. You are president now, and this project is now your project and at your discretion."

"Thank you, Mister Secretary. Given that preface, I suppose I should know what I am now responsible for. Lead on, Mister Secretary."

"Very well, Mister President. If he was here, I think President Roosevelt would agree that this development project began in August 1939, the 2nd to be precise, with a letter from renowned physicist Albert Einstein. Doctor Einstein warned the president that the Nazi regime was working on a fission explosive."

"Fission?"

"Nuclear physicists in Germany, Denmark, and England hypothesized that certain heavy atoms could be split with fast neutrons into smaller constituent atoms with the release of significant energy. Further, a calculated mass of heavy atoms, called a critical mass, would generate its own neutron flux that would very rapidly generate the energy release of millions of atoms in a spontaneous explosion."

"OK. I think I understand all that."

Stimson nodded. "As a consequence of the Einstein letter, President Roosevelt initiated a nuclear weapons development program within the National Defense Research Committee. Shortly after we entered the war, the president decided to transfer the development program to the War Department and my cabinet-level supervision. General Groves, who managed the construction of the Pentagon, took over direct leadership of the program. We formed the Manhattan District within the Army Corps of Engineers to be the cover for the development program. As a result, the program became known as the Manhattan Project. Any questions so far?"

"I don't know enough to have questions. Continue."

"With your permission . . ." The president nodded his consent. ". . . I will ask General Groves to give you the executive summary."

"Thank you, Mister Secretary. In the early days, Mister President, we had countless obstacles to overcome. While we had successful experiments to confirm the physics, we had to translate the physics into engineering and build a functional device. To boil down all the gory details, we settled on the decision for what we call the gun design. We have a high degree of confidence that it will work, but that design uses the 235 isotope of uranium. The uranium isotope is more stable but is fairly difficult to produce—quite slow and laborious. Plutonium 239 is easier to produce, but it is less stable. We abandoned the plutonium gun design in the summer of '43 because we could not get the plutonium to satisfy the stability requirements for the gun design to work as designed. Doctor Oppenheimer, the leader of our scientific and engineering team, developed an implosion design using a plutonium core. We can produce the core sphere with a stable density. Then, using conventional explosives, we uniformly compress the plutonium sphere from softball to tennis ball size beyond the critical mass threshold. The physics calculations suggest the plutonium implosion design will be more efficient as an explosive, and given the production rate of plutonium, we can produce more weapons much faster. The big 'but' here is that the physicists are less certain of the design with its critical components. The team performed a number of experiments and proved the compression of the explosive lenses, but we are not absolutely certain of the plutonium."

Stimson picked up the briefing. "I presented our case to President Roosevelt a month ago. We proposed a full-scale live test of the plutonium implosion design. The president approved the test, and we proceeded with planning. We selected the best site for the science experiment—a remote uninhabited valley of the Alamogordo Test Range in New Mexico. We are scheduled for a calibration test using a cube of 100 tons of plastic explosive."

"One hundred tons . . . two hundred thousand pounds. That sounds like a very big bomb," Truman interjected.

"Yes, it is, Mister President . . . to our knowledge, the largest detonation in history. The Calibration Test is intended to give our instrumentation array a known event, so we will measure exactly how that known event shows up on the instrumentation—pressure, temperature, shock, and such. The Calibration Test is on track to execute in two weeks."

"I see no problem with that," the president said. "Proceed."

"Thank you, Sir. The full-scale test unit . . . we call it Trinity . . ."

"As in the Holy Trinity?" asked Truman.

"The name was Doctor Oppenheimer's choice," Groves added. "He is a great fan of the spirituality in John Donne's poetry." Truman nodded his head. Groves looked at Stimson.

"The full-scale test is provisionally scheduled for two months after the Calibration Test. The test unit is an engineering device we call The Gadget, but the functional mechanism resembles an operational unit. The Trinity device will be hoisted up atop a 100-foot tower. The Trinity unit is calculated to yield the equivalent of nearly 20 kilotons of explosive force."

"Dear God above!"

"Yes . . . a very large explosive bomb."

"My understanding of the war's progress tells me Germany will surrender any day now. So, we shall vanquish Germany before this atomic weapon is proven, which means it will be potentially used on Japan."

"That is our assumption," Stimson responded. "The Target Committee meets the day after tomorrow. The uranium gun device, we call it Little Boy, is built and essentially ready to go. It will be assembled before it is loaded on the bomber. The pieces for the plutonium implosion weapon are nearing completion with the assumption that Trinity works. We've all called the first operational plutonium unit Fat Man, and we'll have the 2nd device a couple of weeks behind the 1st bomb. The 3rd and 4th plutonium units will be a month after that."

"A bomb like that could end the war entirely."

"That is our expectation."

"How soon?"

"Trinity is tentatively planned for early July with your approval. It will take the scientists a couple of weeks to analyze the Trinity results. Assuming the best, that would mean the earliest field use would be mid to late July. The delivery unit, General?" Stimson asked, looking at Groves.

"The 509th Composite Group was formed in the States. It is a nearly self-contained, independent B-29 heavy bomber unit. A handful of their bombers have been modified to carry both Little Boy and Fat Man weapons. They have been practicing with weighted shapes to rehearse the procedures, especially the safety procedures. The delivery group will begin deployment to Tinian to complete their preparations. They'll be ready before the weapons are."

"That is an awful lot to digest. I've been in this job for two weeks. I've gone from zero to a thousand miles an hour in a heartbeat. The ethics of this thing are weighing on me, and I need time to think."

"We fully understand, Mister President. This new explosive presents new and unique morality questions. The Manhattan Project team has nearly completed its original charge from President Roosevelt. You will have the tool, Mister President. Your ultimate decision will be to employ the tool when and where you see fit."

Truman stared at a spot between Stimson and Groves for several minutes. "I need time to think," the president repeated. "Secretary Stimson, please schedule a meeting for us next week with Miss Conway. I want to discuss the expected effects of this weapon. What do you expect the consequences will be for its use? My imagination suggests a bomb this powerful will kill a lot of innocent people."

Rose Conway had joined Vice President Truman's administrative staff in February, as his personal secretary. She moved into the West Wing along with President Truman when he became president by succession. President Roosevelt's personal secretary Grace Tully had been most gracious in assisting Rose assume the duties of personal secretary to the president.

Stimson started to speak but stopped. He nodded and then said, "I will do so. Thank you for your time, Mister President."

Stimson and Groves stood. Truman stared straight ahead. The secretary and the general departed to schedule the president's requested follow-up meeting.

—

Friday, 27.April.1945
Room 3D512
Pentagon Building
Arlington, Arlington County, Virginia
United States of America
08:40 hours

The interior, lower level, windowless, guarded conference room added a feel of secrecy to the meeting. The selected members assembled in the closed room. The members of the Manhattan Project Target Committee were:

-- Major General Dick Groves

-- Deputy Chief of Air Staff, Army Air Forces, Brigadier General Lauris Norstad, USAAF [USMA 1930]

-- Deputy Director, Manhattan Project, Brigadier General Thomas Francis Farrell, USA CEC

-- Dr. John von Neumann, PhD (Mathematics) [born Neumann János Lajos, a Hungarian Jew refugee, and naturalized U.S. Citizen}

-- Dr. Robert Rathbun Wilson, PhD (Physics)

-- Dr. William George Penney, PhD (Mathematics) [British Citizen]

-- Dr. Joyce Clennam Stearns, PhD (Physics)

-- Dr. David Mathias Dennison, PhD (Physics)

"OK, gentlemen. Let's get to work," Groves commanded. "So we are all on the same page in this important work, I will say the secretary and I met with President Truman two days ago. It was our initial briefing for the president. He is grappling with drinking from the fire hose. Until we get clear guidance from our new president, the secretary and I agreed to proceed as planned until or if we are told otherwise. Any questions?" Several members shook their heads. Others remained silent. Groves nodded his head several time in acknowledgment. "To the meat of it . . .

"We agreed at our pre-meeting to the broad conditions for target selection. We now have satisfied several of those conditions. One, both Little Boy and Fat Man had to fit within the modified bomb bay of the B-29. Two, the target had to be within the range of the B-29 with either device.

"We also agreed to the principal criteria for target selection. A valid target must be larger than three miles in diameter around ground zero and an important target to the Japanese. The geography of the target needed to be comparatively flat for the blast wave to create effective damage. And we need a fresh target, one that was unlikely to be attacked by August 1945. With that, Doctor Stearns over to you."

"Before we jump into Joyce's findings," said von Neumann in heavily Hungarian-accented English, "I would like to have a word."

"I don't see why not," responded Groves.

"In our preparatory discussions, several thoughts seemed to coalesce in our work. Beyond the physical properties of any potential target for the bomb, we agreed that psychological factors in the target selection were of great importance. For scientific purposes, precision is essential."

"So, daylight, visual bombing only," interjected General Norstad, "which in turn means the weather will be a significant factor in mission constraints."

"Is that a problem?" asked General Farrell.

"Nope . . . just another element of the decision matrix for the delivery crews."

Silence filled the room for several seconds. Von Neumann picked up his contribution. "Our target choices should achieve the greatest psychological effect against Japan, to end the war with the fewest number of these things as possible. The initial use must be sufficiently spectacular so that the importance of the weapon is recognizable internationally. We think the world must know so that the Japanese cannot deny the event."

"I think we can all agree to those . . . thoughts," commented Groves. He looked at each committee member. No one chose to add more. "Anything else?"

"No Sir."

Groves nodded to Stearns.

"With the help of Army and Navy Intelligence and the O-S-S, the geographic survey of a dozen plus potential targets was completed. The geographic survey became the baseline for our work. Several cities were eliminated straight away—Tokyo being the prime example.

"We then stepped through our criteria and narrowed down the potential targets on the Japanese Home Island to Hiroshima, Kobe, Kokura, Kyoto, Nagasaki, Nagoya, Osaka, Yawata, and Yokohama, and we a ready to discuss each target in detail."

The committee spent the day vigorously discussing target attributes and detractors. They took a break for lunch and avoided the topic they were engaged in. The afternoon brought their work together and into focus. The committee agreed to the summary of the day's work. General Groves thanked the committee and went to fetch the secretary for a debriefing. While they waited for Groves to return with Secretary Stimson, several men talked about the early standings in Major League Baseball.

When the secretary arrived, General Groves introduced him to each committee member. Stimson knew the military officers and a couple of the scientists.

"Thank you for joining us, Mister Secretary. The committee has completed its charge of identifying and prioritizing targets for employment of the Manhattan Project special weapons. Doctor Stearns has been selected to summarize the committee's findings and recommendations."

"Thank you, General. Mister Secretary, before I jump into the findings of today's deliberations, would you like me to review the criteria we utilized to assess our target selections?"

"No, thank you, not necessary. Proceed."

Stearns nodded. "The committee has spent most of the day reviewing the preliminary data and maps from various intelligence sources. We had spirited discussions at times, but we have unanimously agreed on the following findings in priority order.

"Our number one target is Kyoto—designated Able One. The former capital of Japan is in an ideal geographic setting and has attracted many people from Tokyo and other cities that have been hit hard by the 20th Air Force. Industries are now being moved there as other areas are being destroyed. From the psychological point of view, there is the advantage that Kyoto is an intellectual center for Japan, and the people there are more apt to appreciate the significance of such a weapon as The Gadget.

"With the selection of Kyoto, we excluded Osaka and Kobe since they are close enough to realize the effects from a Kyoto ground zero. The decider was the Navy's need for quality port facilities, which Osaka has, and they are mainly untouched by Air Force bombing. While Osaka will feel the blast effects, the city is far enough from Kyoto to avoid serious damage to the port facilities.

"Our number two target is Hiroshima, Able Two, and has the advantage of being of such a size and with the possible geographic focusing from nearby mountains that a substantial portion of the city may be outright destroyed. The city is the location of an important army depot, a regional home defense army headquarters, and a large urban industrial area. It is also an excellent radar target, should the need arise.

"Able Three is Kokura. The city has one of the largest arsenals in all of Japan and is surrounded by urban industrial structures. The arsenal is important for artillery, light ordnance, anti-aircraft, and beachhead defense materials. Our study of aerial reconnaissance photography indicates that if the bomb is properly placed above the arsenal, the higher pressures immediately underneath the bomb could offer additional blast effects for destroying the more solid structures at the arsenal and nearby buildings. Concomitantly, the amplified blast damage could successfully affect more feeble structures farther away.

"Nagasaki is Able Four on the primary list. The city is a major port in southern Kyushu and the site of the Mitsubishi Shipyard, which built two of Japan's largest battleships, *Yamato* and *Musashi*."

The IJN *Musashi* had been sunk on 24.October.1944 by U.S. Navy carrier aircraft during the Battle of Sibuyan Sea, part of the much larger Battle of Leyte Gulf. Her sister ship, *Yamato,* had been hit in the same battle but remained afloat and made it back to Japan for repairs. *Yamato* had been sunk on 7.April.1945, by U.S. Navy carrier aircraft as she sortied for a suicide run at the Fifth Fleet assembled off Okinawa.

Stearns continued, "Nagasaki also had the largest torpedo production factory in Japan, as well as numerous other armaments factories. A significant detractor is a large prisoner-of-war camp on the outskirts of the city.

"Last on the primary list is Niigata, the port on the northwest coast of Honshu. Its importance is increasing as other ports are damaged. Machine tool industries are located there, and it is a potential center for additional industrial dispersion. In addition, Niigata has major oil refineries and substantial storage facilities.

"We pushed Yokohama to the alternate 'B' list due to its proximity to Tokyo. The city, Baker One, is an important urban industrial area that has so far been untouched, with Tokyo taking most of the attention. Yokohama's industrial activities include aircraft manufacturing, machine tools, docks, electrical equipment, and oil refineries. The damage to Tokyo has forced other industries to move to other cities like Yokohama. The city has the disadvantage of the most important target areas being in the heaviest anti-aircraft network concentration in Japan. For us, it has the advantage of an alternative target for use in case of bad weather and being rather far removed from the other targets considered. Tokyo Bay makes radar bombing distinctive should it become necessary.

"Lastly, we moved Yawata from the primary list when we looked at the survey data for the same reason we removed Osaka and Kobe from the primary list—proximity to Kyoto. For the purposes of this meeting, we classified Yokohama as Baker One, Osaka as Baker Two, Nagoya as Baker Three, Yawata as Baker Four, and Kobe as Baker Five. If we need more than five events to end the war, we have sufficient data to activate the alternate list in short order and even a tertiary list if necessary."

Stimson stared at Doctor Stearns for a dozen seconds, and then he flashed a glance at Groves. Stimson looked each committee member in the eyes before he spoke. "Thank you very much, gentlemen. Excellent work. From what I know of Japan, it seems to me that you have captured the essential targeting factors. Therefore, I can accept this listing with one exception.

"I have been to Kyoto. As you noted, it is perhaps the spiritual and cultural center of Japan, the former capital. It is an elegant and gorgeous city, perhaps unique in the world. I cannot accept Kyoto on the target list . . . at least not at the outset."

"That should be no problem, Mister Secretary," responded Groves. "I can't imagine the Japanese standing against one or two of these weapons. We aim to end the war as quickly as possible, not obliterate Japan."

"Well said, General Groves. With the committee's consent, I shall present the target list to the president."

Groves looked at and pointed his right index finger at each committee member. One by one, each member nodded his head or spoke his concurrence. "We're unanimously agreed,"

Stimson nodded. "Thank you, gentlemen, for your excellent work. As soon as the president approves the target list, it will become our working baseline. As information changes, we can adjust the list. I expect the committee to review, consider, and recommend any changes. I'll notify the chairman once the president has approved the list."

"Thank you very much, Mister Secretary. We're standing ready to assist should there be any future questions. With your permission, Sir . . ." Stimson nodded. "We are adjourned."

Secretary Stimson and General Groves shook hands and thanked each committee member as they made their separate way out of the Pentagon maze.

—

Chapter 7

We have met the enemy,
and they are ours.

-- Commodore Oliver Hazard Perry, USN

Wednesday, 2.May.1945
Cabinet Room
No.10 Downing Street
Whitehall, London, England
United Kingdom
16:15 hours

The War Cabinet and the Defense Committee had assembled in toto and were seated on both sides of the large, green felt covered, U-shaped conference table. Several members stood as the Prime Minister entered the room. Some clapped until Churchill held up his left hand for quiet.

"Let us not be premature in this matter," Churchill announced.

"We all heard the broadcast last night," said Greenwood.

"As did I . . . interrupted a late dinner, I must say. While Hitler's death is a positive sign, the war in Europe is not done until we have the signatures of the bloody bastards on the surrender document. And, speaking of that, what do we know from the front?"

Secretary of State for War Sir Percy James 'P.J.' Grigg leaned forward. "The Red Army broadcast that they have secured Berlin. We know from the intelligence that they are not quite secure. They are continuing with mopping up operations, dealing with pockets of S-S and Hitler Youth. The Red Army controls the whole of the city – all districts. Gestures of surrender are coming from all quarters. Field Marshal Montgomery and the other Army Group commanders have their instructions. They have authority to accept the surrender of German forces in their area of operations – not beyond that."

"That is what was agreed to with the supreme commander," added Churchill.

"Yes Sir. German armed forces resistance has ceased. Local army and air force units are surrendering to local commanders. A colonel from the staff of Army Group B confirmed the suicide of Field Marshal Model on the 21st. He dissolved the command on his death. The German colonel stated they were without guidance or leadership. To put it quite bluntly, they do not know what to do or how to surrender. Monty expects a representative from the German High Command, but the man has not presented himself yet."

"Thank you, P-J. But, Anthony, first, welcome back," Churchill said.

Foreign Minister Eden leaned forward. "Thank you, Prime Minister. Under Secretary Hall relieved me after we got the United Nations Conference on International Organization kicked off. The draft charter is in good shape.

"It is important to report that M-I-6 has confirmation from multiple independent sources that the broadcast message last night is genuine and accurate. Hitler and his mistress Braun were married in some macabre private ceremony and then committed suicide, we have from alternative sources. Goebbels killed all six of his children before he and his wife committed suicide as well."

"Macabre is an understated word for the despicable obscenity of these Nawzee killers."

"Yes, without debate. From that broadcast, Admiral Dönitz was apparently designated by Hitler himself to be his successor, after the dictator excommunicated Göring and Himmler for their efforts to supersede him or seek peace terms. The Soviets have not reported on the location of Bormann, who would be the other Nazi leader of interest. The National Socialist apparatus is rapidly disintegrating. With perhaps the exception of *S-S-Obergruppenführer* Karl Wolff, representing the German forces in Northern Italy, we should focus on the armed forces to execute the unconditional surrender."

Prime Minister Churchill looked at each man present. "I think we are in unanimous agreement with that recommendation."

"The end is here," Eden stated. "It is just a matter of executing the instruments of surrender and laying in place the administration of the occupied zones."

"We need a Big Three conference once the initial surrender process is completed. Can we organize it for next month or July at the latest?"

"We will start to get things organized," answered Eden.

"Let's get the surrender business concluded as quickly as possible, so we can publicly celebrate the war's end in Europe. We still have to finish off Japan before this repulsive war is done."

"Winston," Attlee said. All eyes turned to the Deputy Prime Minister, "I have another matter . . ." He stopped and stared at Churchill's eyes, clearly consumed by his thoughts. "Never mind. It can wait . . . until the peace is concluded."

Churchill nodded, not wanting to press the matter on Attlee's mind. "Let's get this done. We are adjourned."

—

Thursday, 3.May.1945
Oval Office
The White House
Washington, District of Columbia
United States of America
15:30 hours

Events in Europe were moving quickly. The instructions to General Eisenhower were clear, concise, and precise. The German capitulation was close. Their leader and several of his henchmen were dead. Others had fled.

This meeting was about Japan. Secretary of State Stettinius and OSS Director Donovan arrived together. President Truman was still grappling with the question of whether to employ the new Manhattan Project bomb. He asked for the Japanese government's status, given Germany's impending surrender. Stettinius and Donovan brought their assessments.

"So, to my question, gentlemen," the president said.

"As you know, Mister President," Stettinius began, "General Tojo resigned as premier and war minister after the fall of Saipan and the Marianas last summer. Nevertheless, he exercises considerable influence through loyal officers and public service personnel. Kuniaki Koiso replaced Tojo and attempted to reform the military's command structure to eliminate the corrosive rivalry between the Army and Navy. Baron Kantarō Suzuki replaced him a month ago. We know the Suzuki government has made discreet low-level diplomatic overtures to the Soviet Union." Stettinius looked at Donovan and nodded to pick up the briefing.

"We have information, some corroborated and some not yet verified, that confirmed the secretary's information and assessment by separate independent means. From our perspective, the Japanese do not see the Russians as adversaries . . . yet. We suspect they are aware of our efforts to redirect the Red Army to the east. We think they are looking for a negotiated peace."

Truman considered the words of his diplomatic and intelligence chiefs. "I do believe President Roosevelt and Prime Minister Churchill were very clear and exact. After what the Axis powers have inflicted upon our precious planet and so many innocent people, there would be no negotiated peace. They can't just say, oops, sorry, let's just forget that last few years. Ain't gonna happen, as we say in Missouri." Truman thought for a moment. He looked at Stettinius. "Have the Soviets contacted us, or the British, on behalf of the Japanese?"

"No. Not yet."

"Then, all we have are some hints. Men are still dying on Okinawa. We are not going to wait on the Japanese. Nonetheless, keep an eye on the Japanese government as best you can. They will surrender unconditionally and submit to Allied governance. We will vanquish the Japanese as we have done with the Germans and Italians. The Japanese did not consult us before starting the war. We are not going to consult them on the peace."

"Very well, Mister President," Stettinius responded.

"We'll keep an eye on things," added Donovan.

"Thank you both. We must end this nasty business as soon as possible but on our terms. Now, Ed, if you will excuse me, I need a private word with Bill."

"Of course, Mister President. Thank you for your time." The secretary of State stood and left the Oval Office, closing the door behind him.

Truman cleared his throat and smiled at Donovan. "I finally got to your proposal. I read it carefully several times. I will tell you upfront that I am not too keen on spies or spying, but your proposal leaves me with the impression that it is an abbreviated version, like shorthand between you and President Roosevelt. So, let's start this discussion with the rest of the story."

Donovan nodded. "Yes Sir, I suppose it was. The proposal was written for President Roosevelt. He knew the history. And, I understood what he was looking for." The president started to speak but stopped and gestured impatiently for Donovan to continue. "The genesis of the O-S-S dates back to 1935 when President Roosevelt asked me to keep my eyes open during my international travels. I had a number of private conversations with the president over those pre-war years. Our exchanges remained low-key, private, and conversational. When the Germans annexed Austria and Sudeten Czechoslovakia, the president began to sense the inevitability of war in Europe and wanted to know what to expect. That was not an easy task. I was a one-man band, and I was trying to run my law practice. I did the best I could, given the constraints. Our agreement changed dramatically when the Germans invaded the Low Countries and France. He sent me on a personal mission for him to one, assess the capacity of Great Britain to withstand the inevitable German attack and two, to learn as much as I could about a national-level intelligence agency. President Roosevelt thought M-I-6 was a worthy model. His relationship with Prime Minister Churchill was essential to that endeavor. From that mission, the president asked me to construct a presidential strategic intelligence organization. The project simmered until the Germans invaded Russia. The surprise of the German onslaught, especially after the pre-war non-aggression pact between them, induced some rapid changes. President Roosevelt created the Coordinator Of Information, C-O-I organization, by executive order. After Pearl Harbor and the Washington ARCADIA Conference, President Roosevelt decided to significantly expand the charter of C-O-I, changed the name to O-S-S, Office of Strategic Services, and moved the organization to the War Department. We have been operating successfully under those changes since the summer of '42. I can summarize our wartime missions."

"That is not necessary, General. I'm certain I'd learn a lot, but I think I know enough for this purpose. It would've been much better for me in my current position if the president had shared the decisions he made. There are far too many of these surprises, but the Constitution does not give me a transition period."

President Truman lapsed into thought for several minutes. Then, when he was ready to speak, he looked at Donovan and continued, "I have read enough reports to have a pretty good feel for the successes of the O-S-S under your leadership, General. I respect the Medal of Honor you hold. I also know enough not to switch horses in the middle of the stream. We will see this to the end . . . together."

"Thank you, Mister President."

"That said, and to be blunt, I do not see a place for such a wartime agency as the O-S-S in the post-war period. This will be a different peace. I fully support the new United Nations, which we remain on track to sign next month in San Francisco. I believe it will be a new peace."

"I know that is the hope and the expectation, Mister President, but from the indicators we have, Marshal Stalin has a far different view of the post-war peace."

"That may well be, General, but that is not the view of things I have. The Soviet Union will be a signatory to the United Nations Charter, as we will be and the other Allies."

"That may well be, Mister President. The Soviets will likely show us what they intend soon enough. May I ask what it is about the current O-S-S and our proposed central intelligence service that does not suit your vision of the intelligence services needed by the Office of the President?"

"I will answer your question succinctly. The O-S-S is an important part of the war effort. The war is going to end eventually. Without a war, there is no need for the O-S-S or any successor service."

Donovan nodded his head. "I serve, we serve, at your pleasure, Mister President. Can we make changes to suit your vision and intelligence needs better?"

Truman chuckled softly. "No, General. I don't see the need. I will wait until the war is concluded before I rescind the original order and issue an order to terminate the O-S-S."

Donovan stared at Truman. "Very well, Sir. I'll prepare to liquidate the service upon your order."

"Thank you, General. That will be all."

Donovan stood, nodded his head, and departed the Oval Office

———

Friday, 4.May.1945
Headquarters, 21ˢᵗ Army Group
Lüneburg Heath, Lower Saxony
Liberated Germany
18:30 hours

The gestures of surrender, or at least peace, had been arriving at numerous locations at a rapidly increasing frequency. The signs that the end of the war in Europe was in sight became apparent in the aftermath of the very serious assassination attempt on Hitler's life and the following *coup d'état* attempted out last year by dissident elements of the armed forces. The failure of the desperate German Ardennes offensive five months ago, along with the death-knell convulsion of the German Air Force at the turn of the New Year, sealed the military fate of Germany. Even the staunch Nazi, heir apparent and Hitler's executioner *Reichsführer-SS* Heinrich Luitpold Himmler made his first outreach for capitulation negotiations in February with Count Folke Bernadotte, leader of the Swedish Red Cross, at Hohenlychen Sanatorium in Lychen, Brandenburg, Germany. The Red Army entered the outskirts of Berlin last month and now controlled the fallen German capital. Newly appointed *Reichspräsident Großadmiral* Karl Dönitz broadcast to the world Hitler's death. The Third Reich was finished. German military resistance ceased; however, pockets of fanatical *Schutzstaffel* and *Waffen-SS* units persisted in their hopeless fighting. The first formal effort toward unconditional surrender came yesterday in the form of a delegation sent by Dönitz and led by the newly appointed, Dönitz successor as Navy commander, *Generaladmiral* Hans-Georg von Friedeburg.

The Germans had offered the unconditional surrender of all German forces yesterday. Field Marshal Montgomery had refused, informing the delegation that he could only accept the surrender of German troops in his area of operations, and further that German forces in the east should surrender to the Russians. Friedeburg had indicated he did not have that authority and had to seek guidance. He had stated they expected to return the next day.

The notice of approach arrived two hours ago. Admiral Friedeburg appeared at Montgomery's command tent shortly before six in the evening. With the admiral were: *General der Infanterie* Eberhard Kinzel – chief of staff of the northwest German Army, and *Konteradmiral* Gerhard Wagner – chief of operations for the German Navy, along with two staff officers.

"Do you have your instructions?" asked Montgomery directly and tersely.

"Yes," Friedeburg answered in English. "We are present to surrender the Navy and the northern armies."

"And, what of the remainder of German forces?"

Friedeburg reverted to his native German, which was translated for the gathering. "We have complied with your instructions of yesterday. We have the authority of the president to surrender the northern forces. It is my understanding from the president that arrangements are underway to surrender all German forces to the supreme commander as soon as the appropriate coordination can be completed."

"Very well." Montgomery glanced down at the single sheet of paper on the table in front of him. He turned the paper and pushed it to Admiral Friedeburg, who was seated to his right at the small square table in the center of the large general-purpose tent. "This is the instrument of your surrender."

Friedeburg read the paper and checked with his translator several times to ensure he understood what he was asked to sign.

---

1. The German Command agrees to the surrender of all German armed forces in HOLLAND, in northwest GERMANY including the FRISIAN ISLANDS and HELIGOLAND and all other islands, and in SCHLESWIG-HOLSTEIN and in DENMARK, to the C-in-C, 21 Army Group. This is to include all naval ships in the areas. These forces are to lay down their arms and to surrender unconditionally.
2. All hostilities on land, on sea, or in the air by German forces in the above areas to cease at 0800hrs. British Double Summer Time on Saturday 5 May 1945.
3. The German command to carry out at once, and without argument or comment, all further orders that will be issued by the Allied Powers on any subject.
4. Disobedience of orders, or failure to comply with them, will be regarded as a breach of these surrender terms and will be dealt with by the Allied Powers in accordance with the accepted laws and usages of war.
5. This instrument of surrender is independent of, without prejudice to, and will be superseded by any general instrument of surrender imposed by or on behalf of the Allied Powers and applicable to Germany and the German armed forces as a whole.
6. This instrument of surrender is written in English and in German. English version is the authentic text.
7. The decision of the Allied Powers will be final if any doubt or dispute arises as to the

meaning or interpretation of the surrender
terms.

Admiral Friedeburg looked directly to Field Marshal Montgomery and nodded his head. He picked up the fountain pen placed before him and signed the document. The German unconditional surrender process had begun. There would be more to follow before it was completely done.

Thursday, 3.May.1945
Oval Office
The White House
Washington, District of Columbia
United States of America
17:45 hours

"Thank you for making time for me, Mister President," Bill Donovan said as he entered the Oval Office and walked to the president's desk. "We just received this ULTRA, and I wanted to bring it over myself." Donovan extracted the single pink paper with bold red border stripes. He handed it to the president and stood beside the desk.

TOP SECRET - ULTRA

```
TOP SECRET ULTRA
SECRET
DATE 0417 03 MAY 1945
TO EMB TOKYO
FROM FO
BREAK
YOU ARE DIRECTED TO INFORM JAPAN GOV THE
LEADER IS DEAD BREAK GERMAN GOV TO SURRENDER
UNCONDITIONALLY WITHIN HOURS BREAK SUBMARINE
WITH SPECIAL CARGO DEPARTED 25 MARCH 1945 IN
ROUTE BREAK GOOD LUCK END
SECRET
DECYPHERED 0837 03 MAY 1945
TOP SECRET ULTRA
```

MOST SECRET - ULTRA

"So, surrender is imminent," Truman stated.

"Yes Sir. It appears so. We have verified that the supreme commander has the information."

"Good. He has his instructions and the agreed wording of the surrender instrument." Truman reread the ULTRA message. "What is this special cargo they mention?"

"We do not have the submarine's identity or the special cargo. The best we have is unverified rumors or gossip that various crates were loaded in Kiel prior to the vessel's departure. We believe whatever it is must be very valuable and important for the Germans to go to this level of effort with a vital asset."

"I assume we are looking for this sub?"

"Yes Sir. We have conferred with M-I-6 and D-N-I at Admiralty this afternoon. Both the Royal Navy and our Navy have been informed. Orders were issued to all naval forces in the Atlantic. M-I-6 and O-S-S have cued up our agents at all usual and likely ports on both sides of the Atlantic to look for support ships. The submarine is not likely to refuel and replenishment in any port, no matter how friendly to them but rather at sea from a supply ship. We're doing everything we can to find that boat and neutralize it"

"The Atlantic . . . not the Pacific?"

"Given the U-boat's departure from Kiel, the boat is still in the Atlantic, although the Pacific Fleet has been alerted as well. The sub will likely take the Cape of Good Hope and Indian Ocean route to reach refueling sites in Argentina and Southeast Asia before making her run to Japan."

"Well beyond me. I shall trust the Navy." Truman looked back to the message and then at Donovan. "If I read this correctly, did it take just four hours to decipher this message?"

"The time zones are not included, so a little bit of additional knowledge is required to answer your question. Great Britain, actually G-C-&-C-S Bletchley Park, remains on double summertime, which is two hours ahead of normal time. Berlin did not change the clock time. Thus, London is one hour ahead of Berlin on the clock, which means it took three hours to decipher the message."

"Amazing." Truman's expression instantly went cold. "Anything else, General?"

"No Sir." Donovan secured the ULTRA decrypt. "By your leave, Sir, good day." Truman nodded. Donovan departed and closed the door behind him.

German submarine U-234 departed Kiel, Germany on 25.March.1945, under the command of *Kapitänleutnant* Johann-Heinrich Fehler. The undersea boat was a Type XB mine-laying submarine equipped with a snorkel and new radar warning devices. After hearing fragments of British and American radio broadcasts announcing the German surrender and finally receiving Admiral Donitz's order to surrender, the captain decided to comply rather than complete his assigned mission. On 14.May.1945, Fehler surfaced off Cape Cod and surrendered the boat, her crew, passengers, and cargo to the USS *Sutton*.

Inside the mine silos, the submarine carried engineering drawings and samples of a new electric torpedo, a crated Me262 jet aircraft, a Henschel Hs293 glide bomb, and lead containers filled with 550 kilograms of uranium oxide, also known as yellow cake, refined but not fully refined uranium (^{238}U). More importantly, substantial captured documentation gave the Western Allies invaluable insight regarding numerous advanced research and development programs, including the German atomic weapons effort.

Several passengers were aboard U-234 as well. The senior officer, *General der Flieger* Ulrich Otto Eduard Kessler, was en route to his new posting as Chief of the *Luftwaffe*-Liaison-Staff Tokyo and Air-Attaché at the German Embassy in Tokyo. Three other specialists traveled with the general to aid the Japanese with the materials the Germans were providing.

Two Imperial Japanese Navy lieutenant commanders accompanied the treasure trove of German technology—*Kaigun-shōsa* Hideo Tomonaga and *Kaigun-shōsa* Shoji Genzo. However, both lieutenant commanders chose suicide rather than submit to capture.

—

Monday, 7.May.1945
Forward Supreme Headquarters, Allied Expeditionary Force
Collège Moderne et Technique de Reims
12 Rue Lesage
Reims, Grand Est
Liberated France
02:41 hours

After the partial surrender to Field Marshal Montgomery a little over two days ago, numerous lower-level conferences had been held with various German delegations to conclude the full, complete and final unconditional surrender of Germany to the Allied powers.

When General Eisenhower had been notified who would represent the remnants of the German State for the surrender ceremony, he decided immediately and unilaterally that he would not attend. Admiral Dönitz had assigned Generaloberst Alfred Josef Ferdinand Jodl, Chief of Operations Staff, German Armed Forces High Command. With General Jodl were Admiral Friedeburg, and the general's aide and translator Major Wilhelm Oxenius.

Eisenhower felt it was inappropriate for him to accept the surrender from a junior officer. The Supreme Commander had selected Chief of Staff, Supreme Headquarters, Allied Expeditionary Force, General 'Beetle' Smith to represent SHAEF and the Allied powers. Chief of the Soviet Liaison Mission to SHAEF Major General Ivan Alexeyevich Susloparov would sign for the Red Army, and Chief of Staff of the French Forces of the Interior *Général de division* François Sevez would witness the surrender document on behalf of the Free French Army.

General Smith and the allies sat across the large, rectangular, conference table from the Germans and opened the proceeding by addressing General Jodl, "Are you prepared to sign the Act of Military Surrender for the German government?"

"Yes," Jodl answered in German.

Smith nodded and a staff officer placed the document in front of Jodl. The blank variables were written in ink. Oxenius read the English document in German to Jodl.

ACT OF MILITARY SURRENDER

1. We the undersigned, acting by authority of the German High Command, hereby surrender unconditionally to the Supreme Commander, Allied Expeditionary Forces and simultaneously to the Soviet High Command all forces on land, sea and in the air who are at this date under German control.

2. The German High Command will at once issue orders to all German military, naval and air authorities and to all forces under German control to cease active operations at 2301 hours Central European time on 8 May and to remain in the positions occupied at that time. No ship, vessel, or aircraft is to be scuttled, or any damage done to their hull, machinery or equipment.

3. The German High Command will at once issue to the appropriate commander, and ensure the carrying out of any further orders issued by the Supreme Commander, Allied Expeditionary Force and by the Soviet High Command.

4. This act of military surrender is without prejudice to, and will be superseded by any

general instrument of surrender imposed by, or
on behalf of the United Nations and applicable
to GERMANY and the German armed forces as a
whole.

5. In the event of the German High Command
or any of the forces under their control
failing to act in accordance with this Act
of Surrender, the Supreme Commander, Allied
Expeditionary Force and the Soviet High Command
will take such punitive or other action as they
deem appropriate.

Signed at *Rheims at 0241* on the *7th* day of May,
1945.   *France*

On behalf of the German High Command.
JODL

IN THE PRESENCE OF
On behalf of the Supreme Commander, Allied
Expeditionary Force, W.B. SMITH
On behalf of the Soviet High Command,
SUSLOPAROV
F SEVEZ, Major General, French Army (Witness)

General Jodl nodded his acknowledgment of the reading, and without
further hesitation, signed the document. The document was retrieved and taken
to the far side of the table. The Allies signed the document at the appropriate
places.

With consent nods from his colleagues, Smith looked back to Jodl.
"These proceedings are concluded," Smith announced. "In accordance with
paragraph two of the Act of Military Surrender, you are directed to return to
your headquarters by the most direct and expeditious means and to remain
there until proper Allied authority directs you otherwise."

Jodl bowed to recognize his orders. The three Germans turned and
departed.

The war in Europe was officially concluded. Now, the Allies faced the
aftermath of the most devastating war in human history, tending to the peace,
and managing the sustainment and reconstruction of a prostrate nation.

"'Ike' would like to see us in his office," General Smith said.

The officers who attended the brief surrender ceremony followed General
Smith upstairs and assembled in General Eisenhower's spacious office. 'Ike'

smiled broadly, like the enormous burden of the war had instantly been lifted from his shoulders, as congratulations flowed freely. Chilled champagne also flowed freely, with corks popping for nearly an hour. The euphoria lasted until the lightening shades of morning twilight illuminated the eastern horizon.

General of the Army Dwight Eisenhower chose to let his staff enjoy the brief moment of celebration without the dampener of refocusing their attention on the redeployment of a large portion of the Allied Expeditionary Force to the Pacific Theater. Operation DOWNFALL had been in the planning stages for many months – the invasion of the Japanese Home Islands. He was all too aware of the bloody slog that the 10th Army remained mortally embroiled in on Okinawa with Operation ICEBERG. Okinawa and Iwo Jima before it gave the Allies a bitter foretaste of what they faced with DOWNFALL. While much of his thinking had turned to the Pacific, Eisenhower also knew they had to set a strong foundation for the occupation forces in Germany. While they celebrated the war's end in Europe, the war was not over.

—

Monday, 7.May.1945
Trinity Test Site Control Bunker S-10000
Alamogordo Bombing and Gunnery Range
La Jornada del Muerto
Socorro County, New Mexico
United States of America
04:00 hours

Manhattan Project Director Major General Groves could barely contain his frustration and irritation. The calibration test shot had been scheduled for this day and this time for several months, and yet, here he was with his chief scientist and Director, Los Alamos Laboratory Julius Robert 'Oppy' Oppenheimer, PhD, delayed because the airborne observation aircraft was not in position.

All 108 tons of military-grade, Composition B, high explosive had been tightly stacked into a 20-foot cube on top of a 20-foot, heavy-duty, wooden platform located 800 yards south-southeast of a 100-foot steel trellis tower intended for use in a full-scale 'Gadget' device test planned for two months hence. A special liquid radioactive trace material had been pumped into an embedded grid of pipes within the pile of wooden boxes. All the test setup and preparations had been carefully thought out to test the elaborate sensor array.

The Control Bunker had been built 10,000 yards virtually due south of the Trinity test tower – 5.7 miles – thus, the S-10000 designation for the control station. There were two similar bunkers north and west of the test tower to manage the vast array of instrumentation scattered across the valley floor and the logistics supporting the intended full-scale test and its aftermath. There were also two planned observation sites prepared for the actual full-scale test – one at 10 miles for most of the Los Alamos scientific and engineering team and the main observation site at 20 miles from ground zero on Compañía Hill for dignitaries and the project brain trust. Only the photographers and two test support personnel occupied the observation sites this morning.

"The observation aircraft had a mechanical problem," Dick told Oppy after hanging up the telephone. "You would think they could have told us."

The Army Air Forces B-29 heavy bomber would serve as the airborne observation platform for both the calibration and full-scale tests. On board, like at the ground observation sites, special motion picture and still film photographers, as well as several witnesses from the scientific team, would observe and record the scheduled event of the morning.

"The aircraft is in the air and should report in position in 10 minutes," Groves added.

"OK," Oppenheimer acknowledged. Then, the chief scientist turned to his test director. "Let's get back on the test card," he commanded.

"Yes Sir," the test director responded. The man returned to the bound test procedures book. He flipped two switches, checked the large wall clock, and turned to an assistant. "Fire the green flare."

Groves and Oppenheimer looked out the thick reinforced window to see a green flare arc through the dark, pre-dawn sky. The signal meant all test personnel and observers should take cover, don their protective goggles and assume their assigned positions.

The test director continued to step through the established procedures they would use for this test and the full-up version. Everything, including the firing circuits, would be precisely the same for both tests – a dress rehearsal all the way around.

All stations reported their readiness to proceed. All of the lights on the control panel were green except for two that remained red. The director looked to Oppenheimer, who nodded his consent to proceed. The director flipped the next to the last switch, arming the firing circuits.

"Twenty seconds to firing," he broadcasted to the entire system. Loudspeakers at each site announced the broadcast. "The automatic firing sequence has been activated."

They watched the secondhand tick down and then looked through the window to ground zero.

04:37 hours

The bright orange fireball briefly and silently illuminated the desert landscape. The fireball ascended into the night sky as it dissipated. In a matter of seconds, the darkness returned. The shock wave from the massive explosion reached them 27 seconds after the fireball bloomed before them and shook everything shakable.

"That looked like a success," reflected Groves.

"It appears so," Oppy answered with solemnity. "It will take us a few days to a week to analyze the data, but that should give us a good metric for a point one kiloton explosion and the dispersal of radiation byproducts. As we discussed, I expect to have the review meeting in two weeks."

"Well done."

"I must admit, General, I was against this test as an unnecessary distraction. However, I suspect this calibration test may well provide essential data for us to assess the full-scale test in July."

"That is the expectation."

"We shall know in a few days . . . after we've analyzed the data."

"Again, well done, Oppy. A great start to the day and week, I must say."

—

Monday, 7.May.1945
Oval Office
The White House
Washington, District of Columbia
United States of America
10:30 hours

"I understand we have good news," President Truman said in an effervescent voice as he stood from his desk and walked to the door.

"Yes, Mister President," announced Secretary of War Stimson.

Truman shook hands with each man – the service secretaries, the service chiefs, and the Secretary of State. "So, it is official."

"Yes Sir," answered General Marshall. "We received confirmation from General Eisenhower an hour ago." Marshall actually chuckled. "It seems they were having a bit of celebration early this morning. The Act of Military Surrender was signed this morning by General Jodl at 02:41, Central European Time, on behalf of President Dönitz."

"Well, hell, yes, they are entitled to a celebration. This is a momentous day." Truman gestured to the long couches. "Please, gentlemen, let's take a load off." Then, as the small assembly took their seats, President Truman asked, "Who took the surrender?"

"General Smith, Sir," answered Marshall.

"'Ike's Chief of Staff?"

"Yes Sir. Ike felt it inappropriate for him to take the surrender from a junior officer."

"Well, I'll be damned. Good for him."

"We do have one glitch to the euphoria," interjected Secretary of State Stettinius.

"Well, damn, Ed . . . always the wet blanket," Truman laughed. "What is this glitch, you say?"

"The Russians have protested the surrender signing in Reims as not being the definitive instrument of surrender."

"How so?"

"The Soviet Foreign Office, Molotov specifically from San Francisco no less, now claims General Susloparov was not authorized by Marshal Stalin or the Red Army High Command to sign the Reims document on their behalf."

"Well, that did not take long. I suppose it is wrong of me to expect they could have done that coordination before the morning ceremony."

"To be candid and direct, Mister President, the coordination was done. Yesterday afternoon, the Foreign Office designated Susloparov as the signatory for the Soviet government. However, it appears Stalin wanted better, more complimentary symbolism. He insisted the definitive surrender could only be accomplished in Berlin – the fallen German capital."

"Which the Red Army now holds. He wants us to come to him."

"To put a sharp point on it, that is precisely how we see it."

"So, are we going to do anything, and if so, what are we going to do for this so-called 'definitive document'?" asked Truman.

"That is being worked out with London, Moscow, and SHAEF, as we speak. We anticipate another signing ceremony in Berlin tomorrow afternoon or evening . . . probably at the headquarters building of the Soviet Military Administration in Germany . . . a former high command officer's mess hall, from what I am told. Also, I must say, Stalin is insisting that no official statement be made until after the definitive document signing and that the announcement should be simultaneous in all three capitals. Churchill is livid. The British people have filled every available space in Whitehall, expecting the official announcement."

"And, rightly so," Truman added.

"Yes, well, Eisenhower and his staff are working feverishly to accommodate the Soviet sensitivities."

"Disgusting, if you ask me." Truman lapsed into contemplation for a few seconds, and no one bothered him. "Resistance to this foolish nonsense will detract from the public celebration everyone is entitled to after this accomplishment. Please keep me immediately informed of progress. Let's get this done, so we can let freedom ring."

"Yes Sir," Stettinius responded.

"We have more good news," added Stimson. Truman gestured impatiently for him to get on with it. "We received confirmation from General Groves two hours ago that the calibration test in New Mexico was near perfect. Of course, they have several days or weeks of data analysis to complete before they officially declare success, but apparently it was quite a spectacular explosion in the pre-dawn hours."

"What time?" Truman asked.

"It occurred at 4:37 this morning."

"Perhaps, General Groves can give us a thorough briefing once his team has reached their findings and conclusion. As I recall your briefing two weeks ago, this was the last milestone before the full-scale test."

"Yes Sir. That is correct," Stimson replied. "I will ask Groves to brief us on the details of the full-scale test when he delivers the calibration test results."

"Excellent. Please pass our congratulations to General Groves and his team. Now, what is the situation in the Pacific, and specifically on Okinawa?"

Secretary of the Navy Forrestal picked up the response. "The Japanese are staying true to form in their suicidal fanaticism. These damnable kamikaze attacks are tragic on an epic scale. Admiral King talked to Admiral Nimitz last night. Admiral, if you would . . ."

All eyes turned to the Chief of Naval Operations. "In short, Mister President, they are in one helluva fight. Admiral Turner, the amphibious task force commander, continues to report ground operations along the Shuri Line at the southern end of the island as desperate. Nearly all the Marine units have been redeployed from the north end of the island, which is now considered secure, to assist in the assault on the south. As we saw this fanaticism on Iwo Jima, the casualty rates are mind-numbing. As Secretary Forrestal indicated, the kamikaze threat remains quite serious. Admiral Turner has deployed Marine fighter squadrons to secure land-based airfields in order to maintain the fighter cover and close air support for the 10th Army, while he has shifted his carriers north in an effort to intercept the kamikazes before they reach the invasion support ships. The Army Corps of Engineers and Navy Seabees are working non-stop to improve the airfields for general-purpose air operations. Nonetheless, the 20th Air Force redeployed a heavy bomb group to the island and began bombing operations from Kadena Air Base on the 17th of last month against Mainland Japan and specifically the kamikaze air bases on Kyushu and Shikoku."

"This is nasty business," the president interjected.

"Yes," answered King, "I think this qualifies. I believe we are on your calendar for the 18th of next month to present the plans for Operation DOWNFALL – the invasion plan for the Japanese Home Islands."

"Do you believe the end is in sight on Okinawa, Admiral King?"

"The end is inevitable. The Japanese have no means of supply or support on the island. They will be ground down until resistance ceases. However, none of us would be so bold to predict that date."

"Well, then, it is not like we are looking for things to do." Everyone actually laughed. "That should be sufficient for now. I would like the Okinawa campaign to be concluded. The troops will need plenty of rest, replacement of losses, and refit, and we must move our European forces to the Pacific staging areas. Let us enjoy the moment of joy that the war in Europe is over. After all, the dirty, laborious slog to win the peace and rebuild Europe must begin in earnest quite soon. One more question, if I may." He paused, but no one replied. "Where is General Eisenhower on his redeployment of forces planning?"

General Marshall responded, "They have been working on those plans for several months now. Part of the redeployment plan depends upon our approval of the Operation DOWNFALL plan; however, barring any untoward surprises, he is preparing to move the 1st and 3rd Armies and the 8th Air Force from Europe as early as next month. I must tell you Prime Minister Churchill is none too happy about these plans."

"I know. I got an earful last week. He is quite worried about being left alone with the Red Army so close. Stalin's shenanigans of the last few months have heightened his concerns and mine, quite frankly. We have already notified the British and Russian governments of our intentions to cease Lend-Lease operations, so that we can refocus our efforts on Japan to end this whole sordid affair as quickly as possible and save lives. I shall carry the water for the team with our cousin Mister Churchill, as his concerns are largely political."

"Thank you for that, Mister President," Stimson interjected.

"Very well, then, I must move on. Thank you for your time, gentlemen. Please keep me informed on all these matters as we move forward to a just and lasting peace on our tired planet."

The men rose and departed, leaving President Truman alone with his thoughts. He had much to consider.

———

Monday, 7.May.1945
St. Regis Hotel, Suite 1906
2 East 55ᵗʰ Street
Manhattan, New York City, New York
United States of America
12:30 hours

OSS Director Donovan had scheduled the meeting in his retained New York City suite with a friend, colleague, fellow traveler, and Head of British Security Coordination (BSC), Sir William Samuel 'Intrepid' Stephenson, Kt, MC, DFC. The BSC has operated as an innocuous front organization for MI6 in New York City. Stephenson was often referred to as Little Bill for his shorter stature than Big Bill—Donovan.

The two men finished their served lunch and settled on the plush couch in front of the large window looking north across the majestic Central Park.

"Thank you for an exquisite lunch, Bill."

"You are most welcome and thank you for coming over here. I thought we should chat in private and more socially about what lays ahead for both of us. I have not discussed any of this with 'C,' D-N-I, or Lord Selborne, as yet. I shall trust you with the information and treat it accordingly." Stephenson nodded, and he remained stoic and contemplative. "President Truman has made it crystal clear that he does not support a central intelligence service as I proposed last fall to replace the O-S-S for the post-war world."

"Well, that is most unfortunate news, Bill. Needless to say, I think that is a tragic mistake. Winston was spot on correct 15 years ago when he sounded the clarion on Hitler's hegemonic intentions. The world has suffered an unimaginable horrific loss of human life as a consequence. He is not wrong about Stalin, Bill."

"That is my read as well, but I have been resoundingly incapable of helping the president realize that reality."

"Winston has not yet met with Truman. Perhaps he might be more successful in illuminating Stalin's intentions."

"Or, he might succumb to the Siren's Song as Roosevelt did. They want to believe him. But, it will be too late once he sees reality—Stalin is saying one thing and doing altogether another."

"Is there anything we can do to assist?"

"Not that I can see. From my brief interactions with the new president, Truman is a straight-up, no-nonsense, just-the-facts-ma'am, kind of guy. He has it in his mind that we fought this terrible war for a far more expansive and durable peace."

"I think we all wish that."

"Yes, precisely . . . except Joe Stalin. We believe he has a far different vision of what peace means to the Russians and the Soviet Union. I have a similar impression of Mao Zedong in China. Unfortunately, Chang is far too dismissive of Mao's organization. The demand for intelligence was intense during the war. I'm afraid it will be exponentially more intense once Stalin and Mao make their subsequent moves, and far more profusive and effusive than what we faced with focused adversaries."

"I can agree with that assessment."

"In that light, the president's rejection of a strategic central intelligence service seems quite like unilateral disarmament. The president has not pulled the trigger, so I suppose there is always hope until there isn't. He has given me a warning order to prepare for the liquidation of the O-S-S when the war is concluded. I will do so. We may not have the capacity to deal with the Soviet and Chinese actions after the peace treaty is signed. We were grossly ill-prepared for the war that came to us. I feel we are comparably ill-prepared to deal with the complexities of the peace that will come. We may have to recruit German intelligence officers who specialized in Russian operations."

"I suspect," Stephenson said with a pause, "you are aware that Hitler dismissed Gehlen last month."

Generalmajor Reinhard Gehlen had been the commander of Foreign Armies East [*Fremde Heere Ost* (FHO)]—the main German intelligence apparatus in the East operating against the Soviets.

"Yes."

"We must find the means to keep him and his officers out of the hands of the Red Army. They will not be kind to the Germans. The F-H-O was very effective against the Soviets. Hopefully, if we capture him and his officers, we can convince them to assist us."

"I'd hate to think we might have to turn over an asset like that to Army Intelligence. But these are the cards we are dealt. I will contact General Carney and at least get him primed to pick up the ball if we get lucky and turn F-H-O."

"The first step is finding Gehlen."

"Quite so."

"Well, even if O-S-S goes away, the B-S-C will not last much longer."

Both men laughed and abruptly stopped with a determined knock on the door. Donovan went to the door and slid the metal flap aside, opening the door's peephole. It was his aide. Bill opened the door. "Yes, George."

"We just got the news, and I know you would want to know immediately. The Germans have surrendered unconditionally. I called E Street, and Colonel Buxton confirmed the information."

"Hallelujah!" exclaimed Donovan. Stephenson came up behind Donovan. Bill turned his head and announced, "The Germans have surrendered."

"Hallelujah indeed!"

"Two down. One to go." Donovan went to the telephone and ordered up two bottles of the hotel's best champagne and three glasses. They had plenty of reasons to celebrate, and they did just that.

—

Monday, 7.May.1945
USAAF Station F-356
Saffron Walden, Essex, England
United Kingdom
18:10 hours

None of the 4th Fighter Group squadrons had even a single day pass. The pilots remained at their respective operations buildings playing cards, checkers, or chess, reading a book, and just dozing in the sunshine of a near cloudless sky.

Major Brian Drummond and the other Group commanding officers had spent the day at 8th Air Force Headquarters at High Wycombe. The sheer number of officers in the large hangar offered a marker of the scale of the European operations. These were just squadron commanding officers and above in just the 8th Air Force.

The gathering of commanders received a summary briefing from General Doolittle, who confirmed the unconditional surrender of German armed forces at SHAEF earlier in the morning. The general allowed the cheers and jubilation to go on for several minutes before he continued. He indicated he had approved a number of celebrational flights in June, and between now, and then they would stand down the squadrons for extended leaves in England to rest and enjoy the moment of victory. They broke up into smaller groups to review the plans for transfer to the Pacific and agree upon the actions of each unit. The general wanted them to understand and appreciate the complex logistics of what lay ahead.

Brian was the only commander to return to Debden Officer's Club. The others went their separate ways after debarking from the C-47 transport airplane returning the commanders to their bases. Only Brian made it to the O'Club Bar, where most of the Group pilots assembled before the evening meal was served in the Mess. He grabbed a pint of beer and went to his usual open seat in the corner of the back table. A few gulps had the desired effect—refreshing. Roughly half of the 334FS pilots took the other chairs. Others pulled up chairs or stood behind the seated pilots as if Brian was holding court.

"How'd it go, Skipper?" Sweet asked straight away.

"I'll brief the squadron tomorrow morning. First and foremost, General Doolittle confirmed Germany's unconditional surrender early this morning."

"Yeah!" "You betcha!" "Fuckin' A!" "Yea baby!" The various spontaneous shouted exclamations attracted other pilots to the audience.

When the assembly began to quiet, Corn asked, "What happens next?"

"None of us have received taskings from headquarters, but according to the general, some of us will participate in celebratory demonstration flights, and we'll all cycle through extended leave periods. A comparative few Fighter Command squadrons will be selected to remain in Europe and probably transfer to Germany or Eastern France."

"For what?" asked Sweet.

"Air defense for our ground forces that will remain for the administration of our sector of Germany."

"Air defense . . . against who?" Rolo asked.

"Unspecified, but I think that potential can be deduced."

"Just say it, Boss," Antler coaxed.

"Nope." Brian took another swallow of his beer. "The general also told us that fighting on and around Okinawa continues with no signs that the Japanese are going to surrender anytime soon. Thus, as we have been warned previously, we must prepare ourselves for transfer to the Pacific Theater to participate in the invasion of Japan's Home Islands. According to General Doolittle, the initial phase of the invasion operation is being planned for later this year."

"Where would we go?" Antler asked.

"Iwo Jima or Okinawa."

"Holy shit!" exclaimed Sweet. "They're still fightin' and dyin' on Okinawa, and Iwo is just a little speck in the vast Pacific."

"You said extended leave," interjected Rolo. "What does that mean?"

"We haven't been told yet, other than something more than a day pass. We will be restricted to England, well, Great Britain, but it will be more than a few days. So, if anyone wants to travel around and learn more about this great country, this will be the time. I'll ask each of you to keep the ops desk informed of where you are at, just in case we have a general or specific recall."

"And you're going home to Momma," Hole added with a loud laugh, inducing the others to laugh as well.

Brian took a few swallows of his beer and waited for the laughter and jabs to diminish. "Yep," which generated more laughter. "If any of you malcontents want to get your hands dirty and do some farm work, you're welcome to come down to the farm. We'll put you to work straight away."

"You said rest and relaxation, Skipper," responded Antler. "Not more work."

"Your choice. The offer is there. We've plenty to do, and you'll get fed well."

"When do we start?" Rolo asked.

Brian stared at Rolo for several seconds and then grinned. "When I get direction from Group. Until then, we remain on duty."

"But not flying," interjected Sweet.

"Nope. No taskings. Those machines are not our personal toys. We use them for the Army's business, and the Army has no business for us right now. So, we wait for instructions."

"How are we going to get to the Pacific?" Antler asked.

"I need another beer for that answer."

"I'll get it," offered a lieutenant from one of the other squadrons.

"Thanks," Brian said to the retreating backside of the lieutenant.

"What are you going to do when the war is done?" Corn asked Brian while they waited for a new beer.

Hunter smiled. "I don't know what's going to happen tomorrow, set aside when the war is done."

"Deal with what comes . . ." Sweet contributed.

"Exactly," said Brian.

"Here ya go, Major."

"Thanks, mate." Brian took a good swallow. "To the question on the table . . . We discussed several options, which depend upon numerous variables. I don't have time or intention to cover a day's worth of contingency planning. Thus, if y'all will allow me, our fighters and the pilots that fly them must get from here to there. The options cover going west through the States or East through the Suez Canal and Indian Ocean. Headquarters wants to give us a break regardless of the direction of our transport. The aircraft are going to get depot maintenance. We don't know who will fly the demos next month. We may or may not be selected. If we do not fly a demo, our aircraft will be partially disassembled and crated up as we did in the summer of '42."

"Summer of '42?" Antler protested. "I had just finished West Point and started flight training. So what the hell happened in '42?"

"Hunter and I," jumped in Sweet, "were still in 7-1 Squadron—the Eagle Squadron—and the Air Ministry decided to ship us off to Russia to help them fight off the Germans. A U-boat torpedo sank the ship carrying our Spitfires."

"No planes, no reason to go to Russia," Corn commented.

"Exactly," Sweet responded.

Antler looked at Hunter. "No U-boats. No torpedoes."

"That wasn't the point of Sweet's story," Brian answered. "First, the Japanese still have functional submarines and torpedoes that work, I do believe. Second, the crating of our aircraft is the point of the story. We don't have orders to box up the aircraft yet, and we don't have orders to travel west or east. We stay here until we're told to move."

"Got it, Boss," Antler said.

The dinner bell rang.

"Let's eat," commanded Sweet.

Brian decided to wait for most of the bar to clear as he finished his beer.

Corn, his steady wingman, remained with his leader. "I'm not too keen on going to the Pacific . . . too much water."

"Can't you swim?"

"Not very well. I've never been a water person."

Brian chuckled softly. Corn eventually joined Hunter. "We'll have to make sure you don't land in the water then, won't we." They both laughed harder. "Now, we'd better get a seat at the table if we expect to eat."

The pilots headed to the dining room and two adjacent seats. They were treated to an excellent steak dinner complete with baked potatoes with all the fixin's and assorted fresh vegetables, including green beans, Brussels sprouts, broccoli, and stripped corn. The dinner felt like the celebration it was.

After dinner, Brian felt the strong urge to call Charlotte. She answered the telephone in great spirits. She had heard the news as well. The day she had waited for six years had finally arrived . . . sort of. Brian did not feel like deflating her exuberance with the ill-defined potential of transfer to the Pacific Theater of Operations. Fellow pilots began to stack up outside the telephone booths, and Brian felt compelled to end the call and allow others to make their calls.

Brian next decided to do some reading and go to bed when he began nodding off. Two weeks ago, he had completed his reading of the English translation of Jules Verne's epic novel, *Around the World in Eighty Days (Le Tour du Monde en Quatre-vingts Jours)*. The book inspired him to read Verne's 1865 novel, *From the Earth to the Moon (De la Terre à la Lune)*—a fascinating story.

———

Tuesday, 8.May.1945
Sowjetische Militärverwaltung in Deutschland
    (SMAD, Soviet Military Administration in Germany)
Karlshorst (Karl's Nest)
Rheinsteinstraße 1
Lichtenberg, Berlin
Soviet Sector of Berlin and Occupied Germany
21:00 hours

The Soviet government had objected to the German surrender in Reims and labeled the action as preliminary or provisional since it did not include the Soviet government. Foreign Minister Molotov claimed Susloparov had no authority to sign an official document for the Soviet government, and the Soviet Union was not represented as an equal allied partner in the capitulation of Germany.

Major General Ivan Alexeyevich Susloparov had been posted as the Soviet Military Liaison to SHAEF at the liberation of Paris last year. General Eisenhower had provided the full text of the surrender document the day before. Susloparov had sent the text to Moscow for review and instruction. Unfortunately, no instructions had arrived by the time the surrender ceremony was to take place, and General Susloparov decided to sign the document.

During the ensuing frenetic communications between Reims, London, Washington, and Moscow, the Western Allies bowed to Soviet sensitivities and agreed to another capitulation ceremony in Berlin at the Soviet headquarters in Karlshorst, Berlin.

The various delegations began to arrive in the morning to finalize the official ceremony. They haggled over the wording for several hours. The delegates also debated whether to include the French, given the nation's checkered conduct during the war, but ultimately, the Big Three agreed, and the French took their place in the official German surrender. They also negotiated seating, arrangements of flags, and just about all the other details of the impending ceremony.

The so-called definitive instrument of surrender was exactly the same as what the Soviets called the provisional instrument of surrender except for an added 6th paragraph that stated, "This Act is drawn up in the English, Russian and German languages. The English and Russian are the only authentic texts." The resultant document would be the so-called definitive German capitulation instrument.

The various delegations, designated witnesses, observers, and the Press assemble in the large banquet hall of the headquarters. Satisfied that the necessary participants were present and ready, the ceremony's host—Marshal Zhukov—called the event to order.

22:43 hours

The authorized German representatives were escorted into the hall from a separate building. For the German government in Flensburg, a city in Schleswig-Holstein and only a couple of miles from the Danish border, the delegates were:
-- Field Marshal Wilhelm Bodewin Johann Gustav Keitel, Chief of the General Staff of the German Armed Forces (*Wehrmacht*) and representing the German Army,
-- *General-Admiral* Hans-Georg von Friedeburg, Commander-in-Chief of the German Navy,

-- Colonel-General Hans-Jürgen Stumpff, representing the German Air Force.

Marshal Zhukov looked directly at Keitel and asked in Russian, "Are you authorized to represent the German government in this matter?"

"Yes," answered Keitel in German.

"Are you prepared to sign the instrument of capitulation for the unconditional surrender of Germany?"

"Yes."

A different Allied aide for each language read the exact words of the document in Russian, then English, and lastly in German.

Zhukov asked, "Do you understand and accept the terms of unconditional surrender on behalf of the present German government?"

"Yes," answered Keitel.

"Sign the document," Zhukov commanded.

Each of the German delegates signed their name. Once complete, the document was passed to the Allied signatories. Marshal Georgy Konstantinovich Zhukov signed the document on behalf of the Supreme High Command of the Red Army and the Soviet Union. Air Chief Marshal Sir Arthur William Tedder, Deputy Supreme Commander of the Allied Expeditionary Force, represented the Supreme Commander, the United States of America, and the United Kingdom. General Carl Spaatz, Commanding General, United States Strategic Air Forces, and General Jean de Lattre de Tassigny, Commanding General, First French Army, signed the document as witnesses. After the signing of the surrender document, the Germans were dismissed to their detention, confinement, and eventual prosecution.

The large banquet hall in which the official signing was completed was cleared and reconfigured. For the next six hours, the representatives present for the surrender were treated to an opulent celebratory banquet hosted by the Soviets. They consumed a sumptuous meal and bountiful alcohol in the form of wine, champagne, and vodka. Generous toasts were exchanged. The war in Europe was over. Now, they had to win the peace.

Later, Keitel and Jodl would be tried before the Nürnberg Tribunal, convicted of war crimes, and executed by hanging for their crimes. A broad array of Allied tribunals were held over the following years to prosecute Nazi leaders, the SS, military personnel, doctors, engineers, and scientists. Accountability was careful, methodical, and relentless. Many would be executed. Others would be imprisoned. Some were acquitted of criminal conduct and returned to German society. A comparatively small number of German experts were recruited into a program called Operation PAPERCLIP that would protect them and transition them to serving the United States. Among those PAPERCLIP Germans were

SS-Sturmbannführer Doktor Wernher Magnus Maximilian *Freiherr* von Braun and *Generalleutnant* Reinhard Gehlen. Von Braun would lead the design engineering team that would build the massive Saturn V moon rocket. Gehlen brought a trove of personnel and documents to assist the Central Intelligence Agency in thwarting Soviet hegemonic ambition in what would become the Cold War between the Soviet Union and the Western Allies.

—

Chapter 8

All things change,
and you yourself are constantly wasting away.
So, also, is the universe.
-- Marcus Aurelius

Wednesday, 9.May.1945
Oval Office
The White House
Washington, District of Columbia
United States of America
15:15 hours

President Truman enjoyed a comparatively quiet afternoon, catching up on his reading. He was a realist and recognized he would likely never reach the end. Greater net outflow remained his current objective. The progress of the military administration of Germany continued to advance nicely, although the president recognized that the division of administrative sectors between the Big Three and France would likely take several months to fully achieve. The supreme commander held firm control over Western Germany and worked diligently on a daily basis to deconflict the frontier with Soviet-occupied Eastern Germany. While combat operations had ceased in Europe, spots of mop-up actions continued against die-hard *Waffen-SS* units scattered about.

General Eisenhower felt the greatest and largest problem facing the AEF was the immediate health care and well-being of the camp survivors, their registration, and eventual repatriation to their home countries. They also had to feed the surviving German people. Lastly, they had millions of German prisoners of war to feed, process, and sort through for potential war crimes prosecution.

The various SHAEF reports regarding the displaced persons matter continued to give him the chills. The enormity of the situation staggered the imagination. Fortunately, he had a powerful and resourceful army to maintain peace and control in Europe, and a cabinet full of ministers to ensure the AEF had what it needed to fulfill its mission.

The knock at the door preceded Rose Conway's entrance. "Excuse me, Mister President, but Secretary Stettinius has arrived unannounced, rather breathless I must say, and asked to see you."

"Must be important. Please show him in Miss Conway."

Conway gestured to the anteroom for the secretary to enter.

Stettinius stepped into the Oval Office three paces, looked over his right shoulder, and nodded to Rose. She knew what he was waiting for and closed the door. Ed walked to the president's desk, opened his metal case, and removed a single piece of pink paper with red border stripes. "We just received this MAGIC decrypt," he said as he handed the form to the president.

TOP SECRET - MAGIC

```
T O P   S E C R E T   M A G I C
SECRET
DATE 19450508 2341 HOME
TO AMB MOSCOW
FROM SCDW
T O P   S E C R E T   M A G I C
BREAK
YOU ARE DIRECTED TO APPROACH USSR FO TO ACT
ON OUR BEHALF BREAK WE WISH THE USSR GOV TO
ACT ON BEHALF OF SCDW TO SEEK PEACE TERMS FROM
THE USA BREAK JAPAN FO WILL CONTACT USSR AMB
TOKYO WITH SAME REQUEST BREAK UNCONDITIONAL
SURRENDER NOT VIABLE OPTION BREAK WE MUST
NEGOTIATE END
SECRET
DECYPHERED OP20C COMM 082347Z MAY 1945
T O P   S E C R E T   M A G I C
```

TOP SECRET - MAGIC

"Nobody said they don't have balls," Truman said with a grunt. "They are getting a little more aggressive with their initiatives, but the bottom line must be, have we, or anyone, heard from the Russians?"

"No Sir, not to my knowledge."

"Maybe we should reach out to the Japanese?"

"We can't do that, Mister President. If we made any move, the Japanese would likely suspect we are reading their mail, which would end MAGIC's bounty."

"Good point." Truman looked at the message again. "Time to educate the boss. Who is SCDW?"

Stettinius chuckled a few times softly. "SCDW stands for the Supreme Council for the Direction of the War. In the original Japanese, it is *Saikō Senso Shidō Kaigi*. Prime Minister Koiso established the SCDW when he replaced Tojo. Prime Minister Suzuki continued the Council when he replaced Koiso.

The Council is equivalent to the British War Cabinet or Defense Committee. It is comprised of the prime minister, the foreign minister, the defense ministers, and military chiefs of staff."

"What do we know, if anything, about the terms they seek?" the president queried.

"The person closest to answering your question is Director Donovan, but I do believe he would answer the same as me. I don't know."

"Guess."

"That's always precarious in my line of work." Truman gestured impatiently for Stettinius to proceed. "My best guess is their paramount concern is the status of the emperor and the government. They may well seek to preserve their way of life."

"Ain't gonna happen, Ed. They seek our terms. There is only one requirement—unconditional surrender."

"They want negotiations."

"There is no negotiation to be done. Their choice is surrender or oblivion."

Stettinius opened his mouth to speak, but no sound came out. He thought for a few more moments, and then he said, "Then, I guess we wait for the Russians. There is no sign yet that they have approached other nations like the Swiss or Swedes."

"Ed, as you noted, we can't reach out to the Japanese. Now that I think of it, such an initiative alone would likely be seen as weakness by the Japanese. Therefore, we will proceed with our plans to defeat the enemy outright on the battlefield."

"We'll keep our ears to the ground and won't play our cards."

"Thanks, Ed. Have a great rest of your day."

"Thank you, Mister President. And to you as well, Sir." Stettinius made his way out of the Oval Office and West Wing.

———

Thursday, 10.May.1945
Site Y (Los Alamos National Laboratory)
Los Alamos, Los Alamos County, New Mexico
United States of America
09:00 hours

"Good morning, Oppy," Groves said, greeting his chief scientist.

"Is it?" Oppenheimer responded with a tone of gloom.

The two Manhattan Project leaders sat across the desk from each other.

"How's the preliminary data looking from the Calibration Test?" asked Groves.

"In a word, enlightening. We mapped the pressure wave precisely, as well as the thermal registers across the grid. We are still analyzing the trace radiation data. Based on the team's progress, we should be complete early next week. Once we have all the data, I want to do a full review to compare the calibration data to our calculated yield of the Gadget from dud to full output. The review might turn up some adjustments to the instrumentation array. We'll be ready before the Gadget is ready."

"Can we move the Gadget test forward?"

"Most of the parts are ready, but we are still working on refinement of the core and the seed. The lenses are nearly complete, but we're going through our measurements and quality checks. Once we complete the data review, I'll have a head session with the department heads to see what we can do to tighten up the schedule."

"The sooner we provide the tool, the sooner we can help end the war. The president just approved the target list, and the 509th should be operational on Tinian by the end of the month."

"Is this really necessary, Dick?"

Groves looked askance at Oppenheimer. "Why do you ask . . . here . . . at the 23rd hour of this development effort?"

"I guess I sense we are closer to achievement, and the morality of this thing is becoming more graphic. At first, my motivation was intellectual curiosity—was spontaneous fission possible? Then, it was the engineering challenge of transforming physics into functional physicality. I'm also mindful of the mounting dissent among some project physicists. So far, they've kept their opinions inside the project, but none of us can promise it will stay that way. We have a good plan to camouflage the Gadget test, but when we drop one of these things on a live city, there will be no hiding what we've done. Are we doing the right thing with this physics?"

Groves nodded. "That's not our question, Oppy. In this instance, that belongs squarely on the shoulders of the president. Our task is to provide the instrument. We will test that tool in two months' time or less. After that, the political leaders must decide whether and how to use the tool."

"We're producing more than one of these things."

"Yes, we are. We are operating at capacity. Oak Ridge is producing sufficient material for a Little Boy device per year. Hanford is achieving a rate to generate material for four devices a year. I think President Roosevelt was fully prepared to use the tool to save lives. I'm still up in the air about President Truman, but I suspect he is far more concerned about the lives of Americans he must send into combat than the devastation of a Japanese city or two to convince the enemy government to surrender and end the war."

"That is a rather brutal thing to say, Dick."

"Yes, it is because war is brutal, Oppy. War is brutal." The physicist nodded in agreement. "Yes, the weapons we are building will claim many lives in an instant, but they will also save millions of Japanese and American lives by avoiding ground combat on a far larger scale than Iwo Jima and Okinawa."

"I'm having some difficulty rationalizing that concept."

Groves again nodded, and this time lapsed into contemplation. "I was taught at West Point to accept the reality of our business. We knew that we were trained instruments of the president. We trust him to use those precious tools wisely. To put the facts bluntly, we were trained to lead soldiers and kill as quickly and efficiently as possible to achieve the president's objectives. We can debate the morality of killing 100,000 enemy people. Does it matter whether the killing is done in a second, a day, a month, or a year? Innocent people are still dead."

"One innocent should not die for political foibles of distant men."

"Oh so true, Oppy, but perhaps 100,000 people must die in an instant to save the lives of millions upon millions of other innocent people. As von Clausewitz so succinctly and accurately stated, 'Politics is the reason, and war is only the tool, not the other way around. Consequently, it remains only to subordinate the military point of view to the political.' We remain subordinate to our political leaders. We will deliver the tool. Our political leaders must decide if or how to use that tool."

"Well said, Dick, but many of us tussle with the morality of one innocent person."

"As rightly we should." Groves thought for a moment. "Do we have a problem here?"

"Just my conscience, I'm afraid."

"We are so close to finishing our tasking. I would hate to see an indiscretion. I have no objection to our team members voicing their concerns within the confines of the team, but we are governed by stringent security protocols that do not allow public dissent."

"I will emphasize that point to the department heads, but I do not think we have that problem. We shall do our part to avoid that issue."

"Eye on the ball," added Groves.

Oppenheimer nodded. He followed Groves' lead and stood. Their schedule told them they were going to make a tour of the test site as much to see the physical effects of the calibration test on the ground at the test site. The two leaders would spend most of the daylight hours at the test site.

—

Friday, 11.May.1945
Oval Office
The White House
Washington, District of Columbia
United States of America
15:15 hours

The president had called the meeting to convey his decision. Accordingly, Secretary of State Stettinius and Director of the Foreign Economic Administration Leo Thomas Crowley entered the famous executive office together.

The Lend-Lease Administration had formed after the passage of An Act To Promote the Defense of the United States (AKA Lend-Lease Act) [PL 77-011; 55 Stat. 31] on 11.March.1941. The act was initially intended to support Great Britain when she stood alone against the Germans. The government expanded the program to provide material support to the Soviet Union after the Germans invaded the country and to the Chinese in their fight against the Japanese. Ed Stettinius had been the administrator, and W. Averell Harriman had been the program liaison to the United Kingdom and stationed in the country. Supervision of the Lend-Lease Program transferred to the Foreign Economic Administration in September 1943.

"Welcome, gentlemen, and good afternoon to both of you," the president greeted Stettinius and Crowley.

"Good afternoon, Mister President," the visitors responded in unison.

Truman gestured to the facing couches and sat across from the other two. "This shouldn't take long. I have decided to terminate the Lend-Lease Program immediately in accordance with the law."

Both tried to contain their shock. "Mister President," Stettinius responded, "with all due respect, that is rather abrupt."

"Yes, it is, which is my duty. The war in Europe is over," Truman declared. "The need for the program as established by law is no longer present."

"Thank goodness for that mercy," Ed said. "Much of Europe is devastated. They have little, if any, food production capacity. Great Britain received several shiploads of coal and oil a year just to heat homes and buildings. Unfortunately, they do not have the manpower to refresh their production. We are just now assessing the humanitarian needs of Germany alone—the people, the prisoners of war, and the displaced people in those dreadful camps."

"As I read the law, Mister Secretary, the program was intended to provide military assistance. No war, no assistance. Once the supreme commander can tally up his needs, we'll present the demand to Congress. We need more appropriate legislation and funding to support the humanitarian needs in Europe."

"Mister President, if I may," Crowley interjected. He waited until the president nodded his consent. "The Lend-Lease Program may have mutated, but we have been providing fuel and food from the effort's inception. The British alone need our help."

"We have several matters here, gentlemen. One, the law does not support what we are doing. A new law is required. Two, we cannot continue. The purpose of the Lend-Lease Program has ended, and I am compelled to abide the law. Three, shipments at sea or loading can complete their deliveries, but the shipments must conclude by the end of this month. Four, when you can articulate the humanitarian need of Europe and eventually Asia with Japan, draft the necessary legislation for Congress to consider. Simply put, we can't continue down the path we are on . . . executive orders and unilateral extensions of existing law. Am I clear?"

"Yes Sir," both men answered together.

"That will be all, gentlemen. Have a good day."

"Thank you, Mister President. Good day.

———

Saturday, 12.May.1945
Standing Oak Farm
Winchester, Hampshire, England
United Kingdom
13:10 hours

Brian's journey home to Charlotte had been more tortuous than usual and certainly more than he remembered since he had been in England. People were moving around more so than even the prelude to OVERLORD. It seemed like a flood, and Brian felt like he was swimming upstream, weaving his way through the ebb and flow of humanity. Civilian men, women, and children moved among the menagerie of uniformed men and women of all services and many nations.

Upon arrival at Winchester Station, Brian waited at the entrance for his favorite cab driver, Morty Jurdy, to show, which he knew would eventually happen. The wait lasted just over a quarter-hour. Finally, Morty saw Brian and drove up directly to him. They greeted each other like old friends. As he drove, Brian listened with pleasure to Morty's ebullient enthusiasm for the war's end in Europe. Morty shared his family's military history, from the Boer War and the Great War to his sons' and nephews' participation in the current war. Two were serving in the 21st Army Group in Northern Germany, while another served in Burma and the youngest in India, preparing for the invasion of Japan. Morty stopped at the crest of the ridgeline overlooking the farm. As Brian got out of the automobile on the sunny early afternoon, Morty switched off the cab and joined Brian in front of the car.

"It is gorgeous country," commented Morty.

"Oh my, yes, Morty. I have been in love with this place and the woman who owns this land since I descended into that lake." They both laughed. "In fact, me and the bits of my Spitfire breaking up passed just overhead, landing in the field beyond the hill on the far side of the lake."

"You are a genuine hero, Major," Morty pronounced.

"For getting shot down over this farm?"

Morty laughed nervously. "Oh dear me, no, Major. You are a decorated ace and one of The Few. We all owe you enormous gratitude for what you have done for our freedom."

"Thank you, Morty, but I was just doing my duty."

"You were a volunteer, Sir. You did not have to be here."

"*Au contraire, mon ami,*" Brian said in the best French he had tried to learn from Charlotte. "British freedom was American freedom. I felt that obligation.

"Bless you for that service, Sir."

Just then, Brian saw Charlotte step outside the main door and wave to Brian and Morty. Both men waved back.

"I'd better get you down to the Missus."

Brian nodded, and both men got back into the cab. Morty drove smoothly down the gravel road and into the forecourt of the main house. Brian jumped out before Morty came to a complete stop. Charlotte leaped into her husband's waiting arms. They enveloped each other, kissed, and whispered intimacies to each other.

"Morty's waiting," Charlotte whispered into her husband's ear as she looked over his shoulder.

"I'd better pay him, huh." The two lovers untangled. Brian went to the cab. "My apologies, Morty." Brian paid three times the fare. "Thank you for your patience and expertise, Morty. Have a great day."

"Thank you so much, Major. You are most generous." Morty looked around Brian and waved to Charlotte. "Great to see you again, Miss Charlotte."

"Likewise, Morty. Thank you for bringing my husband home safely."

Jurdy nodded and drove away.

"Are you hungry, my sweet?" Charlotte asked.

"Nope. I got a sandwich at Waterloo Station."

"Then, let's go to the bench so we can chat."

Brian gestured toward the massive oak tree. They walked together hand-in-hand.

"How long do I have you this time?"

"Other than I am subject to recall at any time, we were given a 30-day leave."

"Thirty days!" Charlotte nearly shouted in surprise.

"Yep . . . quite the change from what we've endured for the last six years, isn't it."

"A welcome change, I must say."

As they reached the bench, Brian gestured to the fire pit. Charlotte nodded as she sat on the bench. Brian made quick work of getting a modest fire going. Satisfied with this effort, Brian sat next to Charlotte on the wide bench and grasped her hand.

"Do you have anything you need or want to do on your leave?"

"Make love to you as often as we can."

"We can handle that one. Anything else?"

"I'd like to go work at each task on the farm. I need to learn."

"That's easy enough to execute as well. So, what lies ahead for your service."

Brian thought for a moment. "The answer is a little more complicated. Preparations are underway to transfer the Group to the Pacific."

"When?"

"I don't know. When they tell us to go. It's kinda like that time in '42 when the Air Ministry was going to ship us off to Russia . . . but farther. We were also told they will select some squadrons to move to Germany to support the occupation, but most will be transferred to the Pacific for the invasion of Japan."

"Oh, dear God above, Brian, when will it end?"

"The Germans have surrendered. The Japanese will surrender eventually. How soon, I don't know." Brian lifted her enveloped hand and kissed the back of it. "This too shall pass."

"Not soon enough. Every time we reach an elation along comes a valley. It has been a difficult five years with you so close and yet so far, and in serious danger almost every day of those five years. I held onto the fact that you were a few hours away . . . and it helped. The thought of you being weeks or months away . . . well . . . that scares me."

"I'm not too keen on the prospect either, but we need to finish this job."

Charlotte stood, walked around the fire, picked up a stick to poke the coals to bring the flames to life, and then she added another split log. When satisfied, she looked at Brian, smiled briefly, and then sat back down next to him, clasping his hand. "We will do what has to be done, but I don't like it."

Brian only nodded. "I want to take advantage of the time we have. What have you heard from Bobby?"

Charlotte smiled in recognition of Brian's swift change of subject. "No word from the government, although Bobby senses the situation is not positive. He confirmed that he is proceeding with the full commercialization of B-A-S. Bobby is also working on a refinement study to identify potentially profitable routes to avoid competition with the large established airlines. He indicated that he feels good about the recruitment of pilots, aircrew, and mechanics. Bobby expects to have an expansion proposal for our review in a couple of weeks."

"Excellent. I look forward to his ideas," Brian responded.

"Me as well. We also have another sale offer, not contiguous, and an interesting proposal for a partnership, a confederation if you will."

"What's in it for us?" asked Brian with genuine curiosity.

"Well, as they say, the devil is in the details, but the first approach suggested a mutually complementary relationship."

"Do you see it?"

"No, but I think it is worth exploring."

"I trust your judgment, sweetheart," Brian added. "I'll help as much as I'm able."

"Which isn't much." They both laughed.

"You are doing a smashingly good job, I must say."

"Thank you, darling. I do try. I will continue to explore the options. Now, what do you say we take two horses out for a ride before the afternoon milking."

"Works for me. Let's saddle up."

Charlotte and Brian did just that and headed out on an assessment tour for Brian to see the latest addition to their greenhouse array and other changes.

—

Monday, 14.May.1945
Hill 230
Okinawa, Okinawa Prefecture
Imperial Japan
10:35 hours

The 10th Army had been slogging it out with the Japanese since the 1st of April. They butted up against the Japanese 32nd Army's primary defensive line, anchored by Shuri Castle and known as the Shuri Line. The line offered interlocking artillery, machine gun, and small arms fire with an underground tunnel network to allow for rapid, protected reinforcement. On the left flank of the Shuri Line, on the northern reaches of Naha city, lay a group of three hills that were not particularly imposing. They were Hill 190, called Horseshoe, Hill 220, named Half Moon, and Hill 230, the Marines called Sugar Loaf.

Captain Owen Stebbins, USMC, commanded Company G, 2nd Battalion, 22nd Marine Regiment, 6th Marine Division, III Amphibious Corps, 10th Army. He led his company in the initial assault on Sugar Loaf Hill. The Americans thought the Marines would make quick work of the Sugar Loaf Complex. They were wrong.

The Battle for Sugar Loaf Hill took eight long days and nights of butcherous hand-to-hand combat. While Sugar Loaf has been recorded in the historical annals of the 22nd Marines, many other battles like Cactus Ridge, Kakazu Ridge, Wana Draw, Wana Ridge, Maeda Escarpment, also known as Hacksaw Ridge, recorded the glory of the 10th Army on Okinawa. They eventually broke through the Shuri Line by mid-May. The end of the Japanese 32nd Army became inevitable, but the last 10 miles to the southern tip of the island would take another five weeks of brutal combat ahead.

—

Monday, 14.May.1945
No.10 Downing Street
Whitehall, London, England
United Kingdom
11:30 hours

The Defence Committee gathered for a closed-door, secret meeting at the prime minister's request. All three service ministers and chiefs of staff stood as Prime Minister Churchill entered the small conference room with General Pug Ismay in tow.

"Sit, please, gentlemen." The attendees took their seats in the middle of both sides of the table. Churchill sat in the prime minister's chair at the center of the near side. "Thank you for making time on such short notice, gentlemen. I've been thinking, and that is always a volatile endeavor. For many years, I have voiced my concerns about Stalin's intentions in Eastern Europe. My concerns have come to fruition regrettably, and I am afraid it will only worsen as time passes. I say Stalin's intentions because he is for all intents and purposes a dictator. We went to war six years ago for Poland. I'll be damned if we are going to standby as the Poles trade one form of dictatorial oppression for another.

"I have been mulling over what to do about the situation for months now, especially after his performance at Yalta last February. An epiphany came to me last weekend at Chequers.

"The Western Allies are the strongest we are likely to ever be, right now, at this moment in history. While we are still mopping up and consolidating our holdings, the supreme commander will be issuing orders soon to withdraw our forces from occupied land in the Soviet-assigned sector based on the ARGONAUT Conference at Yalta.

"I do not have the authority of the supreme commander, but I do have the authority over His Majesty's armed forces. As such, I'm directing our forces in Germany and elsewhere to properly store and maintain all confiscated weapons, from pistols to warships and aircraft."

"Whatsoever for, if I may ask, Prime Minister?" asked Sir Percy.

"The succinct answer is, we may need them." A confused expression and a 'what' gesture from Sir Percy stimulated Churchill to continue briefing. "To be clear, I am directing the Defence Committee to plan what we will call Operation UNTHINKABLE quickly. All work on this plan will be classified as Most Secret – FAILINGS. The objective will be to push the Soviets back to the pre-war border of 1939."

"Prime Minister," responded General Brooke, "I certainly admire your insight, initiative, and audacity. I also support the wisdom of your objective. The world would be a better place with that achievement. However, I am compelled to illuminate here that we have insufficient forces to accomplish such a task. Even if we could convince the Americans to join us, we would still have insufficient forces."

"I will say it a little more emphatically," Sir Percy interjected, "not only do we not have sufficient troops, even if we recalled all of our forces scattered about the world, we have insufficient industrial capacity to support such an endeavor. Only the United States could take on such a task. Lend-Lease extension would be a mandatory requirement at a minimum."

"The world is tired," added First Lord of the Admiralty Albert Victor 'A.V.' Alexander, CH, PC, Member of Parliament for Sheffield, Hillsborough Division. "We've carried on a global war for six long years. The people have sacrificed so much for the war effort. They are celebrating in the streets, in their homes, and in our churches; they are celebrating, and rightly so. You are suggesting we should start another war before this one is done . . . and with one of our allies no less."

"I do not seek war," Churchill replied with solemnity. "I only seek justice for the people of Eastern Europe. I know with as much certainty as one can have in situations like this that if we do not push the Red Army back to their borders now, they will sink deep roots and be far harder to dislodge. They have annexed all the Baltic states, Ukraine, and Belarus, and installed puppet governments in Poland, Romania, and Bulgaria. They will quite likely do so in Hungary, Czechoslovakia, and Eastern Germany. Stalin will dominate all Eastern Europe as he has done in Russia . . . with brute force, submission, and subjugation. It is now or likely never to push them back to where they belong. It is now or never, gentlemen."

"Will this be total warfare against the Soviet Union?" asked the first sea lord.

"The plan should assume so."

"Should the plan include the special weapon?" asked Secretary of State for Air Sir Archibald Henry Macdonald 'Archie' Sinclair, Bart, Kt, CMG, PC, Member of Parliament for Caithness and Sutherland.

Churchill stared at Sinclair, who had been His Majesty's Government's Air Minister since Winton became prime minister. "The device has not yet been proven. When it has, then yes those things should be in our tool kit."

"That is a monstrous thing to say," the first lord protested.

"Far less monstrous than the subjugation of the people from an entire region, A-V. President Roosevelt and by his succession, President Truman, signed the Atlantic Charter in 1941. We are about to sign the United Nations Charter. We are committed to peace, the freedom of all peoples to choose their form of governance, and not to have oppression imposed upon them."

"How is this directive not just an extension and transformation of global war?" Alexander pressed.

"Look, gentlemen, at this juncture, there are two key points in the background. One, I am asking for a plan. This is not an order to execute military operations. We need to see what it would take to do what is right. Two, no one seeks war, but sometimes it is necessary to achieve lasting peace. Stalin is a common street thug who murders his opponents and has the Red Army at his will. I do not presume this will be easy, or without pain, but we made a solemn promise to the Polish people, and we must not fail them simply because the task to help them is difficult or painful." Churchill paused, looking down at the green felt covering the large conference room table. Then, he looked up and at each man in the room. "I recognize and appreciate your collective abhorrence to what I am suggesting here. I will respect your counsel, but we need to see what such a plan looks like. To that end, I want the preliminary plan for Operation UNTHINKABLE in two weeks. . . by Monday, the 28th of May at the latest."

"Yes Sir," came their unified response.

"Thank you, gentlemen. Good day."

———

Monday, 14.May.1945
Oval Office
The White House
Washington, District of Columbia
United States of America
07:45 hours

Bill Donovan arrived early for President Truman's morning intelligence briefing and was ushered directly into the Oval Office. As usual, the president gestured to the facing couches rather than remaining at his desk.

Donovan jumped right to it. "We have heard nothing new from the Japanese initiative with the Soviet Government. M-I-6, and we are pressing our agents in Moscow to pick up whatever hints we can about the request for terms, but to our collective knowledge, the Soviets have made no move to present the request or reject it. They are silent. Our collective opinion is rapidly solidifying. They are stonewalling for some reason."

"What could those reasons be?"

"We have quite a spectrum of possibilities. They might wish the Pacific war to continue for a host of reasons, not least of which might be to force us—the British and us—to transfer major military units from Europe to the Pacific, to thin our forces in Europe, or to buy time for them to decide whether to join the fight in Asia. But, at the end of the day, we do not know what Stalin's intentions are."

"That does not help much, does it, Bill?'

"No Sir. Unfortunately, neither the British nor we have a reliable source in the Soviet premier's inner circle of advisors. I must add at this point that we are beginning to pick up members of German intelligence in the East. As we gather the personnel and their work, we might learn more about the Kremlin. Army Counterintelligence has been alerted and engaged in the process. We continue to watch and listen for the Soviets to move on the Japanese request. It is certainly possible that the Japanese regime might reach its threshold of frustration and reach out to neutral nations, Switzerland or Sweden, for example. The neutrals have no axe to grind, so they might be a more reliable conduit. The ball remains in the hands of the Japanese. Our experts, along with the British, believe the Japanese cannot contact us directly to avoid losing face."

"Face? We're talkin' about people dying."

"Very true. Death before dishonor seems to be their catchphrase."

"That is a very costly attitude."

"To them, it is a necessary and historical stance. To them, *bushido*, the warrior way, is what has kept them safe from invaders over the millennia of their history. We cannot expect them to abandon the history at the core of their culture. I can also say there are conflicting and confrontational forces at play within the Japanese government. The civilian diplomatic corps wants peace to end the war, but the military faction still holds considerable sway. The emperor has made no overt intervention."

"What is the emperor's position on the situation?"

"He has made no public statement. We've heard subtle indications that he wants the suffering of his people to end, but he has chosen to remain aloof."

"Thank you for the education, Bill. This government's policy is and will remain the same. We will not dance to their tune. They will surrender on our terms. They will also pay a terrible price for their pride. What's next?"

"The Allied Expeditionary Force is picking up an increasing number of S-S officers fleeing Germany."

"The rats and the sinking ship."

Donovan chuckled softly. "Precisely, Mister President. Himmler and his cronies formed an organization they initially called The Spider. In August of last year, just before the liberation of Paris, they changed the name to The Organization of Former S-S Members. The acronym of the German words is ODESSA—*Organisation Der Ehemaligen SchutzStaffeln Angehörigen* (ODESSA). Even the name is very close hold. Only senior S-S officers are even aware of it. The fleeing S-S are not surprised or unusual, rats from the ship and all, but the twist you need to be informed of is, we are finding an increasing number of connections to the Vatican and the Catholic Church."

"The Catholic Church?" asked Truman with an air of incredulity.

"My apologies, Mister President. I should have been more precise. We have mounting evidence that a few, more than one, Catholic priests and at least one bishop and cardinal are aiding and facilitating the escape of S-S officers and Nazi-sympathizing industrialists."

"Escape to where?"

"Predominantly South America—Argentina, Brazil, Chile, Peru, and other Southern South American nations."

"I presume you are working with the F-B-I to track them down."

Donovan cleared his throat. "I am reticent to discuss this aspect."

"But, please do, General Donovan," commanded the president to emphasize the chain of command.

"Director Hoover and I do not see eye-to-eye. He believes categorically that the Western Hemisphere is his domain and has made his resentment of our work in South America crystal clear. I have repeatedly tried to reconcile some playground rules with him without success. Accordingly, I have taken my charter from President Roosevelt as overriding. As such, I have directed our agents and sources to avoid interaction with the F-B-I."

"That hardly seems like a wise policy."

"No, it's not, but it is the reality of our situation. We are pressing our intelligence collection activities on all continents except Antarctica. The information we are gathering will be available to all governmental consumers of such data . . . including the F-B-I, when the time and circumstances warrant."

"That is a tall order."

"Yes, it is, Mister President, but these are the times in which we live."

The president's desk telephone buzzed. Truman went to the phone. Donovan stood. "Yes. Fine. I'll finish this meeting now." The president hung up the phone. "I'm sorry, Bill, but our time is up. I would like to know more about this ODESSA business. Until told otherwise, please press on with your work in South America. Thank you for your time, Bill. Good day." Truman did not wait for a response, sat in his desk chair, and immediately turned his attention to papers arrayed on his desk.

"Good day, Mister President." Donovan departed and passed Treasury Secretary Morgenthau on his way through Conway's anteroom.

—

Wednesday, 16.May.1945
No.10 Downing Street
Whitehall, London, England
United Kingdom
11:00 hours

"Great to finally see you again after the historic day," Churchill greeted General Eisenhower. "We'll meet with the Chiefs of Staff Committee in 30 minutes. First, I am compelled to inform you that we shall face an election early next July. Attlee agreed to extend our coalition government until after the surrender of Japan, but the Labour Party rejected this recommendation, thus forcing the election in six weeks. Once the Labour Party confirms its position, I will likely tender my resignation to the King on the 23rd. If so, the election will be six weeks hence—the 5th of July. The election campaign will take more of my time than usual."

"Surely you will be re-elected after all you accomplished in the last five years," Eisenhower replied.

"There is no such thing in political elections. I certainly want to finish this war, but I do not decide these things. I shall campaign hard with no assumptions."

"I wish you the best of luck, Prime Minister."

"Thank you, Ike. I shall do my best. I also want to discuss the upcoming meeting briefly. Two days ago, I tasked the chiefs to develop an operational plan with a single objective . . . to push the Soviets back to the pre-war borders."

"No one will accuse you of thinking small, Winston."

"You've heard my speeches on the subject. You know what and why I believe what I do. Yet, a question I have not asked you until now . . . you've dealt with the Red Army as supreme commander. Do you trust them?"

"The problem is not the Red Army. The problem is Stalin, the N-K-G-B, and the N-K-V-D. Even Marshal Zhukov does not do anything without approval from the Kremlin, and apparently quite often approval from Stalin himself. I'm quite mindful of the purges of the 30s. Zhukov and the other Soviet generals I've dealt with are competent professionals, but they are dominated by Stalin and the Kremlin hierarchy. Case in point is the whole surrender process."

"So, do you believe the Soviets are going to let the countries of Eastern Europe know freedom, to choose their form of governance freely, to choose their alliances, and all other things sovereign states do?"

Eisenhower considered Churchill's question for a score of seconds. "No. I do not."

"My point precisely. His Majesty's Government promised to defend Poland. We failed in 1939. As His Majesty's prime minister, I have sought to restore that promise, but so far, I have failed as well. Eastern European nations deserve to be free."

"I'm certain you recognized the import and consequences of what you are proposing."

"Yes, but I see no other choice. All our diplomatic efforts have failed to convince Stalin. Of course, he will claim he is encouraging democratic elections, but I think we all recognize that he will have a very heavy thumb on the scales in the form of the Red Army."

Eisenhower nodded. "Our best intelligence indicates the Soviets have roughly double the combat divisions as the A-E-F in Europe. To take on the Red Army, we would need approximately four times the number of divisions we have now. That would be an unprecedented mobilization beyond what we have created to date. Whether either of our nations possesses the political will to start a different war with an ally, no less, before this war is done is a question far beyond my sphere."

"New topic for the time we have remaining. Where are you on the occupation sector boundaries?"

"Our immediate task is the mop-up a few hot spots of fanatics who refuse to surrender without a direct order from Hitler."

Churchill chuckled visibly but not audibly. "He's dead."

"Exactly. We will end the resistance one way or another. The next task is imposing martial law in the territory we hold. We are coordinated with the Red Army, but tensions are increasing. We are working on the withdrawal plan to the ascribed sector boundaries defined in the Yalta Conference, to begin by the middle of June."

"As you may be aware, I cabled President Truman five days ago proposing a Big Three summit conference by the end of May to close out several open issues from Yalta. We will meet in Potsdam, outside Berlin, in the middle of July. One of those issues is the refinement of sector boundaries based on the current disposition of forces."

Eisenhower nodded. "I was unaware of a new summit conference, so thank you for sharing that fact. I do not think . . . ," the general said with a knock on the prime minister's office door. Both men looked at the door as Churchill's private secretary stepped halfway into the room.

"Excuse me, Prime Minister," said Jock Colville. "The chiefs have arrived for your half eleven meeting. They are assembled in the Cabinet Room."

"Very well. Thank you, Jock." Churchill looked at General Eisenhower. "We'll continue this with the other chiefs."

Both leaders moved to the conference room without words. Eisenhower greeted his colleagues. The generals, including Eisenhower, sat across the table from Prime Minister Churchill.

The prime minister opened the meeting. "You've had a couple of days to cogitate on the UNTHINKABLE task. I have included the supreme commander in this discussion since he may well be involved in one way or another. What say you?" Churchill asked, looking directly at Field Marshal Brooke.

"First, by your direction, we are preserving and storing confiscated German weapons. From that, the stark reality, Prime Minister, even if we withdrew all our combat divisions from around the world and abandoned our various colonial holdings, we would still be woefully short of the forces necessary to push back the Red Army. We are looking at an alternative strategy to drive a wedge across Northern Poland to the Baltics. We would have to defend our exposed right flank, but it would be a demonstration of our earnestness . . . to encourage local support and give the diplomats a few more tools to convince the Soviets to withdraw. Our evolving strategy does not require American involvement other than to defend the territory they hold."

Churchill looked at Eisenhower but did not have to speak his question. "I have no orders to withdraw from the territory we occupy. I do have orders to prepare for the transfer of U-S units to the Pacific. Doing so will alter our ability to defend the American sector from any concerted, coordinated attack. I must say here that I appreciate your engagement of me in this plan, but I hope you recognize that I must alert the American command structure. They need time to come to grips with the expanse of this effort."

"Ike, I must ask you to hold on that initiative. I have asked the chiefs to give me a preliminary plan by the end of this month. I want to see that plan before I talk directly with President Truman."

Eisenhower stared at Churchill for a handful of seconds. "Out of respect for you, Prime Minister, I will do so. You have placed me between you and President Truman. I'll trust you to respect my position in all this. Don't leave me hanging out in the cold."

"Absolutely, Ike . . . mutual respect."

The general nodded. "I didn't finish my answer to your earlier statement. I do not think it wise to wait until the middle to end of July to withdraw our forces from the anticipated Soviet sector of East Germany. As I indicated, tensions between the Russians and us are increasing. They insist on their control of areas we occupy, which they believe are within their sector. I shall not interfere with your UNTHINKABLE planning. After all, we do all kinds of planning for all sorts of situations. Yet, I am an American general, and I do not want my government backed into any war, no matter how warranted or righteous. I also remain the supreme commander of the Allied Expeditionary Force. I will carry out my orders to the best of my ability until I am relieved of command, or my orders are changed."

"We would expect nothing less, Ike. We have been through too much together. It would be disrespectful to withhold such drastic planning for operations within your command domain."

"Thank you for that."

"Now, I would like to hear the first blush from the sea and air," Churchill said, looking at the first sea lord.

Admiral Cunningham nodded. "Our first look, should such a plan reach the executable phase, suggests that we could close the Baltic and Black Seas in short order. The Arctic and Pacific Fleets are more problematic and would most likely require preemptive action to bottle up the Arctic Fleet at Archangel and Murmansk, and the Pacific Fleet at Vladivostok. The Soviet Navy is not what the *Kriegsmarine* was, but we must act on them with respect. They remain formidable. At first glance, the Navy thinks it is doable."

"Sir Charles, your assessment," Churchill said.

Chief of the Air Staff Marshal Sir Charles Portal responded, "The Red Air Force has grown and proven itself against the *Luftwaffe*. The air force is a little less contained and three-dimensional. We'll need to hit all the runways within one thousand miles of our forward bases to open the plan. We will likely only get one pass unopposed . . . assuming we can maintain secrecy and surprise.

Fighter Command will have to deploy as many squadrons as possible to forward bases in Central Europe and yet maintain sufficient air defense forces to protect the Home Islands. To put the air position in analogous terms, we will be poking the hornets' nest, and we must be prepared for the consequences."

Churchill nodded his acknowledgment and thought for a few moments. He looked into the eyes of each general. "We are all cleared PARAMOUNT in this room, so I feel safe and appropriate to raise the issue. What if we use the special weapon as a force multiplier once we poke the hornets' nest, as Sir Charles suggests." None of the generals jumped to respond. "Very well. Brookie, you're first. Your counsel?"

"We've not seen what these things will do, but if the scientists are correct, one of those bombs will destroy a lot more than a passel of assembled tanks, including a good deal of innocent civilians. Plus, we would contaminate the ground we're trying to liberate. That hardly seems like a reasonable trade. We beat the Russians back, liberate Eastern Europe, and render the land unusable for generations. Prime Minister, pushing the Russians back to the pre-war border is a worthy and necessary task, but the task is a bridge too far . . . like MARKET GARDEN and the Arnhem crossing. While we have more work to do in planning, at this juncture, I am not in favor of pressing to execution of UNTHINKABLE, with or without special weapons." Brooke looked at Eisenhower. "Even with the full A-E-F, we have half the force of the Red Army, and the Americans are planning to move the major of their divisions to the Pacific. We are supposed to be going with them to finish off Japan. From the Army's perspective, we have insufficient forces to take on the Red Army, and we should use our European forces as the Americans intend to do and finish off Japan. Then, we can consider pushing the Red Army back."

"It will be too late by then, Brookie."

"We cannot do both, Prime Minister."

"Sir Andrew?"

"I think Alan offered a precise, poignant assessment. I might choose different words, but I would say the same thing. We do not see the Navy as a major player in UNTHINKABLE, but rather a blocker to isolate the battlefield. We have already deployed significant resources to the Pacific to participate in ICEBERG, and we would expect to play a serious role in DOWNFALL *in toto*. Given the maintenance of existing forces, our initial look-see planning indicates we can cover both demands. The key for the Navy is the containment of the Arctic Fleet. If we lose surprise, the dispositions could dramatically change. Thus, secrecy remains a vital requirement." The first sea lord nodded to the prime minister.

"Sir Charles," Churchill said.

Portal cleared his throat. "In this discussion, I am the odd man out. I see the quickest path to ending the war or achieving the objective. While we await the functioning and explosive potential, the estimates are quite sobering—good city destroyers, but less so against dispersed armies. Small devices and more of them would be more useful against airfields, bridges, concentrated forces, and such. I think atomic weapons have an important place in our kit bag. The Red Army likes to mass its forces, which makes such assemblies prime targets. As the prime minister suggested, atomic weapons are or can be a force multiplier, and to that end, will be a useful weapon to wage war successfully."

"How would you use them?" asked the prime minister out of curiosity.

"The Air Force has done some abstract thinking, but until we know the characteristics of those weapons, we don't know how best to use them. They will not be a general-purpose weapon . . . most assuredly."

"Thank you, Sir Charles. What say you, Ike?"

"From the scientific description, it is Dresden in a single bomb. We are not talking about the destruction of military targets or support infrastructure. This is the destruction of everything—man, woman, and child. I am against destruction on that scale and with such indiscrimination."

Churchill nodded as he thought. "Thank you for your candid counsel, gentlemen. I eagerly anticipate your plan. Thank you for your respect, Ike. We will have many more discussions before we reach the approval stage or the execution phase. Again, thank you for coming and sharing your perspective at this moment. Now, if you will excuse me, I have other matters begging for my attention. I assume I shall see you all at dinner this evening."

"Yes Sir," the generals answered in unison. The prime minister turned and departed the room smartly.

———

Friday, 18.May.1945
Oval Office
The White House
Washington, District of Columbia
United States of America
16:20 hours

President Truman had asked OSS Director Donovan to return since the morning intelligence briefing exceeded the allotted time by more than half and put the president's daily appointment calendar behind from the outset. Donovan tried to avoid conflicts with the president's thinking, but he also felt a significant obligation to the intelligence. The president absorbed intelligence more so than

President Roosevelt, but he also held more hardened positions on issues. One of those calcified stances dealt with Soviet intentions in Eastern Europe.

Reports coming in from Eastern Germany daily seemed to amplify Prime Minister Churchill's assessment, or perhaps it was a premonition, about Stalin's objectives in Eastern Europe. The Red Army had become more confrontational by the day. Even the Soviet Air Force had begun intercepting Allied aircraft entering their sector and heading to Berlin. After a rather contentious discussion in the morning, the president asked Donovan to reassess the facts they had and come back in the afternoon.

Donovan arrived early as he usually did and sat in one of the padded chairs on the other wall from Rose Conway's desk. He had been in the chair for five minutes when the telephone rang.

Miss Conway answered and said, "Yes Sir," twice in rapid succession. Then, she looked directly at Donovan. "The president will see you now, General Donovan."

As the director opened the door and entered, the president walked around his desk. Truman gestured for Donovan to close the door and sit on the couch across from him. "Good afternoon, Mister President."

"Afternoon, Bill. So, let's jump to it. We don't have much time. Have you changed your assessment?"

"No Sir. Since this morning's briefing, I have conferred with our Russia and German desk chiefs, and the station chiefs in London and Bern." Donovan had considered sharing his discussions with Menzies at MI6 and Lord Selborne at SOE, but he was not confident the president would receive the information in the spirit with which it was shared. "The Soviets have not been and are not now acting like an ally. On the contrary, they are acting behaving like an antagonist, or adversary. It is like they believe Berlin is theirs, and they resent our presence in their territory. Both our Germany and Russia desks, as well as SHAEF G-2, have articulated growing suspicions that the Soviets may decide to press their numerical advantage to the west."

"Excuse me, General. That sounds distinctly like warmongering."

"No Sir. I am simply trying to present the available intelligence and associated analysis by our experts. Where we do not have hard corroborated facts, we are offering our best assessment of what we think the available facts mean."

"I am telling you my impression, General. The O-S-S belongs to a nation at war. This war will soon be over . . . one way or another. As I have stated before, I can see no place for the O-S-S in America at peace. I shall be blunt here . . . the image evolving in my mind is a service intent upon ginning up a war to justify the agency's existence."

Donovan stared intently into Truman's bespectacled eyes as he struggled to contain his emotion and urge to lash out. "Mister President, you deserve to have an intelligence service and director you can trust and have confidence in. The situation in Europe remains volatile and unstable. You need the best intelligence information possible delivered by a man you can believe. I am sorry I am not that man, but I fully understand, and I serve at your pleasure alone. I shall tender my resignation immediately."

Truman retained his stern, intense expression. "I have no intention of accepting your resignation, General. You can see this to the end. It is regrettable that my candid opinions have offended your sensitivities. I respect your Medal of Honor earned in brutal combat. I appreciate your intellect and sense of duty. I confess to my inability to believe that an ally seeks confrontation with us."

"Mister President, likewise, I shall confess to my frustration in my efforts to help you appreciate the information we are providing. I am plainly spoken and do not embellish opinions to make a point. Nevertheless, I feel like I am failing you. You need the best information available, and the O-S-S is not providing the information you need."

"Why don't you let me judge that, General."

Donovan held the president's eyes as he considered what he wanted to say. "I see the evolving Soviet threat and the duplicity of the Russian leader. I know enough Russian people—lawyers, engineers, doctors—to have a feel for the Russian people. They do not agree with or support Stalin. They are not communists. They are also realists who recognize the reality of the N-K-V-D. They live in fear. They try to make the most of their situation one day at a time. Stalin and his N-K-V-D, his N-K-G-B, and his cronies are not Russia. But they are the leaders of the largest nation on the planet. And they are not satisfied with the land and resources of the largest nation on earth. They want more. They are driven by greed. That greed may appear different from the greed of Wall Street, capitalism, and corporate America, but it is the exact same greed. Hitler told us the reasons for his hegemony. Stalin will not be so generous. He just smiles, tells us what we want to hear, and then does what he wants to extend his greed. Stalin only draws up when confronted with overwhelming force."

"That seems like a rather cynical view of one of our principal allies in this world."

"Perhaps, Mister President. Time shall tell the tale. If you wish, we can compile a comprehensive listing of the events that lead us to these conclusions. Perhaps if you can see what is happening at the individual level, soldier to soldier, the situation might become clearer. The most glaring example is the very surrender episode. General Eisenhower went out of his way to include the Soviet Union, but no, that was not enough. They insisted that the German surrender be publicly executed on their terms, at their headquarters. The same efforts to dominate anyone and everyone only vary in scale. The dispute between soldiers at a remote checkpoint hardly compares in scale to the surrender of an entire nation at war, but they are both indicative of a common behavior—a schoolyard bully."

"I do not see the connection and do not have the time to read such tedious information."

"That is exactly why you need a man in this position whom you trust to give you the best assessment of the available information."

President Truman considered Donovan's statement. "You are not the issue in this discussion, General. The agency you lead is. My earlier statement stands. Thank you for your time, General. We shall stay the course."

"Understood, Mister President. Is there anything else I can do for you?"

"No. You are dismissed."

Donovan nodded, stood, and departed, closing the door behind him. He spoke to no one as he passed through Conway's anteroom office and exited the West Wing.

—

Saturday, 26.May.1945
Standing Oak Farm
Winchester, Hampshire, England
United Kingdom
14:25 hours

Husband and wife had decided to take the afternoon for a mounted tour of the farm. They made a point of visiting each greenhouse in the impressive array of structures and greeting each employee. Mabel had done an extraordinary job assembling a group of dedicated, enthusiastic employees, many of whom Brian had never seen set aside met before. The greenhouse production process was humming along nicely and expanding the offerings to include green beans, Brussels sprouts, broccoli, squash, and spinach. They were still considering whether to tackle corn. Mabel and her crew had done a masterful job of staggering the crops in each building to achieve a continuous yield for biweekly and, in a few cases, weekly deliveries. The U.S. Army still purchased the majority of the farm vegetable production, but they also allowed 10 to 20 percent of each crop to be sold locally. Mabel and Charlotte both remained confident they could transition the farm's production to local consumers when the U.S. military eventually withdrew from Europe.

From the greenhouse complex, they sauntered their horses through a small forest section of their property. Without looking at her husband, Charlotte asked, "You've been here two weeks now. How do you like being a farmer?"

Brian laughed softly. "I'm not done with service yet." He took a more serious expression and tone with a smile. "I appreciate your concern, my love, but I will be just fine. I've loved being home with you. While this war is not done yet, it is finished in Europe, and it will be over soon against Japan. I've dreamed of having more than a few days with you. I'm ready for the rest of our lives."

"Can you give up flying?"

"Whoa, now, let's not go that far."

This time Charlotte laughed robustly. "I just thought I would ask."

"I know you've been concerned about what's next for quite some time now. We own aircraft. I'll find a way to fly . . . in time. Who knows, you might get the bug if I teach you to fly."

"I've never flown in an airplane, Brian."

"I know. I just need to introduce you slowly and carefully."

"We'll see. I want to make sure that whatever we do, you are happy."

"That's my line . . . I want you to be happy with whatever we do."

"I will be happy as long as we are together."

They crossed a shallow creek in trail. On the far side, Brian moved up beside Charlotte.

"Will we move to America?" Charlotte asked as they broke out of the forest to the edge of one of their many pastures.

"That decision is a way off and dependent upon many variable factors . . . with probably the prime factor whether I remain in the Army. I think it's fairly certain that most of the 8th Air Force and U.S. military will transfer to the Pacific to finish off Japan. Even once that is done, I cannot imagine or see the bulk of American forces remaining in Europe. Whether my squadron is chosen to remain for the occupation is beyond my knowledge but will eventually be determined and implemented. If that happens, I assume you will go with me wherever that may be."

"I should hope so. That is my expectation. Mabel and June can run the farm. They did quite well . . . when . . . when I was incapacitated with grief."

"Regardless of what happens, I would like you to visit Wichita and Kansas as soon as we can make that trip. We can both explore our holdings and what we want to do with everything we own."

"Will we take a ship or fly?"

"Taking a ship might be difficult with troop movements and all, but that is another decision to come when we know more. Right now, there are just too many variables we do not control."

"Brian, you can resign from the Army."

The question silenced Brian for several yards of perimeter fence and wall of their property. "When the war is finally over, I suppose I could. I'm not aware of any service obligation I might have. They might just discharge me as part of demobilization. I'll have to ask."

"Would you?"

"What?"

"Resign from the service?"

"Good question." They sauntered along for another few yards as Brian considered his answer. "When the time is right, yes, I would. I am not particularly interested in some staff job in Washington. But first, I made a personal and moral decision to leave home, defy the government, and volunteer for the R-A-F. That commitment still exists. I intend to see this affair to the end."

"I understand and respect your pledge. I am talking about after Japan surrenders."

"Then, my answer depends upon what the Army expects of me, and we will not likely know that expectation until the war is done. For now, I want to enjoy my time with you at home. This is my home. It feels like home, and it's all because of you . . . from that very first day I met you in July'40."

Charlotte giggled softly as they rode smoothly on their tour. "Actually, my love, I met you in the pond that Wednesday morning. We did not meet until four days later while you were in the hospital."

"Minor detail. You've been my angel since that day."

"That is a very heavy cross to bear. And the problem is, I didn't think. I just reacted. God brought us together, and we are together for life."

"My thoughts precisely."

The horses were doing well. The rich smell of fertile land mixed perfectly on the light breeze with the variety of spring fragrances. The perimeter fencing and walls remained well-maintained. The land was in great shape.

Charlotte took a quick glance at the position of the sun. "It's getting close to milking time."

Brian glanced at his wristwatch. "Yep, quarter to four."

"We'd better pick up the pace."

Brian did not question nor object. They both stimulated their horses to a comfortable gallop but stayed on the perimeter.

The dairymen were nearly finished with their setup for the afternoon milking. While Horace and the men tended to the cows. Charlotte and

Brian ensured the collection equipment and storage tanks were ready for the afternoon's product. When the equipment was ready, they checked on their cheese in various stages of production. Business was good.

—

Chapter 9

The glory and the nothing of a name.

-- George Noel Gordon, Lord Byron

Friday, 1.June.1945
Room 5E766
Pentagon Building
Arlington, Arlington County, Virginia
United States of America
08:00 hours

General Groves changed the name of the Target Committee once the target list had been defined and approved by the president. The Target Committee was now the Interim Committee, to take a more innocuous form but no less significant. The president tasked the committee with sorting through the various pros and cons of the potential employment.

"Take your seats, gentlemen," pronounced General Groves. He waited for everyone to settle around the conference room table and quiet. "As we discussed at our last transition meeting, the president wants our recommendation on employment. Doctor Stearns, why don't you start us off."

"Sure thing, General. As the reality of a workable fission explosive gets closer, the physicists on the project have begun to face that reality. The spectrum of opinion is as broad as it gets. Some advocate for direct, immediate use as the weapon as intended. Others at the opposite end of the spectrum don't want us even to test the device. I do not want to speak for my scientific and engineering colleagues, but I think if we," he said, looking at and gesturing to the scientific members of the committee, "took a vote, the majority would select the test and a demonstration event to show the Japanese the potential of the technology."

"Demonstration?" asked Groves.

"Yes Sir," answered Doctor Wilson. "We think showing the Japanese what this device can do will convince them to surrender without us having to use it on an industrial site in a population center. We also think they won't believe what they don't witness."

"You're suggesting we detonate one of only two devices we'll have by that time," General Farrell interjected, "over the ocean or Tokyo Bay?"

"The ocean," answered Wilson.

"How do you suggest this demonstration will work?" Farrell pressed.

"First, we test the Gadget as planned as soon as it is ready to prove the functionality of the implosion design. Once we are convinced the design is functional, we propose to notify the Japanese government by various means that we will demonstrate a new bomb ten miles off the coast at a precise time, location, and altitude. We think they will surrender immediately when they see this thing explode."

"What if the device is a dud?" Farrell said. "The O-S-S Japan Desk believes Japanese culture will see a demonstration as a sign of weakness. That we did not have the courage to fight like a warrior."

"The physics tells us one of these things detonating over a city will vaporize tens if not hundreds of thousands of innocent people," von Neumann stated.

"Isn't that the point?" asked Farrell.

"Men, women and children . . . the properties of a fission device will not discriminate."

Doctor Penney raised his hand.

"No need to raise your hand," Groves said. "You're an equal member of this committee. Just speak up."

Penney nodded. "I believe most of us want to see the Gadget test completed to answer the last 10 percent. Will it work? We want to know if all our calculations and experimentation will function as we expect. We will cover the Gadget test in every possible manner within reach of contemporary technology. What if we send the Japanese government the test report, the complete test report, the film, and all the data from every angle we record? We should send the scientific report without any of the politics, or embellishment, or couching . . . like we would to any physicist colleague. In addition to the government, we should send the report to Japanese physicists working in the particle physics and quantum mechanics areas."

"Nice idea, Doctor Penney," General Groves interjected, "but both governments decided at the outset of this project that we would not share the design with anyone. By our definition, the design includes the physics calculations that contribute to the engineering."

"We don't have to give them the design or supporting data . . . just the results." Penney paused to look around the room. "There is no guarantee that they, or anyone else, will believe the data, but it would take an extraordinary amount of work to correlate the data. To such people, the only thing that will be undeniable until they see the results for themselves." He paused again to think. No one else spoke. Penney continued, "Many of us would feel better, conscience-wise if we did everything humanly possible to avoid the use, but we also have brothers, uncles, nephews, and sons who are serving under arms. We acknowledge the need for such a devastating weapon, but we simply feel we must give the Japanese every opportunity to come to their senses before we have to use his horrible weapon."

Several of the physicists clapped.

"Perfect, Will," Stearns pronounced. "Well said."

The committee continued a vigorous, thorough debate over options, outcomes, and risks for nearly two more hours. The committee chewed through all the options they could think of, coupled with the potential effects and accumulated risks.

The debate pressed on for several hours with only a 15-minute relief break at 10 o'clock. The committee finally reached a decision before lunch.

"OK, I think we have attained a conclusion," Groves declared. "I do believe we have three recommendations for the president. One, the bomb should be used against Japan as soon as possible. Two, the target should be a war plant in a densely populated area where the bomb would have the greatest possible psychological impact. And three, it should be used without prior warning. Does that properly state the committee's recommendations? Or, perhaps stated in better form, are there any objections to these recommendations?" Groves pointed and looked at each member. He received a form of negative response from each man. "Very well. We are unanimous. We will present our recommendations to the secretary. I'll add that the report will reflect the committee members' concerns. I appreciate your candor and contributions. We are concluded."

The committee members began to make their way out of the Pentagon building while General Groves went to Secretary Stimson's office to give him a preliminary briefing on the committee's deliberations and recommendations.

—

Friday, 1.June.1945
Office of Strategic Services
E Street Complex
Washington, District of Columbia
United States of America
08:30 hours

The department heads gathered for the daily organizational meeting. Donovan and Buxton entered on time, and everyone was present. Wild Bill sat at the head of the table. Ned sat to his right.

"OK, gentlemen, let's get started. Documents?"

"Nothing new, Boss. We are up to date on the archive."

Donovan nodded. "Experimental?"

"Nothing new *per se*, General, other than we are closing out our field trials per your instructions."

"Thank you. Foreign Nationals?"

"We've closed the tap, but we continue to get applicants in large numbers, mostly Japanese and Chinese Americans in impressive numbers. We are processing and registering them as long as they meet the entry requirements. We put those qualified individuals on standby status. There are some impressive men and women in that lot, I must say."

"Keep going in the holding process until we tell you otherwise. Maritime?"

"Nothing new to add, Chief."

"Morale Operations?"

"The same, Boss."

Donovan nodded. "Operational Group?"

"London is consolidating nicely in support of the occupation forces. Bruce's fellas are still trying to situate Berlin Station, but there are very few undamaged buildings in the American sector. I must also report we are finding a disturbing number of Russians snooping about, trying to determine what we are doing. A handful have spoken believable German when confronted, and a couple have spoken passable English with a slight New York accent. As we have discussed in the last few weeks, the guys on the ground are not liking the feel of the Reds in our sector . . . far too much probing with expertly trained agents. They are saying it is not friendly curiosity.

"Our situation in the Pacific is more static. The field agents are making good progress on Mindanao, but on Luzon, the guys are being overtly constrained by the Army. Taiwan's resistance is growing nicely, and the lads are working on the Japanese security services to help the resistance. The team staging in Australia is ready to activate Tokyo Station as soon as we get a sufficient foothold on Kyushu and Honshu. The team has their eye on several buildings still intact near the palace compound. They continue to make overtures to MacArthur's staff, but so far, they've been repeatedly told they're on their own."

"Don't press," Donovan interjected. "We know MacArthur's disposition. No point in poking the bear. Instruct the team to take the initiative. They are to let us know immediately if they encounter any roadblocks they can't manage."

"Yes Sir. Oh, one more item, Bern has been working intensely with Swiss forces to pick up fleeing S-S officers mostly. A few senior enlisted troopers have been caught, but no rank-and-file men so far. They've still not found any hard evidence of ODESSA, but they have incidental or anecdotal signs of an organized effort. The ratline is real. The question is whether there is supervising or facilitating organization like the notional ODESSA orchestrating the escape process."

"Stay on the issue. Make sure we pass all leads to South America. They need a heads-up if the bad guys make it out of Europe. Anything else?"

"No Sir."

"R & A?"

"We've closed out most of our tasks. The few remaining efforts will be closed by the end of the month."

Donovan nodded. "Intelligence?"

"We received confirmation from M-I-6 that Himmler was captured on the 20th of last month. As he and his companions were being processed at the detainment facility, a British military doctor was conducting his induction medical examination, and Himmler bit down on a cyanide capsule. He was pronounced dead at 23:04 on the 23rd. They were all dressed in common civilian attire and carried false papers. The only identification they had was their left arm blood group tattoo. Unfortunately, we did not get to interrogate the man. He deserves a war crimes trial and a proper punishment. Also, and of perhaps more significance to our ongoing intelligence operations in Europe, Reinhard Gehlen surrendered to C-I-C troops in Bavaria."

"Excellent. We must work swiftly and carefully with C-I-C and Army G-2 to interrogate him. With the Soviet actions in Berlin and on the sector boundaries, I suspect Gehlen and his officers may be of vital assistance to us. Therefore, let's stay very close to Gehlen until we can get a proper arrangement in place."

"We're working on it, General. We've got two top-notch field agents at the confinement facility and closely coordinating with the C-I-C commanding officer. We have participated in every interrogation session. The Army has remained open and cooperative. I think they recognize that we are better suited to handle Gehlen."

"It's time for me to have a follow-up conversation with General Nungesser to clearly establish our rules of the road for dealing with Gehlen and his men. I'd like to talk to Gehlen myself."

"I'm not sure that's a good idea, Boss. But I'm also sure you and General Nungesser can work out whatever deal you need."

"Thanks for your vote of confidence," Most of the men in the rooms chuckled at the thought. "I see the potential for Gehlen to fill in a gap or two on our collection process . . . especially with Russia. Let's make sure General Gehlen gets properly vetted and treated with respect. But, most importantly, let's make sure the Russians get nowhere near Gehlen. I suspect he is public enemy number one in Moscow."

The head of the Secret Intelligence Branch scribbled a few lines in his notebook. "Nothing else, Boss."

"Very well. Security?"

"Nothing new. Business as usual."

Donovan nodded. "Special Operations?"

"We are making good progress withdrawing our field teams. All the Jedburghs have been recovered. However, we are still missing half a dozen solos. We're working the radios. We may need to send a recovery team into their areas in our attempt to reconnect."

"How long has contact been broken?"

"The worst over a month. The last three weeks . . . right after the surrender. We'll keep working to recover every man and woman."

"Keep at it. European operations should be winding down. Schedule a separate meeting with Ned and me to discuss redeployment. We have new requirements in South America and China."

"Yes Sir. Straight away."

"Special Projects?"

"We have shut down all projects except the B-A-S contract."

"We need their aircraft. That contract stays open."

"No problem, Sir."

"Last but not least, X-2?"

"Counterintelligence continues to work the four cases we discussed previously. Nothing new since our last meeting."

"Good work, guys," Donovan pronounced. "We have lots of cleanup in Europe. Let's help SHAEF settle things down in Europe. Next, we'll deal with the evolving threat. One more time, pump everyone to keep their eyes out for fleeing Germans of any sort. Once in custody, we'll filter the bad guys from the ordinary, but we must get them into an interrogation room. South America is becoming a haven that needs attention. Lastly, we still have one enemy in the field fighting, and regardless of the commanding general's mindset, we really need to help the troops. Do your best. That will do for this morning's daily. Let's hop to it." As the branch heads stood and left the conference room, Donovan gestured to Ned to remain. When the room was clear, although the door was still open, Donovan swiveled his chair to face Ned Buxton. "I'm heading out at noon. I've asked for a refresh stop in Wichita. I want to talk eye-to-eye with Mister Sales on our situation with B-A-S. Depending on how this Asia tour goes, we'll take the long way back. Once complete, I'll stop for a chat with our hero about his place in whatever the future holds. The stop at Pearl will focus on Admiral Nimitz and the plan for Japan. He has fairly effectively cut off MacArthur. They are close to securing Okinawa, which is much closer to the Home Islands than the Philippines or even Taiwan. What I don't think I've shared with you, I'll be making a day stop on Tinian to chat with the Project ALBERTA leaders and the C-O of the 509th Composite Group. I coordinated with General Groves so they know I'm coming."

On the recommendation of the Manhattan Project, the War and Navy Departments created the Project ALBERTA team to run interference for the 509th Composite Group that would deliver the special weapons to their targets in Japan. The senior officers of Project ALBERTA were commonly known as the "Tinian Joint Chiefs." They were Rear Admiral William Reynolds Purnell, USN [USNA 1906]; Brigadier General Thomas Francis Farrell, USA CEC; and Captain Sterling 'Deak' Parsons, USN [USNA 1922].

"I'll leave my itinerary with associate location codes so that I can keep you up to date on my progress. The B-A-S crew will be authorized to report their position to their headquarters, but destinations will remain classified. I created a WILD compartment for my travel plan, which will remain T-S-WILD for the duration, and you and I will be the only access. Any changes to the itinerary will be passed to you via a T-S-WILD message. The radio gear on the B-A-S Connie is not that reliable. I'll have a T-S-S-C-I secure communication specialist with me to handle the radio for me and B-A-S. Send a parallel missive to the chief of my next station just in case."

"No problem, Bill. We'll hold down the fort and track you down when necessary."

"Thanks, Ned. Keep things calm," Donovan said as he stood.

The two men went to their offices to proceed with the day. Bill would head to Anacostia in a few hours. The Asia trip would be nearly a month-long, and Bill Donovan acknowledged to only himself that the journey might be his last.

—

Saturday, 9.June.1945
Royal Albert Hall
Kensington Gore, South Kensington, London
United Kingdom
21:35 hours

Charlotte and Brian walked hand-in-hand through the hustle and bustle of the disgorging concert hall. The soft cacophony of the myriad muffled conversations, shuffling feet, and rustling dresses offered a discordant background sound that made comfortable conversation difficult. The Drummonds made their way out of the famous concert hall. The couple walked leisurely in the dry, mild, late spring air to the north end of the building. They crossed South Carriage Drive to the ornate, gothic Albert Memorial. They had agreed to meet up with the others on a large park bench near the southeast corner of the memorial square. The Drummonds were the first to arrive, so they sat next to each other on the south end of the bench.

"What did you think?" asked Charlotte.

"In one word . . . incredible. I've never heard anything like that. Such joyous music."

Maestro Ludwig von Beethoven's Symphony No. 9 in D minor, Opus 125, also known as the choral symphony, had been chosen as the celebratory work primarily for the Fourth Movement, otherwise known as Ode to Joy.

"I felt you moving throughout the symphony," Charlotte giggled. "I simply could not disturb your absorption in the music."

"Have you heard it before?"

"No, not the whole symphony. I've heard portions over the years but never the whole symphony until now. After that, I understand why it is such a celebrated musical composition."

"I'd never heard it nor knew of its existence, I must confess. Yet, when that chorus hit those words, which I do not understand, in full voice, I felt shivers and floods of gratitude and revelry. I'm embarrassed to say that glorious music brought tears of pure elation. Amazing! Absolutely and gloriously incredible!"

"A very apropos selection for the end of the war in Europe after six long years," Charlotte added.

"Oh my God, yes! Perfect! I'm so glad you convinced me to go."

"I knew you would like it."

"There's Mud and Marilyn." Brian stood, followed by Charlotte. Within a few yards, Major Drummond turned and smartly saluted Air Commodore Morrison, who returned the salute in fine British fashion. The two couples embraced in the European manner. Brian pointed to Jonathan and Linda, who just crossed South Carriage Drive. The foursome remained standing for the Kensington's join-up. Brian rendered a proper salute to now Group Captain Kensington, his best friend . . . next to Charlotte, of course.

"What did you think of the concert?" Linda asked the group.

"Fantastic beyond description!" Brian nearly shouted in ebullient exclamation.

The group cheered and applauded as other folks walking past them glanced disapprovingly until Jeremy shouted, "His first time," pointing at Brian. Several passersby smiled and nodded. "It was fun, huh?' Jeremy said to Brian.

"That was way beyond fun. What a glorious piece of music!"

"Shall we hail a cab," asked Jeremy, "or would a pleasant walk through the park on this fine late spring evening be preferable?"

"We could go to Shepherd's for a nightcap before returning to the hotel," suggested Marilyn.

As the others began to discuss the pluses and minuses, Charlotte leaned to Brian and whispered, "What do you want to do?"

"I want to be in bed with you, enjoying a night of wedded bliss."

Charlotte elbowed him gently in the ribs. "Oh you nasty boy." They both giggled quietly together. "We rarely get the group together. I think we all ought to go."

Brian nodded.

"We're in," Charlotte said to the group.

"Excellent," Jeremy responded. "Now, we just need to decide, walk or ride?"

The three women looked at each other, nodded, and then said in unison, "Walk."

Linda knew the park the best. She guided the group along various tree-lined promenades toward the east. The six friends almost danced as they walked, laughing, kidding, telling stories common to the group, and engaging passersby with joviality. The walk proved to be their own entertainment. The three Few and their wives entered Shepherd's Pub with a contagious effervescence.

The famous pub's clientele seemed substantially thinner than during the heyday when RAF Fighter Command stood alone against the German onslaught. Brian quickly scanned the bar area, as did Jonathan and Jeremy. There were no recognizable faces. Jeremy ordered and paid for pints for all six of the group.

"Not quite like five years ago," Jonathan observed softly.

"The times are a-changin'," added Jeremy.

"My gosh, ya got that right," Brian declared. He noticed a few unknown faces among the mostly junior RAF officers who displayed expressions of recognition of the air commodore and the group captain, but there were no indications from a mere handful of junior U.S. Army pilots clumped at the far end of the bar. Brian preferred his anonymity. While some of the young pilots appeared to recognize Jeremy or Jonathan, none of them had the chutzpah to approach the senior pilots.

"Not much goin' on, is there?" Marilyn said.

"Nope," responded Jeremy quickly.

"Oddly," Jonathan said, "I kinda miss the energy of those desperate days. We were living so close to the edge . . . we were all a bit frenetic back in those days."

"Indeed! Those were the days, but peace is so much better," added Jeremy.

We still have Japan to deal with, guys. I never asked them if they were facing transfer to the Pacific. I'm sure as hell not going to ask them now, with the ladies present. "Kinda dull," Brian said. "Let's blow this pop stand." The pronounced induced laughter erupted among the six of them. "I've got other things I'd rather be doing." Brian's statement instigated another elbow poke in his ribs from Charlotte.

"Oh dear," Jeremy interjected, "a bit randy, are we?"

They all laughed hard. Charlotte blushed. Those who wished to finish their beer did so. Brian was among those. They placed the remainder of their drinks on the bar.

Outside in the cool evening air, the group decided a walk to the hotel was too much. They managed to crowd into a cab with the wives sitting on their husband's laps. Brian was the first out and paid the cab fare plus a handsome gratuity. They were all staying at the Hotel Dorchester and agreed to meet for a mid-morning breakfast before they split. Jeremy had to return to Fighter Command Headquarters, so Brian and Charlotte would ride the train with Marilyn as far as Winchester. Marilyn would continue to Hamble. Linda and Jonathan would retrieve toddler Julia and her nanny for a few days at his parents' home outside Newcastle-upon-Tyne. Charlotte and Brian would enjoy their opportunity for carnal knowledge.

—

Sunday, 10.June.1945
Supreme Headquarters, Allied Expeditionary Force
I.G. Farben Building
Grüneburgweg 1
Frankfurt am Main, Hessen
American Sector, Occupied Germany
15:00 hours

Supreme Commander General of the Army Eisenhower had invited the newly appointed military governor of the Soviet Sector of occupied Germany to his headquarters. Marshal Zhukov had commanded the 1st Belorussian Front, which had been the central Red Army force in Vistula-Oder Offensive and the Battle of Berlin. He was the closest to an equivalent commander to Eisenhower.

The two counterparts enjoyed a cordial social lunch together with only their interpreters in attendance after Zhukov's arrival in Frankfurt. The two generals quickly knit the threads of comradeship born in the rigors of war. Their luncheon conversation centered on family and children, surprisingly. The victorious Russian general proved to be affable, humorous, and outgoing once they passed the bravado.

"*Nam nuzhno spuskat'sya na parad, Georgy*," Eisenhower said in his best attempt at Russian.

Zhukov briefly showed a shocked expression, and then a broad smile bloomed across his face. "I . . . we . . . we . . ." He waved his hand in frustration, and then he spoke in Russian.

Ike's interpreter spoke softly in English. "I am very impressed by your adequate Russian, my dear Ike. I wish my English was better. Yes, we should go down to your parade. I am eager to see your successful troops. I am honored to review your parade."

"*Spaseeba*," Eisenhower replied.

Zhukov smiled, nodded, and stood, gesturing to the door. The two generals with their interpreters in trail walked to and rode a well-functioning elevator to the ground floor in silence. Both men straightened their uniforms and waited for the PA announcer to introduce them to the small audience. The sound of the outdoor speakers was muffled but audible. The announcer read through the approved script and finally introduced General Eisenhower and Marshal Zhukov. The door opened. Both generals marched smartly in step to the reviewing stand.

The program opened with a low altitude parachute drop of a company of paratroopers from C-47s in the large green grass field in front of the building. The announcer introduced each unit in the air and on the ground as they approached. Squadrons of B-25s, Mosquitos, B-24s, B-17s, Lancasters, Wellingtons, Hallifaxs flew past, and then battalions of tanks, artillery, combat troops, and even a company of Redball Express trucks that kept the armies supplied.

"Most impressive," Zhukov pronounced through Eisenhower's interpreter. "Now I understand why your expeditionary force was so successful. We will parade the Red Army, especially for you, when you come to Moscow."

"*Spaseeba, Georgy*," Eisenhower answered. "We still have more," Ike said and pointed to the east.

The fighters would close the parade and airshow. The first pass of fighters included a squadron of P-47 Thunderbolts and Spitfires. Next up was a squadron of P-38 Lightnings, followed by a squadron of Typhoon fighter-bombers. The finale of the afternoon's event was an entire group of P-51 Mustangs in an open delta formation of three squadrons, with each squadron and each flight in diamond formations. Once they flew past the Farben building, the left and right squadron smoothly transitioned to climbing turns to orbits above and clear of the reviewing area. The lead squadron split into separate flights. The last flight at the base of the squadron diamond broke into a climb sharply away from the building and shifted into a trail formation. Each fighter rolled nearly inverted and dove to simulate a strafing run, in front of the reviewing stand. Each fighter climbed away to reform and established a third up-and-away orbit.

The next flight transitioned to the landing configuration and maintained slow flight. As the flight reached the reviewing stand, another flight in finger four left formation passed at high speed directly overhead the slow flight.

Just as the slow flight began to clean up and clear to the west, the remaining Mustang flight approached at top speed on half-cardinal headings.

They intersected in front of the reviewing stand with only a 100-foot altitude separation. The sight was so impressive that Marshal Zhukov clapped and cheered like an excited schoolboy at his first airshow. The fighter on the southeast heading pulled into a 45-degree climb and rolled twice for a victory roll, and then the pilot broke right, heading west to join up with the rest of the group for their flight back to their home base in England.

"That your famous Mustang?" Zhukov said in halting English.

"*Da*."

Zhukov switched back to his native Russian. Eisenhower's interpreter translated. "A most impressive aircraft," Zhukov said as he pointed at the retiring fighter. "No wonder you beat the Germans with such machines." Eisenhower simply nodded. Zhukov continued through Ike's interpreter, "I am most grateful for your invitation to review your forces."

"You are most welcome, Georgy. We are honored to have such an important ally join us." Eisenhower paused to allow for the translation. The announcer added his closing statement, and the parade/airshow was over. "We have planned for a break to allow us both to tend to the work we do." Again, he paused for translation. Zhukov nodded and smiled. "We will re-assemble for dinner, celebration, and awards."

Zhukov stepped to his left, turned to face his host, and came to a crisp position of attention as he saluted Eisenhower, who did exactly the same for his guest. The two generals shook hands, and then they returned side by side to the building. Zhukov and his aides were escorted to their guest quarters. A sumptuous dinner and celebration were planned in a few hours for Zhukov and his entourage with the senior SHAEF staff.

———

Friday, 15.June.1945
OSS London Station
Nos. 70-72 Grosvenor Street
Mayfair, London, England
United Kingdom
17:00 hours

"Good evening to you, Major," the sergeant of the guard greeted Brian as he entered the small security reception lobby. "The chief is expecting you." The sergeant handed Brian his visitor's badge, which Brian clipped to the lapel of his uniform tunic.

Arnie Clark had called Brian at the farm to inform him that it was necessary to recall all three of the group's squadron commanders. They had been recalled three days early to plan for a tasking received from Air Force headquarters. The mission had actually come from the Office of the Prime Minister on behalf of the King.

All the squadron pilots returned on time. They had completed two rehearsal flights for their portion of the Saturday midday airshow over London Center. Upon their return to Debden after the last rehearsal flight at Duxford, Brian released the pilots for the day when the call from Colonel Bruce came. He had asked Brian if he could come into the station for a discussion, but no topics were offered.

"Nice to see you again, Sergeant."

An armed private appeared. The sergeant of the guard said, "Private Walton will escort you to the colonel's office."

Brian knew the way, having been to the station numerous times, but he also knew all visitors had to be escorted.

"Major Drummond to Colonel Bruce's office," the sergeant announced.

Brian followed the private up three floors and to the corner office. The private introduced Brian. Two men stood. Brian saluted Colonel Bruce. It took him a second to attach a name to the familiar face of the other man—*Captain Edward Vernon 'Eddie' Rickenbacker, U.S. Army Air Service, Medal of Honor recipient and Ace of Aces.*

"Glad you could join us, Brian," Bruce said. "Allow me to introduce Eddie Rickenbacker. Eddie, this is Major Brian Drummond."

Rickenbacker extended his right hand to Brian, which he grasped firmly and enthusiastically.

"It's an honor to meet you, Sir," Brian said with discernible excitement.

"Please, Brian, Eddie is sufficient. May I call you Brian?"

"Yes Sir. Yes Sir. Sorry. Sure thing, Eddie."

Bruce gestured to three of four top-tier leather chairs. Brian and Eddie sat facing each other, with David in the middle.

Rickenbacker said, "I understand we have several mutual friends, Brian."

Who is he talking about? Brian's slightly confused expression induced a soft chuckle in Rickenbacker.

"Bill Donovan and Howard Hughes." Brian nodded. "And, if I am informed properly, you are acquainted with Marlene Dietrich."

Damn! I wonder if he knows Marlene as Bill, Howard, and I know her?

Rickenbacker laughed robustly. "I suppose this is a lot to absorb, and for that, I am sorry." Brian could only nod. "I'm in England for a variety of reasons. One of those reasons is to meet you and discuss a matter of mutual interest."

Brian shook his head. *I've no idea where he's going with this.*

Bruce picked up the conversation, looking at Brian. "You may or may not know that since the Great War, Eddie has been very active in business and specifically the aviation business. He bought the predecessors to and built Eastern Air Lines." Rickenbacker waved his hand dismissively. "Eddie had approached General Donovan with an unsolicited offer to provide air services to the O-S-S, which is why he's here. Bill thought the two of you should talk."

Rickenbacker took over the conversation. "Bill informed me of the work Bainbridge Air Services has done for the O-S-S during the war. The more I examined B-A-S from afar, the more I was impressed and learned of your government work. In addition to meeting an accomplished ace fighter pilot with one less victory than me, I want to make an offer to buy B-A-S or a mutual partnership merger of our two airlines."

"A couple of immediate thoughts, if I may. First, I'm not a Medal of Honor recipient, and I'm not much of a counter of things like aerial victories. I'm most certainly not in your league, Eddie." Rickenbacker started to speak but stopped. "Second," Brian said and looked directly at Bruce, "I was not aware that B-A-S was not fulfilling our contract with the government."

"No!" both men protested simultaneously.

"That is not it at all," Bruce continued. "The O-S-S has been quite pleased with the air support we've received from B-A-S."

Rickenbacker jumped in. "Bill thought we should give you a way out if you wish to take it."

"Does all this mean there will be a follow-on need for air support?" Brian asked Bruce.

"I can't answer that question because I simply don't know. President Truman and General Donovan are in discussions about the future of the intelligence service after the war, but neither of them has shared what that future is. I can't answer that question for either of you . . . for any of us."

"My offer is not dependent on any government contract, Brian. As I said earlier, I've been impressed with B-A-S and your general manager Mister Sales. I can't see your classified operations, but from what I can see of your commercial operations, I think your aircraft and route structure would complement Eastern nicely. I must say that I discussed this potential acquisition with Howard. He's considered the same potential for T-W-A. When I talked to him, I had not decided to make an offer for B-A-S, so this might catch him off guard."

"I'm not deciding anything like that this evening. I'm not convinced I want to sell."

"No problem, Brian. I've no intention of being adversarial. On the contrary, it's a friendly offer. Would you like to know my valuation?"

Brian held up his left hand palm out. "No need, Eddie. No point if I'm not interested in selling at this juncture."

"May I ask what you intend to do after the war?"

"We've already issued instructions to Bobby to the effect that we intend to operate and grow the airline regardless of any potential business contract with the government. So we're going to press on with or without the government."

"Excellent! Hell, regardless of my offer on the table, perhaps we can create a mutual sharing arrangement."

"Sure. I can see that . . . as long as it's not exclusive."

"As my daddy always told me, the devil is in the details. We'll work it out." Rickenbacker paused. "Earlier, you mentioned 'we.' Do you have partners I can't see?"

"No. I own B-A-S outright. I do have an operating board of directors."

"Who are they, if I may ask?"

"We are a private company, but for you . . ." Brian smiled. "Bobby Sales, my wife and life partner Charlotte, Gertrude Bainbridge, and myself."

"I really must meet your wife, Brian. Bill has told me great things. Tell me a little about Miss Bainbridge."

"She's the widow of Malcolm Bainbridge."

"Wait! Malcolm Bainbridge, you say, of 4-3 Squadron, the Fighting Cocks, perchance?"

"One and the same."

"I'll be damned. I know him from our days in France during the Great War." Rickenbacker's expression turned dark in an instant. "You said widow. Malcolm has passed?"

"Yes . . . in March 1940. He got caught in an ice storm and couldn't get on the ground fast enough."

"Too bad. He was one helluva pilot, eight fighters and two balloons, as I recall."

"Correct. He was my flight instructor."

"Well, now, you learned from the best."

"I think so," Brian responded. "When he passed, Gerty deeded his aircraft to me, and that was the beginning of Bainbridge Air Services."

"Ah, now, I understand the name."

"You two could go on, and I could listen all night, but I'm afraid I need to break up this little coffee clutch. Can you join us for dinner, Brian?" asked Colonel Bruce.

"Thank you for the invitation, Colonel, but I've got a squadron to lead, and we have a mission to fly tomorrow. So, I'll have to beg your forgiveness."

"No problem."

"If you're in town tomorrow, my squadron, the 334th Fighter Squadron, will be the high-speed Mustang squadron. We'll be passing up the Thames, over

London Center, Buckingham Palace, and Hyde Park, and underneath a B–17 squadron at the center of the city. Our time mark overhead London Center is 13-oh-five tomorrow."

"We'll go up to the roof right on the flight path," Bruce added.

"Perfect," Rickenbacker said. "I'll be watching, Brian."

All three men stood and shook hands. The private who escorted Brian to Bruce's office was waiting for him. The man escorted him back to the front lobby and out of the building. Brian walked directly to the Bond Street Underground Station to begin his return to Debden.

———

Friday, 15. June. 1945
Oval Office
The White House
Washington, District of Columbia
United States of America
14:30 hours

President Truman entered from his adjacent study. Secretaries of State, War, and Navy, along with the OSS Director, stood and greeted the president. Truman gestured for the others to sit and sat in a plush center chair. The four men split, with Donovan taking the left couch with Stimson.

"Let's jump right in," the president announced. "I presume we've heard nothing more from the Japanese since the last MAGIC intercept on the 9th of May."

"Correct," responded Donovan.

Truman shook his head. "Are there any new circumstances that might alter or affect our communications with or rather from Japan?"

"No Sir," Stettinius answered. "Nothing has changed or moved since that last message from the S-C-D-W to the Russians via the Japanese ambassador in Moscow."

Looking at Donovan, the president said, "Is there any supposition as to why we are not hearing anything? That last MAGIC message was pretty emphatic, it seems to me."

"Yes, it was," said Stettinius. "There could be many reasons. The simplest might well be that the Russians have no interest in being an intermediary in what they see as a U-S war with Japan.

"That seems like a rather narrow, self-centered attitude."

"Yes, well, the Russians have not been known for their engagement. The Russian people are extraordinarily generous, but that attribute does not translate to the leadership."

"Does the intelligence community have any additional insight into the Japanese position?"

"No, Mister President," Donovan quickly responded. "We have a number of initiatives in play in our efforts to answer that question, but as of this moment, we have no yield."

"Press your sources without risking their lives."

"Yes Sir, we will."

"What is the latest from the fighting on Okinawa?"

"This morning's daily situation report from Admiral Turner," answered Forrestal, "the amphibious task force commander, indicated the ground forces are within a few miles of the southern tip of the island. He anticipates securing the island in the next week or two."

"We have lost so many good men," the president mused softly. "Where are we on the special weapons?"

Stimson cleared his throat. "The Little Boy device components are finished, and the components for Fat Man will be finish by the end of the month. We do not plan to move the components to Tinian until after the Trinity test, which is now scheduled for the 16th of July. We satisfactorily completed our calibration test on 7th of May. The project team is ready for the initial full-scale test. The Gadget, as the team calls it, is an engineering test unit that will utilize the same technique at the Fat Man device."

"Thank you, Henry. I am reticent to push for advancement of the deployment because of the complexity and criticality of the engineering. But, with lives in the balance, I must ask if we can move the project dates or the deployment of the operational weapons to the left?"

"Understandable question, Mister President. I've been over the schedule and plan numerous times with General Groves in the last couple of months. Depending upon the result of the Trinity test, we could be operational in a couple of weeks after that. The bomber delivery group is in place and rehearsing the mission plans with weighted shapes. They will be ready before the weapons are. The transportation phase of the plan is ready and will move at the fastest prudent speed. We expect to have all the components on-site for execution at the end of July, beginning of August."

"Excellent. I shall not ask for more. To all of us, we must keep a very close eye on all communication media to end this affair as quickly and peacefully as possible." Truman paused and looked at each minister. "I want it clearly understood by this government that our terms are and will remain the unconditional surrender of Japan and post-war administration by the military. They are not going to squeak out of the corner in which they have placed themselves. We have lost far too many precious American lives from Pearl Harbor to Iwo Jima and now Okinawa.

Those magnificent Americans will not have died in vain. We will proceed with the deployment of our special weapons as soon as they are ready for use. I have thought a great deal about what their use means, and I am at peace with the consequences. People and historians will question and rationalize my decision, but our objectives remain crystal clear. We seek to end the war as quickly as possible to stop the killing on both sides. I hold no doubts or reservations regarding the use of these terrible weapons. We will proceed to the end with all prudent swiftness . . . to save as many lives as possible."

"Yes Sir," the ministers responded in unison.

"Does anyone have anything they wish to add?"

"No Sir," they said again in unison.

"Very well, gentlemen. Please keep me posted. Events may move very fast. Our course is set. The ball is in Tokyo. Good day."

The secretaries offered their departing salutations.

—

Saturday, 16.June.1945
USAAF Station F-356
Saffron Walden, Essex, England
United Kingdom
11:15 hours

The mission briefing had been the same for the last three days, but Brian stepped through every element as if this was their first effort. The only difference was the location of the checkpoints. The airshow plan was ambitious and expected to be a broad entertaining exhibit.

"All right, fellas, we know what to do. Let's mount up and give 'em a great show," Brian commanded. The cacophony of shifting chairs, muffled conversation, and rustling flight equipment filled the room.

Their freshly painted and cleaned up aircraft were ready, and each crew chief was standing by. Newly promoted Staff Sergeant Larson Tomlinson stood by the tail of Brian's QP-G Mustang. "Lookin' sharp, Larson."

Tomlinson saluted his pilot, and Brian returned the salute. "Thank you, Sir. We wanted you in sweet appearance for the show. Say hi to the King and prime minister."

Brian chuckled softly. "Will do. I'll bring her back safe and unharmed." They did a walk-around together and found nothing, not even a spot leak. Each aircraft was full of fuel and had no ammunition or wing stores. The plan called for them to loiter at their staging area at the mouth of the Thames Estuary from 30 to 60 minutes before their first show time gate. Brian would take them up for a couple of high-speed formation runs out over the North Sea before they took up their staging position.

Larson helped Brian with his seat and parachute straps and various connections to the aircraft as he often did. Brian thanked Larson, who then jumped down and positioned himself in front of the left wing to do his part in the engine start process. Satisfied that everything inside the cockpit was ready, Brian checked his wristwatch. They still had four minutes to their planned start time. He looked down the line of fighters. All eyes were on him. The squadron was ready.

At the appointed time, Brian signaled for engine start. Each pilot brought their powerful Merlin-derivative Packard engines to life. With electricity coursing through the multiple wire bundles and all the switches properly set, sixteen majestic Mustangs were eager for flight.

Brian radioed the tower for a squadron takeoff by sections. They were in fine form. The 334FS performed their starburst finale maneuver, and then they formed up for a high-speed run to their staging area. Brian was satisfied. The weather was perfect—CAVU, as the aviators like to say. Clear And Visibility Unlimited. The distinct shape of the Thames Estuary remained readily identifiable. Brian slowed the squadron and reformed them into finger-four flights in trail at their assigned altitude.

Other earlier aircraft had already completed their flyby and returned to their home base. As they loitered in a slow orbit, they watched a squadron of Lancaster heavy bombers with Tallboy shapes installed and escorted by a squadron of Hurricanes on the left flank and a squadron of Spitfires on the right flank. The next to last event in the airshow was a squadron of Typhoon fighter-bombers in a finger-four formation of finger-four flights. The flight of four B-17 heavy bombers arrived from the north at their assigned altitude of 1,000 feet.

Brian commanded the squadron to reform into their diamond formation of flights, each in diamond formation. He signaled to increase speed. Brian scanned the squadron. *Excellent!* The bombers called the initial point passage. Brian waited the prescribed 20 seconds and turned for their run-in to the initial point. "Here we go, lads. Look sharp," Brian radioed. They pressed their acceleration to be at top speed prior to reaching the initial point. Brian kept his engine at maximum continuous power. He dove the squadron slightly to help with acceleration and reach their assigned altitude of 500 feet.

Brian radioed, "Cobweb, I-P." They were on speed and on time.

They were overtaking the bombers nicely, just as they had rehearsed. Brian checked over both shoulders. *Perfect.* The Mustangs roared underneath the bombers at London Center. They drew ahead of the bombers nicely. As they approached Buckingham Palace, Brian radioed, "Cobweb, ready, ready, break." Brian pulled up smoothly to 30 degrees straight ahead and pushed his throttle through the emergency gate. Once he was well clear of the other airplanes, Brian rolled his fighter twice for a nice punctuation victory roll. He could not see the other aircraft, but he knew each of the others had taken their assigned and rehearsed heading and climb angle for what had to be a dramatic starburst ahead of the bombers.

At 5,000 feet, Brian leveled off as he turned to the heading for Debden and throttled back to help the join up. One by one, each fighter rejoined in position.

"Cobweb, Cobweb Six, flights in trail and right echelon." The aircraft began to shift positions as directed. He did not wait for the completion of the formation shift. "Switch Button Baker." He waited several seconds for each pilot to punch the red 'B' button on their SCR-522-A VHF Radio. "Carmen, Cobweb, sixteen for the break."

"Cobweb, Carmen, the pattern is clear, Altimeter three zero one two. Wind one two zero at five. You are cleared for the break and landing runway one zero.

"Roger Carmen. Cobweb is cleared for the break and landing one zero."

Brian led the squadron to a three-mile straight-in, turned to align straight down the runway, leveled off at 500 feet, and maintained 300 MPH. At the approach numbers, Brian rolled crisply to 90 degrees left, pulled his throttle back to idle, and pulled to four g's. As his airspeed declined past 170 MPH, Brian lowered his gear handle and felt the gear transition to down and locked. At 160 MPH, he lowered his flaps. He rolled out just prior to the threshold and landed smoothly, allowing his speed to carry him to the end of the runway. As he taxied off the runway's upwind end and cleared to the taxiway, Brian looked back to see two more Mustangs on the runway and a beautiful string of Mustangs at various stages of landing transition.

Larson jumped up on the wing after the aircraft stopped and before Brian secured the engine.

"She was perfect," Brain pronounced.

"Excellent. We'll feed her and put her to bed."

"Thanks, Larson."

By the time everyone completed their short debriefing, Brian had contacted Group. They were released for the remainder of the day. The pilots were in high spirits, and rightly so. Most of the pilots decided to go into London to celebrate a mission well done. Brian decided to call Charlotte and then call it a day.

—

Monday, 18.June.1945
III Marine Amphibious Corps Headquarters
Okinawa, Okinawa Prefecture
Liberated Japan
13:15 hours

General Geiger stood in front of the large wall map showing the southern third of the island. The grease-pencil markings on the cover acetate displayed the latest dispositions of his command and the flanking Army units. They were down to a few remaining pockets of resistance at the island's southern tip. The end was near, but there was still fighting and dying ahead.

Major General Roy Stanley Geiger, USMC, held unique status in the United States Marine Corps. He enlisted in 1907 after earning a Bachelor of Laws degree from Stetson University College of Law. In 1909, he tested for and received his commission as a second lieutenant. By 1916, Geiger applied for and was accepted into the fledgling naval aviator training program at Pensacola, Florida. He became the 49th naval aviator and the fifth Marine aviator in history. Geiger served as a squadron commander in the First Marine Aviation Force attached to No.5 Group, Royal Air Force at Dunkirk, for which he was awarded his first Navy Cross. During the interwar years, he was instrumental in the development of Marine aviation and served as assistant naval attaché in London prior to the U.S. entry. Geiger became commanding general 1st Marine Air Wing in direct support of the Marines during the Battle of Guadalcanal and now commanded a corps of Marine divisions.

As the general considered shifting forces to overwhelm a couple of hotspots, the captain of the communication center entered. "Excuse me, General. We just heard on the 10th Army Secure Net that General Buckner has died."

"What the hell? What happened?" Geiger asked.

"It's rather confusing," the captain answered, "and the guys are still listening. The general was apparently at a forward O-P to watch the attack of the 8th Marines on Ibaru Ridge when an enemy artillery shell hit the O-P. Unfortunately, his wounds were too severe for the corpsmen to save him."

Geiger lapsed into thought. No one spoke. After several seconds, a switch flipped in Geiger. "OK, fellas, the task force commander will sort it out. We've still got a determined enemy in front of us. Let's get back to the fight."

General Buckner had indeed stopped at a forward observation post of the 8th Marine Regiment, 2nd Marine Division. At 13:15, while Buckner watched the progress of the fighting on Ibaru Ridge, a shell from a Japanese Type 1 47mm dual-purpose gun exploded directly above the observation post. A fragment of coral, broken off by the explosion, struck General Buckner in the chest. He collapsed immediately and died ten minutes later.

Admiral Richmond Kelly 'Kelly' Turner, USN [USNA 1908], commanded Task Force 51, the amphibious task force for Operation ICEBERG. As soon as the news was confirmed, Admiral Turner contacted Admiral Nimitz with the information and recommended that General Geiger assume command of the 10th Army. Nimitz approved

The day after Buckner's death, General Geiger was promoted to lieutenant general and given command of the 10th Army. He became and remains the only Marine and only aviator to command a field army.

—

Monday, 18.June.1945
Cabinet Room, West Wing
The White House
Washington, District of Columbia
United States of America
15:30 hours

Once again, President Truman waited for the assembly to gather before he joined them. This particular meeting was closed and highly classified. The only attendees by direct invitation were the secretary of State, the service secretaries, the joint chiefs of staff, and OSS Director Donovan. The only exception was Deputy Commander of the Army Air Forces and Chief of the Air Staff Lieutenant General Ira Clarence Eaker, USAAF, who had been approved to represent the ailing chief, General Arnold. The sole topic was the operational plan for the final invasion of Japan.

Truman entered. Everyone stood. Truman commanded, "Seats, gentlemen." He stepped smartly to and took the middle chair of the long conference room table with his back to the window side of the room. "We have a lot to cover, but I want to make a preface statement. We have waited for the Japanese to accept the terms of surrender. To my knowledge, we have not seen any indication of the Japanese initiative since the May 9th message. Is that correct, Mister Secretary?" Truman asked, looking directly at Secretary of State Stettinius.

"Correct, Sir," Ed responded.

"We've waited long enough," the president pronounced. "This meeting is to discuss and hopefully approve our operational plans for the invasion and the final defeat of Japan. For the purposes of this meeting, we will assume that the special weapons of the Manhattan Project are not a factor, either because they did not function properly, or that the Japanese government decided to persist in its resistance. Therefore, we will proceed with the best prudent speed to end this sordid affair. With that as a basis, let's hear the plan."

Army Chief of Staff General Marshall began the briefing. "Before we jump into the invasion plan, I'm obligated to recognize the overarching strategic question. I cannot speak for Admiral King and the Navy, but I think I can summarize the contrast our thinking represents. The Army knows it is boots on the ground that wins wars and holds the ground. In contrast, the Navy argues for a blockade and bombardment strategy to compel surrender rather than direct frontal ground combat."

"General Marshall stated the question and issue accurately," Admiral King added.

"Interesting," Truman commented. "At first blush, the Navy's approach would seem less costly . . . in terms of lives and casualties."

"We'll get to the casualty estimates as well as other related matters."

"Continue," the president declared.

"The overall operation is carried under the title DOWNFALL. It is composed of two principal components, OLYMPIC and CORONET. OLYMPIC is the code name for the invasion of Kyushu. CORONET is for the invasion of Honshu and decapitation of the Japanese government. I'll summarize each.

"OLYMPIC is notionally planned with a D-Day on the 1st of November. We intend to land on three beaches on both sides of the southern end of the island. Current intelligence indicates the Japanese deployment is the 16th Area Army to defend the entire island, with the majority of their forces stationed around the northern and eastern industrial centers. The terrain favors the defense, which is why we will deploy a full army to pinch off the southern end of the island and establish a hard defensive line using complementary terrain. The initial assault would involve ten Army and Marine divisions, with four divisions in reserve and follow-on support. The plan entails securing the southern third of the island with its airfields. The purpose is to move tactical air support closer to the CORONET beaches for timely ground support of the primary phase.

"CORONET is tentatively planned for the 1st of March the following year. The assault force is currently planned to be 15 divisions. They will land across several beaches on the Kanto Plain and move as quickly as possible to surround Tokyo and capture the imperial palace with the emperor.

"Depending on the results, we can shift forces as needed. We don't expect it will take ten divisions to hold the designated occupation zone on Kyushu. If so, then we can release divisions from OLYMPIC for support of CORONET. The current plan does not include European Theater units, only Pacific Theater already available forces. The movement of European forces will be required if we do not achieve the quick decapitation objective of the CORONET portion of the DOWNFALL plan. We have coordinated with General Eisenhower, and he is preparing to issue appropriate orders. We recommend General MacArthur for command of Army Forces Pacific and Operation DOWNFALL."

General of the Army Douglas MacArthur, USA [USMA 1903], had evacuated from Corregidor to Australia in 1942 before the fall of the Philippines. Shortly afterward, he had been appointed Supreme Commander of Allied Forces in the Southwest Pacific Area (SWPA). As SWPA, MacArthur advocates for the main thrust across the Dutch East Indies, through the Philippines and Formosa to the Home Islands of Japan.

On the other hand, Fleet Admiral Chester William Nimitz, Sr. USN [USNA 1905], as commander-in-chief Pacific Ocean Areas (CINCPOA) had advocated for a direct island-hopping campaign aimed at the heart of Japan. Nimitz's strategy proved to be more efficient than MacArthur's approach and put American strategic air forces within striking distant of the Home Islands.

President Roosevelt had reviewed and approved both Pacific strategies in July 1944. The president divided his available forces for the two-pronged attack.

Marshall continued, "We will use existing in-theater transports to move as much equipment and personnel as possible, and we will supplement that lift capacity with commercial contract shipping.

"Our best estimate of casualties for the planned 90-day campaign to solidify our hold on the OLYMPIC occupation zone of Kyushu is 350,000 and 100,000 killed. Our estimate for CORONET is 1,200,000 casualties, with 267,000 fatalities."

"Dear God above! You're talkin' about one point five million casualties with four hundred thousand dead." President Truman drifted off into thought. No one spoke. A score of seconds later, the president looked up. "What would the Navy's approach accomplish?"

Admiral King leaned forward. "With the 3rd, 5th, and 7th Fleets, we believe we can choke off all external supply from any direction. We think we can control the sea and air, isolating the whole nation."

"Blockade?"

"Yes Sir."

"Lay siege to an entire country of hundreds of islands?"

"Yes Sir."

Truman looked at Marshall. "And the Army does not think the Navy's approach will work?"

"Oh, it will be successful in part, Mister President. I think Admiral King is correct in that the naval and air forces can do what he has described.

However, I'm compelled to point out that people under siege often will bear unspeakable hardships to defend their motherland. Case in point, we have but to look at Leningrad, Stalingrad, and even London during The Blitz. It might take years to induce surrender by blockade, and even at that, the Japanese may still seek terms acceptable to them. To achieve surrender on our terms, it will take boots on the ground."

"But nearly half a million dead Allied soldiers."

"That is our estimate. I will say we continue to refine the plan as we gain intelligence and resources. We will examine better ways until it is time to execute. We seek to achieve the Allied objective—unconditional surrender. The Navy's approach is certainly less costly in terms of human life and would work if we changed the objective."

"No!" the president barked. "That is not an option on the table, General. We must end this. The fascist government that sucked us into this war cannot be allowed to exist in any form."

"If I may, Mister President," interjected Secretary Stimson, "we know the War Council is looking for a way out. We also know there is considerable conflict within and around the War Council, but the militant nationalist wing remains dominant. To our knowledge," Stimson said, glancing at Donovan, "the emperor has not taken sides." Donovan nodded. "The special weapons may well convince the emperor to swing the internal leadership conflict for peace."

Truman again lapsed into contemplation. He returned more quickly this time. "I tend to agree with General Marshall; we are only going to force unconditional surrender with boots on the ground, but the casualty estimates are simply unacceptable. We test Gadget in less than a month. Preparations for deployment are progressing nicely. We'll have two bomber-deliverable weapons by the end of July." Truman paused to choose his words. "If I understand the plan as it stands today, DOWNFALL does not require A-E-F forces."

"Correct," answered Marshall.

"Then, let's continue to refine the DOWNFALL plan and hold on the transfer of the A-E-F until at least we know whether the Gadget works. Stalin, Churchill, and I have agreed to a summit conference at Potsdam in mid-July. We'll knock off a few of the variables by then. Depending upon events or any significant changes in the plan, we'll hold here and plan to reconvene upon our return from the TERMINAL conference. Thank you for the briefing, gentlemen. We are concluded for now." Truman stood, causing the remainder of the room to stand as well. No one moved farther until the president left the room. None of them spoke as they filed out and went their separate ways.

—

Friday, 22.June.1945
Okinawa, Okinawa Prefecture
Liberated Japan
09:45 hours

Inside of Hill 89, Mabuni Hill, the command cave just to the east of the south tip of Okinawa, Major General Mitsuru Ushijima, Commanding General, of what was left of the 32nd Army, Imperial Japanese Army, and his deputy Brigadier General Isamu Cho, committed *seppuku* (ritual suicide), including being decapitated by a trusted designated master swordsman, in this instance Captain Sakaguchi. The Battle of Okinawa was finally over.

The three-month battle caused 50,000 American casualties, including 12,500 killed in action. Estimates placed the Japanese and Okinawans killed at 110,000.

Twenty-three (23) Medals of Honor were awarded to Army, Navy, and Marine Corps personnel for extraordinary courage in combat beyond the call of duty during the battle.

The 10th Army did not waste time in the massive engineering work to safe and transform the island into a vital staging area for ground, naval, and air forces for the pending invasion of the Japanese Home Islands.

—

Friday, 22.June.1945
Oval Office
The White House
Washington, District of Columbia
United States of America
09:00 hours

Secretary of War Stimson and Secretary of the Navy Forrestal arrived after a quick telephone call requesting an urgent unscheduled meeting. Stimson carried a metal case chained to his left wrist. Miss Conway, with the president's consent, rearranged the schedule. "Go right in," Conway said as the two ministers walked into her anteroom. "The president is waiting for you."

"Thank you, Rose," Stimson answered and led the two service secretaries into the Oval Office. "Good morning, Mister President," he said as the president rose from his desk and gestured to the facing couches. Stimson and Forrestal sat across from President Truman.

Stimson did not wait. "We received several messages in quick succession that we both thought you needed to see directly. Okinawa is finally secure." Stimson opened the case. "The first message was sent in the clear."

```
DATE 19450622 0432 HOME
TO ALL 32 ARMY
FROM CDR 32ARMY
BREAK
MY BELOVED SOLDIERS BREAK YOU HAVE FOUGHT
COURAGEOUSLY FOR NEARLY THREE MONTHS BREAK
YOU HAVE DISCHARGED YOUR DUTY BREAK YOUR
BRAVERY AND LOYALTY BRIGHTEN THE FUTURE BREAK
THE BATTLEFIELD IS NOW IN SUCH CHAOS THAT
ALL COMMUNICATIONS HAVE CEASED BREAK IT IS
IMPOSSIBLE FOR ME TO COMMAND YOU BREAK EVERY
MAN IN THESE FORTIFICATIONS WILL FOLLOW HIS
SUPERIOR OFFICERS ORDER AND FIGHT TO THE END
FOR THE SAKE OF THE MOTHERLAND BREAK THIS IS MY
FINAL ORDER BREAK FAREWELL END
```

"As the next message amplifies, that is General Ushijima's last message to his remaining troops."

"This is what we'll face with DOWNFALL," the president observed.

"Yes Sir, that and much more. Okinawa is like some distant hinterland to the elite Japanese. They fought hard and desperately as they did on Iwo Jima. But I'm afraid the chiefs may have understated the aggressiveness with which they will fight to defend the Home Islands."

"A foreshadow of what is to come on Kyushu and Honshu," the president nearly mumbled.

"Yes Sir. More likely, the fighting will be more desperate." Stimson paused. "That said, the next message is a decipher of the last message from Ushijima to the Japanese high command." Stimson extracted a single piece of paper with a red-striped border. "This one is a little more direct." Stimson handed the message to President Truman.

TOP SECRET - MAGIC

```
T O P   S E C R E T   M A G I C
SECRET
DATE 19450622 0432 HOME
TO HQ IJA
```

```
FROM CDR 32ARMY
BREAK
INTRA ARMY COMMUNICATIONS HAVE CEASED BREAK
AMMUNITION WATER AND FOOD NEARLY EXPENDED BREAK
I WILL DIRECT A FINAL LAST STAND IN WHICH I
WILL APOLOGIZE TO THE EMPEROR WITH MY OWN DEATH
END
SECRET
DECYPHERED OP20C COMM 212308Z JUNE 1945
T O P   S E C R E T   M A G I C
```

TOP SECRET - MAGIC

"This is the general's suicide note to the high command," observed Truman.

". . . and his family," added Forrestal.

"Has the 10th Army confirmed the commander's suicide?" the president asked.

"No, to our knowledge, Mister President," Forrestal replied. "It takes time to clear those caves. They should get there in the next few days."

"My only concern here is not curiosity about the general's macabre end, but rather the dissemination of such information as a lure to ambush our soldiers."

"Valid point, Mister President," Stimson said. "I'm certain they will be careful and cautious."

"The general's order for his remaining troops to disperse and begin guerilla operations is more than a little troubling."

"Yes Sir," responded Stimson. "But the order is consistent with Japanese operations in other areas. General Geiger and his men will deal with what comes."

"I'm sure you're correct. Anything else?"

"Yes Sir. We thought you would want to read the summary message from General Geiger." Truman nodded. Stimson removed the last message from the manacled case and handed it to the president.

SECRET

```
KM
5FLT NR 1483
S 220162Z JUN 45
FM CTF 51
```

TO SO FEW - Victory   235

```
TO PACCOM
CC 5FLT PACFLT FMFPAC NAVY WAR
S E C R E T
URGENT
BT
CG 10ARMY DECLARED ICEBERG OBJECTIVE SECURE X
SMALL POCKETS OF RESISTANCE BEING DEALT WITH
X ENGINEERS WORKING AT MAX HASTE TO REPAIR
NAHA HARBOR X ALL AIRFIELDS BEING RESTORED AND
IMPROVED TO HANDLE HEAVY BOMBERS ASAP END
BT
NNNN
```

SECRET

———————————

"Excellent. Okinawa is a key base for DOWNFALL, so the sooner its facilities are up and running, the better for our follow-on operations."

"Yes Sir. That's it for us," Stimson said.

"Very well. Thank you both. Good day," Truman said and stood.

Stimson and Forrestal stood, thanked the president in unison, and departed. Truman returned to his desk. He did not have much time before his next meeting.

———

Chapter 10

Change is not made without inconvenience,
even from worse to better.

-- Richard Booker

Friday, 6.July.1945
Office of the Director, Office of Strategic Services
E Street Complex
Washington, District of Columbia
United States of America
15:40 hours

"We just received the J-C-S memo authorizing Operation OVERCAST," Ned Buxton announced as he passed through the open door.

"Have you read it?" asked Donovan.

"No, just out of the mailbag. Do you want me to read it first?"

"No, not necessary," Bill answered and extended his left hand. "I'll pass it back to you when I'm done."

Buxton handed the document to Donovan. "I'll leave you to it. Door open or closed?"

"Closed. Thanks, Ned."

Buxton left the director to his reading and closed the office door behind him.

The JCS memo was titled: Exploitation of German Specialists in Science and Technology in the United States. The document provided the structure of Operation OVERCAST and the operating guidelines for the program. The process allowed for the designation and immigration of specifically qualified specialists, scientists, engineers, and other uniquely skilled German and Austrian individuals and their families. Individuals identified as potential OVERCAST people were separated from prisoners of war and other detainees. The project was as much to deny those designated specialists from the Soviet Union as it was to aid the United States.

Donovan pushed the appropriate button on his intercom array. "Jim, Bill, please come to my office."

"On the way," came the tinny response.

Then, Bill summoned Ned back to his office since he had the shortest distance to cover. Bill had recruited and appointed James R. 'Jim' Murphy as the branch chief for counterintelligence since the early COI days. The X-2 Branch, as it was known within OSS, had done a magnificent job thwarting numerous attempts by enemy operatives from penetrating OSS units. However, in the last five months, X-2 had picked up mounting efforts, especially in Europe, by Soviet agents, including native Germans working for the Soviets. From the X-2 work and experience alone, OSS operations were changing dramatically.

Ned arrived first. "Whatcha got, *Jefe?*"

"I called Jim Murphy to join us for a chat. I finished reading the J-C-S memo." Donovan pushed the document across his desk to Buxton, who immediately began reading. Ned continued reading when Murphy arrived. Donovan gestured to the chair next to Ned. When Buxton finished, he passed the document to Murphy. When he finished reading, Murphy looked up at Donovan.

"Interesting. So we're actually going to do it," commented Murphy,

Donovan smiled. "I take it you read the memo as I do."

"We are going to engage with surviving Germans . . . to exploit their knowledge."

"Yes. OVERCAST is a go. The obvious applications are rocket and aircraft engineers, physicists, perhaps medical doctors, and such. I want your unbiased opinion. Does this memo," Donovan said, pointing at the document in Murphy's left hand, "include intelligence and counterintelligence personnel?"

Murphy smiled broadly. "Oh my, I see where you're going, and I like it. In my opinion, yes, emphatically so."

"That's not just wishful thinking?"

"No Sir. These guys are no manual laborers. They're highly skilled and experienced operatives, analysts, and equipment specialists. They are every bit the experts in their field."

"How do you read it, Ned?"

"Exactly the same."

"What is the latest status on Gehlen and his men?"

"Safe . . . in one word. We've worked well with C-I-C. Excellent cooperation. They know we can do things they can't. Currently, the general and a dozen of his senior staff are sequestered in a commandeered hotel that lends itself to layered perimeter security."

"Where?"

"On the outskirts of Stamberg, south-southwest of Münich, on Lake Stamberger. C-I-C managed to get an M-P company assigned for security, and they are a serious bunch. So we are using the location as our local station for now, and we're looking for a more permanent facility that gives more in-depth protection, support facilities, and operating potential."

"Excellent. Do the Reds know you're there?"

"No Sir, not yet, but based on what we've seen in Berlin, Soviet probes are inevitable. We also believe those probes will come sooner rather than later if they discover Gehlen's location. The general is a marked man."

"Gehlen has successfully completed his interrogation and vetting, correct?"

"Yes Sir . . . in fine fashion

"Excellent," Donovan repeated. "Press on with all prudent speed. Do what you think is necessary. Let's get him and his officers into OVERCAST as quickly as possible. Follow the guidelines precisely."

"Yes Sir."

"If you encounter any obstacles of any kind, let me or Ned know immediately. We must not waste time. We have huge gaps in our intelligence collection relative to the Soviet Union. They've decided to take a far more adversarial and aggressive stance since they surrounded Berlin. We need far better eyes and ears on what they are doing in Eastern Europe and elsewhere. Gehlen and his experience against the Soviets is our best hope at plugging those gaps."

"Understood, General. We'll get it done."

"Thanks, Jim." Donovan had chosen not to place the burden of the president's predisposition, but he felt the ticking clock of the president's threatened dissolution of the OSS more than anyone. He wanted a solution to the intelligence blind spot before the dissolution, so whoever inherited the strategic intelligence functions of the OSS would have a working process.

—

Monday, 9.July.1945
Standing Oak Farm
Winchester, Hampshire, England
United Kingdom
15:50 hours

The 8th Air Force rotated groups for week-long passes for more to relax and explore England if they wished. This was the 4th Fighter Group's turn. Brian had arrived home yesterday and synchronized swiftly with the farm's routine. They had read the news in the newspaper and heard the news on the BBC Home Service. Brian, Charlotte, and Mabel ensured the farm's entire crew, permanent and temporary, were aware of the partial eclipse of the sun this afternoon and the necessary precautions.

The farm's owners decided to saddle up and ride to the highest spot on the farm's 385 acres. They had arrived at their chosen spot well ahead of time. Brian had spread out a tarp and a heavy blanket. They had enjoyed their picnic lunch with a nice bottle of wine and relished their moments of affection.

Brian sought the counsel of their local intelligence chief to get the precise times and protections. He had been supplied with two over-exposed transparency sheets to protect their eyes while observing the eclipse.

They lay on their backs and held the heavily tinted sheets over their faces. The sky above them remained devoid of any clouds.

"I've heard about these," Charlotte observed, "but I've never actually seen one."

"Me either. The experts told me it's only a partial eclipse for us."

"It's beginning. Do you see it?"

"Yes, sweetheart. I see it."

They watched in silence as the moon drifted in front of the sun. The path of the total eclipse passed north of them, through Greenland and Scandinavia. The best they would see was a 50% eclipse at the farm.

"This is so fascinating, Brian, knowing that it is the moon passing between the sun and us."

"The majesty of the solar system."

"Dear me, yes."

The entire eclipse took a little over seven minutes for the Drummonds.

As the last of the moon's shadow disappeared, Brian cast aside his viewing sheet and rolled toward his wife. They kissed with progressively more intimacy. Their touching grew in intimacy as well.

"I can't," Charlotte declared softly.

"I know . . . but don't fault me for trying."

Charlotte giggled softly. "You nasty boy. They can see us from the house."

"I love you, Charlotte."

"You must, Brian, and I love you more than I can ever express. Thank you for arranging all this. I never would have watched without you."

—

Friday, 13.July.1945
USS Augusta
At sea
48° 13' North – 15° 40' West
09:45 hours

Admiral Leahy knocked and entered the flag stateroom that served as the president's quarters and office during the transit. "We just received a MAGIC that finally answers the question."

Truman extended his left hand.

Leahy handed the special folder to the president.

TOP SECRET - MAGIC

```
T O P   S E C R E T   M A G I C
SECRET
DATE 19450713 1727 HOME
TO SCDW
FROM AMB MOSCOW
BREAK
REGRET TO INFORM PREMIER STALIN DIRECTED USSR
FO NO ACTION ON OUR 9 MAY REQUEST TO SOVIET
GOVERNMENT UNTIL AFTER BERLIN CONFERENCE END
SECRET
DECYPHERED OP20C COMM 131249Z MAY 1945
T O P   S E C R E T   M A G I C
```

TOP SECRET - MAGIC

"Two months just to say that," observed Truman. "I must say, the more I watch the Russians, the more I think Wild Bill Donovan may well be correct about them."

"That is Churchill's position as well."

"I'll give every man the benefit of the doubt until he shows me a reason not to do so. I've met neither Churchill nor Stalin, as yet, so I'm not predisposed to distrust Stalin, but regardless of my feelings and opinions, he has not been particularly helpful so far."

"If I may ask, Mister President, has Bill Donovan given you any intelligence regarding why the Soviets are delaying? Why are they not helping?"

"No. None. He claims they are working on the question, but nothing to date. Trying to determine why Stalin is doing what he is doing is not an easy nut to crack."

"I'm sure it's not, but that is his job."

"Yes, for now," Truman said matter-of-factly.

"You're still planning to dissolve the O-S-S at war's end?"

"Yes . . . along with force reduction, withdrawal, and spending cuts."

"Our policy remains unconditional surrender."

"Yes."

"Then I suppose there are no negotiation of terms necessary, which in turn means DOWNFALL or . . . the other thing."

"Yes. The Trinity test is scheduled for early Monday morning, in the pre-dawn hours."

"This is the biggest fool thing we have ever done," Leahy declared with vigor. "I understand the attraction to such a device. Of course, we all want the war to end now, or as soon as humanly possible, but the wholesale slaughter of hundreds of thousands of innocent people is simply morally reprehensible."

"I appreciate your candor, forthrightness, honesty, and clarity, Bill, but I see this in a balance scale analogy—100,000 enemy dead versus one point five million American lives."

"With respect, Mister President, it is not that simple."

"Isn't it?"

"No Sir. There has to be a better way to end the war without such destruction."

"I intend to propose that the Big Three should issue an ultimatum to Tokyo . . . surrender or else. They will have the opportunity to surrender."

"How would they know such an ultimatum is not just a simple bluff?"

"Their choice, Bill. Their choice."

"It is your decision, Mister President, and I respect that fact. You know how I feel about these things. To me, they are no different from chemical or biological weapons—indiscriminate wholesale death."

"Yes, I do." Truman placed the MAGIC message back in the cover folder and handed it to his chief of staff. Leahy took the clue and left the president alone with his paperwork.

———

Saturday, 14.July.1945
Supreme Headquarters, Allied Expeditionary Force
IG Farben Building
Grüneburgweg 1
Frankfurt am Main, Hessen
American Sector, Occupied Germany
09:45 hours

"Well, it's official," General Eisenhower proclaimed. "SHAEF has been dissolved, disbanded, and subsumed by U-S Forces European Theater (USFET). We are now the occupation forces of the American Occupation Zone."

"And you are the military governor of the American Zone," Beetle Smith observed.

"So it seems."

"What do you see as our biggest obstacles?" Smith asked.

"Our first priority is to reestablish law and order. Coupled with that task is feeding the people and reconstituting the necessary infrastructure to sustain the population. The task to repatriate the displaced persons in our care will undoubtedly take years to complete if they have a home to return to. Further, some of those in our care may not wish to return to their native countries because they are now occupied by the Red Army. We still have not completed cleaning out the Obersalzburg region of the S-S members who made it down there. While it is not our top priority, we also carry the burden of reformed and restored democratic governance of our zone, and hopefully, with our allies, return at least West Germany to local governance."

"That must be a long way off."

"Perhaps, but it is still part of the charge given to the military governor of the American Occupation Zone. And now, to our shock and disappointment, one ally, or perhaps I should say former ally, has started to rattle his saber. Now, Marshal Zhukov won't take my telephone calls to dampen the tension. Bill Donovan has had the knowledge, experience, and foresight to build our intelligence capacity with respect to that . . . that ally. We are walking a very fine and crooked line, Beetle."

"What do you think we should do?"

"My inclination is to diffuse the situation and eliminate whatever it is that is stirring up the Soviets. Donovan is working to convince General Gehlen to help us. I suspect convincing him will not be difficult. Georgie Patton is about one step short of enlisting German soldiers to take up arms in defense of the American Zone, if not the whole of West Germany."

"Aren't those initiatives a provocation to the Soviets?"

"As I said, it's a fine line. The Russians tell us one thing, and the troops on the ground do another. In this aspect, I agree with Bill Donovan; those troops live in fear and do not act on their own *démarche*. They have orders, and those orders come from Stalin. We are not going to be lulled into quiescence by their protestations."

Eisenhower wanted to share Churchill's Operation UNTHINKABLE planning effort, but he knew better and could not. His doubts about Churchill's thinking were swiftly evaporating under the intensity of facts on the ground that none of them could ignore.

"By the way, I know this does not need to be stated, but I'm compelled to do so. These are private thoughts I've shared with a friend, Beetle. They must not go any farther."

"You're correct, Ike. It does not need to be said, but I appreciate your concern here. How long do you think we'll be here, in the American Zone?"

"Good question, Beetle. I do believe that is a political matter. What I do know it I'm going to do my duty. The task at hand is the administration of the American Zone of the former German *Reich*."

"As we all will do."

"So much depends upon what happens with Japan and when? Those decisions are being made in Washington or soon Berlin. I intend to meet the president in Antwerp when he arrives tomorrow morning. I may add here I may hear more from him, but I do not expect any reassignment . . . at least for now. In broad measure, the reconstruction of Germany will take a decade or more, depending on what the Russians do. If Donovan is correct, things are going to get very complicated and dicey rather quickly, which will extend the transition. Stalin made it quite clear in Tehran last year that he expected reparations, and the pasteurization of Germany to achieve that objective was appropriate."

"The Morgenthau Plan."

"Yes, or the Russian version, at least."

"That does not bode well for the surviving Germans."

"No, it doesn't. I thought if I could connect with Zhukov, we might find a workable accommodation, but that notion fades by the day. He follows his orders just as we do. So we'll see what the president may share, and I'm able to pass along."

"Good luck, Ike. We'll keep the gears turning while you're gone."

"As you've always done, Beetle. I can't thank you enough."

———

Sunday, 15.July.1945
USS Augusta
51° 25' North - 3° 34' East
Mouth of the Scheldt Estuary
05:47 hours

President Truman made it a point to rise early for the view he now witnessed out the transparencies on the forward bulkhead of the flag bridge. Admiral Leahy stood with him.

"We've officially entered the Scheldt Estuary," announced Leahy. "We should dock in Antwerp in an hour or two."

"This part of the estuary is Holland, correct?" the president asked.

"Yes Sir. Most of the estuary is Dutch. The border lays a few miles north of Antwerp city at the mouth of the river."

Truman pointed to the north and the thin ribbon of land. "And that must be Walcheren Island?"

"Yes Sir. A rather nasty fight last fall. The Germans had sufficient forces on the island to deny us access to the Scheldt even though we held all of Antwerp, which consequently denied us use of the great port city for several months. The Canadian II Corps finally cleared the island's defenses in November. Antwerp port was up and running just in time for the Battle of the Bulge."

"That is history, now."

Dock 1742
Antwerp, Liberated Belgium
07:35 hours

The president saw a line of Army staff cars and trucks standing at the dock to transport the necessary personnel and materials to Berlin as the heaving lines were cast ashore. The docking had begun at just before seven.

The distinctive figure of General of the Army Eisenhower stood alone with his fists on his hips in a conventional khaki service dress uniform. Truman waved. Eisenhower snapped to the position of attention and saluted crisply.

Truman watched with a genuine interest in the docking process as it progressed swiftly and expertly. The warship was soon secured to the dock, and the gangway was installed and secured. The American Zone military governor was the first person to board the warship. No honors were rendered, perhaps by the general's request.

Eisenhower appeared on the flag bridge a few minutes later. After introductions, the general followed the president and chief of staff to the flag conference room.

"So what is the plan, General?" the president asked.

"The Sacred Cow, your dedicated C-54 transport, is guarded and standing by at Brussels airport. Antwerp airport is not yet operational. As soon as you are ready, we have an armed convoy ready to drive you to Brussels, which will take a couple of hours. The flight to Berlin-Gatow will take a couple of more hours. Your residence in Berlin is secure, and I must say it has been checked several times for any potential bugs."

"Bugs?"

"Listening devices."

"Will you be able to travel with me? We've much to discuss."

"I stand at your command, Mister President."

"Excellent. Before we head out on the next leg of our journey, I want to personally convey my sincere, heartfelt gratitude for your service to the nation and the freedom-loving people of the world."

"Thank you, Sir."

"Your leadership of the Allied Expeditionary Force will be studied and admired for decades. That said, let's get on the road."

The president, admiral, and general made their way to the quarterdeck. Honors were rendered to the president as he disembarked. The three leaders were ushered to a well-appointed Cadillac staff car painted in Army olive drab. While the disembarkation of the president's entourage would take another couple of hours, the president departed.

Two heavily armed half-tracks with support troops took the lead and trail of the five staff cars. They loaded quickly, without fanfare, and were soon on the road. Truman and Leahy sat in the forward-facing passenger seats, while Eisenhower sat in one of the aft-facing seats in front of the president.

"Please give me a quick summary of your plan for the administration of the American Zone of Germany and the American Sector of Berlin."

"Yes Sir. Our primary functions have quickly transitioned from combat to police and logistics supervision. We continue to find diehard S-S men in various locations, but that is generally when they are cornered. For the most part, the S-S, Nazis, and associated believers have tried to evaporate and disappear. We have an enormous number of prisoners of war, and displaced people who are predominantly survivors of the concentration camps. As you may know, the primary death camps used by the Nazis were in Poland. While we have found plenty of dead in Germany, they are primarily by starvation or summary execution, like Admiral Canaris, the military intelligence chief for most of the war. While we work through the vetting of the prisoners and registration of the displaced persons, our most significant single task is feeding the German people.

"I have directed our troops to maintain law and order. We simply cannot tolerate looting and crimes. The people are desperate, so we are trying to show compassion, but we must get a supply structure in place to sustain all categories of people under our charge. So far, we are implementing local organizations for the direction of the logistics effort. We have found a number of former government officials the Nazis turned out that have been most helpful in recovering the communities to a sustainable standard of living. As a result, reconstruction in some of the lesser damaged areas has begun."

"Excellent work, General. Tell me about your relationship with the Soviets?"

"The joint Allied Control Authority was established and staffed by all four constituent nations a month ago. The growing number of confrontations between the Soviet and Western Allies have increased daily, on the ground and in the air. I requested the Control Authority to establish safe corridors for ground and air traffic to and from Berlin."

"What is the basis of the Soviet confrontations?" Truman asked.

"They apparently see their Zone as exclusive."

"We're allies, partners, for Christ's sake."

"Yes Sir, but Marshal Stalin has directed this stance. He doesn't want us in his Sector or Zone."

Truman stared intently at Eisenhower. "You know this how General?"

"I've tried to build a working relationship with Marshal Zhukov. He has confided in me that Stalin makes all the decisions down to a very low level. He conveyed his frustration. When I tried to work out a functional procedure to de-conflict our transits, he responded exactly, 'My hands are tied.' We've tried to respect their sensitivities where we can, but I cannot tolerate the Soviets choking off our Sector of Berlin."

Truman continued to hold Eisenhower's eyes studiously. "That is a rather stark assessment."

"That is my view as well. Of course, I wish it was not so, but I must deal with the situation as it stands."

"Perhaps I can find some accommodation with Marshal Stalin."

"I shall pray for your success, Mister President. We can use all the help we can get."

Truman nodded. "I'd like to hear about your experience with this organization that General Donovan calls ODESSA."

"We've not yet found a conclusive document or definitive links, but we have ample examples of S-S officers, senior enlisted, political Nazis, and others using disguises, false documents, and various techniques of evasion. The C-I-C troops are working very hard to track down every lead. They have identified several waystations in what they call the ratline. Appropriately named, I must say. Most of the ones we've captured so far are not good men. That lot has all qualified under the rules for prosecution by the tribunals. This is a crazy business, Mister President."

"I'm certain I only know a mere fraction of their crimes against humanity, but they must be held to account for their crimes. The initial tribunal is being established in Nürnberg, and we expect the first trial of the surviving leaders should begin next year. Justice tells me there will likely be dozens of trials for groups of S-S camp commanders, doctors, judges and lawyers, party leaders, and such. Finally, those evil men will feel justice for what they've done."

"We'll do our part."

"Allow me to ask a direct question, General. How has the O-S-S fit into your operations before and after the surrender?"

This time, it was Eisenhower's turn to study the president's eyes and face in search of the purpose of his question. "I'm a soldier, not a politician, Mister President. I . . ."

"I'm not asking a political question, General," Truman interjected. "I want to know what the O-S-S has done and is doing for you as a field commander."

"I have not seen or even heard of much of what they do, but I can say when the O-S-S has given me actionable intelligence, they have been correct. For example, they gave us the best intelligence they could before the German Ardennes offensive last fall. They warned us, but it was not enough, clear enough, to act upon. There are many other examples. If I was in your position, I would want the O-S-S working directly on my intelligence needs."

Truman smiled. "Who knows, General, one day you may well have my job, but for now, I'm in the hotseat." He looked around Eisenhower. "It looks like we've arrived."

They arrived at Brussels airport and went directly to the C-54 transport airplane with the words "Sacred Cow" painted on the nose. The three men boarded straight away. The crew began starting their four engines. They were airborne in ten minutes and on their way to Berlin. A flight of four P-51 Mustangs joined up to escort the transport to its destination—just in case.

—

Sunday, 15.July.1945
Haus Erlenkamp (Little White House)
No.2 Kaiserstraße
Babelsberg, Potsdam, Brandenburg
Soviet Zone, Occupied Germany
12:45 hours

The landing of the Sacred Cow at Gatow airfield had not been the smoothest any of them had experienced. The runway repairs made the field operational but far from ideal. Destroyed hulks of German aircraft littered the entire airfield. Most of the previous buildings were damaged to unusable levels. A small tent village had been constructed for the personnel to run and secure the visiting aircraft.

The drive to Babelsberg had been surprisingly pristine, with thick vegetation hiding whatever damage might be behind the trees and bushes. The roadway was generally undamaged. Gatow was only a few miles from Potsdam and Babelsberg. There were no signs of war damage of any sort in the area once they left Gatow airfield. They made a slight detour off the main road to drive by *Schloss Cecilienho*f, where the main conference would be held. The large royal palace appeared to be more than appropriate for a summit conference. They passed through Potsdam to the adjacent community of Babelsberg. All three leaders had been assigned to large villas on the shore of the long and narrow *Griebnitzsee*. President Truman's residence for the conference was the former

'*Haus Erlenkamp*,' which had been constructed in 1892 and was soon dubbed the '*Kleines Weißes Haus*'—Little White House.

As the president and his chief of staff were given a tour of the mansion and grounds, Secretary of War Stimson pulled General Eisenhower aside and whispered, "A private word, if I may." Eisenhower nodded and followed the minister to a small room that appeared to be a makeshift office. Stimson gestured for Eisenhower to close the door, which he did. They sat in comfortable chairs facing each other. "It's going to be a hectic week, so this may be the only opportunity for this chat." He did not wait for an acknowledgment. "The reason we issued a hold order for the transfers to the Pacific is what is going to happen tomorrow morning." Eisenhower did not react in any manner. "In the pre-dawn hours of rural New Mexico, we will conduct a full-scale test of the atomic weapon. If that test is successful, we will immediately move the components of two operational bombs. Those devices will be deployable by the 26th or 27th of this month. We expect the first detonation to cause shock, confusion, uncertainty, and doubt. If so, we will be prepared to detonate the second device, which should eliminate any remaining doubt. The command expectation is these atomic bombs will end the war swiftly. Of course, if that happens, the need to transfer forces is eliminated."

"Has the decision to deploy been made?" Eisenhower asked.

"No. First, we need the results of the full-scale test. We need to know this thing will work and do what the scientists' calculations say it will do. There is no small uncertainty on that question alone. Second, the president intends to raise the issue at the summit and expects to release a joint ultimatum to the Japanese government—unconditional surrender or else. Depending on the Japanese response, the decision to execute will be based on those facts yet to be obtained."

Eisenhower nodded his head. "The designation and schedule for transfer of the required units have been set. They are ready to be activated."

"Excellent. Thanks, Ike. The hold will remain in place until we know what the Japanese are going to do, no matter which course is chosen. We reviewed the operational plans for DOWNFALL with the president last month. He has approved the full plan for both phases. The A-E-F units are not required for OLYMPIC or CORONET unless they do not achieve their objectives. We do not have much doubt in the ability of Pacific Forces to achieve a sustainable beachhead and foothold, but if the Japanese refuse to surrender, we will need the A-E-F units to fight the fight."

"We're ready to go when you send the signal."

"Excellent. Now, the last topic I wanted to discuss is personal and private." Eisenhower nodded. "You've done a magnificent job as supreme commander.

I remember those discussions in late '43, and they were not pretty. More than a few of the national leaders believe a combined force command was an impossible assignment. Many were convinced joint command could not work. The president, George Marshall and I believed in you, and I must say you proved the doubters wrong. My point is not to sing your praises, but rather to assure you that the sky is the limit for you. You can do anything you want, including the presidency. The Republican Party has asked me to assure you of their support. The choice is yours."

"Wow!" Eisenhower exclaimed. "I don't know what to say."

"You don't have to say anything, Ike. You need time to think about what you want to do. What do you want your future to be?"

"Mister Secretary, I remain a serving military officer. I am not and will not be another George McClellan. Even if I wanted to be president, I would not run against a sitting president."

"Don't jump to judgment. The next presidential election is not until 1948. You have time. We all have time. A lot can happen in three years, not least of which is the mid-terms next year. My task, on behalf of the Republican Party, was to plant the seed and water it. Just think about it, Ike. You can do whatever you want after your success with OVERLORD and the defeat of Germany."

"I will think about it, but please do not overlook my conditions."

"We won't. Like you, I have my duty. As the ministerial supervisor of the Manhattan Project, I intend to see it to the end. I must say, my days in this administration are nearing an end. I will quite likely resign shortly after the war is done."

"Thank you for sharing all of this with me. I will think about all of it."

"We can ask no more, Ike. Now, we should adjourn. We don't need to stimulate speculation."

The president was not quite complete with his tour of the mansion. Eisenhower waited in the foyer, since he expected to accompany the president on his planned tour of the damage in Berlin.

American Sector, Berlin, Occupied Germany
14:30 hours

The president had requested a tour of the damage in the German capital. As the military governor and senior general officer, Eisenhower was obligated to accompany the commander-in-chief. A similar small armed convoy as the transit from the ship to the airport had been arranged for the president's tour.

They made their way to the main thoroughfare into Berlin center. They passed through several forested regions with very few signs of combat. As they reached the outskirt of the city and entered the American Sector, American soldiers lined both sides of the roadway, or what was left of it. Sherman tanks interspersed the soldiers.

"Why the troops?" Truman finally asked.

"A precaution, Mister President."

"Against what?"

"The war in Europe has been over for two months, but we still find S-S members in all their variants and sympathizers. The hardcore believers are convinced *der Führer* is still alive, and the empire will rise again and be reconstituted. They are capable of anything, and we are minimizing the risk."

"Thank you for that, Ike. Who are the troops with?"

"Second Armor, Mister President."

"Please thank them for their diligence."

"I will, Mister President."

They made it barely a mile into the American Sector before the destruction became graphically apparent. The damaged buildings were nearly universal in what was once a grand capital city. The piles of rubble that began to increase in frequency were all that remained of what had once been multi-story buildings. There was rarely a clear straight section of roadway. Instead, they weaved their way around piles of rubble collected to offer some path through the debris.

"My God, Ike! The destruction! This is the Western Front in France. Some parts are not recognizable as human."

"The consequences of five years of bombing. The first mission was 80 British aircraft, and the last one involved more than 900 bombers with the 8th Air Force during the day and RAF Bomber Command at night. But even this destruction did not bring the Germans to surrender. Troops with rifles and machine guns brought the end."

"This is what Japan faces, what we face in Japan if we can't convince them to surrender."

"I imagine so, Mister President."

"Have you found any useable buildings?" the president asked with genuine concern.

"The engineers have been very busy non-stop assessing structures. The farther we move away from the city center, the more likely we find serviceable buildings. We are finding portions of buildings that can be made usable with shoring and enclosing a few of the remnants, but those are few and far between. Most of the city will have to be razed, trucked away, and replaced with new buildings. There are still people living in the rubble with no heat, water, sewer, or food supply."

"Who is in command of the American Sector?"

"General Clay and his 2ⁿᵈ Armor Division provided initial command. Ten days ago, General Parks was appointed as the military governor of the American Sector of Berlin."

The convoy came to a halt, and the lead half-track moved to the side of the cleared area. President Truman looked down the road ahead and noticed the large sign erected at the right margin of the roadway.

YOU ARE LEAVING
THE AMERICAN SECTOR
ВЫ ВЫЕЗЖАЕТЕ ИЗ
АМЕРИКАНСКОГО СЕКТОРА
VOUS SORTEZ
DU SECTEUR AMÉRICAIN
SIE VERLASSEN DEN AMERIKANISCHEN SEKTOR
U.S. ARMY

"My gosh, Ike, is that really necessary?" Truman asked as he pointed at the sign.

"Yes Sir, I'm afraid it is. The confrontations I mentioned earlier generally occur when curious or intoxicated soldiers cross that painted line on the pavement adjacent to the sign. The U.S. command has spent inordinate hours trying to recover those individuals. The Soviets inevitably claim they are spies and even threaten a few of the more belligerent individuals with summary execution as spies."

"I had no idea. These confrontations sound quite serious."

Eisenhower chuckled softly. "To the men involved, I am certain they feel the seriousness. The Soviets are not gentle or tolerant. We strive to move quickly to resolve the situation. General Parks felt a warning was necessary. That sign has reduced but not eliminated transgressions."

"Where are we?"

"We are on *Friedrichstraße*, and the cross street just ahead is *Zimmerstraße*. There are several makeshift bars and cafes near this intersection. General Parks has considered closing those establishments, but he is trying to find some balance. Working in Berlin is very stressful and, in some places and circumstances, can be dangerous. The troops need some relief from that stress."

"Not much relief if they become guests of the Red Army."

Again, Eisenhower chuckled. "Quite so."

"Let's go ahead."

"I would not advise that, Mister President. First, the Soviets have not been particularly diligent in returning infrastructure to a minimum operating level.

Second, our experience in these confrontations tells us they are not especially respectful of anyone they detain in their sector."

"None of that suggests their conduct or behavior is not that of an ally or even a remote friend."

"No Sir. I think that is an accurate assessment. While I have not detected that attitude with Marshal Zhukov or his senior staff, your observation is quite accurate at the working on the ground level."

"What does Zhukov say when these confrontations are detected?"

"He claims he has not heard of any problems. We give him and his staff the physical evidence we have, but it achieves nothing we can detect. It seems Zhukov wants to ignore the problem. The pervasive territorial possessiveness is impossible to ignore. That said, my guidance to General Parks is to do what he can to avoid confrontational situations."

A half dozen armed Red Army soldiers appeared as a cordon across the path ahead. They all displayed serious, confident expressions of what looked like defiance rather than resolve. The troops on the half-track were visibly alert but took no overt defensive action.

"General Donovan has informed me of probes by Soviet agents."

"Correct. They occur every day . . . mostly N-K-G-B and N-K-V-D agents, but we have seen military incursions. The military events are generally to recover their soldiers before they reach our custody. Of those we have detained, all of them without exception have sought asylum."

"That says a lot right there. Have we had any soldiers seek asylum in the Soviet Sector?"

"No Sir, not that we've detected."

"I would really like to see their administration."

"Understandable, but it is too risky. If you wish, I can contact Marshal Zhukov and try to arrange a sanctioned visit. But, while the rules allow for inter-sector transit and travel, the ensuing confrontations with local guard units are simply too problematic."

Truman thought for a moment. "I have enough on my plate. This tour is sufficient. Let's head back. Those troops," Truman said and gestured toward the Red Army soldiers, "don't look especially friendly."

"They are sending a wordless message." Eisenhower said to the driver, "Let's reverse and head back to the Little White House."

"Yes Sir," the driver replied and then signaled the convoy with a circular overhead hand gesture outside the car's open window.

The drive back was not without obstacles to circumvent but was generally uneventful. As they reached the city's outskirts and the pristine forest, President Truman thanked General Eisenhower for arranging the tour and serving as his guide.

When they arrived at the president's residence, Admiral Leahy stood outside and engaged the president with the immediate actions awaiting his attention. The president's work was never done.

—

Monday, 16. July. 1945
Control Bunker S-10000
Trinity Test Site
Alamogordo Bombing and Gunnery Range
La Jornada del Muerto
Socorro County, New Mexico
United States of America
02:00 hours

The final assembly of the device, the development team called The Gadget, had been completed three days earlier. The six-foot diameter sphere was an implosion-type device with a grapefruit-sized plutonium core buried in spherical segments of specialized conventional explosive material, designed to compress the core to a critical mass, inducing the explosive release of vast energy. The Gadget had been hoisted to and secured at the top of a 100-foot steel tower located at 33° 40' 38" North – 106° 28' 31" West – a precise point the test team called ground zero. The electrical connections of the complex firing circuit had been checked at least a dozen times in the last two days. At the top of the tower just a few hours earlier, the special Model 1773 Exploding-BridgeWire (EBW) detonators, all 32 of them, had been carefully installed, secured, and connected to the firing circuit. The device and the test systems were ready.

Most of the working test team had been on sight for nearly a week during the final assembly and completion of the test setup. General Groves and Doctor Oppenheimer arrived at the control bunker shortly after midnight and received a rather disappointing weather forecast. Thunderstorms had already formed west-southwest of the test site and were moving toward their location. Like the calibration test, the full-scale Gadget test had been scheduled for 04:00 local time.

By 02:00, all the observers, witnesses, and test personnel, 250 specifically invited people in all, as well as the security detail of double that number, were registered and confirmed at their designated locations and stations. Every possible entry point within 25 miles of ground zero had been blocked and protected with small units of specially trained, heavily armed, very serious, Army military police.

At the Compañía Hill VIP observation site, the Manhattan Project Deputy Director Brigadier General Farrell hosted the dignitaries, including

Vannevar Bush, James Conant, Ernest Lawrence, Enrico Fermi, and the senior British physicist Sir James Chadwick. A heated field tent kept the group comfortable in the morning chill.

The rain had begun shortly after their arrival. The rumble of thunder and the ominous flashes of lightning across the Jornada del Muerto valley made everyone uneasy, tense, and agitated. Perhaps, it was the long-standing name of their location – Journey of Death – that added to their unease or the knowledge that the firing circuits were all electrical that amplified their jitters during the passing thunderstorms. Doctor Fermi initiated a betting pool in an attempt to lighten up the mood at the Compañía Hill observation site. Would this thing really work? If it did, how big would the resultant explosion be? None of them knew. Most of them guessed from zero – a dud – to the full, calculated, theoretical yield.

03:30 hours

"OK, Oppy," announced General Groves as soon as he placed the telephone handset in its cradle, "the meteorology experts at Alamogordo confirm our assessment. These thunderstorm cells will clear the 25-mile radius by 4:30 or 5 at the latest. So let's delay the test to 5:30 to give everyone plenty of room."

Oppenheimer looked to his test controller, who nodded his head in concurrence. "Very well, Dick." Oppenheimer walked to his test controller. "You heard *el Jefe*. Let's reset T-zero to 5:30."

"You got it, Oppy."

Oppenheimer returned to the thick observation window alongside Groves. They stared at the receding lightning flashes. "At least our design and construction proved sufficient to endure nature's wrath."

"So it would appear," Groves responded softly.

"All locations informed," announced the test controller.

"Very well."

"I understand you took zero in the betting pool," Groves said with an unusual and uncharacteristic smile.

"I felt I had to. I have too much invested in the experiment. The scientist in me expects to be wrong."

"We all have so much invested in this project, not least of which is the billions of Treasury dollars."

"Yes . . . that too."

"OK, Oppy, I'm going to head to my station," Groves said. The plan called for General Groves to be at the Base Camp 10 miles south-southwest of ground zero. Most of their contingency services were staged at the Base Camp site to deal with any of the potential outcomes.

Oppenheimer nodded in acknowledgment without taking his eyes off the exterior scene. Groves departed the S-10000 Control Bunker for the Base Camp. Only the whirr of the electronics' cooling fans could be heard. The chief scientist remained isolated in his thoughts. They had come so far in three short years. They had accomplished so much – unprecedented theoretical and practical physics, gargantuan engineering design work, unimaginable experimentation at the detail level, and historical construction and manufacturing efforts across the country.

"We're approaching auto-time," the controller announced.

"Proceed," was the simple command from Doctor Oppenheimer.

The distinctive green flare arced into the pitch-black night sky. Some observers decided to lie down prone on the ground. They had 20 seconds to time zero. Then, the protected eyes of the observers and witnesses turned to the known point. Data recorders and cameras were automatically triggered during the final countdown.

05:29:45 hours

The electrical pulse firing command went to all 32 EBW detonators as close to simultaneously as the best electrical engineering design could produce. The explosive lens sent a focused spherical shock front inward, compressing the grapefruit-sized plutonium sphere into a dense, tennis-ball-sized critical mass. The compression squeezed the beryllium-polonium initiator at the center of the plutonium sphere that spewed millions of neutrons into the plutonium, splitting atoms and accelerating the enormous energy release of the near-instantaneous chain reaction.

In an instant, the sun appeared on earth, 100 feet above the desert floor. The brilliant flash of light brought daylight to the night for a few long seconds. The heat made it feel like an oven had enveloped them. Then, the shock wave violently shook everything 27 seconds after the detonation.

05:40 hours

"We are all sons of bitches," Oppenheimer said aloud. The fireball ascended into the night sky as it gradually dissipated and disappeared from visual detection. He added in almost a murmur for no one in particular and only to express the thought that held his mind. "Now, I am become Death, the destroyer of worlds" – the well-known line from the Bhagavad-Gita, the most revered of all the Hindu texts,

Subsequent analysis of all of the test data over the following weeks would determine the explosive yield from The Gadget to be 21 kilotons of equivalent TNT – 200 times the explosive power of the calibration test and 2,000 times the power of the British "Grand Slam" conventional bomb – the largest conventional explosive bomb ever dropped from an airplane to date – from a device a mere fraction of the size of the calibration test pile or the "Grand Slam" bomb. It worked! So began the nuclear age.

———

Monday, 16.July.1945
Golden Gate Bridge
Between San Francisco and Marin Counties, California
United States of America
08:20 hours

Yet another grey warship made its way out of San Francisco Bay like hundreds of Navy ships had come and gone in the last four years of the war. This one had a hull number '35' on both sides of her bow. The ship no longer sported the dazzle camouflage exterior paint scheme she had when she entered the famous harbor for the Mare Island Shipyard and mandatory repairs of battle damage from Okinawa. What no observer on the bridge, Fort Monroe, the shoreline, or the few small boats and ferries in the vicinity could possibly know was the constructed gray container welded to the deck of the ship's fantail contained a unique special weapon the scientists, engineers, and technicians who design and assembled the device called Little Boy. The only items missing from the container was the initiator and the core required to transform the assembly into a bomb of unimaginable power.

The wake behind the USS *Indianapolis* began to boil before the heavy cruiser passed beneath the historic bridge. No observer of the scene could know this warship's destiny and its precious cargo. The device was the first, and so far the only, gun-type uranium fission bomb. The cruiser had been tasked to carry the main components of the precious item at the best prudent speed to Tinian, where a specially trained group waited to assemble and deliver the new bomb.

———

Monday, 16.July.1945
Little White House
No.2 Kaiserstraße
Babelsberg, Potsdam, Brandenburg
Soviet Zone, Occupied Germany
14:37 hours

The activities of a remote executive office blossomed as soon as the station's active message had been sent. The secure communications center to support the president's and government's summit conference location had been up and running, in part, by two and a half hours after the president's arrival yesterday afternoon. The service was fully functional by midnight last night. As always, the president's communications service operates 24 hours a day, seven days a week. Moreover, they had sufficient qualified and cleared personnel, so there was not a second gap in operations.

Secretary of War Stimson received a particular classified message and immediately came to brief the president. He was asked to wait for a few minutes, and then he would be squeezed into the president's busy pre-conference meetings. Stimson entered the small room the staff had set up as the president's office in the stately, undamaged mansion.

"Good afternoon, Mister President."

"And to you, Henry. I assume you've something important."

"Yes Sir, I do." Stimson handed the yellow message paper to the president.

SECRET

```
MP
MP NR 2113
S 161029Z JUL 45
FM MANHATTAN
TO SECWAR
S E C R E T
URGENT
BT
BABIES BORN
BT
NNNN
```

SECRET

"Plural?" Truman asked.

"Typographical error, I do believe," said Stimson. "Teletypes are incapable of punctuation, and I think General Groves attempted a contraction, which did not work. I think the intended message was 'baby is born.'"

"So, it worked. The damn thing worked!"

"Yes Sir. That is the meaning of this message."

"I'll be damned!"

"This is an agreed to initial message. There were four short, coded messages to represent full success to complete failure. The project team will send expanded reports as they know more. General Groves informed me that they will go through a series of levels of data review. For example, developing and reviewing all the film coverage will take days. We should expect to get progressively expanded messages as they complete each level of assessment."

"But the damn thing worked!" the president repeated his exclamation. "This changes the equation. Where are we in the deployment plan?"

"The sail order was issued by Jim Forrestal for the heavy cruiser *Indianapolis* to cast off just after the Trinity test was successful. She is carrying the main bodies of Little Boy and Fat Man. The uranium and plutonium cores will be flown to Tinian separately. Once all of the components are in the custody of the 509th, they will hold on assembly until they receive the execute order. We didn't want the functional pieces to be together until actionable authority is provided."

"Yes, I recall. Wise move. When will all the pieces arrive at Tinian?"

"Barring unforeseen events, that date is the 26th of July by the plan. It would take another day to prepare for and assemble the devices, so your executable date is the 27th."

"This news brings my decision much closer," Truman said and looked at his shoes in thought.

"Yes Sir."

"Show the message to Churchill tomorrow as the situation permits before our preparatory meeting."

"What about Stalin?"

"Hold on that for now."

"Yes Sir. I expect more messages on the test to come in quickly, so we'll keep a close eye on the message traffic."

"Thank you, Henry."

18:50 hours

Stimson's expectations were spot on correct. Truman had just finished his evening meal when Stimson returned with more relevant messages. They chose to talk in Truman's closed office.

"What have you, Henry?"

"First, we just received confirmation that Churchill landed earlier this hour at Gatow. He's en route to his quarters. We haven't received notice of Stalin's arrival, but we know he left Moscow by rail on the 13th. Second, I just received another Trinity message." Stimson handed the light pink paper to the president.

TOP SECRET

```
WA
WAR 32887
TS 161519Z JUL 45
FM WAR OPS SPEC
TO SECWAR
T O P   S E C R E T
URGENT
BT
FOR SECWAR EYES ONLY
OPERATED ON THIS MORNING X DIAGNOSIS NOT YET
COMPLETE BUT RESULTS SEEM SATISFACTORY AND
ALREADY EXCEED EXPECTATIONS X LOCAL PRESS
RELEASE NECESSARY AS INTEREST EXTENDS GREAT
DISTANCE X DR GROVES PLEASED X HE RETURNS
TOMORROW X WILL KEEP YOU POSTED END
BT
NNNN
```

TOP SECRET

"This is just an expanded version of the initial message."

"Yes Sir, exactly. The keywords in this message are 'exceed expectations' and 'extends great distance.' Here is the press release referred to in that message." Stimson handed the white paper to the president.

```
WA
WAR 32888
U 161525Z JUL 45
FM SECWAR OFC
TO SECWAR
UNCLAS URGENT
BT
PRESS RELEASE 16 JULY 1945
SEVERAL INQUIRIES HAVE BEEN RECEIVED CONCERNING
A HEAVY EXPLOSION WHICH OCCURRED ON THE
```

```
ALAMOGORDO AIR BASE RESERVATION THIS MORNING X
REMOTELY LOCATED AMMUNITION MAGAZINE CONTAINED
A CONSIDERABLE AMOUNT OF HIGH EXPLOSIVES AND
PYROTECHNICS EXPLODED X THERE WAS NO LOSS OF
LIFE OR INJURY TO ANYONE AND THE PROPERTY
DAMAGE OUTSIDE THE EXPLOSIVES MAGAZINE WAS
NEGLIGIBLE X WEATHER CONDITIONS AFFECTING THE
CONTENT OF GAS SHELLS EXPLODED BY THE BLAST
MAY MAKE IT DESIRABLE FOR THE ARMY TO EVACUATE
TEMPORARILY A FEW CIVILIANS FROM THEIR HOMES
BT
NNNN
```

"And this has already gone out?" Truman asked.

"Yes Sir. As indicated in the previous message, the light and sound of the test event immediately generated calls to police stations within range. We don't yet know what that distance is, but General Groves rightly wanted to get ahead of any speculation with a plausible story."

"I'd say he accomplished that. Good initiative and thinking. It is a very believable story. It is a little disturbing of the notion of 'gas shells.'"

"Quite so, but he needed something more than just an explosion for any potential evacuation orders."

"Ah, yes, that makes sense, but it is still disturbing. The immediate question stemming from those words is, what kind of gas?"

"If the query comes, they will claim chlorine . . . a familiar gas from the Great War and again within the plausible sphere."

Truman nodded. "It sounds like Groves is handling the unique event in fine fashion. I'm sure we will learn more in the next few days. I presume we will receive a readiness message once all the components are in place."

"Yes Sir. Absolutely! With the success of Trinity, the gears for deployment are turning according to plan. Relative to deployment, no news is good news. Yet, I will also add that the project team and my office know we need as much information as can be safely transmitted. I think the full report will come by courier, thus, it will take a few more days of transit. The official project report will probably not be available for several weeks or a month since the scientists need time to analyze their collected data."

"They have time. After all, it's not like we've nothing to do."

Stimson chuckled, which induced a laugh from the president. "That's it for now, Mister President. I'll keep you posted as we learn more."

"Thank you, Henry."

Stimson left the president to his reading.

21:20 hours

"Back already," President Truman said lightheartedly as Stimson reentered the office.

"My apologies, Mister President, but I thought you would want to see this one just in from D-C." Stimson removed the pink paper and passed it to the president."

TOP SECRET

```
WA
WAR 32902
TS 161948Z JUL 45
FM WAR OPS SPEC
TO SECWAR
T O P   S E C R E T
URGENT
BT
FOR SECWAR EYES ONLY
DOCTOR HAS JUST RETURNED MOST ENTHUSIASTIC
AND CONFIDENT THAT THE LITTLE BOY IS AS HUSKY
AS HIS BIG BROTHER X THE LIGHT IN HIS EYES
DISCERNIBLE FROM HERE TO HIGHHOLD AND I COULD
HAVE HEARD HIS SCREAMS FROM HERE TO MY FARM X
BABY HEALTHY AND KICKING X PARENTS VERY PROUD
IN ALL ASPECTS X DOCTORS WILL TAKE A FEW DAYS
TO FULLY ASSESS THE BIRTH X EXPECT FULL REPORT
WITHIN A WEEK END
BT
NNNN
```

TOP SECRET

"OK, this one is beyond my deductive powers, Henry."

Stimson chuckled visibly but silently. "Understandable, Mister President. Nature of the beast, I'm afraid. The first part tells the designs for both Little Boy and Fat Man are set and ready for deployment once the order to execute is sent. Highhold is my farm on Long Island, which means light from the explosion was seen and detected 250 miles away, while the sound of the explosion was reported 40 miles away. That is farther for both sound and light than our most optimistic estimates. The team is telling us the Gadget, the equivalent of Fat Man, performed better than expected, which means we are on track to meet the deployment readiness."

"The 27th."

"Yes Sir, exactly."

"Excellent news. Thank you, Henry. Now, get out of here. Get a good night's sleep. We have a full day tomorrow . . . well, actually, for the next two weeks." Truman chuckled.

"Thank you, Mister President. Have a good night."

—

Chapter 11

Even the final decision of a war is not to be regarded as absolute.
The conquered nation often sees it as only a passing evil,
to be repaired in after times by political combinations.

-- Carl von Clausewitz

Tuesday, 17.July.1945
Schloss Cecilienhof
Im Neuen Garten 11
Potsdam, Brandenburg
Soviet Zone, Occupied Germany
16:40 hours

As the delegates gathered for the first plenary session of the TERMINAL summit conference, Secretary Stimson watched and waited for an opportunity. The objective of his attention was Prime Minister Churchill, who was using the pre-conference minutes to socialize with diplomats he had not seen in years. Stimson wanted to fulfill the president's charge to inform the prime minister before the conference began.

The moment came when Churchill looked for his next conversant. Stimson stepped toward his back and gently touched the prime minister's left elbow. Churchill turned. "Good afternoon, Henry. Great to see you again."

"Good afternoon to you, Prime Minister. May I have a private word before the conference begins?"

"Yes, certainly." Churchill and Stimson left the main room and found an unoccupied small conference room.

Stimson closed the door. "Thank you for your time, Sir." Churchill nodded. "The president asked me to show you this message and brief you on what we know so far." Again, Churchill nodded. Stimson removed the folded message from the inside left breast pocket of his suit jacket and passed it to the prime minister, who unfolded it and read the initial succinct report.

The puzzled expression on Churchill's round face induced a modest chuckle from Stimson. "I've no idea what this means," Churchill pronounced.

"It means The Gadget test in New Mexico was successful."

"Plural?"

Again, Stimson chuckled softly. "President Truman had the same reaction. We believe it was a message transmission typographical error since our teletype machines are incapable of punctuation. General Groves meant the baby is born, which was the code phrase for a successful detonation."

"Dear God above, this is the second coming in Wrath. The day is finally upon us."

"Yes Sir, exactly. The test took place yesterday morning before dawn. The test team is still collecting and analyzing the instrumentation data. We expect to receive a more detailed report from General Groves in a few days."

"Excellent. Is President Truman going to announce the results at the conference?"

"No Sir. He asked me to brief you only. He hopes to discuss this news with you privately after the official dinner."

"What about Stalin?"

"He is not inclined to inform the premier, at least not until he has conferred with you. The press release issued by the test team should quell any Press speculation."

"So, the damn thing worked."

"Yes Sir, it did. And based on the initial message, the test was equal to or better than the calculations. Like I mentioned earlier, we expect to receive more details in a few days. The official final report may be more than a month or more away."

"What about the operational units for Japan?"

"From the initial report, orders were issued to move Little Boy and Fat Man components to Tinian for potential delivery. General Groves informs us that the date for use is currently the 27th of this month."

"Ten days hence."

"Yes Sir."

"How will we proceed?"

"That is one of the topics for your private discussions with the president. I do not want to preempt the president. I hope you understand."

"Certainly, Henry. Quite the heavy burden for my first meeting with the new president."

"Yes Sir. They do not get much bigger than this."

"Indeed. So, the end of the dreadful war is within sight."

"We believe so. The current thinking is that the Japanese will likely be shocked into uncertainty, confusion, and doubt, which is why we decided to stage the second device to eliminate any lingering doubts."

"Follow-on devices?'

"The second Fat Man device is three to four weeks behind, and the next one a month after that. Oak Ridge is still working to produce sufficient core material for another Little Boy version toward the end of the year. We have agreed on five primary targets. We are prepared for additional deliveries as devices become available and the political decisions for deployment are made.

As expected, the extent of employment is in the hands of the Japanese Supreme Counsel."

"Quite so. Anything else?"

"Only if you have additional questions, Sir. We do not yet have the technical details, but they will, of course, be available to you as soon as we have them."

"My current questions are for President Truman."

"Thank you, Prime Minister."

Churchill nodded and gestured to the door. The two men returned to the main conference room as the attendees shuffled toward their seats at the table or the periphery. The TERMINAL conference's first plenary session was about to begin.

—

Saturday, 21.July.1945
Little White House
No.2 Kaiserstraße
Babelsberg, Potsdam, Brandenburg
Soviet Zone, Occupied Germany
15:00 hours

In the mansion's sunroom, Stimson finally got his chance to sit down with President Truman and Secretary of State Byrnes.

James Francis 'Jim' Byrnes replaced Ed Stettinius as secretary of state on 3.July.1945. He had served as a representative, a senator, and an associate justice of the U.S. Supreme Court before joining the federal Executive Branch as the director of Economic Stabilization and then War Mobilization in the Roosevelt administration. More importantly, Jim was a confidante and mentor to Harry Truman.

"I received a more detailed report on the Trinity test from General Groves. If you will permit me, I would like to read the report so that each of us hears the information at the same time and can ask questions as they arise."

"Sure, Henry. We will listen," responded Truman.

Stimson opened the folder and read aloud to his audience of two.

TOP SECRET - PARAMOUNT
WAR DEPARTMENT
WASHINGTON

18 July 1945

MEMORANDUM FOR THE SECRETARY OF WAR.
SUBJECT: The Test.

1. This is not a concise, formal military report but an attempt to recite what I would have told you if you had been here on my return from New Mexico.

2. At 0530, 16 July 1945, in a remote section of the Alamogordo Air Base, New Mexico, the first full scale test was made of the implosion type atomic fission bomb. The bomb was exploded on a platform on top of a 100-foot high steel tower.

3. The test was successful beyond the most optimistic expectations of anyone. Based on the data that it has been possible to work up to date, I estimate the energy generated to be in excess of the equivalent of 15,000 to 20,000 tons of TNT; and this is a conservative estimate. There were tremendous blast effects. For a brief period there was a lighting effect within a radius of 20 miles equal to several suns in midday; a huge ball of fire was formed which lasted for several seconds. This ball mushroomed and rose to a height of over ten thousand feet before it dimmed. The light from the explosion was seen clearly at Albuquerque, Santa Fe, Silver City, El Paso and other points generally to about 180 miles away. The sound was heard to the same distance in a few instances but generally to about 100 miles. Only a few windows were broken although one was some 125 miles away. A massive cloud was formed which surged and billowed upward with tremendous power, reaching the substratosphere at an elevation of 41,000 feet, 36,000 feet above the ground, in about five minutes, breaking without interruption through a temperature inversion at 17,000 feet which most of the scientists thought would stop it.

4. A crater from which all vegetation had vanished, with a diameter of 1200 feet and a slight slope toward the center, was formed. In the center was a shallow bowl 130 feet in diameter and 6 feet in depth. The material within the crater was deeply pulverized dirt. The material within the outer circle is greenish and can be distinctly seen from as much as 5 miles away. The steel from the tower was evaporated.

5. One-half mile from the explosion there was a massive steel test cylinder weighing 220 tons. The base of the cylinder was solidly encased in concrete. Surrounding the cylinder was a strong steel tower 70 feet high, firmly anchored to concrete foundations. This tower is comparable to a steel building bay that would be found in typical 15 or 20 story skyscraper or in warehouse construction. Forty tons of steel were used to fabricate the tower which was 70 feet high, the height of a six story building. The cross bracing was much stronger than that normally used in ordinary steel construction. The absence of the solid walls of a building gave the blast a much less effective surface to push against. The blast tore the tower from its foundations, twisted it, ripped it apart and left it flat on the ground. The effects on the tower indicate that, at that distance, unshielded permanent steel and masonry buildings would have been destroyed. I no longer consider the Pentagon a safe shelter from such a bomb.

6. The cloud traveled to a great height first in the form of a ball, then mushroomed, then changed into a long trailing chimney-shaped column and finally was sent in several directions by the variable winds at the different elevations. It deposited its dust and radioactive materials over a wide area. It was followed and monitored by medical doctors and scientists with instruments to check its radioactive effects. While here and there the activity on the ground was fairly high, at no place did it reach a concentration which required evacuation of the population. Radioactive material in small quantities was located as much as 120 miles away.

7. For distances as much as 200 miles away, observers were stationed to check on blast effects, property damage, radioactivity and reactions of the population. While complete reports have not yet been received, I now know that no persons were injured nor was there any real property damage outside our Government area. As soon as all the voluminous data can be checked and correlated, full technical studies will be possible.

8. The test had been originally set for 0400 hours and all the night through, because of the bad weather, there were urgings from many of the scientists to postpone the test. Such a delay might well have had crippling results due to mechanical difficulties in our complicated test set-up. We held firm and waited the night through hoping for suitable weather. We had to delay an hour and a half, to 0530, before we could fire. This was 30 minutes before sunrise.

9. Because of bad weather, our two B-29 observation airplanes were unable to take off as scheduled from Kirtland Field at Albuquerque and when they finally did get off, they found it impossible to get over the target because of the heavy clouds and the thunderstorms. Certain desired observations could not be made and while the people in the airplanes saw the explosion from a distance, they were not as close as they will be in action. We still have no reason to anticipate the loss of our plane in an actual operation although we cannot guarantee safety.

10. Just before 1100 the news stories from all over the state started to flow into the Albuquerque Associated Press. I then directed the issuance by the Commanding Officer, Alamogordo Air Base of a news release. With the assistance of the Office of Censorship we were able to limit the news stories to the approved release supplemented in the local papers by brief stories from the many eyewitnesses not connected with our project.

11. My impressions of the night's high-points follow:

By 0330 we decided that we could probably fire at 0530. By 0400 the rain had stopped but the sky was heavily overcast. Our decision became firmer as time went on. At 0510 I left Dr. Oppenheimer and returned to the main observation point that was 17,000 yards from the point of explosion.

At about two minutes of the scheduled firing time all persons lay face down with their feet pointing towards the explosion. As the remaining time was called from the loudspeaker from the 10,000 yard control station there was complete silence. Most of the individuals in accordance with orders shielded their eyes in one way or another. There was then this burst of light of a brilliance beyond any comparison. We all rolled over and looked through dark glasses at the ball of fire. About forty seconds later came the shock wave followed by the sound, neither of which seemed startling after our complete astonishment at the extraordinary lighting intensity.

12. A large group of observers were stationed at a point about 27 miles north of the point of explosion. Individual reports will be included in the final report.

13. I have informed the necessary people here of our results. I informed Lord Halifax that I was sending this report to you and that you might wish to show it to the proper British representatives.

14. We are all fully conscious that our real goal is still before us. The battle test is what counts in the war with Japan.

15. May I express my deep personal appreciation for your congratulatory cable to us, and for the support and confidence that I have received from you.

16. I know that Colonel Kyle will guard these papers with his customary extraordinary care.

L.R. Groves
L. R. GROVES,
Major General, USA.

Enclosures:
Pictures
News Release

TOP SECRET - PARAMOUNT

"That is rather sobering," Byrnes reacted first.

"Thank you for your reading, Henry. Fifteen to twenty thousand tons of explosives is a very large bomb."

"Yes Sir. That is the range the physics calculation determined. From that information, we can safely say The Gadget achieved or exceeded the calculations."

"Now, imagine a thriving populated city under one of those things," Byrnes mused.

"I think we are all keenly aware of the destruction these bombs can inflict. We can hope and pray we do not have to use them. Of course, we will give the Japanese ample opportunity to surrender unconditionally, but I want it clearly and emphatically understood that it is the policy of the United States that I will not sacrifice one point five million American lives to avoid using this tool. From this information, these bombs will do what we need them to do if Japan refuses to or hesitates to surrender. I have made my peace with these things, and I do believe we all want this war to end as soon as possible."

"Yes Sir, we do, but in a single bomb from a single bomber, we will cause the indiscriminate deaths of so many innocent people."

"Jim, I appreciate your sensitivity; however, you must see the balance. I see this question in unambiguous terms." President Truman held his hands out, palms up, and moved them like a balance scale. "One thousand innocent Japanese lives versus one point five million American soldiers—sons, husbands, fathers, and even grandfathers. The choice is clear."

"I understand the reasoning, Mister President, but the scale of these things is mind-boggling. Until now, these devices were theoretical and imaginary. Today, they are very, very real. They scare me."

"They should scare us all. They are horrible weapons of human creation based on the physics of nature. That said, let me ask you, what is the difference between one thousand B-29 bombers dropping their payloads of explosive and incendiary bombs and a single B-29 dropping one bomb?"

"The dead are dead."

"Exactly . . . no matter the method of their destruction. They certainly did not respect the lives of our people on the 7th of December."

"Mister President, not to be argumentative, but Pearl Harbor was a military attack on military targets. While there are legitimate military targets in each of the approved target cities, the majority of the population is not so employed."

"A distinction with no difference from my perspective." Truman paused and held Byrnes's eyes until the secretary shook his head to indicate he had nothing more to add. The president shifted his gaze to Secretary Stimson. "Henry, we will proceed with all prudent speed with the deployment plan. Unless you tell me otherwise, the earliest deployment date is the 27th of this month."

"Correct, Sir," Stimson confirmed. "All the components are en route. We are tracking to plan."

"Very well. Prime Minister Churchill has been informed. He deserves to review this report from General Groves. I will say, at this juncture, I am inclined to at least verbally brief Premier Stalin. I would like him to have a few days to think about all this because I would like at least the Big Three as signatories to the ultimatum for the Japanese."

"The Soviets might not be particularly amenable to that notion," Byrnes added.

"Why?"

"Simply put," Byrnes continued, "they are not at war with Japan."

"And, we have repeatedly asked them to join the Pacific campaign," interjected Stimson. "Having listened to the words and actions of the conference so far, I'm beginning to feel that approaching the Soviets to join the fight was a mistake. Now that we have atomic bombs of such power, I'm becoming convinced it's a mistake. As they are doing in Eastern Europe, they do not want peace and freedom. They want more land and buffer states for their sense of security."

"We certainly see signs, Henry," said Byrnes, "that your words are not without substance, but as a diplomat who has worked with the Soviets, I can't agree with your rendition of the facts. Let's be very careful how we deal with the Soviets. They are a suspicious bunch as a whole, verging on paranoia. They see enemies everywhere in every form. This is not a new behavior, and we've adapted our efforts to their sensitivities. I only urge caution. Any resistance or tension on our part will only play to their sensitivities."

"What about this?" Stimson asked, holding up the Groves report.

"I will inform Stalin myself. But, for now, I want that report confined to PARAMOUNT. In my opinion, so far, he deserves to know as an ally, but I do not want to risk any compromise of ALBERTA. We're close to the end of this horrific affair. We will be careful how we tread.

"Now, we've got the fifth plenary session in a few minutes, so we need to get over to the palace. Thank you for your time and counsel, gentlemen. We're adjourned."

The three leaders rode separately across the lake to the afternoon's joint session of the summit conference.

—

Tuesday, 24. July. 1945
Schloss Cecilienhof
Im Neuen Garten 11
Potsdam, Brandenburg
Soviet Zone, Occupied Germany
19:30 hours

President Truman had sent a request to *Villa Herpich*, Stalin's residence for a personal meeting. The Soviet premier accepted the president's invitation. The president's guest arrived on time prior to their private dinner. After greeting his guest, Truman gestured to the well-appointed sitting room overlooking the lake. The two leaders sat across from each other. Their interpreters sat in simple wooden straight-back chairs at the right shoulder of each leader. Both leaders spoke in their native language and conversed via the interpreters.

"I asked to speak to you privately about a unique and serious matter." Truman waited for the translation. Stalin only nodded. "A week ago, we tested a new military explosive of unprecedented power."

"Congratulations, Mister President."

"We intend to issue an ultimatum to the Japanese government—unconditional surrender or else."

"You will use this new explosive as the 'or else'?"

"Yes."

"It must be a very big explosive. The Japanese are not easily intimidated."

"Yes, it is, and no, they are not. We have considerable experience with the Japanese principle of *bushido*." After translation, Truman continued, "I will raise the ultimatum matter at tomorrow's plenary session to ensure the conference is aware and to give you the opportunity to be a signatory of the ultimatum."

"Thank you for the courtesy. As you know, Mister President, the Soviet Union is not at war with Japan." Stalin paused for translation. "We are keenly aware of your request to join the invasion of Japan." Another pause. "We are transferring major units to our eastern provinces in anticipation of assisting your efforts." Pause for translation. "When we have sufficient Red Army forces in the East, we will carry out peripheral support operations."

"You will not join us for the invasion of the Home Islands?"

"Are you asking us to lead a joint combined invasion force?"

"No, I'm asking you to join us."

Stalin stared intently and sternly at Truman. "I am the only commander of the Red Army."

An awkward silence surrounded the four men. Truman was not satisfied with Stalin's position toward finishing off Japan, but it was his near-total lack of curiosity about the atomic bomb that truly puzzled him. Regardless, the president chose not to push the topic.

"Shall we head to the dining room?"

"Of course. Lead the way."

The evening meal between the Big Three leaders proved to be light-hearted, jovial, and devoid of rancor, tension, or confrontation.

After dinner and the departure of his guests, President Truman called for the Secretaries of State and War to join him and his chief of staff as soon as possible. The president recounted the pre-dinner conversation with Stalin.

"When I told him of the atomic explosive test and our intent to use the bomb to subdue Japan, he seemed uninterested in the technology. He asked no questions, and I chose not to offer more information without specific questions." Truman shook his head.

"Maybe he didn't understand," Byrnes suggested.

"Then why didn't he ask questions?"

"Perhaps he already knows?'"

"Spies?" asked Truman.

"Impossible!" Stimson protested. "The Manhattan Project is the most secret and secure operation in the world."

"Well, something was dreadfully wrong. I wanted to make you both aware while my impressions are fresh. We have so many issues in play. I don't see this exchange altering our path. We will raise the ultimatum issue at tomorrow's session and release it to the Japanese as soon as possible thereafter." Truman looked at Stimson. "You might have your security folks relook at security."

"Yes Sir."

In February 1943, the U.S. Army's Signal Intelligence Service, the forerunner of the National Security Agency (NSA), began a counterintelligence program to decipher Soviet communications as concerns about the activities of the Soviet NKGB, NKVD, and GRU pushed suspicions beyond the threshold of tolerance. The highly classified and compartmented program was known as VENONA.

It was VENONA decrypts that eventually uncovered the massive Soviet espionage effort to penetrate the Manhattan Project. The Soviets became aware of the Allied atomic weapons program in 1941, when German refugee, British physicist Klaus Emil Julius Fuchs informed a fellow German-Soviet agent of the British and American atomic explosive effort.

VENONA would eventually uncover the Cambridge Five spies in England and the pervasive Soviet penetration of the Manhattan Project. Individual Soviet spies like Fuchs, Hall, the Rosenbergs, Podolsky, McNutt, May, Pontecorvo, and others were identified.

Marshal Stalin was not impressed or interested in President Truman's disclosure because he had known for years and directed a similar Soviet weapons development program based on the mounting intelligence being collected. He most likely knew more about the inner workings of the Manhattan Project and the evolving atomic bomb design than either Roosevelt or Truman. Counterintelligence agents in the United States and Great Britain eventually uncovered the extent of Soviet penetration.

—

Wednesday, 25.July.1945
Villa Urbig
No.23 Ringstraße
Babelsberg, Potsdam, Brandenburg
Soviet Zone, Occupied Germany
12:30 hours

Prime Minister Churchill had requested the 9th plenary session be moved up to allow Attlee and himself to return to London. The election results were due to be publicly announced the following morning.

The plenary session began at 11:00 and concluded at 12:15. The Polish sovereignty issue dominated the morning discussions. Poland represented the fate of all Soviet-occupied Eastern European nations. At the session's conclusion, he said goodbye to the leaders and attendees and hoped to return in a day or so.

Churchill had chosen to leave his personal baggage at his conference residence in Germany. He expected the Conservative Party to win a clear majority and his premiership continued as the war was not yet done. Churchill had felt the Labour Party's decision to dissolve the War Cabinet before the war's end and force elections had been a political mistake, which he was happy to deal with. Despite his optimistic perspective on the election, the occupation and continuing war effort in the Pacific seriously diluted and distracted his election campaign, but he felt he had done the best he could. The voting by the British people was done. They now needed to receive the decision of the voters.

The prime minister said goodbye to the staff, waited for Attlee to arrive, and departed for Gatow Airbase. They would fly together in the prime minister's plush C-54B transport known as Paralos.

The aircraft would take off at 13:23 and land at RAF Northolt at 14:45. Churchill would have a nice family dinner at the Annexe with Clementine, Mary, and Randolph. He remained pensive and distant but still enjoyed the family gathering. The British war leader confessed to his family about the cloud he felt looming over his sense of the future.

—

Wednesday, 25.July.1945
Office of the Chief of Staff
Pentagon Building
Arlington, Arlington County, Virginia
United States of America
14:30 hours

The order to execute Operation ALBERTA had arrived last night from Secretary of War Stimson in Potsdam. Deputy Chief of Staff General Thomas Troy Handy, USA [VMI 1914], had been acting chief of staff since General of the Army Marshall departed Washington with President Truman on the 6th.

The Office of the Chief of Staff prepared the necessary document. General Handy read through the letter one last time and signed it as directed by the secretary's message.

TOP SECRET

WAR DEPARTMENT
OFFICE OF THE CHIEF OF STAFF

WASHINGTON, DC

                                        25 July 1945

TO: General Carl Spaatz
    Commanding General
    United States Army Strategic Air Forces
    1. The 509 Composite Group, 20th Air Force
will deliver its first special bomb as soon as
weather will permit visual bombing after about
3 August 1945 on one of the targets: Hiroshima,
Kokura, Niigata and Nagasaki. To carry military
and civilian scientific personnel from the War
Department to observe and record the effects of
the explosion of the bomb, additional aircraft
will accompany the airplane carrying the bomb.
The observing planes will stay several miles
distant from the point of impact of the bomb.
    2. Additional bombs will be delivered on
the above targets as soon as made ready by

the project staff. Further instructions will
be issued concerning targets other than those
listed above.

    3. Dissemination of any and all information
concerning the use of the weapon against Japan
is reserved to the Secretary of War and the
President of the United States. No communiques
on the subject or releases of information will
be issued by Commanders in the field without
specific prior authority. Any news stories will
be sent to the War Department for special
clearance.

    4. The foregoing directive is issued to
you by direction and with the approval of the
Secretary of War and of the Chief of Staff,
USA. It is desired that you personally deliver
one copy of this directive to General MacArthur
and one copy to Admiral Nimitz for their
information.

Thos. T. Handy
THOS. T. HANDY
General, G.S.C.
Acting Chief of Staff

TOP SECRET

General Handy buzzed Marshall's office assistant.

"Yes Sir?"

"Please ask the duty courier to come see me directly."

"Yes Sir, right away."

The courier office was two floors down and a fifth of the way clockwise around the building. Handy worked on letters and message traffic requiring the chief's signature while he awaited the courier.

"Sir, Captain Adamson is here from the courier's office."

"Send him in, please."

The captain appeared wearing a crisp, pristine, pinks and greens uniform with General Staff lapel insignia and no ribbons or badges. He stepped smartly to a position of attention and saluted. "Captain Adamson, reporting as ordered, Sir."

Handy returned the salute. "At ease, Captain. You will hand carry and deliver this Top Secret letter," holding the classified execution order, "to General Spaatz personally and without exception or interference."

"Yes Sir."

"Upon delivery, you will return to this office and report your mission completion to me and me alone."

"Yes Sir."

General Handy folded the letter and placed it in an envelope. The captain took the proffered envelope. "Dismissed."

Adamson saluted, performed a perfect about-face, and marched out of the chief's office.

——

Thursday, 26.July.1945
Buckingham Palace
Whitehall, London, England
United Kingdom
19:00 hours

The 1945 election results had been a crushing defeat for the Conservative Party and Prime Minister Churchill. The Conservatives won 212 seats, including Churchill's new district of Woodford. Labour won 393 seats, and the Liberals won 12 seats. Labour had an outright majority, and Clement Attlee would soon become prime minister.

When the results were announced as final, Clementine sought to cheer up her husband as the depth of the election defeat sank in. She had told Winston, "We must look at the positive in this. These results, my dear husband, might well be a blessing in disguise."

Churchill had grimly replied, "At the moment, it seems quite effectively disguised."

Clementine had recognized the signs of deepening depression in her husband, but she knew he needed to work through the gloom.

As required by protocol in service of King George VI, the prime minister requested and was granted an audience with the King. The King's Aide-de-Camp Colonel Lord Harewood, 6th Earl of Harewood, met Churchill at the main entrance to the palace. "Welcome back to Buckingham Palace, Prime Minister." He immediately turned to escort Churchill to his meeting.

"Thank you, Colonel."

They walked together up the main staircase to the Gold Room. The colonel knocked and opened the left side of the large double door. "Your Majesty, Prime Minister Churchill."

Winston stepped toward the King, stopped two paces from the sovereign, and rendered a modest bow. The King extended his right hand to his first minister. "It is my duty to tender my resignation as your prime minister, Your Majesty, having failed to achieve a majority in the most recent election."

The King gestured to facing couches. Churchill sat across from the King after the sovereign sat. King George began, "You know, I must confess, I was not in favor of your premiership in 1940. I will also confess to you personally that I was dreadfully wrong. There is no man alive who could have done what you did in those dark days of 1940 and the Blitz. It has been the distinct honor of my life to witness the majesty of your words and the effectiveness of your leadership through the war. We, and here I believe I speak for myself and all our people, cannot possibly thank you sufficiently for saving the kingdom from the tyranny of fascism."

"It was my honor to serve, Your Majesty."

"I must further tell you, my dear Winston, I intend to establish a new earldom for you."

"I am flattered and honored by your gesture, Sir, but I am compelled to tell you that I am a son of Commons, not Lords. Commons is my home."

"You deserve at least an earldom, if not a dukedom, but I appreciate your position. We shall table this for now. Would you accept a knighthood?"

"With respect, Your Majesty, I just lost an embarrassing and devastating election. I may well lose my leadership of the Conservative Party after such an electoral defeat. Now is not the time, Your Majesty, but thank you very much for the expression."

"I am troubled by your humility, Winston. You stood strong, virtually alone, through our darkest days. You won the greatest war in our noble history. There is no one more worthy of the sovereign's recognition."

"Thank you for understanding, Your Majesty."

King George nodded and smiled. He stood, and Churchill did as well. "Very well, Mister Churchill, you stand relieved." The two shook hands. Churchill stepped backward four paces, turned, and departed. His premiership was done.

———

Thursday, 26.July.1945
Little White House
No.2 Kaiserstraße
Babelsberg, Potsdam, Brandenburg
Soviet Zone, Occupied Germany
20:15 hours

Once the president's Cabinet-officer attendees gathered in the modest room rearranged to serve as the makeshift Cabinet room, President Truman began the follow-up meeting. "To say I am disappointed in the Soviet stance is seriously understated. Despite his facial cordiality, Stalin is acting more like an adversary than an ally."

"Excuse me, Mister President," Secretary of State Byrnes interrupted, "I appreciate and share your disappointment. However, as your chief diplomat, I am compelled to note here that the Soviet Government has steadfastly maintained that Japan did not attack the Soviet Union. They have clearly stated publicly and privately their neutrality with respect to Japan. Therefore, for them to join in the ultimatum would be tantamount to a declaration of war against Japan. Further, as Marshal Stalin has repeatedly and consistently stated for the record, they are willing to join the fight to subdue Japan, but only after they have moved sufficient forces to the east. Expecting more from them is unreasonable."

Truman noted Stimson stirring in his chair as if being bitten by some unseen insect. "Do you have something to contribute, Henry?"

"Yes Sir. With the success of Trinity, the equation has changed. I now believe encouraging the Soviets to join the fight against Japan will not serve our long-term interests in the region."

"How so?" Byrnes challenged.

"As we've seen in Eastern Europe, Stalin and the Soviet Union have shown no signs of rehabilitating the nations they now occupy. I believe we should expect the exact same behavior in Asia. They will likely use our invitation as justification to carve out as much territory as possible from Japan. With Trinity, we do not need them, and I suspect we will regret bringing them into the fight."

"I see the merit in both arguments. However, we will proceed with the ultimatum as we discussed and agreed at today's plenary session."

"Allow me to check on the document," Byrnes said. Truman nodded. Jim left the room for a few minutes. When he returned, he distributed copies of the ultimatum. The original to the president and mimeographed copies to each of the ministers. Each man read the intended words.

```
(1) WE — THE PRESIDENT of the United States,
    the President of the National Government
    of the Republic of China, and the Prime
    Minister of Great Britain, representing
    the hundreds of millions of our countrymen,
    have conferred and agree that Japan shall
    be given an explicit opportunity to end
    this war.
```

(2) The prodigious land, sea and air forces
    of the United States, the British Empire
    and of China, many times reinforced by
    their armies and air fleets from the west,
    are poised to strike the final blows upon
    Japan. This military power is sustained and
    inspired by the determination of all the
    Allied Nations to prosecute the war against
    Japan until she ceases to resist.

(3) The result of the futile and senseless
    German resistance to the might of the
    aroused free peoples of the world stands
    forth in awful clarity as an example to
    the people of Japan. The might that now
    converges on Japan is immeasurably greater
    than that which, when applied to the
    resisting Nazis, necessarily laid waste to
    the lands, the industry, and the method of
    life of the whole German people. The full
    application of our military power backed by
    our resolve, will mean the inevitable and
    complete destruction of the Japanese armed
    forces and just as inevitably the utter
    devastation of the Japanese homeland.

(4) Following are our terms. We will not deviate
    from them. There are no alternatives. We
    shall brook no delay.

(5) There must be eliminated for all time the
    authority and influence of those who have
    deceived and misled the people of Japan
    into embarking on world conquest, for we
    insist that a new order of peace, security
    and justice will be impossible until
    irresponsible militarism is driven from the
    world.

(6) Until such a new order is established
    and until there is convincing proof that
    Japan's war-making power is destroyed,
    points in Japanese territory to be
    designated by the Allies shall be occupied
    to secure the achievement of the basic
    objectives we are here setting forth.

(7) We do not intend that the Japanese shall be enslaved as a race or destroyed as a nation, but stern justice shall be meted out to all war criminals, including those who have visited cruelties upon our prisoners. The Japanese Government shall remove all obstacles to the revival and strengthening of democratic tendencies among the Japanese people. Freedom of speech, of religion, and of thought, as well as respect for the fundamental human rights shall be established.

(8) The occupying forces of the Allies shall be withdrawn from Japan as soon as these objectives have been accomplished and there has been established in accordance with the freely expressed will of the Japanese people a peacefully inclined and responsible government.

(9) We call upon the government of Japan to proclaim now the unconditional surrender of all Japanese armed forces, and to provide proper and adequate assurances of their good faith in such action. The alternative for Japan is prompt and utter destruction.

"I do believe this is our agreed to document," Truman declared. "Churchill agreed to the language before his departure, and Attlee has not yet returned from the election. Therefore, if there are no objections, please transmit this document to Japan and the Supreme Council as soon as possible."

"Upon your command, Mister President," Byrnes responded.

—

Thursday, 26.July.1945
USAAF Station F-356
Saffron Walden, Essex, England
United Kingdom
21:00 hours

Most 4th Fighter Group pilots were off base on an extended evening pass. Many of those who remained, including Major Drummond, had gathered in the Officer's Club bar for a beer or two, but they also knew the election results in Great Britain and the expected concession speech of Winston Churchill were due to be broadcast.

Brian sat by the radio with several other pilots. When he heard the tone, he commanded in a shout, "Quiet!" The room instantly went silent, and most of the room's occupants gathered around the radio.

"Good evening. This is the BBC Home Service. Mister Churchill has asked to speak to the nation. Mister Churchill . . ."

The distinctive and familiar voice of the former prime minister greeted all those listening.

"The decision of the British people has been recorded in the votes counted today. I have therefore laid down the charge, which was placed upon me in darker times. I regret that I have not been permitted to finish the work against Japan. For this however all plans and preparations have been made, and the results may come much quicker than we have hitherto been entitled to expect. Immense responsibilities abroad and at home fall upon the new Government, and we must all hope that they will be successful in bearing them.

"It only remains for me to express to the British people, for whom I have acted in these perilous years, my profound gratitude for the unflinching, unswerving support, which they have given me during my task, and for the many expressions of kindness, which they have shown towards their servant."

The silence remained in the room and on the radio. Brian expected more from Churchill's words.

"That concludes Mister Churchill's statement. We return to current programming." Classical music of some sort Brian did not recognize came through the radio. Brian switched it off.

"Well, damn!" Brian exclaimed.

"He lost, Major," someone responded.

"Yeah. The Conservative Party lost, and he will no longer be prime minister, but he deserves so much better."

"The British people took a sharp left turn," another pilot observed.

"What do we care? We're going home soon. The British have made their choice."

"I can't believe the British people would vote against Churchill, but they voted for the Labour Party candidates in most districts."

"Your buddy is still out."

"Not out of Commons but out of Number Ten," Brian responded. "And just a little reminder, Japan has not yet surrendered, and we are still under an alert for transfer to the Pacific. We're not done with this fight just yet."

"The British people washed out the Conservatives and Churchill with them."

"Why do you like him so much, Major?"

"Oh, I don't know. Maybe because he inspired us all during the summer of 1940." Brian looked around at the faces looking at him. "Sweet was the only other pilot currently with us who flew in the Great Air Battle. I think it safe to say Winston Churchill sustained us. There were more than a few voices inside and outside of government who strongly advocated for capitulation to the Nazis. What would have happened if the people had not listened to Churchill? So, yeah, I think the man got a raw deal."

"He still lost."

"No, he didn't. He won re-election in his district."

"Then, why isn't he still prime minister?"

"The British have a different system than we do. The party that wins the majority of seats or can form a coalition for a majority decides who will be prime minister."

"Then, why didn't he just form a coalition?"

"Well, there are 640 seats in Commons. Labour won 393 of those seats. So no coalition was possible in this instance."

"How do you know all this?"

Brian laughed robustly. "I've been here six years. Now, enough of the inquisition. I'm calling it a night." He finished the last long swallow of his beer and left the group.

Brian stopped at one of three open telephone booths. He called Charlotte to wish her a good night. She had listened to Churchill's concession speech on the radio and felt sorry for the wartime leader. The conversation was short but full of love. Brian went to his room and his book.

—

Thursday, 26. July. 1945
Hickam Army Air Base
Oahu, Hawaiian Islands
Territory of the United States of America
11:15 hours

A C-54 Skymaster with only national markings in conventional olive drab livery and no squadron, group, or wing identifiers had landed two hours earlier from San Francisco. The aircraft was assigned to the 509th Composite Group as one of their squadron's worth of identical transport airplanes. The squadron's livery prompted the popular moniker of *Green Hornet*.

The current mission originated at Kirkland Airfield in Albuquerque. The stops at San Francisco and Honolulu were planned for fuel, sustenance, and relief for those so inclined. Their mission plan required a squad of armed MPs to secure the aircraft, but the mission commander refused to leave his charge at either en route stop. Instead, he kept a keen eye on the security detail and anything moving even remotely near the aircraft.

Although the pilots were both senior to the mission commander, Second Lieutenant William A. 'Bill' King, USA CIC, a seasoned prior-enlisted officer, had been specifically chosen by General Groves and assigned as the mission commander for the special air transport task. King was the only passenger on the aircraft. He was the designated courier for a particular metal container called the bird cage, containing the plutonium core for the Fat Man device. His orders were quite specific and precise.

The two pilots returned to the aircraft with a box lunch for King that he would wait to eat once they were airborne and clear of the Hawaiian Islands. Next, the pilots began their pre-flight inspection. As King watched the pilots performing their checks and scanning the periphery around the aircraft, he noticed an Army infantry colonel in field fatigues striding purposefully toward the Green Hornet. He stopped to talk to one of the MPs and pointed at the aircraft several times. King could not hear the words being spoken, but the animation and gestures were sufficient to convey the colonel's intentions. Finally, the lieutenant stepped slowly and casually to position himself in front of the boarding ladder. He sensed what was coming, and he was prepared.

Pushing his way past the MP guards around the plane, the colonel strode smartly toward the aircraft. Then, with the colonel five yards away and closing, King said in a commanding voice, "May I help you, Sir."

"Out of my way, Lieutenant. I'm commandeering this aircraft."

"Stop where you are!" The colonel stopped and then started to take a step toward the aircraft. King did not hesitate and unholstered his M1911 45-caliber, semi-automatic pistol aiming at the man's heart. "You are not authorized to be near this aircraft."

"I'm a fucking colonel, and you're a damn sniveling lieutenant. That aircraft," the colonel said, pointing at the Green Hornet, "has only one passenger—you. I outrank you, and I need this aircraft to take some of my combat troops back to the States."

"I'm sorry, Colonel. Unfortunately, the aircraft is not available."

"I don't care whether it's available or not. It's here. It's empty. And I need it."

"As I said, Sir, it's not available. I'm a designated Army courier, and I'm on a mission authorized by the Secretary of War."

"What are you escorting?"

"I cannot tell you that."

"Why not?"

"You are not granted access to the information."

"Lieutenant, I've had about enough of your insolence. I've got a more important mission to perform, and I'm taking command of this aircraft. Holster that pistol and step aside."

"I will not."

"I am your superior officer, and I'm giving you a direct order."

"My orders come from well above you, Colonel, and my orders take priority."

The colonel started to take another step toward the aircraft.

King had had enough of the colonel's aggressive belligerence. He finally cocked the hammer on his pistol, and said, "You can't come aboard this plane!!" The colonel froze mid-stride. King did not twitch, blink, or waver. The tunnel of the pistol's barrel remained steady as a rock. "Now, I've tried to tell you as much as I'm able and to be as respectful as I can, but I've a mission to perform. You are interfering with my mission. You're welcome to call the secretary of war or the president if you wish. Regardless of what you choose to do, you will clear this area now, or I will drop you where you stand."

"I don't believe you."

"I don't care."

King retained his stern and determined expression while he held his aim. He slowly and deliberately clicked off the pistol's safety to ensure the colonel knew exactly what he was doing. The symbolic message was crystal clear. The colonel held up his hands and stepped backward carefully. King did not budge and tracked the colonel's withdrawal until he was beyond the guards and had turned to walk back to the terminal. King gently and slowly lowered the pistol's hammer, reengaged the safety, and holstered the weapon.

Both pilots had stopped underneath the tail, clear of the confrontation. King signaled for them to board. As they neared the boarding ladder, King said to the pilots, "Get this plane off the ground and out of here, or I'm going to get in trouble!"

The three men and their unique package took off in a matter of minutes. Their last leg was underway.

In a few more uneventful hours, Lieutenant King would accomplish his mission and deliver the plane's precious cargo to the Project ALBERTA team without further incident.

—

Saturday, 28.July.1945
Little White House
No.2 Kaiserstraße
Babelsberg, Potsdam, Brandenburg
Soviet Zone, Occupied Germany
10:10 hours

Secretary of State Byrnes called and requested an immediate meeting with the president. He indicated he had just received the Japanese response to the Allied ultimatum. It was not positive. President Truman asked the other Cabinet secretaries, the joint chiefs, and his chief of staff to join the meeting.

Byrnes arrived just after Stimson, Forrestal, and Morgenthau. All three service chiefs had been the first to arrive, followed by Leahy.

"What do you have, Jim?" Truman asked once everyone was present.

"At three P-M in Tokyo today, which was seven A-M here, Prime Minister Suzuki made a public broadcast to respond to our ultimatum."

"Have they sent any message traffic to anyone . . . us, the Russians, the Swiss, the Swedes, anyone?"

"I made a specific point of urgently checking our communications intelligence folks and the O-S-S, asking that precise question. As of 20 minutes ago, nothing, not even a chirp. It took us a little longer than usual to translate his words and understand the nuances in his word choices."

"OK. What did he say?" Truman asked with impatience.

"We will get a transcript as soon as possible with the nuances noted. He referred directly to our ultimatum of the 26th and called it 'unworthy of consideration,' 'absurd,' and 'presumptuous.' Suzuki closed his broadcast statement with the sentence 'We must kill it with silence,' which to us means they intend to ignore the ultimatum."

"Well, I would say that settles the matter," Truman pronounced. "I suppose they do not believe us. That is their choice entirely."

"I must also add, Mister President, headlines in Asian papers universally stated, Japan rejects surrender ultimatum."

Truman looked directly at Stimson. "Are we ready?"

"Yes Sir. I received the coded confirmation last night. The order has been issued. They are to deliver Little Boy after the 3rd of August on one of the four approved initial targets in priority order as weather permits. Only a direct order from you, Mister President, will stop it now. Silence is consent."

"Should we respond to the Japanese broadcast?" the president asked.

The query induced quick contemplation. Byrnes was the first to respond. "From the State perspective, they may well misread the intent."

"Meaning?"

"That we are bluffing. They have the ultimatum. It states our position. Based on what we know from the broadcast, they offered no actionable counter. They only scoffed at our ultimatum, which suggests to us that they already believe we are bluffing in an effort to intimidate them into surrender. We should avoid adding to their predisposition."

"Anyone else?" President Truman asked and looked around the table. Even Bill Leahy chose not to object. He had not altered his opinion, and he had nothing new to add. "Very well. We shall stay the course." He paused. No one spoke. The president looked at General Marshall. "I need to know what the order cancellation timeline looks like. Presumably, we can recall the mission up to the point the bombardier punches the release button. So, how far in advance of that moment does a recall order have to be issued?"

General Marshall leaned forward onto his elbows. "Such communications usually take a few hours. In this instance, we must refine our communications links." Marshall glanced at General Arnold. "We should be able to setup a streamlined urgent recall message and produce the shortest timeline we can." Marshall again looked at Arnold, who nodded in agreement. "The timeline and delivery aircraft's flight plan will give us a date and time deadline for a recall order."

"We'll ensure the aircraft commander fully understands that he may be subject to recall," Arnold added. "We'll also ensure clocks are synchronized and the time zone differences accounted for between Berlin, Washington, and the aircraft clock."

"Good point," Truman added. "Thank you." He looked at Byrnes. "Make sure State is listening intently. The S-C-D-W in Tokyo might change their mind. If they surrender according to our terms before the recall deadline, I think we all would like to avoid the destruction the special weapon will yield if used. So I will ask here, to ensure no mistakes, perhaps we should run a communications drill to test the system and timeline."

"We should be able to accomplish that," Marshall stated, "test as soon as we have the process established."

Truman nodded. "Can anyone think of anything else we can do to give the Japanese as much time to surrender as possible?"

"We can extend the ultimatum," Leahy suggested.

"No, we cannot. They summarily rejected the original. An extension would only enhance their sense of our weakness. The order to execute has been issued and received by the delivery team. We will proceed as decided."

The meeting was disbanded, and the course of history was set.

—

Chapter 12

The body politic, like the human body,
begins to die from its birth, and
bears in itself the causes of its destruction.

-- Jean Jacques Rousseau

Monday, 6.August.1945
USAAF Station Destination
North Field
Tinian, Mariana Islands
Territory of the United States of America

The 509th Composite Group was an odd unit with only one bomber squadron of 18 Boeing B-29 Superfortress heavy bombers and completely self-contained with their necessary support personnel. They were configured for one mission, or rather one mission type—a special bombardment mission. They also operated C-47 Dakota and C-54 Skymaster transport aircraft. The Group had been activated in December 1944 with then Lieutenant Colonel Tibbets as the commanding officer. He was one of the most experienced combat, heavy bomber pilots in the Army Air Forces. Tibbets had been promoted to colonel in January. The Group developed and rehearsed the handling and delivery procedures in the United States before they deployed. The lead elements of the Group arrived at North Field in May 1945.

The bomber crews flew training missions with practice munitions called "pumpkins" because of their color (orange, for visibility) and unusual shape (resembling the Fat Man device). They also flew combat missions to Japan with conventional munitions to learn the rigors of long-range operations along with the various control procedures. The 509th, secretive and unusual, was not popular with the other groups on Tinian. They did not seem to operate to the same rules as the regular bomber crews, and there was palpable resentment.

The so-called Tinian Joint Chiefs led the deployment of the special mission force to Tinian Island. Four men comprised the leadership of the in situ delivery team.

-- Rear Admiral William Reynolds Purnell, USN [USNA 1908], Deputy Chief of Naval Operations for Materiel. He was the Navy's representative to the Military Policy Committee of the Manhattan Project.

-- Brigadier General Thomas Francis Farrell, USA CEC, Deputy Director for Operations of the Manhattan Project, and General Groves's direct representative on Tinian.

-- Captain William Sterling 'Deak' Parsons, USN [USNA 1922], Commanding Officer Project ALBERTA, the tailored and specifically configured team to deliver the special weapons to their assigned targets in Japan.
-- Colonel Paul Warfield Tibbets, USAAF commanding officer 509th Composite Group, the action unit for Project ALBERTA.

Their direct engagement proved vital in the team's build-up, using their rank and status to break more than a few roadblocks thrown up by the bureaucratic-military support services. The limited port facilities in place to support the 20th Air Force operations had been prioritized, and the four leaders used their presidential authority to ensure Project ALBERTA had the highest level of support. The Tinian Joint Chiefs would be present for every evolution of the logistics and support processes, and this historic day was no different. The entire team was on site for the vital mission, and they were assigned the code name SILVERPLATE.

The order to execute Special Mission 13 had been received two days ago. The Little Boy gun-type uranium weapon had been checked and rechecked multiple times. The conventional-looking, unconventional fission bomb had been loaded aboard the Enola Gay, a Boeing-designed, Martin-built, B-29-45-MO heavy bomber, serial number 44-86292. The aircrews for the three weather reconnaissance bombers were briefed and would take off an hour earlier than the strike crews. One bomber each would be sent to the primary and two secondary targets – Hiroshima, Kokura, and Nagasaki. They would radio back the direct weather observations of all three planned targets as well as the expected weather for the potential T-0 at each site.

00:00 hours

With Admiral Purnell and General Farrell observing, and Captain Parsons with the Enola Gay crew, Colonel Tibbets stood in the large Quonset Hut Group operations room they called the War Room and waited for the inaudible conversational rumble to dissipate. "The day for which we have trained all these months has finally come to us. We're going on a mission to drop a bomb different from any you've ever seen or heard about. This bomb contains a destructive force equivalent to 20 thousand tons of TNT." An inaudible rumbling of disbelief and perhaps awe interrupted Tibbets's mission briefing. Again, he waited patiently for quiet. "Look, fellas, I understand the sentiment, but we've got work to do. We know the procedures, the route, the potential targets on the list, and the control communications. Let's get this briefing done and this show on the road."

The Group intelligence officer covered the weather forecast to T-0 at all three planned targets for the day. None of them were expected to be clear, so the final decision would come from Colonel Tibbets once he received the precise reports from the three, weather aircraft. A spare aircraft would be positioned at Iwo Jima in case one strike aircraft developed a mechanical problem that might preclude mission accomplishment. Of the two remaining strike aircraft, one carried an instrumentation package to assist the scientists in yield determination, and the other carried observers and photographers. They also covered the potential air defenses they might encounter. The five-ton weapon, its support equipment, and extra fuel for the extended missions put Enola Gay 15,000 pounds over the B-29's maximum gross takeoff weight. That reality had been part of their preparations. Six of the Group's other heavy bombers were assigned to support the day's singular mission—enable Enola Gay to deliver the Little Boy weapon to one of the three authorized targets.

Every member of each crew knew precisely what he had to do throughout the planned 11-hour mission. There were no questions. The crews would eat a comparatively sumptuous, steak-and-eggs breakfast before they boarded the trucks to take the crews to their respective aircraft. The three weather airplanes took off at 01:37 in two-minute intervals while the strike crews completed their preflight checks.

Tibbets and his crew strapped in. The engines were started successfully, the systems were brought online, and the aircraft readied for flight.

02:45 hours

Tibbets called for clearance, taxied the heavy bomber to the engine run-up area, and completed the proper checks and preparations for takeoff.

"North Tower, Dimples Eighty-Two is ready for takeoff," Tibbets broadcast.

"Dimples Eighty-Two, position and hold Runway Zero Nine 'Able.'"

"Position and hold 'Able' for Dimples Eight-Two."

"Landing lights," commanded Tibbets. Flight Engineer Staff Sergeant Wyatt Duzenbury, USAAF, of Michigan, flipped the landing light switch up, brightly illuminating the area ahead of the aircraft. Tibbets advanced the throttles for the four powerful Wright R-3350 engines just enough to move the heavy bomber beyond the hold-short line. He carefully maneuvered the massive aircraft onto the runway, to the threshold, to use every foot of the 8,500-foot runway. He slowly turned the bomber to align the nose on the centerline and stopped the aircraft. Tibbets scanned the cockpit. The takeoff checklist was complete. They were ready.

"Dimples Eighty-Two, North Tower, the pattern is clear. The runway is yours. Winds zero nine five at seven knots. Cleared for takeoff. Good luck."

Tibbets looked to his right and Copilot Captain Robert Alvin Lewis, USAAF, of New York, and said, "Let's go." Lewis nodded his head. Tibbets broadcast, "Dimples Eighty-Two rolling." Tibbets pushed all four throttles smoothly forward and listened to the powerful engines approach full thrust. Lewis placed his right hand at the base of the throttle quadrant to back-up Tibbets. The bomber bucked against the brakes. When he was satisfied that everything was as it should be, he released the brakes. The aircraft lurched forward and began to accelerate slowly down the runway. Tibbets pushed the throttles to the stop for every last horsepower the engines could produce. From their rehearsals, he knew he would need every foot of the runway to get the beast into the air. The heavy bomber virtually floated into the night air, gaining altitude slowly. "Gear up," commanded Tibbets. Lewis raised the red gear handle. The sounds could be felt, although not heard over the engines. The other two strike aircraft—The Great Artiste and Necessary Evil—took off singly at two-minute intervals.

As soon as Tibbets had the aircraft configured for and in a cruise climb, he banked the plane, turning to the heading for Iwo Jima.

03:00 hours

With the aircraft stable in level cruise flight at 8,000 feet, Tibbets felt a tap on his right shoulder. He turned to see Deak Parsons, the weaponeer expert for the mission and commander of Project ALBERTA. Deak was a contraction of his nickname acquired at the Naval Academy, short for Deacon, a play on his family name. Parsons joined the Manhattan project in the summer of 1943, growing in the knowledge of Little Boy and Fat Man. He had witnessed every major development event in the last two years of the Manhattan Project. General Groves assigned Parsons to be the field engineer for the first delivery mission. Deak nodded his head toward the aircraft's rear, which signaled that he would prepare Little Boy in the bomb bay.

Twenty minutes later, Parsons returned, tapped Tibbets on the shoulder again, and gave him a thumb's up. Tibbets acknowledged the sign. "Tom, Little Boy's alive. Run your checks," he commanded Bombardier Major Thomas Wilson 'Tom' Ferebee, USAAF, of North Carolina. Tom had been Tibbets' bombardier on Red Gremlin, the 97ᵗʰ Bombardment Group B-17 they flew in Europe and was the natural choice for his crew.

"Wilco, Skipper." Ferebee switched on his arming panel and ran through his rehearsed procedures to verify his control panel's status and the weapon's connection. A few minutes later, Ferebee reported, "Sight's full up. All circuits green. She's ready."

"Thanks, Tom. Let me know if anything changes." While the Little Boy bomb was fully assembled and ready for release, the safety plugs remained in place and would not be removed until just prior to release.

06:05 hours

Passing overhead Iwo Jima Island at 8,000 feet, Tibbets announced over the intercom, "Checkpoint Iwo." He entered a wide orbit over the famous island. The two other strike support bombers joined up in short order. "Course for the common I-P." The common Initial Point was located equidistant from all three targets as they moved closer and awaited the weather reconnaissance reports.

"Three One Six to the common I-P," responded Navigator Captain Theodore Jerome 'Dutch' Van Kirk, USAAF, of Pennsylvania. Dutch was another veteran from Tibbets Red Gremlin crew.

Tibbets banked the massive bomber to the right and leveled the wings. "Steady three-one-six. Did you compensate for winds aloft?"

"Of course, I did, Skipper."

At the last time he would have access to the unpressurized forward bomb bay, Parsons replaced the last red electrical safety plugs with green enabling plugs. Little Boy was now fully enabled and would be armed by the bombardier before dropping from the bomb bay.

"Panel remains all green, " Ferebee stated.

Tibbets initiated another cruise climb with their two companions, this time to 26,000 feet. They checked the interior pressurization system several times to negate the requirement to don their oxygen masks. All systems remained fully functional.

07:30 hours

Tibbets spoke over the intercom to Enola Gay's crew. "OK, fellas, we're carrying the world's first atomic bomb. The weapon is fully ready to release. We have a little less than two hours to go. Get your parachutes and flak suits on, just in case we encounter opposition." Every man complied with Tibbets' instructions.

08:24 hours

Radio Operator Private Richard Hadine 'Dick' Nelson of Idaho carried a handwritten, printed, deciphered message just received from the assigned Hiroshima weather aircraft—Straight Flush—and handed it to Colonel Tibbets.

```
Cloud cover less than 3/10ths at all altitudes.
Advice: bomb primary.
```

He returned the paper to Nelson and held up his right index finger. Tibbets keyed his intercom. "It's Hiroshima. Let's get this done." He looked back to Nelson and said, "Send a single-word message to Iwo and Tinian—Primary." Nelson nodded and returned to his radio station to fulfill the colonel's order. Tibbets initiated another cruise climb to their final delivery altitude of 31,000 feet. They could see Shikoku and Honshu beyond. They were headed directly to their destiny.

09:05 hours

"Ten minutes to the A-P," said Dutch over the intercom. No one responded. Everyone knew what those words meant. The Aim Point, the T-shaped Aioi Bridge over the Ota River, remained clearly visible.

Ferebee straddled his Mark XV Norden bombsight, checked his pre-set settings, and peered through the sight's optics.

Enola Gay was on a heading of 264 degrees at 31,060 feet and an indicated 200 miles per hour airspeed on their final run-in to the target.

"I-P," Dutch announced over the intercom.

No one spoke. Only the drone of the four engines and the aerodynamic noise could be heard by any crew. Colonel Tibbets trusted his highly experienced bombardier and knew Ferebee was doing everything he could. Peering into the bombsight, Tom watched the crosshairs track the AP to the precise, calculated release point for their flight conditions.

Tibbets checked the clock; three more minutes to the proper target. He mentally reviewed his go-around and post-release procedures.

"I've got it," announced Ferebee with a surprising touch of excitement in his voice.

09:12 hours

"Autopilot to Bombardier," Tibbets announced. *This is it! All our training has come to this moment.* "She's yours, Tom."

"Panel remains green. Switches hot. Here we go."

The bomber flew straight and smoothly. Ferebee detected surprisingly little drift, which meant the winds aloft were very close to the expected upper-level winds in the forecast and validated by the weather aircraft. The fine corrections were easy, and he kept the sight crosshairs stable on the briefed aim point—the T-bridge over the Ota River at the city's center.

———

Monday, 6.August.1945
Aioi Bridge
34° 23' 48" North – 132° 27' 09" East
Hiroshima, Hiroshima Prefecture, Chugoku, Honshu
Empire of Japan
09:15:17 hours

On command, the forward bomb bay doors snapped open. Ferebee depressed his release button. "Bombs away," announced Ferebee over the aircraft intercom. The aircraft jumped as the 9,700-pound 'Little Boy' special bomb dropped from the aircraft's bomb bay to its moment in history. "Rather bomb away," Tom said with a slight chuckle in his voice.

Colonel Tibbets flipped off the autopilot switch to take back manual control of the aircraft and rolled the huge bomber hard. He pulled back firmly on the control yoke. He was turning the large aircraft 180° to put as much distance between the impending explosion and the aircraft with his crew. He glanced quickly at the aircraft's clock. "OK, fellas, we have 40 seconds. On goggles," Tibbets commanded with a firm, unemotional voice. "Make absolutely certain your goggles are properly in place. No exceptions. I don't want anyone injured when that device goes off." He expected the whole crew to comply, while he would wait until just a few seconds before detonation. He could barely see the instrument panel and controls when the dark goggles were in place.

09:16:00 hours

When the integral timer reached the calculated fall time, a conventional explosive charge in the tail of the Little Boy bomb detonated, driving the uranium-235 bullet through the barrel into the precise hole of the uranium-235, cylinder target in the nose of the weapon. The combination of the bullet and cylinder formed a critical mass—a near-instantaneous chain reaction released vast energy.

A sun instantly appeared on earth for the second time in a month. The intense light, heat, and shockwave spread out in all directions. Little Boy exploded 1,800 feet above the ground and 800 feet from the intended aim point. Virtually everything within miles of the explosion vanished, vaporized by the vast energy released by the bomb, and what remained was incinerated by fire.

Seconds later, the shockwave reached the retreating Enola Gay five miles from the hypocenter and shook the aircraft violently in three distinct segments. Necessary Evil was 15 miles away and felt the shockwave but not as violently as the Enola Gay.

As the Manhattan Project field agent and mission commander, Parsons's hand printed an immediate report message to Tinian and General Farrell for

Dick Nelson to send once they were safely away with the mushroom cloud rising well above their altitude on their tail.

———————————

```
Clear cut, successful in all aspects. Visible
effects greater than Alamogordo. Conditions normal
in airplane following delivery. Proceeding to
base.
```

———————————

The strike aircraft set a course directly for Tinian. All of them had sufficient usable fuel to make the long return leg of the mission.

North Field, Tinian
14:58 hours

After twelve hours and thirteen minutes in the air, Enola Gay and her crew landed safely back at North Field, Tinian. Among the small crowd of dignitaries on the tarmac to celebrate the success and return of Enola Gay were General Carl Spaatz along with Admiral Purnell and General Farrell. Cheers, handshakes, backslaps, and other celebratory gestures blanketed the entire Enola Gay crew as they deplaned. The band played patriotic songs. Photographs were taken of the crew and the welcoming gathering before they began to disperse. All the other aircraft landed safely as well. The historic mission was done.

—

Monday, 6.August.1945
USS Augusta
39° 55' North – 61° 32' West
At sea
Atlantic Ocean
11:25 hours

President Truman had been working on the text for his intended report to a joint session of Congress on the Potsdam Conference as well as the United Nations and other world issues. As usual, Admiral Leahy continued to be a valuable advisor beyond his duty as the military chief of staff to the president.

The rap of knuckles on the metal hatch to the flag stateroom that the president occupied broke their concentration and interaction. Leahy went to the hatch and opened it to see Augusta Commanding Officer Captain James Hicks Foskett, USN.

"We just received this message for the president," Foskett said and handed the paper to Leahy. After reading the short message, Leahy gestured for Foskett to enter and close the hatch. Bill walked to the president's desk and handed it to President Truman.

SECRET

```
DW
MANTT GAK NR 11903
S 060502Z AUG 45
FM SECWAR
TO POTUS ABD AUGUSTA
SUBJ RETRANS
BT
S E C R E T
S 060431Z AUG 45
FROM SILVERPLATE
TO SECWAR COS MANHATTAN 20AF
S E C R E T
SUBJ PROJECT ALBERTA
LITTLE BOY DELIVERED TO PRIMARY WITH EXPECTED
RESULTS X REPORT TO FOLLOW END
BT
NNNN
```

SECRET

"It's done," Truman said with solemnity.

Leahy nodded, "Yes Sir. It'll be a few days before we get the initial full report of the damage and casualties."

"Bill, you've always been frank and candid with me. I know how you feel, but if this bomb can end the war, think of how many lives we will save."

"I know the argument, Mister President, but we presumably killed a lot of innocent people this morning. We don't know how many yet, and we may never know."

Truman looked at Foskett. "Pardon us, Captain. Do you know what this message means?"

"I've no idea, Mister President, but I gather that whatever it is, it's important."

Truman smiled. "That may be the understatement of the decade, Captain. I could not say so yesterday, but I can tell you today, Little Boy is a unique bomb, an atomic bomb, that exploded over Hiroshima, Japan, with a force equivalent to 20,000 tons of T-N-T."

"My God!" exclaimed Foskett.

Truman chuckled softly. "We all pretty much have that reaction. We eventually . . ." Another knock on the stateroom hatch interrupted the president.

Leahy again went to the hatch. He gestured for a master sergeant from the special communications section to enter. The man went directly to the president and handed a red folder to him.

TOP SECRET - MAGIC

```
TOP SECRET
DATE 19450806 0955 HOME
FROM 12 AIR DIVISION
TO ARMY HIGH COMMAND
HIROSHIMA CITY VIRTUALLY DESTROYED BY A VIOLENT
LARGE SPECIAL TYPE BOMB GIVING THE APPEARANCE
OF MAGNESIUM BREAK MOST OF THE CITY EVAPORATED
BREAK MORE BURNED BY FIRE BREAK THOUSANDS
KILLED MANY MORE INJURED END
TOP SECRET
DECIPHERED HYPO 052135Z AUGUST 1945
```

TOP SECRET - MAGIC

President Truman handed the paper back to the sergeant, who immediately turned and departed. "More of the same," he said to Leahy. "The Japanese now know the meaning of the July 26th ultimatum, and more importantly, what we can do."

"Will this one serve as our demonstration?" asked Leahy.

"That depends upon the Japanese government. The Army has the second device on Tinian, and it's ready for delivery. Stimson tells me the third and fourth devices are in various stages of on-the-way."

"Hopefully, we don't have to use another one of those weapons and kill even more people."

"We can always pray, Bill." Truman paused. No one spoke. "What I do need is the film and radio broadcast equipment set up as soon as possible. I need to broadcast a public statement on this development. Hiroshima was a very public event. News will spread worldwide like lightning."

"Would you like me to handle that, Mister President?" volunteered Foskett.

"Thank you, Captain. Yes, that way, the admiral can help me rehearse my speech a few more times."

"By your leave, Sir, I'll tend to it right away."

Truman saluted. Foskett left the compartment and closed the hatch behind him. The president retrieved his prepared speech with a few tweaks from both men.

———

Monday, 6.August.1945
USAAF Station 356
Saffron Walden, Essex, England
United Kingdom
16:00 hours

As commanding officer, Brian remained on base, just in case, while most of the squadron ran off to London, or to meet up with girlfriends, or to find a willing female for some softer companionship. He considered sitting down with his latest book—*A Connecticut Yankee in King Arthur's Court*. He had read it in high school, but the story brought a different feel to his current circumstances. Moreover, Brian had been pleasantly surprised at how refreshing Mark Twain's writing style and storytelling were. Nonetheless, somehow, at the moment, a few beers became more attractive than the book as they waited for the evening meal.

Brian had no sooner sat down at a table in the bar when the bartender turned up the radio.

"We interrupt our regular programming for a special address from the President of the United States. Ladies and gentlemen, the President . . ."

The announcement got Brian's attention. He moved a couple of chairs closer to the radio since not all the dozen or so pilots in the bar area wanted to listen to the president. The audio tone marked the beginning.

President Truman began, "Sixteen hours ago, an American airplane dropped one bomb on Hiroshima, an important Japanese Army base. That bomb had more power than 20,000 tons of T-N-T. It had more than two thousand times the blast power of the British 'Grand Slam,' which was the largest bomb ever yet used in the history of warfare to this point.

"The Japanese began the war from the air at Pearl Harbor. They have been repaid many fold. And the end is not yet. With this bomb, we have now added a new and revolutionary increase in destruction to supplement the growing power of our armed forces. In their present form, these bombs are now in production, and even more powerful forms are in development.

"It is an atomic bomb. It is a harnessing of the basic power of the universe. The force from which the sun draws its power has been loosed against those who brought war to the Far East."

Brian was becoming progressively more irritated with the noise. "Come on guys! It's the president on the radio. He's talking about some new bomb."

"He's not here," someone shouted, "and beer is more important."

Do I pull rank? These yayhoos should be listening to the president. This is important. Brian tried to listen, but the noise caused him to miss numerous words of the president's speech. *Something very important has happened, and he's trying to tell us.* Out of frustration, he stood, went to the large radio, and turned up the volume. Brian pulled up his chair closer to the radio and sat back down. Several other interested pilots did the same.

Truman's words came through scratchy but clear again. "But the greatest marvel is not the size of the enterprise, its secrecy, nor its cost, but the achievement of scientific brains in putting together infinitely complex pieces of knowledge held by many men in different fields of science into a workable plan. And hardly less marvelous has been the capacity of industry to design, and of labor to operate, the machines and methods to do things never done before so that the brainchild of many minds came forth in physical shape and performed as it was supposed to do. Both science and industry worked under the direction of the United States Army, which achieved a unique success in managing so diverse a problem in the advancement of knowledge in an amazingly short time. It is doubtful if such another combination could be combined in the world. What has been done is the greatest achievement of organized science in history. Moreover, it was done under high pressure and without failure.

"We are now prepared to obliterate more rapidly and completely every productive enterprise the Japanese have above ground in any city. We shall destroy their docks, their factories, and their communications. Let there be no mistake; we shall completely destroy Japan's power to make war."

Damn! What the hell is this thing? An atomic bomb, he said. I've got a lot to learn. I've never heard of such a thing.

"It was to spare the Japanese people from utter destruction that the ultimatum of July 26 was issued at Potsdam. Their leaders promptly rejected that ultimatum. If they do not now accept our terms, they may expect a rain of ruin from the air, the like of which has never been seen on this earth. Behind this air attack will follow sea and land forces in such numbers and power as they have not yet seen and with the fighting skill of which they are already well aware."

"Hey, Major, the radio is interfering with our drunken conversation," an anonymous someone shouted. "We'll buy you a beer if you turn that damn radio off."

"Guess they don't care to listen," said a young second lieutenant pilot he did not recognize.

"We can lead a horse to water, but we can't make him drink." Brian waved his hand dismissively and returned his attention to the radio despite the continuing cacophony at the bar.

"The fact that we can release atomic energy ushers in a new era in man's understanding of nature's forces. Atomic energy may, in the future, supplement the power that now comes from coal, oil, and falling water, but at present, it cannot be produced on a basis to compete with them commercially. Before that comes, there must be a long period of intensive research."

"What is this atomic bomb and atomic energy of which he speaks?" asked the unknown lieutenant.

Brian held up his extended right index finger to his lips.

Truman concluded, "I shall recommend that the Congress of the United States consider promptly the establishment of an appropriate commission to control the production and use of atomic power within the United States. I shall give further consideration and make further recommendations to the Congress as to how atomic power can become a powerful and forceful influence toward the maintenance of world peace."

The radio announcer stated, "That concludes President Truman's address to the nation. We return to our regular programming in progress."

Brian switched off the radio and then looked at the lieutenant. "I wish I knew what they mean. My guess is that the government has a very powerful new explosive. I think we all have a lot to learn. He's clearly warning Japan that more such destruction is coming to them if they don't surrender. Now, I think they just passed the first call to evening meal. Let's eat."

Brian noticed a second lieutenant attired in full pinks and greens service uniform appeared in the double-wide doorway. The lieutenant asked one of the pilots a question. The aviator turned and pointed directly to Brian.

Oh my, this can't be good.

Swimming against the flow of pilots making their way out of the bar toward the dining room, the lieutenant weaved his way to Brian. The boyish-appearing lieutenant stopped two paces short, came to a sharp position of attention and then saluted. Brian returned the salute without standing. "Major Drummond?" the young man asked.

"Yes."

"I was asked to deliver this envelope to you personally."

Brian took the proffered square envelope from the lieutenant. "Is a reply necessary?"

"No Sir. It was not so indicated to me."

Brian nodded. "Very well. Thank you, Lieutenant. Dismissed."

"You don't see that every day," commented Rolo, the Green Flight, 2ⁿᵈ Section leader.

Brian opened the envelope and extracted the card with a handwritten message.

General of the Army Eisenhower

invites

Major and Mrs. Brian Drummond, USA

to join him for a casual evening and dinner

at 17:30 on Wednesday, 5th September 1945

at Telegraph Cottage, Coombe Hill, London

R.S.V.P Mayfair 7715

Brian returned the card to the envelope.

"Something serious, Skipper?" Rolo asked.

"First, it's personal and none of your business. Second, we'll miss dinner if we don't get in gear."

Brian stood and left the bar with a handful of 334ᵗʰ pilots. Brian and his entourage made their way to the Officer's Mess dining room without another word. He resisted questions he could not answer and withdrew to his thoughts as he ate. After dinner, he called Charlotte to check in and did not mention the president's radio address. She did not reference it either. Brian figured it was better to learn more before offering his observations or opinions. With the telephone call completed, Brian chose his book over the pointless raucousness of the evening bar. The book eventually took him to sleep.

Wednesday, 8.August.1945
509ᵗʰ Composite Group
USAAF Station Destination
North Field
Tinian, Mariana Islands
Territory of the United States of America
14:00 hours

Colonel Tibbets had been working through the mountain of messages, to and from the Group, since Monday. His throughput barely exceeded the inflow of traffic arriving after the Little Boy mission. The paperwork gods had to be served. Fortunately, the Press had been kept at bay by Admiral Purnell, and Paul was grateful for that buffer. They were doing their job, and he must do his. The Group's purpose remained active.

Deak Parsons knocked on Tibbets' open office door and entered with Purnell and Farrell behind him. "We just received the order for Special Mission 16," Deak announced and handed Tibbets the single sheet of pink paper.

TOP SECRET - PARAMOUNT

```
WD
TS 080527Z AUG 45 URGENT
FM SECWAR
TO SILVERPLATE
INFO MANHATTAN
       COS
       PACCOM
       20AF
T O P   S E C R E T   P A R A M O U N T
BT
BY AUTHORITY OF POTUS PROCEED WITH SECOND
DELIVERY ASAP X PARTS FOR THIRD AND FOURTH
DEVICES EN ROUTE END
BT
NNNN
```

TOP SECRET - PARAMOUNT

"Can we make it tomorrow morning?" Parsons asked.
"So, the first one wasn't enough for the Japs, huh?"

"Guess not," Purnell answered. "We're not privy to diplomatic exchanges. We execute orders."

Tibbets nodded his head in acknowledgment. "My gosh, Deak," Tibbets responded to Parsons, "I would've thought such a question would be unnecessary. The whole Group has rehearsed this process more than enough times. Of course, we can do it. The crews have been assigned since Monday. Every one of them has done their homework. They know the mission plan backward and forward. The only uncertainties in my mind are the weather and mechanical problems. So, I shall ask all three of you, do we go for a morning delivery?"

"I say go," Purnell answered.

"Me as well," added Farrell.

"The device can be loaded and ready in a few hours. So, I say go as well."

"Very well. We'll get it done," Tibbets announced.

The three men remained in the office as Tibbets directed the operations staff to initiate the Special Mission 16 order.

22:00 hours

The Group's specially trained ordnance men began loading the fully assembled Fat Man weapon on the Bockscar B-29 Superfortress. The procedures had been rehearsed uncounted times. Each man knew precisely his task in the process that would take two hours and 30 minutes to complete with all the checks and crosschecks. The device was Army green like any other bomb. They were no longer practicing with the orange-painted 'pumpkin' weighted shapes. Every man knew they were handling the real weapon they had trained for so many months to load, secure, and prepare. None of the ordnance men knew what was inside the bomb or what would happen when it eventually detonated, but they all understood by the shape and mass of the weapon that it was not a typical bomb.

Only two weather aircraft were assigned to support Mission 16. Enola Gay would cover Kokura, and Laggin' Dragon would have Nagasaki. Like Mission 13, the weather aircraft would take off an hour earlier than the strike birds to provide ample observations of the target weather.

23:00 hours

Tibbets conducted the mission briefing for all crewmembers of the three strike planes. The Rendezvous Point was changed due to bad weather from Iwo Jima to Yakushima, a near circular island roughly 40 miles south of the southern tip of Kyushu. In addition, the altitude at which the planes were to fly was raised to 17,000 feet from the usual 8,000 feet to avoid the weather, which would increase fuel consumption. Colonel Tibbets issued two essential directives at this briefing: wait no more than fifteen minutes at the rendezvous point before proceeding on to Japan and drop the Fat Man bomb visually only. The onboard ground mapping radar could assist, but it was not accurate enough. The weather was forecast to be more problematic in the region, but the weather guessers gave them a sufficient margin above the minimum threshold required to enable the mission.

—

Thursday, 9.August.1945
USAAF Station Destination
North Field
Tinian, Mariana Islands
Territory of the United States of America
02:15 hours

With the ground exterior walkaround complete, Major Charles W. Sweeney, USAAF, of Massachusetts, led his crew in boarding Bockscar. Each crew member completed their pre-takeoff checks and reported their readiness for flight and the mission. The first glitch came from Flight Engineer Master Sergeant John Donald Kuharek of Pennsylvania.

"Boss, we've got a problem," announced Kuharek from his station behind the copilot's seat. Sweeney looked back over his right shoulder. "The fuel pump on the number one reserve tank is inop." The aft bomb bay had two 640-gallon reserve fuel tanks.

"We're not going to carry around 4,000 pounds of dead weight. So let's deplane while the maintenance guys fix it."

The crew deplaned while a Group maintenance crew jumped on fixing the fuel pump.

The weaponeer assigned to tend Fat Man, Commander Frederick Lincoln 'Dick' Ashworth, USN [USNA 1933], from Massachusetts, asked, "What's the problem?"

"A fuel pump for one of the reserve fuel tanks is inop."

"How long will it take to fix it?"

"They said about an hour."

"That's still within our time window," Dick offered.

"Yes. Unless you tell me otherwise, as long as we are within our mission constraints, and we have a bomber that can perform our assigned mission, we will go."

"Sounds reasonable. I'll inform the Chiefs."

"Sure. I suspect they already know. The colonel keeps a pretty close eye on things."

Ashworth nodded and joined his assistant in watching over the closed, forward bomb bay and its unique contents.

03:47 hours

It had taken nearly 90 minutes to replace the defective fuel pump, replace the fuel, perform the necessary checks to ensure system functionality, and to run through the pre-takeoff checklists, again. Finally, they were ready to go and still within their planned launch window.

"North Tower, Dimples Seventy-Seven is ready for takeoff," Sweeney broadcast.

"Dimples Seventy-Seven, position and hold Runway Zero Nine 'Able.'"

"Position and hold 'Able' for Dimples Seventy-Seven."

Several minutes passed. "Dimples Seventy-Seven, North Tower. Wind is one zero five at ten knots. Cleared for takeoff. God bless you and return home safely."

Sweeney pushed the throttle levers forward, released the brakes, and the heavy bomber rumbled down the dark, edge-lit runway, accelerating nicely. They were on their way. The primary target was the Kokura Arsenal.

04:00 hours

As Parsons had done with Little Boy three days earlier, Dick Ashworth replaced Fat Man's red safety plugs with green enabling plugs. The bomb was reported ready, and Bombardier Captain Kermit King Beahan, USAAF, of Missouri, performed and reported his control panel was ready.

09:10 hours

Bockscar reached the briefed Yakushima rendezvous point and entered a wide orbit around the island. They immediately spotted The Great Artiste that joined up in a half-mile trail position, but Big Stink was nowhere in sight. Sweeney initiated a climb to 30,000 feet altitude while he held the orbit and waited for Big Stink to join.

"Let's wait for Big Stink," Ashworth said, kneeling next to Sweeney. "The observers and high-speed cameras are on that bird."

"The most I can give them is 30-40 minutes, and then we'll have to go without them."

Both weather planes reported their weather observations. Kokura and Nagasaki had low broken clouds. Conditions were not ideal, but they were better than the mission minimums, and it would come down to luck—would a hole in the cloud layer be present when they reached the target?

09:50 hours

After orbiting the rendezvous point for 40 minutes and stable at 30,000 feet, Big Stink was still nowhere in sight. Sweeney said over the intercom, "OK, Dick, we've waited as long as we can. Do you agree that we will go without the observer/photo bird?" Their mission orders stipulated radio silence. They could not radio Big Stink. None of them had any idea whether the third strike B-29 was even still flying. The mission was paramount.

"Agreed," was Ashworth's succinct response.

"Van, give me the heading to Kokura. We're going for the primary."

Navigator Captain James Frederick 'Van' Van Pelt, Jr., USAAF, of West Virginia, responded immediately, "Primary bears zero zero eight true from our current location. That's zero zero two magnetic, Boss."

Sweeney banked the big bomber left. "Turning to zero zero two. OK, lads, we're about an hour out. Let's make sure each of you is ready, especially your flash goggles. Kermit, are you ready?"

"Panel's green, no glitches," Beahan responded. "Sight is set, optics good. Bombardier ready."

"It's showtime, folks. No mistakes," Sweeney said to the crew over the intercom.

10:44 hours

"We're at the I-P," announced Van.

"I've got nothing visually. Haze, perhaps smoke, fog, and low clouds," Kermit added. "Nothing . . . no landmarks . . . nothing."

"I've confirmed the primary on radar," announced Staff Sergeant Edward Kenneth 'Ed' Buckley of Ohio, the Group's most experienced radar operator. "Perfect match."

"We've got to have a visual," Sweeney declared. "We're going around." He rolled the bomber into a standard rate turn to the right for a long racetrack pattern to give them another run at the IP in hopes the clouds broke enough for visual release on the aim point.

The second pass yielded the same result as their initial approach, but their airborne situation changed. Several flak bursts bloomed beneath them, which meant the Japanese used radar-directed anti-aircraft guns.

"They're using radar. Can you get 'em, Jake?" Sweeney asked the crew's electronic countermeasures officer.

First Lieutenant Jacob Beser, USAAF, of Maryland, answered, "Workin' on a lock, Skipper." Several minutes passed. "Got 'em. My goodness, this one is just like in school. We're good, Skipper."

"Bandits, six o'clock low and climbing," called out Tail Gunner Staff Sergeant Albert Travis 'Al' Dehart of Texas over the intercom.

"Keep track of 'em, Al," Sweeney responded. "OK, fellas, things are heating up here. After this pass, we're diverting to the secondary. So let's see if we can deliver the Fat Man on this pass." They turned inbound.

"I-P," announced Van.

"Confirmed," Ed added.

A couple of minutes passed. "No joy. I've got nothing," said Kermit. Another minute passed.

"We're past the Aim Point," Van said with solemnity.

Sweeney commanded, "Safe your panel, Kermit."

"She's safe. We're cold. Panel's still green," Beahan replied.

The aircraft banked left. "Heading to the secondary."

"Skipper, we're near bingo," Kuharek interjected.

"Two one one magnetic," said Van. Sweeney adjusted his heading to 211° magnetic.

"I concur with John," added Sweeney's copilot, First Lieutenant Charles Donald 'Don' Albury, USAAF, of Florida.

Ashworth knelt between Sweeney and Albury.

"We have a mission to perform. The country is counting on us, Don. John, calculate our bingo for Iwo and another for Okinawa from Nagasaki. We've gotta deliver Fat Man. John, where are the new bingos?"

"Holding our standard reserve, it's 231 gallons for Yontan and 283 gallons for Iwo."

Albury did not use the intercom and looked directly at Sweeney. "Are you sure, Boss? We're going to be quite thin making it back to base with that bomb," Albury shouted over the drone of the cockpit noise.

"Our mission is the delivery of that weapon," Sweeney said without the intercom, gesturing with his right thumb over his right shoulder to the bomber's rear, "in accordance with our operating instructions. We've got to give it every try until we have no other options."

Albury shrugged his shoulder and looked away, staring out the windshield in front of him.

Sweeney shook his head several times and checked his instrument panel in front of him.

Ashworth tapped the aircraft commander on his right forearm. Sweeney looked. Ashworth leaned close to Sweeney's right ear. "Can you do it?"

"The guys are getting nervous. None of us wants to ditch this beast. Hell, I'm uneasy about this. Everything depends on the weather, and we're likely to face the same weather at Nagasaki as we saw at Kokura."

"Can you drop with radar?"

"Those aren't our instructions."

"I know that, but Fat Man is the only device we have right now. Can you do it?"

Sweeney thought for a moment as he looked at the instrument panel and then looked back at Ashworth. "All of the targets have distinctive radar signatures. Radar is less accurate than with the Norden, which the colonel acknowledged in the briefing. Yes, we can do it, if you authorize us to do so."

"Can we still make it to Okinawa?"

"It will be tight, but yes, I think we can."

Ashworth thought for a moment and then said, "As the mission commander, I authorize you and your crew to release the bomb using radar only if necessary."

"Very well."

11:32 hours

Sweeney keyed the intercom. "OK, fellas, we're going to press on to the secondary. Abe, send a one-word message to Iwo and Tinian—Secondary." Sergeant Abe Spitzer of New York served as the crew's radio operator.

"Wilco, Skipper," Spitzer affirmed.

"Ed, we are now authorized to do a radar release, so get your equipment ready. Track the target as long as you can. We'll get only one pass at the target. Kermit, a visual release is preferred. Give it your best. You're going to have to call it a mile out; that will give Ed 20 seconds to the release if you don't have a visual."

"I can handle that," Kermit answered.

"We're 20 minutes out. Let's make damn certain we're ready. We can make only one pass at the secondary. No mistakes. Van, we'll pass through and head straight to Yontan."

"I'll be ready, Skipper," Van Pelt responded.

Bockscar tracked directly toward the Southern Kyushu port city of Nagasaki. The city was the largest natural harbor in Kyushu and the site of numerous varied war industries, including the production of ships, ordnance, military equipment, and other essential war materials.

11:56 hours

"I've got the target on display," Ed Buckley announced. "Perfect match. Good track. We're 10 miles out and closing nicely."

"Thanks, Ed. Stay on it. Kermit, your show."

"Roger, Skipper. Panel's green. I've got nothing but low clouds at the moment, but there might be a break coming. The device is armed. Switches are hot." A long agonizing silence left the entire crew with only the noise of engines and flight as they flew on.

Big Stink finally found them as Bockscar made the final run to the target. They were at 39,000 feet, rather than 30,000 feet with the other aircraft.

32° 46' 25" North -- 129° 51' 48" East
Nagasaki, Nagasaki Prefecture, Kyushu
Empire of Japan

To everyone's surprise, shock, and even a little relief, Kermit shouted over the intercom, "I've got it!" What he saw in the optics of his Norden bombsight was the distinct shapes of a large sports complex along the Uragami River, two miles (three kilometers) north of the city center.

No one debated Beahan. "Autopilot to Bombardier," Sweeney announced over the intercom. "Get your goggles on," he commanded. "No exceptions." Sweeney looked around him. Those he could see were doing exactly as instructed. He decided to hold his donning until the bomb dropped free. Kermit Beahan's face was attached to the bombsight. The whole crew heard the distinct clunk of the bomb bay doors snapping open.

12:01:17 hours

"Bomb's away," Kermit said as the aircraft lurched up with the release of the five-ton mass from the forward bomb bay. Beahan closed the bomb bay doors, safe'd his bomb control panel, and then he donned his goggles and ensured they were properly in place.

Sweeney switched the autopilot back to his control and advanced the throttles to full power to gain as much distance as possible before detonation. He checked his instrument panel to ensure all four engines were running smoothly, and then he donned his goggles.

12:02 hours

Fat Man detonated at 1,650 feet over the city with a force of 21 KT, 30% greater than Little Boy. As the Enola Gay experienced three days earlier, Bockscar felt three distinct shock waves shake the big bomber, but unlike Enola Gay, they were prepared for the jolts by the debriefing of the Enola Gay crew. The aircraft was still flying. Sweeney pulled his goggles down around his neck, where they would remain until they landed. He retarded the throttles and set power for maximum range.

12:06 hours

"Everyone OK?" Sweeney asked over the intercom. Then, each member of the crew reported his position and status.

"One niner one magnetic to Yontan," Van volunteered.

Sweeney adjusted his heading slightly to the right. "How far?"

"Three hundred miles by my calculation."

"It's going to be close," Kuharek added. "My calculations indicate we'll be into our reserve." The B-29 crews in the Pacific used a standard 40-minute fuel reserve—40 gallons of usable fuel.

"Thanks, John. Abe, get on the radio. Try to raise air/sea rescue. Give them our position, heading, and intended divert destination. Before we might need to, I want everyone to ensure you have your life vest on and properly secured. Make sure the life rafts are secure and ready to deploy. Let's make sure we're ready for a ditching at sea if it comes to that." Several crewmen acknowledged the instructions. "Kermit, get your thermite ready in case we need it." The bombardier had a thermite grenade near his station that would destroy the sight. The bombardiers had trained to place the grenade in a receptacle on top of the sight with instructions to pull the pin and let the lever fly igniting the incendiary contents and melting or igniting everything it came in contact with. Beahan removed the grenade from its container, placed it in the receptacle, and locked it in place.

"Abe, your silence is not good."

"No Sir. I've been at it since you ordered it. Nothing, Skipper, not even a tickle."

"Keep trying. I'd rather have 'em standing by and not need 'em."

"Fuel's tracking, Skipper," interjected John Kuharek. "We're going to be real close."

"Thanks, John. I've got all four engines at max range. Lean 'em out as close as you can. Abe, any luck?"

"Nothing, Skipper. I've tried every frequency I've got. I'll keep trying."

13:00 hours

"We're into the reserve," Kuharek announced, which meant they had 40 minutes until they ran out of fuel.

"Land ho!" exclaimed Kermit.

"Ed, what have you got?" asked Sweeney.

"I'm painting land, but I don't have enough to positively identify what that land is. I'll keep working on it."

"Abe, dial me up Yontan Tower on V-H-F."

Several seconds later, Spitzer replied, "You're up, Skipper."

"Yontan Tower, this is Dimples 7-7." No response came. Sweeney pulled the throttles back to begin a gradual descent. He could now see what looked like green mountains ahead of them. Unfortunately, none of them had anything recognizable. Sweeney repeated his radio call numerous times as they approached the mountainous terrain.

"I've got a good paint on the scope," Buckley announced. "It's Okinawa, and I've got Yontan. Come left four degrees for runway 1-9 at Yontan."

Sweeney adjusted his heading and continued his descent. He finally had the runway in sight and had a good track for a right turn to final. There was no go-around option. Sweeney repeatedly tried to raise the tower or any aircraft on frequency without success. He broadcast a fuel emergency, again without reply. "Ed, get ready to fire a red flare. I'll let you know when. Everyone, keep your eyes out for other aircraft. We've got no comm with the tower, and we've got to get this beast on the ground." Sweeney liked his approach, and with Don Albury, he configured the big aircraft for landing. He initiated a right turn to the lineup on Yontan Runway 19. "Fire the flare, Ed."

"It's gone, Skipper."

Yontan Airfield, Okinawa, Ryuku Islands Prefecture
Liberated Japan
13:20 hours

Sweeney landed a little fast but made it safely. No one was hurt. Before he could turn off the runway onto the taxiway, the number two engine quit due to fuel starvation. "John, shut down three. We don't need to attract any more attention than we already have." The flight engineer did so promptly. No matter what, they were on the ground. The Great Artiste and Big Stink landed behind Bockscar. Their fuel state was better than Bockscar since they had been flying with less weight. An MP half-track and several Jeeps with 50-caliber machine gun pedestal mounts rushed out to greet them before they completed the shutdown.

17:30 hours

Although they did not need full fuel, Sweeney asked for full fuel. They sent the appropriate messages off to Tinian and informed them of their plan to return tonight, along with their expected arrival time. After briefing the other two strike aircraft, they loaded up and took off in two-minute intervals, climbing to 8,000 feet and heading directly to Tinian. The Great Artiste joined up off the left wing. Big Stink was off the right wing.

North Field, Tinian
22:30 hours

The three, strike aircraft were the last mission aircraft to land safely back at North Field. There was no welcoming committee, no dignitaries, no photographers, no band . . . only the ground crewman with their light wands directing them into their parking spots. They had accomplished their assigned mission, not without numerous hiccups. The mission was finally done. Everyone returned home safely. Major Sweeney felt good. It had been a difficult mission, but they made it back to their home base.

—

Thursday, 9.August.1945
Residence
The White House
Washington, District of Columbia
United States of America
06:00 hours

"My apologies for interrupting your morning, Mister President." Secretary Stimson said as he entered the residence and found the president partially dressed in gray trousers and a light blue dress shirt with French cuffs and presidential seal cufflinks.

"Most unusual, I must say, Henry. It must be important."

"It is. Fat Man was dropped on Nagasaki. The crew found low overcast obscuring their primary target—Kokura. According to the initial report, the crew made several passes at the primary target but could not obtain acceptable mission conditions. They identified the target on radar on each pass but could not visually identify the target. Finally, they diverted to their secondary target—Nagasaki. The crew encountered more unacceptable weather, but good fortune brought a break in the clouds of sufficient size for the bombardier to identify the target and release the bomb."

"I assume it functioned properly."

"Yes Sir. The scientists must analyze the collected data, but the initial impression of the observers was that Fat Man was equal to or greater yield than Little Boy."

"I wonder if the Japanese leaders will believe this one?"

"Yet to be determined, Mister President. To my knowledge, we've heard nothing from the S-C-D-W since the MAGIC intercept after Little Boy."

"Have you been able to refine the availability of the follow-on devices?" Truman asked.

"General Groves and I discussed that very question last night. The third device will be available to deploy by the 17th, no later than the 18th. The fourth bomb is expected to be ready for delivery in mid-September. The core of the second Little Boy weapon won't be ready until at least November."

"OK. So, we wait."

"Yes Sir. I imagine the Japanese are cogitating deeply on what was clearly not a fluke to them. The action rests entirely with them."

"They've got nine days before they receive the next dose. I don't want to leave that week plus without attention to them. Please direct the air force to strike Japan one or two times over the next intervening nine days. I want them to know we will continue to strike them until they surrender. I don't think we want atomic and conventional missions to overlap, but we must keep the heat on them between atomic deliveries. According to your earlier statement, we can deliver three or perhaps four special weapons before we must execute Operation OLYMPIC. If they have not surrendered by the third bomb, we will need to issue the appropriate orders to prepare for the execution of OLYMPIC and transfer the majority of the A-E-F to back up Operation CORONET."

"It shall be done. Jim Forrestal and I will meet with the Joint Chiefs later today to ensure they understand the time gates and sequence of events. Hopefully, Suzuki and his comrades will recognize the futility of their position and resistance before we must drop the next one."

"We shall pray for that, Henry."

"I'll get out of your hair and leave you to the rest of your day. Thank you for your time, Mister President. Good day."

The president sat down for his breakfast, which had been kept warm for him. He ate breakfast alone, and then he finished dressing before walking with his Secret Service security detail to the West Wing and Oval Office.

—

Thursday, 9.August.1945
Standing Oak Farm
Winchester, Hampshire, England
United Kingdom
13:15 hours

The 4th Fighter Group had been given a 48-hour pass. Colonel Clark had yet to receive further direction. They stood in limbo between transferring to the Pacific or going home. The fighter groups were being rotated into the American Zone of occupied Germany in case they were needed for the protection of transport aircraft in and out of Berlin as tensions with the Soviets continued to mount. The recent news had piqued curiosity but had not altered the limbo they felt . . . at least not yet.

Charlotte was standing outside as soon as he looked at the house. *She must have seen Morty's cab as it crested the ridge line.* Brian thanked and paid

Morty. After he exited the cab and Morty drove away, Charlotte's expression changed as she pointed to the oak tree and their bench. She was carrying a small picnic basket.

"What's up?"

"I brought a sandwich and a canteen of water so we can talk."

Charlotte started walking to the oak tree without a kiss or even a handshake. Brian quickly caught up to her. "OK. Is something wrong?"

"Not with us. Not with me." Charlotte stopped, stepped forward to face her husband, and gave him a quick peck on the lips. "The news has been very confusing since the last time we talked. Some of it scares me, Brian."

They reached the shade of the massive oak tree. Charlotte sat. Brian pointed to the fire pit, but Charlotte shook her head. She opened the basket and handed Brian his roast beef sandwich with lettuce, cheese, and fresh tomato slices. Before he could convey his amazement and gratitude, Charlotte looked into Brian's eyes and said, "The BBC announced at the noon hour broadcast news that the American air force had dropped another one of those things on another Japanese city. They say it completely obliterated . . . my word . . . both of those cities . . . Hiroshima and Nagasaki, as I recall. What are these things, and what is going on?"

Brian finished his second bite of the sandwich before he answered. He took a good swallow from the canteen. "I don't know. When I called you Monday evening, we had just listened to President Truman's broadcast announcement. He called it an atomic bomb. I've never heard of such a thing. Apparently, it is a new kind of explosive. It must be, since a single bomb appears to have destroyed a Japanese city in each instance."

"What about your transfer?"

"Nothing new. Command has yet to tell us about those bombs and has yet to give us any new information about the transfer orders. So, we are still on hold."

Charlotte frowned and stared straight ahead without any particular object in sight. "That means our plans are on hold."

"Charlotte, we should continue to operate as we have for the last bunch of years. Nothing has altered that course. I doubt nothing will until the Army decides what to do with us. As a precaution, the Army has set up a rotation of fighter groups to stage in the American Zone of Germany. Each group goes over for a week. We're scheduled to deploy to Germany in late September, like we did to Ukraine last year. I've no idea what all this news means to those plans, but we'll continue to do what we are assigned to do." Brian finished the sandwich and drank from the canteen without finishing it.

"I pray every night that this war will finally be over, and they will let you come back to me," Charlotte said.

"At least I'm not being shot at."

"Stop. That's not funny. The news of these terrible bombs and you going to where they are dropping those things scares the bloody hell out of me. You fighting with German fighters worried me because I expected something bad to happen every day. But these bombs are not like being shot at. They are monstrous."

"The best I can say is I'll try to learn more. Until we know more, you really must try to put those thoughts aside. They are not helpful. At the moment, I am here, not there. Let's avoid letting our imagination get too far ahead of where we are."

"Easy for you to say. You're not the one waiting in the dark."

"I will do my best to learn more, my darling. Now, to change the subject, I forgot to tell you last Monday that we got an invitation to dinner with General Eisenhower."

"You forgot!"

Brian chuckled softly. "Yes, I did. The courier delivered the invitation right after the president announced the first bombing."

"Can I see it?"

"Oh here, yes, of course," he answered as he removed the envelope from the pocket of his uniform tunic. He passed the envelope to Charlotte, who immediately removed the card and read it.

"He asked for a response, Brian. You got this four days ago."

"It's not until next month."

"What do you want to do?"

"The general had mentioned such a dinner when he awarded me the D-S-C in April of last year. I guess he finally found some time."

"What does he want?"

"I've not talked to him since last year. The invitation doesn't say. As I recalled, he noted that we were both from Kansas."

"That seems like an odd reason for a general to invite a major and his wife to a private dinner."

"My thoughts exactly, but that's still a handwritten invitation. I think we'll know if it's real when we call the number. What say you?"

"Well, frankly, I would like to meet the man who led our troops to victory over Germany. Yes, I'm in favor. I'd recommend we accept."

"Very well, then. Are we done here? If so, we can go inside and telephone our response."

Both stood. Brian picked up the picnic basket. He kissed Charlotte and thanked her for the delicious sandwich.

—

Thursday, 9.August.1945
Farm Hall
23 West Street
Godmanchester, Huntingdon, Cambridgeshire
United Kingdom
14:00 hours

The Allied intelligence chiefs gathered on at least a monthly basis, if not more often, when the situation warranted. This afternoon's session was a special request from Colonel Thomas Joseph 'Tom' Kendrick, a career intelligence officer within MI6 and founder of MI19, the POW interrogation service.

The four chiefs road up to Farm Hall Cage together. The chiefs at the table with Colonel Kendrick were General Sir Stewart Menzies for MI6, Director-General David Petrie for MI5, Lord Selborne for SOE, and Colonel David Bruce representing OSS. They dispensed with the cordialities promptly.

"Thank you for coming all the way up here, gentlemen. Normally, I would come to you in London, but this one is rather unique."

"We are intrigued," interjected Lord Selborne.

"Yes, well," Kendrick continues, "I think you will find it worth the journey. As we had agreed, the captured German fission research scientists were collected up here at Farm Hall and separated from all other detainees. Farm Hall is quite a bit smaller than Trent Park, but it is wired up to a greater extent."

"I'm so glad we could be of service," Lord Selborne said.

Kendrick smiled and chuckled softly. "This site was formerly an S-O-E training location. The mansion and grounds are ideal for our purposes."

"So what have you learned," Menzies asked with a hint of impatience.

Kendricks nodded. "After we received the daily newspapers that reported on the Hiroshima event, we included and placed the newspapers on their reading table in the sitting room with other unrelated newspapers, magazines, and books. Then, shortly before dinner was to be served to the group on the 6th of August, they gathered in the sitting room for drinks, and we recorded the following conversation.

"The first page lists the detained individuals under our surveillance. The second page is the transcript of their conversation." Each man opened their folder and began to read.

MOST SECRET - ANGEL

Farm Hall's current focus list as of 6th August 1945; 08:00

```
DIE -- Doctor Kurt Diebner, PhD (Nuclear
          Physics)
HAH -- Doctor Otto Hahn, PhD (Organic
          Chemistry); Nobel Laureate
          1944(Chemistry)
HEI -- Doctor Werner Karl Heisenberg, PhD
          (Physics); Nobel Laureate 1932
          (Quantum Mechanics)
WIE -- Doctor Carl Friedrich Baron von
          Weizsäcker, PhD (Physics)
WIR -- Doctor Karl Eugen Julius Wirtz, PhD
          (Physics)
```

MOST SECRET - ANGEL

―――――――――――――

"That's quite a list of scientific knowledge," Bruce interjected.

"Yes, it is, and we are still collecting up these guys as we jointly find them," Kendrick commented. "None of them offered any resistance whatsoever, and with only one exception so far, we found all of them at home with their families."

"These are not the only scientists involved in a fission explosive development," stated Bruce.

"No, they are not," Menzies answered, "just the ones we've found so far."

―――――――――――――

MOST SECRET - ANGEL

```
Excerpt of conversation: DIE, HAH, HEI, WIE, &
WIR; 6th August 1945; 17:41
[ . . . ]
HEI I don't believe a word of the whole thing.
    They must have spent the whole of their
    £500,000,000 in separating isotopes; and
    then it's possible.
WEI If it's easy and the Allies know it's easy,
    then they know that we will soon find out
    how to do it if we go on working.
HAH I didn't think it would be possible for
    another twenty years.
WEI I don't think it has anything to do with
    uranium.
[ . . . ]
```

```
DIE We always thought we would need two years
    for one bomb.
HAH If they have really got it, they have been
    very clever in keeping it secret.
WIR I'm glad we didn't have it.
WEI That's another matter. How surprised
    BENZER(?) would have been. They always
    looked upon it as a conjuring trick.
HAH DOEPEL was the first to discover the
    increase in neutrons.
WEI I think it's dreadful of the Americans
    to have done it. I think it is madness on
    their part.
HEI One can't say that. One could equally well
    say "That's the quickest way of ending the
    war."
HAH That's what consoles me.
[ . . . ]
End of relevant conversation.
```

MOST SECRET - ANGEL

As the last face looked up, Kendrick said, "The general opinion of our experts is they reacted to the news with incredulity. They are convinced in their knowledge that the Allies could not have achieved a functional device. I will add here, I brought our sympathetic ringer up to Farm Hill. Major Ian Monroe, an M-I-19 officer in the persona of Lord Aberfeldy, acted as the Welfare Officer for German generals and notables. Aberfeldy was constructed as a nobleman and distant cousin of King George VI."

"Aberfeldy had a chance exchange with Doctor Hahn yesterday afternoon. He matter-of-factly mentioned the B-B-C announcing that an atomic bomb had been dropped on Japan. Hahn was thoroughly devasted, visibly so, by the news. Hahn declared himself personally responsible for hundreds of thousands of people's deaths because his original research made the bomb possible. Hahn told Aberfeldy that he had contemplated suicide when he realized that his laboratory work had led to such destruction."

"With these men, I think it safe to say that the root question of how close the Germans were to a functional atomic bomb, we unanimously feel they were a long way from such a device."

Menzies looked to the others. "Do we all agree on that assessment?" All the chiefs nodded in the affirmative.

"Thank you," Kendrick acknowledged. "I recommend we summarize the transcripts without referring directly to the facility, the process, or the techniques. Further, I would like to open a new S-C-I compartment for the dissemination of ANGEL information to TUBE ALLOYS and the Manhattan Project. The Alsos team, the exploitation collection fission research group created by General Groves, requested access to the raw data from Colonel Bruce."

"As we agreed, we rejected their request," interjected Bruce. "I will inform the team of our decision here."

"Have these men," said Selborne, "been subjected to proper interrogation to probe more deeply into what they know and exactly how far they got?"

"No Sir," Kenrick answered. "We wanted to ascertain what we could without direct interrogation. We can establish that process in short order."

"That should do," Selborne responded.

Menzies looked at everyone. "Unless anyone has an objection or contribution, I suggest we leave the decision in Colonel Kendrick's experienced hands."

"Agreed." "Yep." "Indeed," came the replies.

—

Thursday, 9.August.1945
Residence
The White House
Washington, District of Columbia
United States of America
20:30 hours

Bill Leahy arrived. President Truman had finished dinner with his wife and daughter 20 minutes earlier. Leahy announced, "Byrnes is on his way over with a message hot off the teletype from the Swiss."

"Presumably the surrender message."

"My guess is yes."

"I guess the second bomb did the trick," Truman responded with a modest chuckle in his voice.

"Perhaps so, Mister President. That is a rather cynical view, even if it is true."

"Yes, well, these are the times in which we live."

The chief duty Secret Service agent opened the residence door as soon as he saw Secretary Byrnes appear from the stairway and announced Byrnes' arrival. The 63-year-old man had apparently decided the elevator took too long.

The breathless Byrnes entered the residence, struggling to catch his breath, and went directly to the president. "The Japanese . . . have . . . accepted . . . the Potsdam terms," he chopped out and handed the message to the president.

```
DATE 09 AUG 1945 2307 CET
FROM SWISS FEDERAL POLITICAL DEPARTMENT BERN
TO STATE DEPARTMENT WASHINGTON DC
ORIGINAL RECEIVED 2302 CET FOR IMMEDIATE
RETRANSMISSION TO SECSTATE GODSPEED
DATE 19450810 0700 HOME
FROM PRIME MINISTER TOKYO
TO SWISS FEDERAL POLITICAL DEPARTMENT BERN
FOR IMMEDIATE TRANSMISSION TO THE UNITED STATES
GOVERNMENT ON BEHALF OF THE EMPEROR AND THE
GOVERNMENT OF IMPERIAL JAPAN WE ACCEPT THE
POTSDAM TERMS PROVIDED THE ALLIED POWERS AGREE
NOT TO ALTER THE EMPERORS PEROGATIVES END
SUZUKI
```

"Well, I may not appreciate the nuance in the chosen words," Truman said, "but I do not believe they have accepted. They still insist on the emperor's prerogatives, which is an unacceptable condition upon our stated terms."

While Byrnes's respiratory recovery continued, Bill Leahy suggested, "May I offer, Mister President, I am certain we can craft a more positive reply that reflects our terms without slapping the Japanese in the face."

Byrnes nodded. As he thought, Truman looked out the concentric, semi-circular window into the falling dusk. "OK. Let's try it," the president decided, looking at Byrnes. He then looked at Leahy. "Until further directed, I want all bombing of or offensive operations against any portion of the Japanese Home Islands to be suspended. ALBERTA will continue their preparations for the third delivery, but they will not act until so ordered."

The gears of diplomacy ground threw the exact choice of every word. They took two days to agree. Finally, in the early morning hours of the 12th, the official reply to the Japanese was transmitted through the Swiss to the Japanese.

SECRET

```
SD
S 121048Z AUG 45 URGENT
FM SECSTATE
TO SWISS FEDERAL POLITICAL DEPARTMENT BERN
S E C R E T
BT
PLEASE CONVEY TO PRIME MINISTER TOKYO
FROM THE MOMENT OF SURRENDER THE AUTHORITY OF
THE EMPEROR AND THE JAPANESE GOVERNMENT TO
RULE THE STATE SHALL BE SUBJECT TO THE SUPREME
COMMANDER OF THE ALLIED POWERS WHO WILL TAKE
SUCH STEPS AS HE DEEMS PROPER TO EFFECTUATE
THE SURRENDER TERMS X THE ULTIMATE FORM OF
GOVERNMENT OF JAPAN SHALL IN ACCORDANCE WITH
THE POTSDAM DECLARATION BE ESTABLISHED BY THE
FREELY EXPRESSED WILL OF THE JAPANESE PEOPLE
END
BT
NNNN
```

SECRET

The Allied reply sent deeper spasms into the Japanese government. The right-wing militant wing rattled their saber.

—

Monday, 13.August.1945
Cabinet Room, West Wing
The White House
Washington, District of Columbia
United States of America
17:20 hours

The Cabinet had assembled early. President Truman saw no reason to wait until the appointed time. He entered early and asked the ministers to sit. Truman waited until he was seated in his usual center seat and in position.

"Thank you for coming. Also, thank you, Director Donovan, for joining us. Let's begin with your report on what we know about the situation in Japan."

"Of course, Mister President. Since our reply on the 12th, we have confirmed their receipt. O-S-S agents in country picked up more than a few indications of a *coup d'état* by a militant faction within their armed forces to depose the emperor and the government. We cannot ascribe the weight of fact to what are at best rumors. Our sources feel the information is likely correct, but we cannot corroborate it as yet. Also, our sources report publicly discernible actions by forces they claim are and remain loyal to the emperor. I think it is safe to say that the emperor has stepped off his position of neutrality and is leaning toward accepting the Potsdam terms without condition. The information suggests he may have resigned himself to submission, but we cannot confirm or verify that assessment. They are struggling with the hardliners, and the signs suggest the emperor is moving toward the diplomats."

"But they have not yet accepted reality," the president said.

"No Sir," responded Byrnes.

"We should be sympathetic," Truman pronounced, "to the elements of peace within Japan. It is encouraging to know there are such forces, and they are working to overcome the fascist faction within the military. Can we find a way to reach out to the peacemakers and help them in any way?"

"Japan is one of the more insular societies through history," Donovan offered. "Such a connection would be a very delicate matter. Keeping such contact beyond the awareness of the militants would be very risky, especially for the Japanese individuals. The *Kempeitai* is the military police arm of the Imperial Japanese Army. In reality, they are far greater and more expansive than military intelligence, predominantly since the Army controlled the government during the war. Tojo and the other generals turned to the *Kempeitai* for state security. In reality, they became the equivalent of the *Gestapo*, and in some respects, a far more effective organization. They are not troubled by politics as the *Gestapo* was. It is not yet clear which side the *Kempeitai* is on."

The Cabinet debated the overtures from Japan and to Japan for more than an hour. Truman listened mainly to the various views of the situation. The ministers were unanimous in their desire to end the war as quickly as possible, but a broad spectrum of paths to peace was voiced.

President Truman reached his point of saturation. He had heard enough. The president struck his fist on the large table like a gavel. "OK. Enough! Thank you all for your counsel. The policy of the United States has not and will not change. It is unconditional surrender, period. Our response of the 12th stands as is. Secretary Stimson, please proceed with the final preparatory steps." The whole room was not cleared for PARAMOUNT information, so his cryptic sentence would have to suffice. "Further, you are directed to order the 20ᵗʰ Air Force to prepare a one thousand bomber incendiary mission. Choose a target not on the other list. The mission will be subject to recall should the Japanese formally surrender before the lead bomber reaches the target. Any questions?" None came. "Please report accomplishment to me directly. Let's keep our ears to the rails. We can only hope the peace faction prevails. Until then, gentlemen, we are adjourned."

The group stood and waited for the president to leave the room. They gathered up their papers and filed out without further words.

—

Wednesday, 15.August.1945
Cabinet Room, West Wing
The White House
Washington, District of Columbia
United States of America
18:30 hours

The telephone call from OSS Director Donovan, who was on his way, had requested the unscheduled meeting with the president. Rose quickly called Secretaries Stimson and Forrestal to attend the unscheduled meeting. Secretary Byrnes was the closest and the first to arrive. Donovan was the next to arrive and joined Byrnes in the Cabinet Room. Truman asked Admiral Leahy to join the group.

"Something new?" Byrnes asked.

"Yep. We picked up a public broadcast by Emperor Hirohito himself."

"Well, that is quite unusual."

"Yes, as in never. I picked the essential paragraphs. I wanted to get the crucial pieces to the president and the defense cabinet. I also have more information on the *coup d'état.*"

"I won't ask you to pass the information twice," Byrnes said.

Stimson and Forrestal arrived together. With greetings exchanged. The four men waited silently across the large table from the president's chair. President Truman entered ten minutes after they were all in the Cabinet Room.

"Seats, gentlemen," the president commanded. "Bess and Margaret are holding supper for me. Let's get this done. Bill, I think you called this coffee clutch. Let's hear it."

"Mister President," Donovan began, "Emperor Hirohito publicly broadcast a radio message to his people earlier today. We will have the full transcript later tonight. We did not have time to type up what we have so far, but I thought I would read the first part of the emperor's broadcast statement if you wish."

Truman chuckled softly. "I've not had a story read to me since I was a little tyke. That said, my curiosity is piqued. So, unless there are any objections, we await your reading."

"Before I read the emperor's message, I should say the loyal palace guard finally got the upper hand on the usurpers early this morning. The *coup* failed. The *coup* attempt was led by a group of hardline junior officers. They tried to seize the palace, capture the emperor, and impose martial law to avoid surrender, as they believed the S-C-D-W was headed. They failed to gain the support of senior officers and government officials. The *coup* leaders, Major Kenji Hatanaka, Lieutenant Colonel Jiro Shiizaki, and others committed ritual suicide, *seppuku*, on the grounds of the Imperial Palace. The *coup* came very close to succeeding, but it ultimately failed. Later this morning, the emperor decided that the time had come for him to intercede for the good of his people."

"Thank goodness for small blessings," Byrnes commented.

"Yes, exactly," Donovan replied with emphasis. "The emperor's statement began . . .

"To our good and loyal subjects:

"After pondering deeply the general trends of the world and the actual conditions obtaining to our empire today, we have decided to effect a settlement of the present situation by resorting to an extraordinary measure.

"We have ordered our government to communicate to the governments of the United States, Great Britain, China, and the Soviet Union that our empire accepts the provisions of their Joint Declaration.

"But now the war has lasted for nearly four years. Despite the best that has been done by everyone—the gallant fighting of the military and naval forces, the diligence and assiduity of our servants of the state, and the devoted service of our 100 million people—the war situation has developed not necessarily to Japan's advantage. In contrast, the general trends of the world have all turned against her interest.

"Moreover, the enemy has begun to employ a new and most cruel bomb, the power of which to damage is indeed incalculable, taking the toll of many innocent lives.

"Should we continue to fight, it would not only result in an ultimate collapse and obliteration of the Japanese nation, but also it would lead to the total extinction of human civilization.

"Such being the case, how are we to save the millions of our subjects or to atone ourselves before the hallowed spirits of our imperial ancestors? This is the reason why we have ordered the acceptance of the provisions of the Joint Declaration of the Powers."

"If I heard your reading properly, Bill, there are several key points. One, he accepts the Potsdam Declaration without qualification or condition. Two, he acknowledges at least one of the atomic bombs. Three, he has not used the words, 'surrender,' 'unconditional,' or any combination."

"Yes Sir," Donovan answered. "That is the way I read it."

"My interpretation as well," Jim Byrnes added.

Truman very carefully looked at each man and received a head nod of agreement. "So, while this is a little unorthodox, we are unanimous that his statement is the unconditional surrender of the Japanese." Again, President Truman looked at each man and received an affirmative nod. "Because of the ambiguity to save face, we must send a confirmatory message immediately without slapping them in the face. My suggestion . . . we send Suzuki a direct unclassified message setting the date, time, and place for the signing of the formal surrender document."

"What do you propose for that date, time, and place?" asked Secretary Byrnes.

"I was thinking Sunday, the 2nd of September, at nine in the morning, on the fantail of the battleship *Missouri*, in Tokyo Bay, so that all Japanese people who can see the harbor will see that battleship."

"That should be no problem. I'll notify Admiral Nimitz and issue the appropriate orders," Jim Forrestal offered.

"I'll notify MacArthur and get him on step as the Supreme Commander."

"Let's take this broadcast as the direct equivalent," Truman declared, "and conduct ourselves as such. My interpretation of the emperor's words is their way of surrendering unconditionally. The emperor did not mention retaining his divine right of kings or any other royal prerogative. If we treat him with respect, he may well be extraordinarily helpful in pacifying the country and transforming the country into a democratic state in good standing within the community of nations. Does everyone agree?"

"Yes Sir," came the unanimous response.

"Very well. Henry, please send the stop and recall orders to all Allied forces in the Pacific and Asia, especially for ALBERTA."

"I'll see to it immediately," Stimson answered.

"I need to make a very public announcement to the nation and the world as soon as possible. The worst war in human history is finally over." The group applauded and cheered. "I will notify Prime Minister Attlee, Marshal Stalin, and Generalissimo Chang. We have reason to celebrate, gentlemen. Well done to all."

—

Thursday, 23.August.1945
Office of the Director, Office of Strategic Services.
E Street Complex
Washington, District of Columbia
United States of America
08:45 hours

Bill Donovan chose to ignore the morning papers after reading *The Times*, *The Post*, and the *Chicago Tribune*. The reporting on the Japanese surrender, despite what they chose to call it, and the progress of the Allied occupation of Germany with the growing tensions between the Soviets and the Western Allies had been reasonably accurate when discounted to the common hyperbole of journalists.

Ned Buxton burst into Donovan's office, which in itself was unusual. "Have you seen this," he shouted, waving what appeared to be a folded *Chicago Tribune*.

"Yes."

"That damn Walter Trohan is at it again."

"Yes, he is."

As the Washington bureau chief for the *Tribune*, Trohan remained an influential voice in the capital and among the newspaper's readers.

"These are outright lies, Bill. They are equivalent to wartime disinformation we employed on our enemies."

"I agree."

"Surely, you must be more upset than this," Buxton said, waving his arm at Donovan.

"I am, Ned. I assure you, but I do not see myself as another Don Quixote."

"Damn, Bill, the title alone is intentionally inflammatory and patently false—'O-S-S Survival Plan Attacked As Plot for U.S. Super-Gestapo – Congress Prepares to Unearth Secrets of Donovan's Mix of Bankers and Reds.' My God, Bill, how low will he go. He goes out and finds a passel of Republican sympathizers who resort to calling us names, for God's sake. He says the O-S-S stands for 'Only Select Slackers' and 'Oh, Strickly Soviet.'" Donovan remained stoic and simply listened without emotion to Buxton's furious rant. They are saying . . . Trohan and the Republicans . . . our proposed central intelligence service is just another form of the Gestapo or the O-G-P-U for Christ's sake."

The OGPU was the Soviet Union's Joint State Political Directorate. It was the intelligence and state security service and secret police from 1923 to 1934. The OGPU transformed into the NKVD.

"What are we going to do?" Ned asked.

"Nothing."

"Nothing!" protested Buxton.

Donovan put down his pen, crossed his arms on his chest, leaned back in his chair, and smiled. "Yes, Ned, nothing."

"Bill, the Trib closed the article with . . . ," Buxton opened the paper to the end of the Trohan article and read, 'Although these documents and those submitted to the White House by General Donovan were made available to the *Chicago Tribune*, they were never officially in possession of this newspaper. They were copied by its representative on paper belonging to the *Tribune*.' They know what they did was wrong and wanted a disclaimer."

"It does not matter. The president stated emphatically that the O-S-S would be disbanded within a month of the war's end. The war has ended. We have the necessary agreements and arrangements to divide our resources and distribute them to the relevant agencies. Our service to the nation is nearly over."

"That sounds so fatalistic . . . quite unlike you."

"Perhaps so, my friend, but we have done our duty. The president has made his position very clear. The time has come for us to retire."

Colonel Ned Buxton, Bill Donovan's long-time friend, colleague, and deputy turned, walked out, and grumbled, "I don't like it one damn bit."

"I don't either, my friend," he muttered to himself.

—

Chapter 13

In war, resolution;
in defeat, defiance;
in victory, magnanimity;
in peace, good-will.

-- Winston Churchill

Sunday, 2.September.1945
USS Missouri
35° 33' 11" North – 139° 53' 16" East
Tokyo Bay, Tokyo Prefecture, Kanto, Honshu
Empire of Japan
09:00 hours

The massive battleship sat at anchor in Tokyo Bay, but the warship was not alone. The famous bay was filling swiftly with a broad array of Allied warships after the approaches and entrance had been swept repeatedly by U.S. minesweepers. The bay's water defenses had been removed, neutralized, or destroyed.

General of the Army Douglas MacArthur had received his appointment as the Supreme Commander Allied Forces Pacific and would accept the Japanese surrender. However, Admiral of the Fleet Chester Nimitz harbored his resentment of MacArthur privately and accepted his role in the ceremony as the designated representative of the United States of America.

There was no confusion or ambiguity with this ceremony, as there had been in the surrender of Germany four months earlier. The United States had carried the majority of the campaign in the Pacific and Asia against Imperial Japan. General MacArthur demanded precision and no debate.

The battleship's massive 16-inch naval rifles in the Numbers 1 and 2 main battery turrets were traversed to starboard 30 degrees. The starboard forward quarterdeck stood on the main deck under the barrels of the Number 1 turret. General MacArthur stood with the officer of the deck beyond the side boys. Behind the general were Admirals Nimitz and Halsey, along with the recently released POW Generals Wainwright and Percival.

Lieutenant General Jonathan Mayhew Wainwright IV, USA [USMA 1906], had become a POW when he surrendered his command of Allied Forces Philippines in May 1942. Wainwright had been freed by the Red Army in Manchuria on August 16th.

Lieutenant General Arthur Ernest Percival, CB, DSO & Bar, OBE, MC, OStJ, DL, had surrendered his command as General-Officer-Commanding

Malaya Command at Singapore on the 5th of February 1942. The action was the largest surrender in British history. Like Wainwright at Corregidor, both generals faced the reality that they were surrounded, had no chance for resupply or reinforcement, and were nearly out of food and ammunition. Percival was in the same camp as Wainwright and other Allied general officers. He was released with Wainwright.

On the ship's starboard side, 01 level next to the Number 2 Main Battery turret, a rectangular table with a green cloth covering and one simple straight-back chair on each side of the table had been set up. The pages of the Instrument of Surrender document had been arranged on the table and awaited the signatories. The signing site was below the ship's bridge and superstructure and just aft of the forward quarterdeck boarding ladder. While the official delegates were formed around the signing table, every available perch above the signing table was filled with curious observers.

The senior flag officers waited to meet the delegation from the Japanese government. The representatives of the Empire of Japan were the last to arrive on board the American battleship. There was no fanfare or announcement on the ship's 1MC broadcast system, and no honors were rendered. The generals led the Japanese delegation up the forward 01 ladder from the quarterdeck to the ceremony site.

With the official witnesses assembled in two groups, one aft of the table and the other to port of the table, a chaplain stepped to the standing microphone and offered a prayer. The "Star-Spangled Banner" was played by the ship's band.

MacArthur stood to the microphone stand. "It is my earnest hope, and indeed the hope of all mankind, that from this solemn occasion, a better world shall emerge out of the blood and carnage of the past, a world founded upon faith and understanding, a world dedicated to the dignity of man and the fulfillment of his most cherished wish for freedom, tolerance, and justice."

At the conclusion of the supreme commander's opening statement, the Japanese delegates stepped forward to sign the surrender documents.

INSTRUMENT OF SURRENDER

We, acting by command of and in behalf of the Emperor of Japan, the Japanese Government and the Japanese Imperial General Headquarters, hereby accept the provisions set forth in the declaration issued by the Heads of the Governments of the United States, China,

and Great Britain on 26 July 1945 at
Potsdam, and subsequently adhered to by the
Union of Soviet Socialist Republics, which
four powers are hereafter referred to as
the Allied Powers.

We hereby proclaim the unconditional
surrender to the Allied Powers of the
Japanese Imperial General Headquarters and
of all Japanese armed forces and all armed
forces under the Japanese control wherever
situated.

We hereby command all Japanese forces
wherever situated and the Japanese people
to cease hostilities forthwith, to preserve
and save from damage all ships, aircraft,
and military and civil property and to
comply with all requirements which may
be imposed by the Supreme Commander for
the Allied Powers or by agencies of the
Japanese Government at his direction.

We hereby command the Japanese Imperial
Headquarters to issue at once orders to
the Commanders of all Japanese forces and
all forces under Japanese control wherever
situated to surrender unconditionally
themselves and all forces under their
control.

We hereby command all civil, military
and naval officials to obey and enforce all
proclamations, and orders and directives
deemed by the Supreme Commander for the
Allied Powers to be proper to effectuate
this surrender and issued by him or under
his authority and we direct all such
officials to remain at their posts and to
continue to perform their non-combatant
duties unless specifically relieved by him
or under his authority.

We hereby undertake for the Emperor,
the Japanese Government and their
successors to carry out the provisions of
the Potsdam Declaration in good faith, and
to issue whatever orders and take whatever

actions may be required by the Supreme
Commander for the Allied Powers or by any
other designated representative of the
Allied Powers for the purpose of giving
effect to that Declaration.

We hereby command the Japanese Imperial
Government and the Japanese Imperial
General Headquarters at once to liberate
all allied prisoners of war and civilian
internees now under Japanese control and
to provide for their protection, care,
maintenance and immediate transportation to
places as directed.

The authority of the Emperor and the
Japanese Government to rule the state shall
be subject to the Supreme Commander for the
Allied Powers who will take such steps as
he deems proper to effectuate these terms
of surrender.

Signed at _Tokyo Bay, Japan_ at _0904_ on the_
Second day of _September,_ 1945.

MAMORU SHIGEMITSU
By Command and on Behalf of the Emperor of
Japan and the Japanese Government

YOSHIJIRO UMEZU
By Command and on Behalf of the Japanese
Imperial General Headquarters

Accepted at _Tokyo Bay, Japan_ at _0908_ on
the_ _Second_ day of _September_ 1945, for the
United States, Republic of China, United
Kingdom and the Union of Soviet Socialist
Republics, and in the interests of the
other United Nations at war with Japan.

DOUGLAS MAC ARTHUR
Supreme Commander for the Allied Powers

C.W. NIMITZ
United States Representative

HSU YUNG-CH'ANG
Republic of China Representative

BRUCE FRASER
United Kingdom Representative

KUZMA DEREVYANKO
Union of Soviet Socialist Republics
Representative

THOMAS BLAMEY
Commonwealth of Australia Representative

L. MOORE COSGRAVE
Dominion of Canada Representative

JACQUES LE CLERC
Provisional Government of the
French Republic Representative

C.E.L. HELFRICH
Kingdom of the Netherlands Representative

LEONARD M. ISITT
Dominion of New Zealand Representative

When the Japanese delegates signed the document and stepped back, General MacArthur stepped forward and sat. Lieutenant General Wainwright and Lieutenant General Percival stood behind General MacArthur as the supreme commander signed and closed the surrender of Japan. He used five ink pens to affix his signature to the document. One pen each went to Wainwright and Percival. Two other pens were reserved for and would be sent to the U.S. Naval Academy and the U.S. Military Academy. MacArthur chose to retain the last pen.

The other signatories—Australia, Canada, China, France, Great Britain, Netherlands, New Zealand, Soviet Union, and the United States—added their signatures to the surrender document as witnesses.

The ceremony took just 23 minutes, and then a formation of B-29 Superfortresses that had brought such destruction to Japan flew over the *Missouri*. Following the bombers, squadrons of carrier aircraft swooped overhead.

The greatest war in human history was finally and officially concluded.

Most folks just wanted to return their lives to some semblance of normalcy as quickly as possible. The Allied leaders knew the signing of the surrender document by the representatives of Imperial Japan marked the end of the combat phase and the beginning of the hardest and least bloody years of what lay ahead – winning the peace.

Later that day, General MacArthur broadcast to the world, "Today, the guns are silent. A great tragedy has ended. A great victory has been won. The skies no longer rain death, the seas bear only commerce, and men everywhere walk upright in the sunlight. The entire world lies quietly at peace. The holy mission has been completed. We have had our last chance. If we do not devise some greater and more equitable system, Armageddon will be at our door." Human beings worldwide were celebratory and hopeful, while frightened about what lay ahead.

—

Sunday, 2.September.1945
Standing Oak Farm
Winchester, Hampshire, England
United Kingdom
20:05 hours

The 4th Fighter Group had completed a duty week in Germany with sporadic flight scrambles to avert various confrontational incidents. For the most part, their duty week had been quiet. They flew a couple of border patrols to show the flag. The Group returned to Debden Saturday afternoon. Brian completed his necessary paperwork Sunday morning, and then he made his way to the farm.

After dinner and the crew dispersed for the evening, Brian built a modest fire in the fireplace and sat with Charlotte, Edith, and Mabel. Todd was safely in bed.

"The B-B-C Home Service announced the Japanese had formally surrendered. Is that true?" Charlotte asked.

"I've yet to hear directly from headquarters, but I believe the B-B-C is correct. The Japanese accepted the Potsdam Declaration on the 15th of August, and we had been told that the formal signing of documents was scheduled for this morning, Tokyo time. So, yes, I think it's true, and the war is finally over."

"Halleluiah!" Mabel exclaimed.

"We will celebrate," declared Charlotte. She retrieved a bottle of champagne from the refrigerator. She got the glasses while Brian opened the bottle. He poured four glasses.

"To peace," Brian said as he held up his glass. All four of them clinked glasses.

"Better, yet," Mabel said confidently, "to Major Brian Drummond, one of The Few who helped bring us this peace." Brian shook his head. *I don't need this. I was just one of millions.* "Hear, hear," Mabel added with a smile and happiness in her voice. They clinked glasses again. Mabel finished her drink. "Now, if you will excuse me, I've got a long day and an early start tomorrow."

"Good night, Mabel," Brian said.

Edith finished her drink and said, "I'll join you," she added.

The two women excused themselves, said good night, and ascended the stairs.

Brian poked the fire and put another split log on the glowing coals.

Charlotte kicked off her shoes and placed her bare feet in her husband's lap. As Brian took to his task inducing moans of pleasure from his wife, Charlotte closed her eyes and eventually murmured, "What happens now?"

"We go to bed and drift into wedded bliss."

"No, you ninny," she replied with a stronger voice without opening her eyes. "Now that the war is officially over, have they told you what is next for you?"

"Well, they have canceled the Pacific transfer warning order and issued transfer orders back to the States for my squadron. Our movement date is currently set for November 9th. We're supposed to go to Selfridge Field near Mount Clemens, north of Detroit, Michigan."

"I guess I need to learn my American geography."

"You'll have time."

"What about you . . . about us?" Charlotte asked.

"We don't have individual orders yet. None of us do. So, until I hear otherwise, we remain here and operate from Debden."

"Are you going to remain in the military? Mary knows John is going to stay as long as he can. Linda says Jonathan wants to stay in. Do you want to remain in the military?"

"I don't know my options, if any, so like I said about the squadron, we'll continue to do what we're doing until something changes. Then, for all I know, they may disband the squadron and discharge all of us. I've never been through anything like the end of a major war." Brian paused. Charlotte's eyes remained closed, and her breathing was slow and steady. "Have you heard anything from Jonas, Travis, or Bobby?" he asked softly.

"None of the above," she murmured faintly. "Their monthly reports are due here any day now."

"No word on the O-S-S contract?"

"None. Bobby is not waiting. Per our instructions, he is proceeding with reorientating B-A-S for full-time commercial service." Charlotte withdrew her feet from Brian's caresses and sat up straight. "Enough of all this boring chatter. I'm sure it's bedtime, and my expectations are high."

Brian smiled broadly. "I shall strive mightily to not disappoint."

Charlotte stood to switch off the lights. Brian followed her after he doused the fire. Finally, the couple headed toward the marital bed and the pleasure that awaited them.

—

Wednesday, 5.September.1945
Telegraph Cottage
Warren Road
Coombe Hill, Kingston upon Thames, London, England
United Kingdom
17:30 hours

Brian thought it rather odd that the cab driver asked if he and Charlotte were expected at the requested address. He had laughed at the question but figured out the driver was serious when he did not drive away. Brian extracted the invitation from his jacket pocket and handed it to the driver. After carefully studying the card, the driver asked, "Is this genuine?"

"Are you serious?' The driver stared in his rearview mirror at Brian and did not blink or twitch. "Yes, it is genuine."

The driver smiled and nodded. "Very well. Please pardon my resistance, Major Drummond. It is an exclusive community, and we've been asked to ensure we're careful with fares to that neighborhood."

"Thank you for being careful." The driver only nodded to acknowledge Brian's statement.

The drive southwest through the city streets and Richmond Park was new for both passengers. They turned off the main road to a small road with a large sign saying it was a private road with entrance by invitation only. Brian touched Charlotte's arm and nodded to the sign as they passed. She smiled and nodded.

The cab stopped in front of a modest, mid-sized, two-story house with a high-pitch slate roof surrounded by lush mature trees. The house was roughly the same size as Standing Oak, although a markedly different design and layout.

Brian paid the fare plus a modest gratuity. He helped Charlotte out of the cab, which drove away as soon as the door was closed. They turned and surveyed the well-lit house. Brian wore his pinks & greens service uniform with only his RAF and USAAF Senior Pilot wings, right and left, respectively, with his taut frame service hat rather than the aviator's crush hat he wore on duty. Charlotte's modest light gray mid-calf, long-sleeve dress complimented Brian's uniform. She chose not to wear a hat on this occasion.

They walked hand-in-hand up the short driveway. Brian rapped the brass knocker three times. An in-uniform navy captain opened the door. Brian saluted, but the captain did not return his gesture.

"Major and Mrs. Drummond." The captain extended his right hand to Brian and Charlotte. "Welcome to Telegraph Cottage. I'm Harry Butcher, Naval Aide to General Eisenhower. Please do come in." Captain Harry Cecil Butcher, USNR, of Iowa, had been the general's naval aide since 1942.

Brian removed his hat, which Butcher hung on a wall-mounted hat rack. Butcher gestured to the living room. Brian recognized General Eisenhower immediately. The general, a British Army colonel and an attractive woman dressed in the uniform of Women's Army Corps (WAC) second lieutenant were standing when Charlotte and Brian entered.

"This is Major Brian Drummond and his lovely wife, Charlotte. Brian, Charlotte, this is Colonel James Gault and Lieutenant Kay Summersby," Eisenhower said, gesturing to the colonel and lieutenant.

Colonel James Frederick Gault, MBE, MVO, of the Scots Guards, had been Eisenhower's British assistant and served as the supreme commander's liaison during the war.

Second Lieutenant Kathleen Helen Mary 'Kay' Summersby, USA WAC, née MacCarthy-Morrogh, had been a member of the British Mechanised Transport Corps when she was assigned to drive General Eisenhower when he first arrived in England in 1942. She remained his driver and assistant, and eventually became his secretary and friend. However, Eisenhower insisted that Kay be transferred to the U.S. Army in 1944.

Butcher served drinks. Then, they took their seats in the living room.

"It is a distinct honor to finally meet you, Mrs. Drummond," Eisenhower said. "May I call you Charlotte?"

"By all means, General," she replied.

"Now, now, Ike is fine. After all, your husband and I herald from the same state."

"Thank you, Ike."

Eisenhower nodded and smiled. "I have sung your husband's praises and yours. It is not every day we meet a civilian holder of the George Cross. And, if I am informed properly, King George himself awarded you for your heroic effort to have rescued young Brian from your lake."

"You were informed correctly, but I still do not understand why. The events of that day remain a blur to me. I just did what had to be done."

"She saved my life," Brian added.

"At the time," Ike said, looking at everyone, "Brian was already an ace fighter pilot, and thanks to Charlotte's quick reactions, Brian went on to become a five-time ace."

"And my husband," Charlotte added, inducing laughter in the group.

"We are expecting another couple for dinner," Ike announced. "Until then, may I ask how your farm is doing?"

Brian looked at Charlotte, who nodded back for her husband to answer. "Charlotte has managed the farm exceptionally well, Sir, while I was off to war. She has expanded the farm's business. We have a pantry full of preserved vegetables. She grows those vegetables year 'round now."

"Enough, Brian. I'm sure our host is not interested in the trivia of farm life."

"*Au contraire, mon ami,*" Ike interjected in perfect French. "I grew up on a farm. We both," Eisenhower said, gesturing to Brian, "are Kansans. Everything is farming in Kansas."

"That and aviation, oil . . ." The distinctive brass door knocker interrupted Brian's additional comment.

Butcher shot up and went to the door. Eisenhower stood, followed by Summersby and Gault. Brian and Charlotte joined the others in standing. Clementine and Winston Churchill entered the modest living room like a brilliant light. Clementine wore a conservative, light blue, lace dress with shoulder jacket. Winston was attired in a well-cut, three-piece dark gray suit with a black bow tie. Captain Butcher handed a tumbler of Winston's favorite Scotch whisky to the former prime minister and a modest glass of gin & tonic to Clementine. The Churchills knew everyone and greeted the group as friends, but they focused on Charlotte and Brian, who they treated as the guests of honor.

"When General Eisenhower informed me he was having you to dinner," Winston said to Brian, "I knew we could not miss the opportunity, and when he added that your exquisite wife Charlotte would attend as well, we simply could not miss the event." Winston turned to Charlotte, "It is an honor and a pleasure to finally meet you, Mrs. Drummond. It is not often I get to shake hands with a holder of the George Cross, and even better, awarded by the King for saving the life of our five-time ace," he announced with a smile and a pat on Brian's right shoulder, before taking and kissing the back of Charlotte's right hand.

"The honor is mine, Prime Minister."

"Oh no," Winston replied, "I'm no longer prime minister, unfortunately."

"My apologies, Sir. You should be."

"Hear, hear," came the chorus of cheers.

"Thank you all for the sentiment, but the people have spoken in resounding fashion, I must add.

Clementine spoke to Charlotte. "I understand you have lost a husband and a son to this war."

"Yes, Ma'am, and my father, my uncle, my father's brother, and I add my mother were lost in the Great War."

"Oh, my blessed Lord!" exclaimed Clementine. "You've done and given so much to the realm, my dear. How can we ever repay your sacrifice?"

"No need, Mrs. Churchill, no need. My family has done our part. It is history and memories now. I have worried about my husband every day he is not with me. The Germans have been shooting at him for five years. You and Pri. . . er . . . Mister Churchill have children in service as well."

"Yes, we do, and blessedly, our children have survived the war."

"I should add here that the Drummond's farm near Winchester in Hampshire," Eisenhower interjected in an apparent effort to soften the mood of the conversation, "has produced a bounty of vegetables and dairy products for the war effort and now the peace in Europe."

"Marvelous," Clementine added.

"Does this mean you are going to become a farmer?" Winston asked of Brian.

"I've not received orders yet. But there is a lot of talk about demobilization, although nothing specific. Everyone expects something to happen now that the war is officially over."

"I'm certain General of the Army Eisenhower, our contemporary Caesar Augustus, triumphant on the battlefield, could put in a good word for you, Brian."

"Of course, I can. Just say the word."

"Thank you, General. We've thought about what's next for us. We've not decided either way. We also agreed to let this phase play out and deal with what comes our way. Charlotte has sacrificed so much for me and my passion. I think it is only fair for me to devote more time to her and our family."

"Are you going to have more children?" asked Clementine.

Charlotte's face brightened with a broad smile. "As many as we can produce," she answered with a bubbly effervescence.

Clementine clapped softly. "Such a glorious future. Good luck to both of you."

"Thank you, Ma'am."

Butcher must have received a signal, nodded his acknowledgment, and then announced, "Dinner is ready. Shall we enjoy a sumptuous meal?"

The group sauntered into the elegantly appointed dining room with formal place settings and name cards for seating. Charlotte sat to Eisenhower's right. Winston sat opposite Eisenhower at the head of the table, while Brian was situated between Kay and Clementine.

The dinner conversation remained social rather than professional. They shared opinions about flowers, gardens, fishing, the soothing sounds of flowing water, and the joy of lights after years of blackout. The jovial conversation complemented the classic Kansas meal of prime rib, green beans, and mashed potatoes, after a Maine lobster bisque and bountiful green salad, and topped off with an exquisite apple cobbler ala mode.

With the meal complete, they moved back to the living room, brandy and cigars for those so inclined. Brian took the brandy but not the cigar. He lasted as long as he could, and then he decided to step out to the rear patio and garden. Once outside, Brian took a couple of deep breaths. The scents of the flower and conifer trees added a seductive aroma to the cool evening air. Before Brian returned to the house, General Eisenhower joined him with his brandy but no cigar."

"The smoke too much?" Ike asked.

"Yes Sir. It gets to me. I needed some fresh air."

"I know the sensation. I thought I would add, to you personally, that my offer earlier was genuine."

"I understood that, Sir. I'm just not too keen on seeking favors. I'd prefer to let the system function as it will."

"If you change your mind, simply call me. We owe you a great deal, Brian, and you most certainly deserve special consideration. Now, I must say that since the first time I heard your story I was fascinated. Moreover, I'm intrigued by your holdings in Kansas. What can you share with me?"

"My parents passed in an automobile accident just after midnight on New Year's Day 1941. I inherited their estate. I had no idea what they had accumulated before and during my childhood."

"I am so sorry for your loss, Brian."

"Thank you, Sir. It was a tragic accident. We were in the middle of The Blitz. The R-A-F allowed me to return home, and they arranged for me to hitch a ride with Mister Hopkins on the PanAm Yankee Clipper flying boat back to New York."

"Hopkins, as in Harry Hopkins?"

"Yes Sir."

"Dear me, Brian, you run in interesting circles."

Brian chuckled softly. "No Sir . . . just lucky or opportunistic."

"Did you get to talk to him?"

"Yes Sir. He asked to talk to me in his compartment. We listened to Churchill's *Give us the Tools* speech, although the radio reception was not the best."

"We could probably spend the rest of the evening talking about that conversation, but my curiosity overwhelms me. I simply must ask, you have land and oil wells?"

"Yes Sir, ten sections with several dozen active oil wells."

"Then you must be a very wealthy man." Brian nodded. "Why on earth did you put yourself at such risk in combat fighter airplanes?"

"First, I love to fly. Second, I'd say I'm a fairly good hunter. Third, I felt a duty, an obligation, to defend freedom. Lastly, I was nearly two years into my service when my parents passed, and they had kept me totally oblivious to their accumulated assets."

"You managed to defy federal law and join the R-A-F just after you turned 18."

"True, but I also received a presidential pardon for my Neutrality Act violation."

"My gosh, Brian, your story gets deeper and deeper with each sentence. This conversation will take . . ." The door opened and Butcher approached. He leaned forward and whispered in Eisenhower's ear. The general nodded. "The rest of our conversation shall have to wait for a later opportunity, Brian. We are being summoned inside. Thank you for the chat."

"Thank you, Sir." Brian followed Eisenhower and Butcher back to the living room.

As they joined the others, the Churchills bid General Eisenhower good night. Brian saw Charlotte give him a subtle chocks-out signal. He nodded. They waited for the Churchills' departure before they paid their respects.

On the cab ride to their hotel near Waterloo Station, Charlotte asked, and Brian recounted his conversation with General Eisenhower. Charlotte told her husband they had been invited to lunch on Saturday at Chartwell with the Churchills, and she accepted the invitation on behalf of both of them.

By the time they reached their hotel, checked in, and made it to their room, it was well after their bedtime. Regardless, they both felt like a celebration of a rewarding day and evening was warranted. They turned to the pleasures of the flesh before sleep consumed them.

—

Saturday, 8.September.1945
Chartwell Manor
Westerham, Kent, England
United Kingdom
12:30 hours

The Drummonds had considered a drive to their luncheon date, but neither of them was confident enough in the fuel supply as the nation continued its recovery from wartime rationing. They decided the train was the most reliable mode of transport.

Winston's valet and now Chartwell's butler Frank Sawyers welcomed the Drummonds when the cab dropped them off at the front door. "Welcome to Chartwell, Major and Mrs. Drummond."

"Thank you," Brian responded.

"Mr. and Mrs. Churchill are in the Drawing Room if you will follow me." Sawyers led the Drummonds down a hallway that jogged to the left and then the right. Winston and Clementine stood in the middle of the Drawing Room. Winston was attired in his characteristic charcoal gray pin-striped suit with black poke-a-dot bowtie, while Clementine wore a beige, full-sleeved, ankle-length dress. "Major and Mrs. Drummond," Sawyers announced.

"Welcome back to Chartwell, Brian," said Winston. "I do believe this is your first visit to our home, is it not, Charlotte?"

"Yes Sir, it is," Charlotte answered. "It is a gorgeous home . . . with extraordinary views."

"Brian was last here in August 1939, before the war began, correct?" Winston asked Brian.

"Yes Sir. Spot on!"

Sawyers handed Winston a glass of what appeared to be whisky. Clementine received a glass of what appeared to be sparkling water with a wedge of lime. Charlotte and Brian declined drinks.

"This place has been our sanctuary for 23 years, except for the five years of my premiership when we had to close it up, since the security folks considered the property too vulnerable."

"At least you are back home now," Charlotte offered.

"You are quite correct, my dear," added Clementine. "As Winnie says, this is our sanctuary. Here, we are at peace in the storm."

"That is how we feel about Standing Oak Farm," Brian contributed.

"Does that statement imply that you intend to remain in England if you are discharged during the demobilization?" Winston asked.

"To be honest, Prime Minister . . ."

"Ah, Ah, my dear Brian, I've been turned out to pasture."

"Excuse me, Sir. Old habit."

"You were saying?"

"We've," Brian said, gesturing to Charlotte, "discussed all the options we can imagine. We'll deal with whatever comes . . . just as long as we are together. We've been apart too long. It is time to be together for a while."

Winston chuckled more visibly than audibly. "I suppose I'm in the same boat."

"Except your work is not here," Clementine interjected. "I do not need you underfoot constantly."

They all laughed at the notion.

"Plus, your heart and lifeblood are in Commons. What's more, you turned down an earldom from the King for that reason alone."

Winston changed the subject. "I know how much you enjoy flying, Brian. No flying on the farm. What do you want to do?"

"I've not gone that far. I want to see what the Army does or decides, and then we will decide what we will do. I know I have a home," Brian paused to chuckle softly, "actually, several homes since we still own my childhood home in Wichita, Kansas."

Sawyers announced the new arrivals, "Air Chief Marshal Sir John and Lady Spencer." They turned to see John and Mary join them.

They all embraced and greeted each other. John wore his service uniform replete with his stack of ribbons under his pilot wings. The Churchills and Spencers engaged the Drummonds as if they were long-time friends beyond the professional service connection. As they laughed and traded salutations, Sawyers handed John and Mary an equally poured glass of whiskey without asking.

Winston looked at Brian. "Now that I see another officer, I am curious, Brian, why aren't you wearing your awards. I know you have more than a few. I witnessed one of your awards—the Military Cross, as I recall."

Brian smiled, looked down at his shoes, and then answered, "They attracted too much attention I would rather not have."

"I suppose I understand, but the King has awarded you at least two medals I know of."

"I mean no offense, Sir. I appreciate the awards I have received."

"You deserve them, Brian. You've done so much for freedom, and you deserve the recognition for your accomplishments. Twenty-five aerial victories are nothing to sneeze at."

"Enough," Clementine interjected. "Has Brian violated some law or rule?"

"No, Clemmie," Winston answered.

"Then, leave him alone. He looks perfectly marvelous in his uniform."

Sawyers appeared and announced, "Mrs. Landemare informed me that luncheon is ready when you are, Mister Churchill."

"Thank you, Sawyers. Shall we take our sustenance?"

Mrs. Georgina Landemare first cooked for Winston in 1905. She began part-time culinary services for the Churchills in 1933 after her husband passed. In early 1940 before Winston became prime minister, Landemare became the full-time chef for the Churchills and continued her service after Winston left office.

The group descended the bilevel stairway to the dining room. Winston sat at the head of the table with Clementine opposite from him. Brian was seated at Winston's right with Charlotte across from him. Mary sat next to Brian and opposite Sir John.

Mrs. Landemare prepared a delicious chicken cordon bleu, au gratin scalloped potatoes, and broccoli & carrot medley with a light Hollandaise sauce. She made a point of using cheeses from Standing Oak Farm. The fact made the meal all the better. The cheeses had remarkable taste and consistency. The meal and the farm's milk and cheese production became the talk of the table.

After lunch, Winston insisted the men join him for a walk of the grounds. Clementine led the women to the drawing room for tea and chat. Winston and John availed themselves of Winston's Cuban cigars. Brian declined the smoke. John had heard his uncle's stories about the development of the garden and grounds. The acclaimed politician remained immensely proud of his bricklaying skills and wall construction. Yet, the coy pond remained his favorite and go-to place for contemplation.

As they stood at the edge of the developed garden and enjoyed the expanse of grass and valley beyond. The view of the Southern Kent countryside exuded peace and tranquility. Brian could not help imagining what the sky above them must have looked like in the summer of 1940.

Winston changed the subject. "When did you return from the Mediterranean?" he asked Sir John.

"A month ago. We were in the process of disbanding the headquarters and moving our tasks to lower units, and to the regenerating of the Foreign Office staff in Italy. I've been reassigned as the operations officer within the Air Ministry. Whitehall is much closer to home, Mary, and the children," John said and winked at Brian.

"Not much operating these days," mused Churchill.

"Quite the contrary, Uncle. Our transports—the Americans and us—are flying constant missions to Berlin to support the ground transport and occasional missions between Zones. We rotate fighter squadrons to escort the transports. The Soviets persist in sending up fighters to harass our transports. They keep us one step short of armed combat."

"So, it is happening," Churchill mused.

"Yes Sir, it appears so, much to our regret."

"My squadron," Brian added, "has taken a couple of rotations with no end in sight so far."

"And to think, we were notional allies just a few months ago," John contributed.

"I gain no satisfaction in the fact that I tried my best to warn our friends, the government, and the people of what lay ahead with Stalin and the Kremlin. I've known the Russian people to be warm, generous, and friendly. The problem lies not with the people but within the walls of the Kremlin." Churchill again shifted gears. "You are going to remain in service?" he asked Sir John.

"Yes . . . as long as I can be of service. What about you, Brian?"

"It's up to Washington. I suspect I'm headed toward discharge as part of demobilization. I do not have a college degree, and apparently, the Army thinks that is important. Plus, they need some filtration criteria to accomplish the downsizing."

"General Eisenhower offered to intercede on your behalf," Winston stated.

"Yes, he did, and I thanked him and you for making the offer, but as I told the general, I would prefer to let the Army do what it will. So, I'm good either way. Plus, in peacetime, I can't imagine there will be much use for fighter pilots."

"You will always have a place in the R-A-F," John declared.

"Hear, hear," exclaimed Winston.

"Thank you both. I truly appreciate your concern, your support, and your friendship. I would not be where I am today without the help of both of you, repeatedly over the years. I can't possibly repay your support."

"Nonsense, Brian," Winston interjected. "It is we who owe a debt of gratitude that is impossible to repay. I will note in this thought that you are one of the few of The Few who won the great air battle and survived the war. You chose to stay and fight, while many of your brethren left their cockpits in accordance with guidelines for less violent duty. No, Brian, it is we who can never repay what you've contributed to peace and freedom. And, to think, your glorious history began with Sir John's vision."

"I would love to take the credit, Uncle Winston, but the true credit belongs to Malcolm Bainbridge, God rest his soul. It was Malcolm who saw the promise in a fledgling aviator."

"Yes," Brian said with a smile, "but it was you who got me to England and into the cockpit of a frontline Spitfire."

"You have a great many friends, Brian," Sir John replied.

"Me included," added Winston.

"I am truly blessed to have such friends."

Winston smiled. "With that conclave of love and admiration, I think I should shepherd you to the ladies as a responsible host."

The three men sauntered back to the manor house and the Drawing Room to rejoin the ladies. With the arrival of the men, Lady Mary opened the departure and appreciation of their hosts for the delightful luncheon and afternoon.

Sir John had an RAF limousine and offered the Drummonds to transport them to their home in Harrow for the night. Charlotte declined the generous offer, but they opted for Waterloo Station and the afternoon train to Winchester. Both John and Mary got out after Charlotte and Brian to embrace and kiss their friends before separating.

The journey progressed without delay. They had the compartment to themselves for the whole rail portion of the trip. Charlotte and Brian exchanged their remembrances of the conversation while they were separated. Charlotte made sure her husband understood how proud she was of his accomplishments.

The Drummonds were disappointed that their favorite cab driver, Morty Jurdy, was not waiting for them, but their arrival at Winchester Station was well after Morty's regular hours. Edith waited up to welcome the Drummonds home and wanted to know how the former prime minister was doing. The three of them talked with a nice fire in the fireplace.

—

Friday, 14.September.1945
USAAF Station F-356
Saffron Walden, Essex, England
United Kingdom
19:15 hours

Brian got the news directly from Colonel Clark late in the afternoon and kept it to himself through the evening meal at the Officer's Mess. He knew what he needed and wanted to do. Brian waited for an open telephone booth. The operators connected him to Charlotte.

"It's official, darling," he said straight away.

"What is?"

"I've orders to be discharged from the service on Friday, the 28th. They don't want me. They wanted to send me back to Wichita, my home of record, but I chose Winchester. So, I'll be coming home to you in two weeks."

"Really?"

"Yes. It's finally official. The war is over, and I'll be a civilian shortly."

"I can't wait. I've waited so long for this day. Do you have to fly between now and then?"

"The squadron is not scheduled for duty in Germany until next month, so unless there is some special mission, I believe the answer to your question is no. We are now setting the plan to transfer the squadron back to the States, but that will be after me."

"Will you be coming home between now and the 28th?"

"I doubt it."

"Are any other guys being discharged as well?"

"Yes, Sweet, Fly, and Swede."

"That seems like a lot."

"Yeah, it does, but we are not in combat anymore."

"Good. I love you, sweetheart. Please be safe and come home to me."

"I will, my darling. Two weeks. I love you."

—

Thursday, 20.September.1945
Office of Strategic Services
E Street Complex
Washington, District of Columbia
United States of America
08:45 hours

The department head meeting had moved swiftly through the day's agenda. Donovan could feel the tone of their day's department head meetings had changed. There was less of everything—energy, problems, issues, enthusiasm, virtually everything. Bill knew why but he refused to acknowledge what he knew was coming any day now. To him, it was business as usual until the end. Wild Bill Donovan tried mightily to exude that mindset to his lieutenants, but he was not going to fight reality.

"That's it, gentlemen," Donovan proclaimed. "Jim . . . a word, please," he said, gesturing with his eyes to his left. "If you would stay, Ned . . ." Buxton remained in his seat. The last one of the others to leave the room was John Magruder. Donovan nodded for him to close the door. He looked at James R. 'Jim' Murphy, head of the X-2 (Counterintelligence) Branch. "I didn't want to discuss this with the whole group. Where are we on Gehlen?"

"We're collectively nearly complete on vetting him and his surviving lieutenants. So far, so good. None of them have even a whiff of any links or connections with war crimes. Everything we know and have found so far points to the fact that they were focused on Kremlin leadership and processes. C-I-C concurs. Initial discussions with Gehlen suggests they are eager to continue their work against the Kremlin."

"How do you see that working?"

"We will need to establish a working command structure for our operations against the Soviet Union. We see Gehlen operating as a working advisor to the command staff. At present, we see retaining his lieutenants as a super advisory staff attached to the command headquarters."

"OK. Press on. We are way behind in our collection work against the Soviets. Gehlen and his boys should help us get caught up."

"Of that, I have no doubt. I've found him to be a calm, cool, competent intelligence officer. He knows the Soviets. He understands them. He will give us insight we do not currently hold."

"The Reds have been very active against us since before the war. Hoover keeps finding more, and I imagine he's finding only the tip of the iceberg."

"That is my opinion."

"Don't waste time. Let's get Gehlen, and his staff settled into an operating structure as soon as possible. Also, let's be overly cautious about his and his group's security. If the Soviets don't already know, they will soon figure out that we have him and, more importantly, that we are integrating his skills into our operations. I'm convinced once they know, they will pull out all the stops short of open combat to eliminate him."

"We are taking extraordinary precautions to protect him."

"Thanks, Jim. I know the next topic is outside your sphere, but I wanted your opinion. Magruder has inserted a team into Indochina and linked up with the Viet Minh. The French are applying serious pressure on the president to support their re-assertion of colonial domination in the region. What is your read of Ho Chi Minh?"

"He's a charismatic, intelligent, and committed leader of Viet sovereign aspirations. They've taken a big step toward that objective when they entered Hanoi three weeks ago and have begun establishing a government. Ho has been an avid, vocal, bold nationalist since the Versailles Treaty days. I think it safe to say he will not take kindly to us supporting the French against the Viet Minh, especially after they were so helpful in our operations against the Japanese. The French were nowhere to be found, but the Viet Minh worked well with our teams."

"Do you think we should side with the Viet Minh?"

"If we hope to have influence in the region, I will say yes, we should."

"That will not sit well with the French."

"What the French are asking for is not consistent with the Atlantic Charter signed by Roosevelt and Churchill. The British have begun the process of independence for most of their colonies. The French should do the same."

"My opinion as well. The Atlantic Charter was quite clear on that matter, and fair is fair."

"Any questions, Ned?"

"No Sir."

"Thanks, Jim. Now, get back to work."

Murphy nodded, stood, and left the conference room.

Donovan looked at Buxton, nodded, and stood. They returned to their offices. Bill had several reports he had not finished reading and immediately jumped back into the process. He had been at it for just 20 minutes and had not completed reading the top report when his secretary knocked and opened the door.

"Mister Stone from the Budget Office is here to see you," she said.

"Is he on the calendar?"

"No Sir. He arrived unannounced."

"Put him in the book and show him in."

Donald Crawford Stone was the assistant director of the Bureau of the Budget. Director Harold Dewey Smith had been President Roosevelt's budget manager since 1939 and continued to serve President Truman. Stone had an almost classical professorial appearance—short combed back light brown hair, thin, almost gaunt, pallid face, rimless glasses, sweater vest, bow tie, and tweed jacket.

"Good morning, Don. How may I help you?"

"I'm just the messenger, General," Stone answered.

Donovan stared at Stone with a common serious stern expression. "Understood. Let's have it."

Stone opened his leather briefcase and extracted a single piece of paper. He stepped forward and handed the letter to Donovan.

CONFIDENTIAL

WHITE HOUSE
BUREAU OF THE BUDGET
WASHINGTON, D.C.

September 14, 1945

TO: Major General W.J. Donovan
    Director, Office of Strategic Services
    E Street Complex

1. By direction of the President, I must officially inform you that all funding for the Office of Strategic Services (O.S.S.) will be reduced to zero effective Friday, September 28th, 1945.

2. As a consequence, you are directed to complete the distribution of O.S.S. personnel and any on-going taskings to the appropriate receiving departments. Your office and its functions are to be transferred to the Secretary of War.

3. Subsequent department secretaries shall
decide upon retention of personnel as they see
fit within their funding and mission statements.
    4. Any reconciliation necessary to carry
out this action will be performed by this office
only.
    5. Report compliance to this office
immediately upon completion.
Respectfully,

Harold D. Smith

Harold D. Smith
Director

CONFIDENTIAL

"So, this is it," Donovan pronounced.

"Yes Sir. I'm afraid so."

"There is no discussion?"

"No Sir. Director Smith stated emphatically that this is final. There are no discussions or negotiations to be had. You have two weeks remaining to comply."

A grim expression darkened Donovan's face. "It is a sad day . . . for a noble and heroic organization of exemplary people, Donald. It is done. I shall carry out the president's order with vigor. It shall be done. Please convey my statement to Mister Smith."

Stone nodded, turned, and departed.

—

Friday, 21.September.1945
Cabinet Room
The White House
Washington, District of Columbia
United States of America
15:30 hours

The State, War and Navy secretaries stood as President Truman entered the conference room. "Seats, gentlemen." The president sat across the table from the secretaries. He pushed the stack of stapled papers across the table. Each man took a packet.

OSS Director Donovan belonged at the meeting, but the order to disband had been issued for execution, so the OSS was considered irrelevant. The president needed a strategic intelligence perspective based on facts and expert analysis, but Wild Bill Donovan was not a participant.

"Henry recognizes his work." Truman looked at Byrnes and Forrestal. "For your benefit, Jim and Jim, what you have now is a memo and cover letter Henry prepared for me. The subject of the letter and memo is the topic of this meeting. Each of you has elements of this issue at the ministerial level on the national and international stage, but we will have only one policy. I would like to discuss Henry's proposal. I want to leave this room with one policy regarding nuclear energy and these special bombs. Any questions so far?"

"No Sir," the three secretaries answered in unison.

"You've had a little less than two weeks to read, review, research, and develop an opinion on the subject. Please take one last quick read-through, and then we'll discuss."

Each secretary promptly read the cover letter.

SECRET

SECRETARY OF WAR

WASHINGTON, D.C.

```
From: Henry Stimson, Secretary of War
To: Harry S Truman, President of the United
    States of America
Date: September 11, 1945
Dear Mr. President:
    In handing you today my memorandum
about our relations with Russia in respect
to the atomic bomb, I am not unmindful of
the fact that when in Potsdam I talked with
you about the question whether we could
be safe in sharing the atomic bomb with
Russia while she was still a police state
and before she put into effect provisions
assuring personal rights of liberty to the
individual citizen.
    I still recognize the difficulty and am
still convinced of the ultimate importance
of a change in Russian attitude toward
individual liberty, but I have come to the
conclusion that it would not be possible to
use our possession of the atomic bomb as a
direct lever to produce the change. I have
become convinced that any demand by us for
an internal change in Russia as a condition
```

of sharing in the atomic weapon would be so
resented that it would make the objective
we have in view less probable.

I believe that the change in attitude
toward the individual in Russia will come
slowly and gradually and I am satisfied that
we should not delay our approach to Russia
in the matter of the atomic bomb until that
process has been completed. My reasons are
set forth in the memorandum I am handing
you today. Furthermore, I believe that
this long process of change in Russia is
more likely to be expedited by the closer
relationship in the matter of the atomic
bomb which I suggest and the trust and
confidence that I believe would be inspired
by the method of approach which I have
outlined.
Faithfully yours,

Henry L. Stimson

> Henry L. Stimson
> Secretary of War

SECRET

The attached memorandum presented Henry Stimson's approach to the
question of atomic weapons and the Soviet Union. The Stimson memo was
a carry-over from the Potsdam Conference discussions once the reports of
the Trinity test success reached them. Great Britain had been and remained
a partner in the Manhattan Project, but the Soviet Union and other nations
were explicitly excluded.

TOP SECRET

SECRETARY OF WAR
WASHINGTON, D.C.

MEMORANDUM FOR THE PRESIDENT

Subject: The advent of the atomic bomb has
         stimulated great military and probably
         even greater political interest
         throughout the civilized world. In a
         world atmosphere already extremely

sensitive to power, the introduction
of this weapon has profoundly affected
political considerations in all
sections of the globe.

In many quarters it has been interpreted
as a substantial offset to the growth of
Russian influence on the continent. We can be
certain that the Soviet Government has sensed
this tendency and the temptation will be strong
for the Soviet political and military leaders
to acquire this weapon in the shortest possible
time. Accordingly, unless the Soviets are
voluntarily invited into the partnership upon a
basis of cooperation and trust, we are going to
maintain the Anglo-Saxon bloc over against the
Soviet in the possession of this weapon. Such
a condition will almost certainly stimulate
feverish activity on the part of the Soviet
toward the development of this bomb in what
will in effect be a secret armament race of a
rather desperate character. There is evidence
to indicate that such activity may have already
commenced.

If we feel, as I assume we must, that
civilization demands that someday we shall
arrive at a satisfactory international
arrangement respecting the control of this
new force, the question then is how long we
can afford to enjoy our momentary superiority
in the hope of achieving our immediate peace
council objectives.

Whether Russia gets control of the
necessary secrets of production in a minimum
of say four years or a maximum of twenty years
is not nearly as important to the world and
civilization as to make sure that when they
do get it they are willing and cooperative
partners among the peace-loving nations of the
world. It is true if we approach them now, as I
would propose, we may be gambling on their good
faith and risk their getting into production
of bombs a little sooner than they would
otherwise.

To put the matter concisely, I consider
the problem of our satisfactory relations
with Russia as not merely connected with but
as virtually dominated by the problem of the
atomic bomb. Except for the problem of the
control of the bomb, those relations, while
vitally important, might not be immediately
pressing. The establishment of relations of
mutual confidence between her and us could
afford to wait the slow progress of time. But
with the discovery of the bomb they became
immediately emergent. Those relations may be
perhaps irretrievably embittered by the way
in which we approach the solution of the bomb
with Russia. For if we fail to approach them
now and merely continue to negotiate with them,
having this weapon rather ostentatiously on our
hip, their suspicions and their distrust of our
purposes and motives will increase. It will
inspire them to greater efforts in an all-out
effort to solve the problem. If the solution is
achieved in that spirit, it is much less likely
that we will ever get the kind of covenant
we may desperately need in the future. This
risk, is, I believe, greater than the other,
inasmuch as our objective must be to get the
best kind of international bargain we can - one
that has some chance of being kept and saving
civilization not for five or for twenty years,
but forever.

The chief lesson I have learned in a long
life is that the only way you can make a man
trustworthy is to trust him; and the surest way
to make him untrustworthy is to distrust him
and show your distrust.

If the atomic bomb were merely another
though more devastating military weapon to be
assimilated into our pattern of international
relations, it would be one thing. We could
then follow the old custom of secrecy and
nationalistic military superiority relying
on international caution to prescribe the
future use of the weapon as we did with gas.

But I think the bomb instead constitutes
merely a first step in a new control by man
over the forces of nature too revolutionary
and dangerous to fit into the old concepts. I
think it really caps the climax of the age
between man's growing technical power for
destructiveness and his psychological power of
self-control and group control-his moral power.
If so, our method of approach to the Russians
is a question of the most vital importance in
the evolution of human progress.

Since the crux of the problem is Russia,
any contemplated action leading to the control
of this weapon should be primarily directed
to Russia. It is my judgment that the Soviets
would be more apt to respond sincerely to a
direct and forthright approach made by the
United States.

My idea of an approach to the Soviets would
be a direct proposal after discussion with the
British that we would be prepared in effect to
enter an arrangement with the Russians, the
general purpose of which would be to control
and limit the use of the atomic bomb as an
instrument of war and so far as possible to
direct and encourage the development of atomic
power for peaceful and humanitarian purposes.
Such an approach might more specifically lead
to the proposal that we would stop work on
the further improvement in, or manufacture of,
the bomb as a military weapon, provided the
Russians and the British would agree to do
likewise. It might also provide that we would
be willing to impound what bombs we now have in
the United States provided the Russians and the
British would agree with us that in no event
will they or we use a bomb as an instrument of
war unless all three Governments agree to that
use. We might also consider including in the
arrangement a covenant with the U.K. and the
Soviets providing for the exchange of benefits
of future development whereby atomic energy may

be applied on a mutually satisfactory basis for
commercial or humanitarian purposes.

  I emphasize perhaps beyond all other
considerations the importance of taking this
action with Russia as a proposal of the United
States - backed by Great Britain but peculiarly
the proposal of the United States.

  After the nations which have won this war
have agreed to it, there will be ample time to
introduce France and China into the covenants
and finally to incorporate the agreement into
the scheme of the United Nations. I urge
this method as the most realistic means of
accomplishing this vitally important step in
the history of the world.

Henry L. Stimson

                Henry L. Stimson
                Secretary of War

TOP SECRET

  When all three finished their read-through, President Truman stated, "I would like to hear your views without my bias. So, as the senior department, Jim, you start."

  Secretary of State Jim Byrnes leaned forward, placing his hand flat on the table on either side of the packet. "I've appreciated Henry's argument from our first substantive discussions in Berlin, but my opinion has not changed. I think Henry is correct in his contention that trusting breeds trust, but what I feel is missing from his proposal remains the existence of bad men, pathological men that will never deserve our trust and will use our trust in them against us. I want to believe, but the reality of the Soviet Central Committee and the Duma, for that matter. We all know and recognize Stalin's consolidation of power as essentially a dictator after The Great Purge of the 1930s. We have witnessed that reality in the conduct of the military, the diplomatic corps, and even in treaty compliance. I was not a direct participant in the diplomatic negotiations at Tehran or Yalta, but I'm a sufficient student to recognize those interactions from the baseline of my involvement at Potsdam. We have no intelligence from the O-S-S or elsewhere that give us definitive knowledge of Stalin's intentions. However, from what we see playing out in Eastern Europe and the Soviet Zone in Germany, we see rather disingenuous actions in each of the Soviet-dominated countries.

Further, we see signs that Stalin holds an ideological zealousness of Soviet governance as preferable and dominant to democracy.

"With that background, I'm afraid I cannot support Henry's proposal. While I laud the idealism of the Stimson proposal, I cannot see how such an approach will be successful, given Stalin's demonstrated position. Further, I cannot see any mechanism to enforce the rules even if we could achieve an agreement. I just do not think the Stimson proposal is practical in our contemporary reality." Brynes nodded his completion.

"Thank you, Jim." Truman looked at Forrestal. "Your perspective, Jim?"

"Since Trinity, the Navy has devoted considerable attention to the consequences of these weapons on our ability to perform our mission as part of the national defense. To put our assessment in blunt terms, the effects of massive explosives can overwhelm our current ship designs and construction. The Navy would prefer these weapons did not exist. We also recognize the Genie can't be returned to the bottle. Rather than leveling the playing field by providing the technology to the Soviets and others, Stalin's conduct suggests he would be more likely than not to use such a monstrous tool to intimidate and coerce those who stood in his way. Imagine, if you will, Hitler having several functional atomic bombs in 1940 when Great Britain was on her knees and hanging on by a thread. That is exactly how I see Stalin. As Jim articulated, I laud Henry's initiative to diffuse the potential arms race, but I suspect it has already begun . . . we just don't know it yet. I have mixed feelings about this question, but at the bottom line, I cannot see my way to support unilateral disclosure, and I do not see a path to substantive verification. Therefore, I must recommend against the proposal."

"Very well, thank you, Jim. Well, Henry, I don't imagine your opinion has changed in a week, but do you have anything to add?"

"Only that long journeys begin with the first step. If we do not take the first bold stride, we'll be turning our backs on the Soviets. We will have sown the wind, and we shall reap the whirlwind."

"That is rather ominous."

"We have seen the early photographs and reports from both Hiroshima and Nagasaki. We've seen the power of these bombs, and if we continue our research and testing, we will make them smaller and more powerful. The Russians will be forced to develop them just to defend themselves in their institutional paranoia."

"We're not going to attack Russia. We've no interests in Russia."

"They will not think so," interjected Byrnes. "They see everything in conspiratorial terms . . . state paranoia, if you will."

"We're not going to reform the Russians. They are who they are. Before we go any farther, do any of you need more time to study or contemplate this matter?"

All three either gestured or spoke in the negative. Truman lapsed into contemplation, staring at the packet on the table in front of him. Finally, the president looked at each minister across the table. "OK. Here are my thoughts.

"Our use of atomic energy will expand into electrical power generation, propulsion, and many other unforeseen areas. I went into the TERMINAL conference last July with an open mind and generous heart. I wanted peace like all of us after such a horrific world war. But, unfortunately, our good wishes and hopeful outlook are not sufficient to overcome the darker intentions of independent men. As I reflect on that moment at *Cecilienhof* when I informed Stalin of the Trinity test success, I felt the sensation that he was not impressed, almost like he already knew the results. In contrast, Churchill's response was excited and energetic, and he knew full well what was coming. I share Jim's opinion, although we don't know precisely, that the arms race with the Russians has already begun, and if my suspicion proves correct, it began years ago.

"I agree with Henry that trusting breeds trust, but that is a two-way street. We did not have to share with the Soviets, but we have unilaterally. We've shared intelligence and massive material support, and we've sent them entire bomber-fighter wings to support their operations in the East. What have they shared with us? To my knowledge, nothing. I appreciate the thoughts and sentiments of your proposal, Henry, but I cannot find a path to support this approach," he said, holding up the memorandum. "I do not trust Stalin or the Soviets. I do not like their approach to the administration of the Eastern European nations. I hold grave doubts about their intentions. We witness highly suspicious activities in Manchuria and Northern Korea.

"Until further discussion and amendment, we will maintain the secrecy of the Manhattan Project and whatever it evolves into. We will also continue our research and development of improved devices. I appreciate your initiative, Henry, but I must reject your proposal. Thank you for your counsel, gentlemen." Truman stood and departed. "We are concluded," he added before he reached the door.

The department secretaries stood. Stimson followed the president.

Oval Office
16:23 hours

"Excuse me, Mister President," Stimson said as he followed Truman into the office.

"What is it, Henry?"

Stimson removed an envelope from his suit jacket's inside pocket. "I must tender my resignation." He handed the envelope to the president.

"Is this because I rejected your proposal?"

"No Sir. I'm 78 years old. I was born just after the Civil War. I've served most of my adult life in government. It's time, Mister President. The war is won. I've done my duty. It's time."

Without opening the envelope, President Truman responded, "Very well, Henry. I accept your resignation. Go with God in peace." The two men shook hands, and Stimson left the Oval Office for the last time.

—

Friday, 28.September.1945
USAAF Station F-356
Saffron Walden, Essex, England
United Kingdom
13:00 hours

The black telephone on Sergeant Ellison's desk rang. "Three Thirty-fourth." "Yes Sir." "I will, Sir." Juli hung up the telephone and went to the CO's office. "Excuse me, Sir. Colonel Clark wants to see you."

"Thank you, Juli." Brian completed the report he had been working on, signed it, and placed it in his outbox.

Brian grabbed his hat and headed to the 4th Fighter Group headquarters building. As he entered, the group adjutant stood and followed him to Colonel Clark's office. The adjutant closed the door. Brian stopped in front of Clark's desk, came to a position of attention, saluted, and said, "Major Drummond reporting as ordered, Sir."

Clark returned the salute. "At ease. Take a seat." Brian sat. "Today is the day. We could not carry out the discharge process without talking to you personally and privately." Brian nodded. "It has been my distinct honor to serve with you, Hunter. There are very few pilots that I respect as much as you. You hold a unique place in Air Force history. I know of no one else who has served in fighter cockpits as long as you have, and you are in a rare group of fighter pilots having recorded 26 ½ aerial victories. When we received your orders two weeks ago, I asked Command why they were discharging one of our most experienced and accomplished fighter pilots? The answer was simple and direct. They had to apply filters to achieve demobilization, and the filter that caught you was no college degree."

"Thank you for asking, Arnie. I figured it would come down to something like that. I'm good with this. I've done my duty, and I've got plenty of other things to do. So, no harm, no foul. Thank you very much for your thoughts. I'm ready to go."

"The adjutant will take you through the paperwork. I understand you've elected to remain in England rather than return to your home of record."

"Yes Sir. Charlotte is here. My home is here now. Can I say one last goodbye to my guys before I head out?"

"Sure you can. You're technically still on duty until you arrive at your home of record or final discharge destination."

Brian stood, came to attention, and saluted. Clark returned the salute and came around his desk, extending his right hand to Brian. They shook hands. Brian completed his paperwork and was officially discharged from the Army Air Forces.

Before heading to the railway station, Brian returned to the Squadron area. Sweet, Fly, and Swede had already separated first thing in the morning. Sweet did not have to go far and returned to his parents' home in London. Swede and Fly were now on a train to Liverpool to board their ship back to the States.

Brian made a point of tracking down Sergeant Tomlinson before returning to the Dispersal building. He offered Larson a job at BAS back in Wichita, if that is where he ended up. There were no orders for his discharge. Brian gave him Bobby Joe Sales contact information should he choose to use it. Larson thanked Brian.

The 334FS had been released for the day and stood down from operations until a new commanding officer was designated and replacement pilots arrived. A half dozen pilots had already departed for London or other destinations on leave.

He shook hands and said goodbye to each pilot remaining in the building. He wrote on the chalkboard his contact information for Winchester and Wichita should any of them need to reach him. With his goodbyes done, he hitched a ride to the railway station and his journey home.

———

Friday, 28.September.1945
Riverside Stadium
26th & D Streets, Northwest
Washington, District of Columbia
United States of America
16:00 hours

The arena was the only facility of sufficient size within walking distance of the E Street Complex. The enclosed, covered stadium had been used in recent years as a roller-skating rink located on the Potomac flats below the OSS headquarters buildings. Roughly 2,000 morose OSS men and women crowded into the arena. Some sat. Most stood. As the large wall clock ticked to the hour, Colonel Ned Buxton stood to the dais and the microphone.

"Thank you all for joining us. Ladies and gentlemen of the O-S-S, it is my distinct honor to introduce our director and leader, Major General Bill Donovan." Some of the audience applauded but most remained silent and motionless. The expressions of most, if not all, of the people, were markedly glum.

Donovan and Buxton exchange places after shaking hands.

"This is our last day in existence and operation. It is a moment of transition. We have done our duty in an extraordinary, exemplary fashion. While this," Donovan swung his arms to signify the entire assembly, "is not the whole of the O-S-S, you are the heart, nervous system, and brain of the organization. Some of our muscle remains in the field, still doing the nation's work that has to be done.

"As you all know, the organization is being disbanded. All the functions and operations have been distributed and accepted by other departments. Your new departments and supervisors will become effective on Monday, the 1st of October. I trust that each of you will continue to perform your work in an exceptional manner.

"Lastly, I wanted each of you to hear it from me personally and directly, the nation will not likely know what you have done because of the secrecy of our works, but I will emphatically state that the United States of America and We, the People, owe each of you an un-repayable debt of gratitude for your service to the nation. You can go with the assurance that you have made a beginning in showing the people of America that only by decisions of national policy based upon accurate information can we have the chance of a peace that will endure.

"Thank you so very much. It has been the honor of my life to serve with you. Go with the blessings of God Almighty." Donovan stepped back from the podium to resounding applause. Buxton moved back to the microphone. Donovan remained standing two paces behind his deputy.

Buxton held up both hands above his head to signal for quiet. When the crowd returned to attentiveness, Ned spoke. "I have known Bill Donovan for better than 30 years. I can tell you there has been no more devoted leader than Bill Donovan. Many of us witnessed the extraordinary, selfless efforts of our general to overcome the strong currents resisting the Coordinator of Information and the Office of Strategic Services but overcome he did. Our work was a significant contributor to winning the war. We operated as a well-oiled intelligence team. I will say in closing, thank you, General Donovan, for your strong and decisive leadership, guiding us through the troubled years of war and supporting us through thick and thin." Applause interrupted Buxton's speech. "I will add my voice to General Donovan's.

Thank you all for the extraordinary work you delivered to the Allied and the nation's war effort. Hold your heads high with pride." Again, applause erupted among the audience as Ned stepped back from the podium.

Donovan and Buxton remained in the arena and shook the hand of everyone who wanted to offer a personal goodbye. Both leaders spoke to each person by name and recognized their work by position. The OSS was done.

—

Friday, 28.September.1945
Winchester Railway Station
Winchester, Hampshire, England
United Kingdom
21:10 hours

Brian Drummond had managed to make it into London, across town, and to Waterloo Station in time to catch the last train to Winchester. He had made the journey from Debden to Winchester countless times, but this trip seemed inordinately long and frustrating, with railcars crowded with service personnel returning from the combat zones. A cornucopia of Allied uniforms occupied every available seat and space.

To Brian's surprise, he found Morty Jurdy standing beside his cab with a broad smile on his face and an OFF-DUTY sign on the roof of his cab.

"Welcome home, Major Drummond," Morty shouted as Brian exited the railway station.

Brian was still in his pinks & greens service uniform, so he did not object to the title even though he was technically no longer in the service. "Thank you, Morty. It's a little late for you, isn't it?"

"Not to worry, Sir. I heard you were coming home for good, and I knew I had to be the one to take you home."

"I am honored by your loyalty and sense of duty, Morty. You've become a friend over these years of war. Thank you for being so devoted."

"You are most welcome, Sir. Now, I suspect the missus eagerly awaits your arrival home in peace. Shall we be on our way to the farm?"

"Absolutely." Brian threw his loaded duffle bag onto the far side of the rear passenger seat and got in next to his bag. Morty closed the door and then positioned himself behind the vehicle's controls.

"Let's get you home."

Brian relished the drive through lighted streets and homes. While the barricades and checkpoints were gone, the signs of wartime England had not yet been removed entirely. Nonetheless, the sight of peace returning to the country stimulated a broad smile. "Please stop at the crest like we usually do, Morty. I've never seen the farm at night in peacetime."

"It'll be my pleasure, Sir."

The last time they had stopped on the crest overlooking the main farm complex, they were in the blackout mandate of wartime. The exterior seemed lit up like a Christmas tree—lights Brian did not recall ever seeing before.

"It is idyllic," Brian muttered.

"Yes, it most certainly is. I've enjoyed every trip I've made over this ridgeline. I've seen the lights before, but they're even more glorious now that the peace is won."

Brian simply nodded. They stood together, looking at just the lights. Brian did not know if Morty had a family waiting for him, but he began to feel guilty. "Go, you have a family waiting for you, Morty."

"I have a lovely, devoted wife and two growing daughters, but do not worry, Sir, they've gone to bed by now."

Brian chuckled softly. "How did you read my thoughts?"

"You are a kind and generous war hero, Major. I just sensed your concern. To be honest, I simply could not pass up this important assignment."

"Thank you, Morty. I appreciate your generous words, but let's mount up so we can get you home."

Standing Oak Farm
21:35 hours

The two men did just that. Brian paid Jurdy for the fare plus a very generous gratuity. The cab started up the hill when Charlotte burst out of the house and leaped into her husband's arms.

They kissed passionately, and Charlotte persisted. She did not want the moment to pass. Brian held her and matched her passion. They eventually sated their enthusiasm. Brian lowered her feet to the bricks of their porch.

"You are finally free," she declared.

"Yes, Ma'am. I am."

"You can take off your uniform."

"I'll take it all off for you right here and now."

"I dreamt and prayed for this day for so long."

"I know."

"What happens now?"

"What do you think? We live happily ever after."

Charlotte wrapped her arms around Brian's neck and lifted herself to his waiting lips. They consumed each other. Charlotte lowered herself to the bricks. "My dear husband, your words are music to my ears."

"We aim to please, my dear."

"And please, you have, but now, I want a different pleasure."

"Oh my." Brian left his duffel bag on the bricks, lifted Charlotte into his arms, pushed open the door with his foot, and carried her to the bed. "Are we going to make a baby now that the war is over?"

"Yes, my darling. We are going to make lots of babies, but not tonight. It's not that time of the month for us."

"We can practice."

Charlotte laughed robustly like Brian had never heard her laugh before. "I want lots of practice with my stud."

"You really want lots of babies?"

"Yes, I do . . . as many as we can produce."

"Wow! That's quite a switch."

Charlotte shook her head. "No, it's not. The war is over. We'll make up for lost time."

"Well, then, we'd better get to it, huh," Brian murmured as he began to undress his wife. Charlotte enthusiastically joined in the process. Within a couple of minutes, they were both stark naked, each with their appropriate anatomical preparedness. Brian opened his mouth to speak . . . *nope, pleasure first.* Brian gently picked Charlotte up in his arms like a precious bundle, stepped to the bed, and laid her slowly onto the cool sheets. She reached for him, and he lowered himself to her embrace. They took to nature's task like ducks to water. Peace had come.

—

About the Author

Cap Parlier

—

Cap and his wife, Jeanne, live peacefully in the warmth and safety of Arizona—the Grand Canyon state. Their four children have established their families and are raising their children—our grandchildren. The grandchildren are growing and maturing nicely with two college graduates so far and another in her senior year.

Cap is a proud alumnus of the U.S. Naval Academy [USNA 1970], an equally proud retired Marine aviator, Vietnam veteran, and experimental test pilot. He finally retired from the corporate world to devote his time to his passion for writing and telling a good story. Cap uses his love of history to color his novels. He has numerous other projects completed and, in the works, including screenplays, historical novels as well as atypical novels at various stages of the creation process.

—

Interested readers may wish to visit Cap's website at <http://www.parlier.com> for his essays and other items or subscribe to his weekly Blog: "Update from the Sunland." Cap can be reached at: cap@SaintGaudensPress.com.

—

www.ingramcontent.com/pod-product-compliance
Lightning Source LLC
Chambersburg PA
CBHW060820120726
47909CB00006B/2004